ACCLAIM for MELISSA

How to Plot a Payback

"The perfect escape for lovers of dogs, second chances, and swoon-worthy romance. Don't miss this one."

—Annabel Monaghan, bestselling author of *Same Time Next Summer*

"Super cute! Melissa Ferguson's romcoms lean more on the com than the rom, and this book is no different, delivering chuckles and giggles with an effortless writing voice, witty dialogue, and a cast of lovable characters. I was totally on board as soon as I read the premise, especially since it's a storyline I haven't already read more than a dozen times (give me all the fresh plots please!). You could say this is a grump/sunshine (although he's really not all that grumpy), enemies-to-lovers (although the hard feelings are only one-sided and misguided at that), slow burn, but I just call it a cute little romp of a book."

—Sarah Monzon, author of *All's Fair in Love and Christmas*

"It was so fun to sit in on the writer's room of a successful sitcom in Melissa Ferguson's delightfully charming and wonderfully quirky romance. There are so many sweet moments and wonderful characters sprinkled throughout, and I'm certain rom-com fans are going to fall in love!"

—Courtney Walsh, *New York Times* bestselling author

Famous for a Living

"Calling all fans of slow-burn, opposites-attract romance! Melissa Ferguson brings another fresh, delightful rom-com in *Famous for a Living*. Cat and Zaiah are an imperfectly perfect match with swoony chemistry and plenty of back-and-forth banter. The gorgeous national park setting provides a lush backdrop for this fish-out-of-water story as influencer Cat hopes to escape a media fallout and finds much, much more. Readers who loved

The Cul-de-Sac War and *Meet Me in the Margins* won't be disappointed in Ferguson's latest read!"

—Emma St. Clair, *USA TODAY* bestselling author

"*Famous for a Living* is a heartwarming and funny read with quirky characters and the occasional moose. It takes the reader on a virtual escape to the mountains and hot springs of Montana and the lofts and busy streets of New York City. Melissa Ferguson has given us a sparkling, sweet rom-com with a lot of heart."

—Suzanne Allain, author of *Mr. Malcolm's List*

Meet Me in the Margins

"Ferguson (*The Cul-de-Sac War*) enchants with this whimsical tale set against the evergreen culture war between literary and commercial fiction . . . An idealistic, competent heroine, a swoon-worthy hero, and delightfully quirky supporting characters bolster this often hilarious send-up of the publishing industry, which doubles as a love letter to the power of stories. This is sure to win Ferguson some new fans."

—*Publishers Weekly*

"A marvelous book on the power of positive feedback, the various struggles of being an emerging writer, and how to find a balance between work and life, this book is a very entertaining read."

—Book Riot

"*Meet Me in the Margins* is a delightfully charming jewel of a book that fans of romantic comedy won't be able to put down—and will want to share with all their friends. Readers will lose themselves in Melissa Ferguson's witty, warm tale of Savannah Cade and the perfectly drawn cast of characters that inhabits her world. This literary treat full of missed opportunities, second chances, and maybe even true love, should be at the top of your reading list!"

—Kristy Woodson Harvey, *New York Times* bestselling author of *Under the Southern Sky*

"Ferguson has penned a lively romance for every bookworm who once longed to step through the wardrobe or sleep under the stairs. *Meet Me in the Margins* brims with crisp prose and crinkling pages as Savannah Cade, lowly editor at a highbrow publisher, secretly reworks her commercial fiction manuscript with the help of a mystery reader—and revises her entire life. You'll want to find your own hideaway to get lost in in this delightful, whip-smart love story."

—Asher Fogle Paul, author of *Without a Hitch*

The Cul-de-Sac War

"Melissa delivered a book that is filled with both humor and heart!"

—Debbie Macomber, #1 *New York Times* bestselling author

"Melissa Ferguson delights with a grand sense of humor and a captivating story to boot! With vivid detail that brings the story roaring to life, *The Cul-de-Sac War* brings us closer to the truth of love, family, and home. Bree's and Chip's pranks and adventures turn into something they never expected, as Melissa Ferguson delivers another heartwarming, hilarious, and deeply felt story."

—Patti Callahan, *New York Times* bestselling author of *Becoming Mrs. Lewis*

"Melissa Ferguson's *The Cul-de-Sac War* is sweet, zany, and surprisingly tender. Bree and Chip will have you laughing and rooting for them until the very end."

—Denise Hunter, bestselling author of *Carolina Breeze*

"With her sophomore novel, Melissa Ferguson delivers hilarity and heart in equal measure. *The Cul-de-Sac War*'s Bree Leake and Chip McBride prove that sometimes it isn't the first impression you have to worry about—it's the second one that gets you. What follows is a delightful deluge of pranks, sabotage, and witty repartee tied together by heartstrings that connect to turn a house into a home worth fighting for. I was thoroughly charmed from beginning to end."

—Bethany Turner, award-winning author of *The Secret Life of Sarah Hollenbeck*

"Witty, wise, and with just the right amount of wacky, Melissa's second novel is as charming as her debut. Competition and chemistry battle to win the day in this hilarious rom-com about two people who can't stand to be near each other—or too far apart."

—Betsy St. Amant, author of *The Key to Love*

The Dating Charade

"Ferguson's delightful debut follows a first date that turns quickly into a childcare quagmire . . . Ferguson's humorous and chaotic tale will please rom-com fans."

—Publishers Weekly

"*The Dating Charade* will keep you smiling the entire read. Ferguson not only delights us with new love, with all its attendant mishaps and misunderstandings, but she takes us deeper in the hearts and minds of vulnerable children as Cassie and Jett work out their families—then their dating lives. An absolute treat!"

—Katherine Reay, bestselling author of *The Printed Letter Bookshop*

"*The Dating Charade* is hilarious and heartwarming with characters you truly care about, super fun plot twists and turns, snappy prose, and a sweet romance you're rooting for. Anyone who has children in their lives will particularly relate to Ferguson's laugh-out-loud take on the wild ride that is parenting. I thoroughly enjoyed this story!"

—Rachel Linden, bestselling author of *The Enlightenment of Bees*

"A heartwarming charmer."

—Sheila Roberts, *USA TODAY* bestselling author of the Moonlight Harbor series

"Melissa Ferguson is a sparkling new voice in contemporary rom-com. Though her novel tackles meaningful struggles—social work, child abandonment, adoption—it's also fresh, flirty, and laugh-out-loud funny. Ferguson is going to win fans with this one!"

—Lauren Denton, bestselling author of *The Hideaway* and *Glory Road*

"A jolt of energy featuring one of the most unique romantic hooks I have ever read. Personality and zest shine through Ferguson's evident enjoyment at crafting high jinks and misadventures as two people slowly make way for love in the midst of major life upheaval. A marvelous treatise on unexpected grace and its life-changing chaos, Cassie and Jett find beautiful vulnerability in redefining what it means to live happily ever after."

—Rachel McMillan, author of *The London Restoration*

"Ferguson delivers a stellar debut. *The Dating Charade* is a fun, romantic albeit challenging look at just what it takes to fall in love and be a family. You'll think of these characters long after the final page."

—Rachel Hauck, *New York Times* bestselling author of *The Wedding Dress*

HOW to PLOT a PAYBACK

Also by Melissa Ferguson

Snowy Serendipity

Famous for a Living

Meet Me in the Margins

The Cul-de-Sac War

The Dating Charade

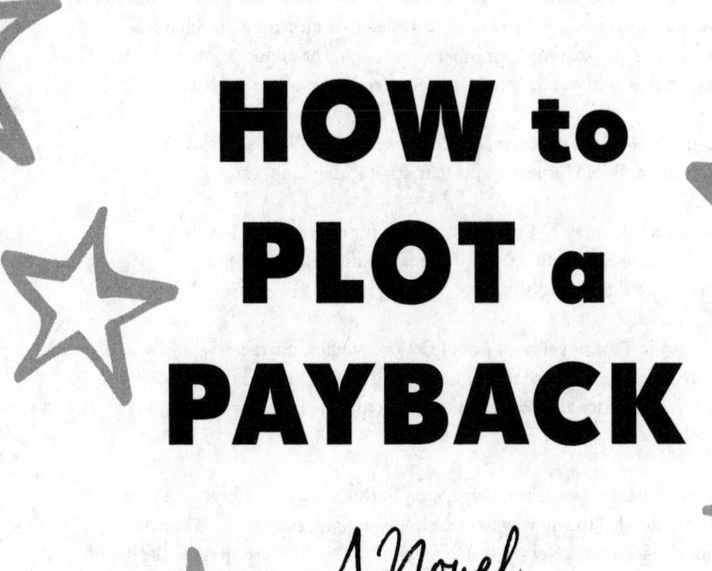

HOW to PLOT a PAYBACK

A Novel

MELISSA FERGUSON

THOMAS NELSON
Since 1798

How to Plot a Payback

Published in Nashville, Tennessee, by Thomas Nelson. Thomas Nelson is a registered trademark of HarperCollins Christian Publishing, Inc.

Thomas Nelson titles may be purchased in bulk for educational, business, fundraising, or sales promotional use. For information, please email SpecialMarkets@ThomasNelson.com.

Library of Congress Cataloging-in-Publication Data

Names: Ferguson, Melissa, 1985- author.
Title: How to plot a payback: a novel / Melissa Ferguson.
Description: Nashville, Tennessee: Thomas Nelson, 2024. | Summary: "She's been muddling his plans for years-now he's the writer for the beloved character she plays on television, and it's time for payback"--Provided by publisher.
Identifiers: LCCN 2023041870 (print) | LCCN 2023041871 (ebook) | ISBN 9780840702913 (paperback) | ISBN 9780840702999 (epub) | ISBN 9780840703002
Subjects: LCGFT: Romance fiction. | Novels.
Classification: LCC PS3606.E7263 H69 2024 (print) | LCC PS3606.E7263 (ebook) | DDC 813/.6--dc23/eng/20230912
LC record available at https://lccn.loc.gov/2023041870
LC ebook record available at https://lccn.loc.gov/2023041871

Printed in the United States of America

24 25 26 27 28 LBC 5 4 3 2 1

This book is dedicated to my marketing manager,
Kerri Potts.

Where would I be without our spontaneous
and encouraging conversations?

Chapter 1

Finn

Murder is just *so* tedious.

The blood, the weapons, the extravagant mess to clean up over and over and *over.* Does anyone even know how much bleach I've had to endure smelling over the years? Gallons. Truckloads. I've lost two pairs of shoes in the past three months to unfortunate missteps.

The desktop screen of my laptop is covered in folders meticulously organized into files labeled Poisons, Burn Phones, Cybersecurity, Brilliant Body-Hiding Spots, Run-of-the-Mill Body-Hiding Spots, and—a fan favorite—Absolutely Bloody Pathetic Body-Hiding Spots.

I could make a killing—pun absolutely intended—selling this computer and all its contents on the serial killer black market.

I've been in the business of murder for eight years. Nothing to brag about in the grand scheme of things, but long enough that I've made a name for myself. A reputation.

And by the age of thirty here I stand, Finn Alexander Masters III, son of proud parents Mary and Finn Masters II of 202 Sommerhill Road, Welling, England, settled for life in the great land of Los Angeles, pigeonholed into the career of my dreams. Murder.

And all I want, the whole reason I'm here at this absurd party tonight, is to get out.

"And then it turned out they *all* were in on it," sputters the man opposite me. Spittle blinds me in one eye. "*Brilliant.*" While holding his appetizer plate, he motions with both hands that his head is exploding. Several sausages quiver and roll onto the rug.

My eyes flicker down to the white shag.

Mr. Henry doesn't seem to notice. "Were you the mastermind behind that—just—absolutely *awesome* twist?"

I crouch (which, mind you, is no simple task in the small, overstarched suit my cowriter Paula pushed into my hands this morning with a *shh* as she shut the wardrobe door behind her). As I collect the tiny sausages, I say what I always say in these moments: "It was a joint effort. Everyone in the writers room is essential."

But yes. I had thought of that plot twist.

And yes, I am secretly quite proud of that one.

"Oh yes. A team effort," he says seriously, as though he knows every detail of life inside the writers room. "Your minds have to be in sync, so much so that you're always finishing each other's sentences."

We never do that.

"That's a pat on the back for the *Higher Stakes* director who hired you all."

Executive producer.

"He had to *know* you could work together. I can just imagine him—"

Her.

"—throwing you all in a room together as he stood behind

some great big mirror, seeing how his creation worked it all out."

We are not monkeys in a lab. She is not God. There is no mirror.

"And now look at you." He throws out a hand—and another sausage. "Writing as a synchronized team for the biggest murder mystery sitcom—"

Sitcoms are comedies.

"—on television today. The Backstreet Boys, so to speak, of Hollywood."

He finishes his monologue and stares at me with a smile that lasts several silent seconds. Then gives fresh attention to the sausages I've returned to his plate.

Pops one into his mouth.

Begins chewing.

Continues smiling at me, now while chewing.

As if at any moment I'm supposed to erupt with a *Bravo! You nailed it.*

I'm just opening my mouth to thrust forward some such reply—because *fine*, the whole point of my being at this party is to win over potential employers—when he adds the fateful words, "The only thing that could possibly top what you've all done would be if Lavender Rhodes was your leading lady."

My body tenses as if he just casually pulled a grenade from his pocket.

"Can you just imagine?" he says wistfully, casting a hopeful glance at the mob of guests around us.

"I'd rather not."

My response is immediate. My tone flat.

He pulls back for a startled moment. Then abruptly he laughs, accompanied by a shake of my shoulder. "You Brits. Such dry humor."

As I'm being shaken like a ragdoll, I cast a sidelong glance at Paula, who has been following the conversation from across the room. She gives two thumbs up in a sort of *Power on! You are doing great!*

I bet this is the sort of gesture nurses give women in labor when they're on hour nineteen and the nurses secretly know they've got at least another ten hours to go.

I take a breath.

There are thirty-four couches in the house hosting this charity event.

Thirty-four couches among the sixteen rooms of this $70 million estate, which looks and feels more like an airport with an open bar crawling with Hollywood elites than the kind of place you'd call home.

And around these thirty-four couches, there *must* be someone of influence who doesn't have a sausage-eating problem and an obsession with Lavender Rhodes.

"*It's called networking, Finn,*" Paula had said when she handed me a ticket two days ago. "*If you really want to move out and up, this is the place they bring the ladders. And if you really want to get on one of those ladders, you're going to have to schmooze your pants off.*"

I brace myself and refocus on him as he continues his lecture. To me. About the art of writing for the telly.

"*Remember, half the guests at this party would cheerfully murder you behind the bushes and take your place if they could get away with it. Remember, Mr. Henry has more money and fresh interest in the affairs of Hollywood than he knows what to do with, thanks to a robust life in business and a recent marriage.*"

I spot a long white carpet fiber on the sausage on his plate.

Watch his eyes gloss over it with disinterest before he plucks it off and bites the sausage in two.

"Did you know, Masters," he says around a mouthful, as his eyes take on a special gleam, "I'm a writer myself?"

I throw an exasperated gaze at Paula.

No.

I survived mention of Lavender Rhodes.

I will not survive the I'm-also-a-writer conversation too.

But Paula throws me a you-stay-right-there-young-man stare. I grit my teeth but stay.

She's a convincing one, that Paula.

Ten years my senior. Mum of four, three of whom are state championship wrestlers, all of whom could pummel me within an inch of my life—including the seven-year-old. She carries a bit of post-baby weight around the middle, which she spent a couple of years declaring she was working off but now just refers to fondly during late-night writing sessions—usually with taquito in hand—as Fred.

She's been a story editor since I began in the lowly ranks of writing assistant. Saw my potential when I was bringing the room caffeine during 2:00 a.m. shifts and frantically taking notes. She takes the credit for pulling me up to staff writer. She befriended me. Mentored me. And also, in her motherly way, terrifies me.

The squint in her eyes just now sends a clear message: *Be pleasant. Remember why you are here.*

I clench my jaw. Pleasant.

"Is that so?" I reply with as much interest as possible. "How long have you been . . ." I pause. "A writer?"

"Oh, decade at least," he says flippantly, as though we're talking about fishing. Or riding a bicycle. "The story first came to me in the middle of the night. *Gripping* stuff. And I just saw the whole thing laid out for me right then"—he manages to put four fingers up in a picture-this style, and I don't even glance as a crab cake drops to the ground—"start to finale. Guess what the murder weapon was? You'll never guess in a hundred years."

I wait.

But he's looking at me with expectation, clearly one of those people who actually likes you to guess a handful of incorrect things.

"Oh. Hmm," I say, feigning to rack my brain. I throw out something so terribly cliché he'll win his little game. "Cyanide."

His face drops.

He looks so wounded I backpedal.

"Which is *very* clever, if that's what you thought of," I say, tweaking both brows. "It can be given surreptitiously with immediate results."

"Yes!" he cries, all wounds forgotten. "It *is* a clever little idea! Dropping a little into a cup of tea at a restaurant would be rather ingenious, wouldn't it? A swap by someone you had *thought* to be a trusty waiter?"

I'm going to just pretend I've never heard of Sherlock Holmes here.

"What's the name of your book? I'll have to look it up."

"Ohhh," he says, pulling a face. "I haven't gotten to writing it down yet. You know how it is. Something's always blocking my way. But it's here." He taps his temple. "Safe and sound."

I stuff both hands in my pockets and rock back on my heels. Swallow hard. "Sure. Sure."

It pains me. Physically pains me to have this conversation.

"And believe me," he says, "I've watched my fair share of that show of yours and I've never seen it done quite like this."

Cyanide shows off the top of my head:

Season 2, episode 11.

Season 4, episode 2.

Season 4, episode 8.

"Right," I say.

"Right?!" he cries, and then with an almighty slap hits me on the shoulder as though he's found someone who finally gets it.

Shakes me a few times.

And then freezes.

Watery eyes staring at me.

Thoughts apparently spinning.

"You know, Finn," he says, leaning in even closer, the sausage on his breath unmistakable. "You might be just the man I've been looking for. With your creative intellect, my guidance, and any luck tonight, a conversation that will draw Lavender Rhodes into a mutually"—he lowers his voice—"*advantageous* opportunity, we could be the start of a little dream team—"

That's it.

"I'm so sorry, Mr. Henry," I interject, disentangling myself from his web as I step back. "A colleague is trying desperately to get my attention. I really must be going."

"Oh?" He turns in the direction of the room behind him and, compelled, I lift a finger towards Paula as if to say, *Yes, I see you. I'm coming.*

She pretends not to see me.

I raise my finger higher and begin to wave.

She—very clearly having zero interest in helping me make my escape—turns her back on me and exits the room.

"It was truly a pleasure," I say, undeterred. "I wish you the best of luck in your future projects."

I'm willing to leave my job for just about any substitute. But there are limits.

And Lavender Rhodes is that limit.

I can't feel too guilty about leaving him, because the moment I step into the crowd, several guests with beady, vulturelike eyes swoop in, and Mr. Henry, with barely enough time to pop another sausage into his mouth, greets them boisterously through a mouthful and begins again.

Now to find Paula.

I maneuver through one room and into another. Then an adjoining one. Then another.

Each as packed as the others.

The house is a melting pot of two distinct types of Hollywood corporates.

Both types in their sequined garb. Both clutching neon-colored liquids in martini glasses and clouding the room with expensive fragrance. But from a mile away, I could pluck them apart. Drop each into his or her designated category.

The glitter or the glue.

Paula and I are Hollywood's glue, those who belong to the behind-the-scenes work: the financing, the developing, the writing. Anyone from the elite creators of the biggest hits on telly to the prop designer on a B-lister who managed to secure a ticket. Yes, we have on the suits and dresses. Yes, Paula looks rather nice tonight with a nest of curls arranged by Chloe in makeup. But no amount of hair, makeup, or clothing can conceal us enough that we could be mistaken for the other type. There's always some clue—the streak of a tan line, the slight hunch in the shoulders, general level of confidence.

And then, of course, there are the glitter. The stars who speak through blindingly white veneers the words we feed them onstage or on set. The ones who don't wither when a crowd looks at them. The ones who can walk in wearing a costume designed to look exactly like a sheet of computer paper with an egg on it as though this is just a typical Saturday.

Two very different worlds.

Four flights of stairs up and down, twenty minutes, and one ominous text from Paula's husband with the words STOP HER, and I find her at the other end of the house. We're in a room that looks like an aircraft hangar, the entirety of one wall raised to reveal the side yard. The sound of barking echoes off the concrete floors, matching the noise level of an aquamarine waterfall outside flowing into a glowing pool on a clifftop overlooking the city. The view of the skyline is majestic, but surprisingly enough, fewer people stand on the green turf admiring it than beside the rectangular booth where Paula stands now. Barking is coming from at least a dozen large bins. Employees race around as men and women lean over the booth, pointing with their glossy nails. A general frenzy pulses through the air. The atmosphere falls somewhere between the Glastonbury Festival and the discovery of the Princess Diana Beanie Baby at a car boot sale in the 1990s.

A banner above the booth reads Paws with a Cause.

Leaflets are scattered on the floor all around, scribbled with words about a therapy-dog charity and where to donate. I don't look long enough to read it through though, because taking up half the sheet is *her* face, beneath the bold words "Rare Appearance by . . ."

Her.

A hundred Lavender Rhodeses on leaflets all around me.

I step around them, careful not to taint my shoes by a touch.

Frankly, I'd leave the room entirely were it not for the need to grab Paula. Or more specifically, save her husband. Because I see now what Mike was referring to in that text.

"Back away from the puppies, Paula," I say, halting behind her.

Paula freezes.

She turns slowly, revealing two cream-colored snowballs in her hands, which, upon further inspection, are living animals. Tiny brown eyes peek out behind the masses of fur. Petite teddy bears, if you will.

A woman beside us reaches towards one. Paula sticks out an elbow protectively, then swivels around to block her.

I may be too late.

"Oh good, Finn. I couldn't hold them off much longer. Here."

"Wha—" I say over the clamor.

And before I know it, I'm being handed off a puppy as if it's a martini.

"What is this?" I say, looking at the thing in my hands.

"That one's for you."

"What? You're joking. Are you mad?"

"Shhh!" Paula hisses, slapping the hand of a man trying to take hold of the dog in my arms.

A man I'm almost certain is Rowan Atkinson.

"Do you realize what this is?" she says in a rush. "These dogs are the goody bags!" She bellows, "*The goody bags!*"

Okay, we've officially entered Princess Diana Beanie Baby–era level.

She rubs the puppy maniacally as she continues, "This is a Chow Chow. They're worth over $11,000! And here they are just *giving* them away." Her eyes run over the bins of puppies labeled with a variety of exotic names. Löwchen. Pharaoh Hound. Tibetan Mastiff. One particularly rowdy bin in the back is peculiarly labeled Program Dropouts.

"Terrific," I reply. "But it's also a dog. And you have four kids."

"So?"

"Two other dogs."

She gives an annoyed what-does-that-have-to-do-with-this? sniff.

"One stray cat. Two snakes," I continue.

Her bottom lip begins to pucker out.

"In a house that's twelve hundred square feet with a dining table that doubles as your office."

Silence.

"Just last week you tried to give away your cat. To me."

The curls nestled at the nape of her neck quiver as she shakes her head. "Mike texted you, didn't he?" she spits out, squinting at me. "You're teaming up on me."

"The last thing you need to add to your life is a puppy. Despite the fact they're worth more than your minivan."

"But—"

Our eyes lock for several seconds. Continuous *ding*s are coming from both our phones, no doubt all from Mike.

Finally, with a massive shrug that sets off all the sequins down to her toes, she groans through her teeth. "Fine." Multiple hands appear magically to take the dog, which she blindly releases. She then plops the dog I'm holding into a second set of hands. "You know, if you ever fall into a bad case of thallium sulfate poisoning, don't come looking for me to bail you out with any Radiogardase antidote." She flings her arms out. "Because *heaven knows* you can't support me despite all I do for you."

A short bark of a laugh explodes behind us, and simultaneously, Paula and I turn.

A man thirty years my senior stands before us, quietly outdressing everyone in the room, including the woman dressed as a sheet of computer paper and egg. A single red rose rests in the breast pocket of his tuxedo jacket. Thick salt-and-pepper brows hover like rain clouds over baby-blue eyes. A frank, permanent crease sits between his brow, as though he's spent much of his life disapproving of people and is unafraid to show it.

But his eyes are bright, earnest even, as he looks at me and stretches out one hand. As we shake, Paula's eyes become round as saucers.

And all at once it clicks.

This is Victor Goodwin in the flesh.

Creator and executive producer for Goodwin Productions. The brains behind fifteen films that have brought in over $2 billion at the box office worldwide. Innumerable TV series. The creator of *Neighbors*, the long-running sitcom for Wagner Television beloved by billions of people around the world.

Victor Goodwin. The legend in the flesh.

Another man moves around us.

No, that's not correct.

He makes a massively wide berth around us, pushing into

others rather than enter our conversation. I cast a quick glance around and suddenly realize everyone around us has withdrawn a good five feet.

"You crime writers certainly have a way with insults," he says.

"Mr. Goodwin," I say, surprise clear in my voice. I give a quick nod. "This is an honor."

"Finn Masters, is that right?" Goodwin replies.

I didn't think Paula's eyes could get wider, but there they are. Her contacts are going to fall out.

"Yes. That's right."

"I must say, I'm a huge fan of your work."

The words hit me like a blow.

A tiny whistle escapes Paula's lips.

For the first time, I'm finding it hard, very hard indeed, to give my patent reply.

"It's . . . a joint effort," I say after a moment. "Everyone in the writers room is essential." After a long pause, I add, "Especially Paula here. She's been on the team since the beginning."

Paula, who's turned quite wooden, teeters under my pat on her shoulder.

"Pleasure," he says, but his eyes don't leave mine. "I've been following you for some time, Masters. You've left an imprint. A mark upon the show."

"For the better, I hope."

"Obviously," he answers with a slight flick of his brow, as though it was stupid of me to ask for reassurance.

"Well," I say unsteadily. "Thank you. That's quite the compliment."

"Not a compliment. The truth."

I see Goodwin is the absolute opposite of Mr. Henry. He's the kind of man who speaks bluntly. Even at parties on a Friday night, he doesn't waste time or words.

"I followed along the first two seasons because I like to keep my eye on the competition," he continues. "Get a clear view of the landscape."

He has to be joking.

Higher Stakes hardly counts as competition.

"But then something surprised me when I started the third season. Right after you were hired on." His eyes grow steely. There's a hardness in his voice as though what he's about to say is of great and unfortunate importance. "I found I was starting to *like* it."

"Th-thank you?" I say.

"I began to look forward to six o'clock, Monday evenings," he adds with a frown.

Several seconds go by.

I'm not sure how to respond to this.

"And then one day," Goodwin says slowly, voice dropping to a foreboding rumble, "I did something inexcusable. I found myself rescheduling a small dinner party."

From cues alone, one would think I was supposed to display shock and cry out, *"No!"* Instead, I wait silently for him to continue.

"Why?" He presses an accusing finger on my chest. "So I. Could watch. Your show. *You*"—he taps on my chest twice—"hooked me on your show."

My eyes flicker to Paula.

"There are plenty of writers on the team—"

"*You* were the change."

Another lengthy silence ensues.

"It's her!" I hear someone hiss in another conversation.

Heads turn toward the side of the house, where windows illuminate the valet in the circular driveway outside. For a moment, I'm tempted to turn my attention away.

"And that," Mr. Goodwin continues, "is why I want to talk to you. Word on the street is that you are looking for new employment."

My chest tightens.

"I'm not sure where you got that information," I say evasively.

I've been careful to only speak to a couple of people.

If my boss found out, I would be sacked on the spot.

"There's Lavender!" somebody cries out.

People begin to move, some slowly, others throwing care and reputation to the wind and rushing in heels with sloshing champagne glasses. Several are taking out their phones. Even the employees clutching leaflets and dogs have made their way outside. Paula, I realize, is no longer beside us.

The room is rapidly emptying but for Goodwin and myself.

I have to tread lightly here.

"What are you hinting at, sir?" I say.

"My supervising producer stepped down last week." He plucks a dog hair off his otherwise impeccable suit. "She decided to"—there's a slight hesitation—"take a sabbatical."

I fight a tilt of my brow.

Goodwin is using the term *sabbatical* pretty loosely. It's no secret he's a workhorse and runs the writers room behind his decade-long sitcom with a perfectionist's eye. Last we heard, Carrie Suja sold all her belongings, including her phone and laptop, purchased a camper van, and now is swerving along the mountainous roads of Colorado with a rabbit in her lap and mushroom tea in hand.

But sure. Sabbatical works too.

"If you're up for the job, I could use you."

And there it was.

Out of the blue, the offer of a lifetime. Not to the lowest rungs of the biggest sitcom in history but as producer. The offer I'd been dreaming of, at my fingertips.

"You want me to join *Neighbors* . . . as supervising producer."

"The rest of the team is adequate to their jobs—"

Adequate? The show has seventy-five Emmy nominations and

twelve wins. Each writer on that team could take my job tomorrow, just sweep it right out from under me if they asked.

"—but the reality is," he continues, then pauses as if deciding whether he really wants to say this aloud. Apparently, what he's about to say is important enough to risk sharing with a total stranger. "We've been on air a long time. America can only handle watching their favorite TV couple repeat a cycle of dating then breaking up for absurd reasons for so long before they give up."

I begin to shake my head. I know what he's saying, but *Neighbors* is a legend. The cast in some measure is on every cover of everything I see in print at any point, any day.

He puts up a hand, halting me. "Nobody's seeing it yet. But ratings have plateaued."

Yes. At the top.

"The writers are blaming it on the holidays. Or saying inane things like, '*Neighbors* is on top. There's nowhere to go.'"

I drop my eyes to prevent him from reading my very thoughts and soul.

"Idiots," he hisses. "It's TV. There's *always* room to grow."

I get it now. I get why Carrie Suja is currently enjoying the winding mountain roads of Colorado in a camper van named *Solo*.

"I've lived long enough, though. And if there's one thing I know, it's TV. I sense change coming. And we need an outsider who can ignite that change. Frankly, I need you."

I look around and for one wild moment the question crops up. Did he know I was going to be here tonight? Even I wasn't sure until the last moment I was going to be here tonight! A creeping suspicion follows that if Mr. Goodwin wanted to find me, he'd find me. By knowing about my whereabouts and finding me at this party. By slipping a pig's head into a cake for me with icing that says, "Work for Me, or Else." One way or another.

As if to answer my unspoken question, Goodwin adds, "I have

a couple other names, but rather fortuitously, I found you here first. And if it's all the same to you, I'd like to just nail down the position tonight."

Tonight.

He wants a decision tonight. As in . . . right now.

Well.

It's simple, isn't it?

It is impossible to turn down.

Absolutely impossible.

Nobody in their right mind would turn down this opportunity. *Everyone* in Hollywood would give *anything* to work for Goodwin. And of course, I have Paula to thank. For giving me that ticket and dragging me here.

I suck in a breath and flick my eyes over.

Paula's on her toes now, craning her neck with her hands on the shoulders of—*is that Melissa Rauch?*—as they all peer through the window.

I at least have to try.

"It'll be a challenge jumping in from the outside. I could use somebody in that room on my side."

Something in his eyes flashes, as though he sees my challenge . . . Does he like my bravado?

Desperation courses through my veins with the urgent plea he likes my bravado.

"You want her?" He tosses a head Paula's direction.

"She's been in the business fifteen years." I pause, throwing out one more bone. "Came up with Cedar Christie's character herself."

Zing.

The crease between his brows eases to a sliver.

Everybody loves Detective Phillips's charming, comedic supporting character. Cedar Christie is the sidekick who brought new life to the show's fifth season.

I can see his tongue sliding over his teeth as he considers my proposition.

He wears the same expression as that guest serial killer we had on last season.

Prodigious thinking.

Lining up the dominos of how things will play one by one and then mentally flicking the first domino and watching how it all falls.

Apparently he likes what he sees, because he blinks and pivots his attention back to me.

"She'll come on as staff writer. If she's worth her salt, she'll move up the ranks as people die off."

Funny.

Most people call that getting promoted.

"But know this, Masters," he continues, and there they are again, those rain-cloud brows moving together forebodingly. "I don't like to waste my time. If you're in, this is an *all-in* position. If you're one of those people who likes nights to themselves—"

Who'd want that? Staying at work late to write is part of the gig.

"—weekends—"

Sure. I am accustomed to occasional Saturdays in the writers room.

"—holidays—"

Whoa now.

"—time off for 'weddings'—"

Why did he put that in air quotes?

"—funerals for your aunt's next-door neighbor's niece—"

Well—

"—and all those other little *extracurriculars*—"

I mean, I'm fairly certain no one in the history of the world has referred to a funeral as an extracurricular.

"—then this job isn't for you. But if you are willing to work, to consider coming in early as on time and leaving late as standard, and the thrill of seeing your ideas come to life and entertaining an *entire generation* is sufficient . . ." He pauses and lifts a finger as if to declare that his next words are key. "If you can give 150 percent to this job, then name your price and I'll double it."

He stops.

And is waiting for me, it seems, to answer.

With an actual number.

I'm tempted to look around me, half expecting this to be some cruel party trick bigwig celebrities play on the lowly nobodies at parties. Which would then be caught on camera.

Then shared, of course, and everyone gets a good laugh.

While I get fired.

But there is the chance.

The deliriously hopeful chance.

"Ten grand per episode," I say.

Bold is the right choice, yes?

I scrutinize his expression in that blink of a moment, hoping I am right.

Mr. Goodwin is stoic for far, far too long.

Then he laughs.

"You'll do it for five," he replies and slaps me hard on the back. "And if you last till June, we'll talk. Now if you'll excuse me . . . I'll see you Monday morning."

And suddenly he's strolling towards the exit doors.

"Where are we meeting?" I call out.

"At work," he calls back, as though the question is an obvious one, and he takes offense at obvious ones. "*Obviously.*"

Right. I'll just figure out that little detail later.

And suddenly, there I am.

Standing alone beneath a slowly revolving disco ball in an empty room. Martini glasses with neon liquids strewn around me. A yap coming from an escaped puppy racing across the floor.

I've just accepted a job. And the job is perfect.

I ignore the open door and, stuffing my hands into my trouser pockets, step slowly over to the window and look out.

Cameras flash like lightning.

A crowd has formed around the circular driveway.

The job is perfect.

I watch as everyone—both the glitter and the glue, all so posh and polished—completely loses their cool as one leg with a four-inch-heeled shoe stretches out of the limo and touches the pavement.

The *job* is perfect, I repeat, chest tightening as I watch the woman take the hand of a man and step out in a simple shimmering silver gown.

Her hair falls over one eye and she pulls it back, giving a winsome smile to the crowd as though they are just the chummiest of friends.

Repulsive.

The job *is perfect.*

Through the window, I can hear the muted cries of people calling, "Lavender! Over here!"

Vomit. In my mouth.

Who told her to choose the name Lavender Rhodes?

What feeble marketing ploy was it to encourage audiences to hear her name and conjure up images of driving through fields of lavender?

It's Mary. Mary Rhodes.

But apparently, the name embodied by millions throughout history—including the Virgin Mother herself—wasn't good enough for her.

I watch from the window as the crowd swallows her.

A weak February rain begins to dot the lawn.

Rain slaps the window and slowly rolls down the pane.

I'm certain from an outsider's perspective I look like an angry old man. The one naysayer among a crowd of enthusiasts. But they don't know her like I do, do they?

This.

Job.

Is.

Perfect.

A career move of a lifetime.

A pivotal moment in my life. Absolutely everything I've ever wanted.

Except for her.

Because I hate—no, it's not a strong enough word—I absolutely *loathe* Lavender Rhodes. And on Goodwin's famed *Neighbors*, Lavender Rhodes is the star.

But . . . the job is perfect.

WEEKLY CAST SCHEDULE

NEIGHBORS

Monday:

9AM Makeup

11AM Shooting Before Live Audience, Stage 2

Tuesday:

9AM Table Read New Episode, Writers Room

Wednesday:

9AM Rehearsals, Stage 2

3PM Run Through Show, Stage 2

Thursday:

9AM Rehearsals, Stage 2

1PM Makeup

3PM First Dress Rehearsal, Stage 2

Friday:

9AM Makeup

10AM Final Dress Rehearsal, Stage 2

Sonya Bhavsoman:

Makeup: ~~Amely Clement, 555.818.3451 Gideon Peck 555.929.2348 Hattie Davis 555.888.2939~~ N/A

Wardrobe: Fay Silverman, *555.588.8192*

PA: Westley Ford, *555.155.2562*

Lavender Rhodes:

Makeup: Chloe Ostrander

Wardrobe: Fay Silverman, *555.588.8192*

~~PA: Selah Wilson~~

Kye Walker:

Makeup: Brenna Bailey

Wardrobe: Fay Silverman, *555.588.8192*

PA: ~~Dave Wahlquist, 555.112.4234~~ Maggie Goodwin, 555.777.2384

Chapter 2

Lavender

Monday, Film Day, Stage 2

One of the most underrated joys in life is watching someone's existence become just a little bit better on account of your efforts.

Writing an anonymous check to pay for the surprise medical bill of an employee at the juice bar you frequent? Lovely.

Surprising the prop designer's wife with a private audition with the casting director who owed you a little favor? Wondrous.

Setting up two lovebirds on a blind date and having the honor of giving the speech at their wedding two years later? Priceless.

There is truly nothing quite so beautiful as not only knowing just what can help someone better their life, but also being the bearer of those things.

"But I don't *want* a puppy!" Sonya cries.

"Yes, but that's the thing. *Yes, you do!*" I say enthusiastically, holding firm to the leashes despite the monumental tug of ten dogs pulling me in every direction.

Sonya, a horrified expression on her face, as though expecting the dogs to draw and quarter me like medieval executioners at any moment, pulls her robe tighter around her body.

It's Monday morning, twenty minutes to nine. Filming day. The day a week's worth of running lines and meticulously crawling through every second of what will become twenty-two minutes of laughs and sighs comes to fruition. I'm supposed to be en route to the makeup chair, and given how I look right now, probably running, not walking.

Instead, I'm standing in the hallway in front of Sonya's dressing room. A clattering of what sounds like a thousand dishes falling to the floor resounds in the distance and all the dogs pause as one to look toward the noise. (*Chef's Kitchen* shoots on Monday mornings, too, and the walls aren't as thick as you would think.)

Sonya's hair is in giant rollers.

A bronzy blush runs up one-half of her face, the makeup brush in her left hand ready to swipe the other side.

It hasn't been confirmed yet, but I believe Sonya holds the world record for running off makeup artists. So many, in fact, that the show stopped hiring them and now she does it on her own.

She was thrilled about this because, according to her, Amely was heavy-handed on the concealer, Gideon got her face confused with a blank canvas and thought he was Michelangelo, Hattie used winter colors, and one-day stay Presley kept forgetting she wasn't a "blond-haired, blue-eyed Barbie . . . No offense, Lavender."

None was taken.

It comes as no surprise to anyone that Sonya applies her own makeup better than them all, though. Whenever Sonya decides to do something, it's as good as done (so everyone get out of the way), and it's done in award-winning fashion.

A moplike dog with strings of gray completely obscuring both eyes rushes towards Sonya, strings bouncing, and she grabs the door and holds it in front her like a shield.

I bend down to pull him back—an immediate mistake, as

they've all learned in the past thirty hours where I hold my stash of treats.

Which is why, moments later, I'm flat on the ground beneath the pile of them, pushing them off as they sniff around my pockets. Sonya doesn't look convinced as I say, "You're going to *adore* him. He's my favorite."

I attempt to reach over for the puppy I handpicked for her. He's currently ripping at the hem of my silk skirt. (Which is just *fine*. Skirts are *things*. And puppies are *lives*.) Once I manage to elbow off the others and get his teeth out of my skirt, I hold him up.

"Isn't he adorable?"

She doesn't speak.

But she doesn't have to.

We all know he is.

Covered in a soft tricolored fluff of black, brown, and white, the Bernese Mountain Dog puppy is swallowed up in fur with just a few dots of black on his otherwise pink nose. His paws are enormously oversized. His tail wags tremendously as his big, honey-brown eyes bore into Sonya's.

He doesn't like to sleep, as it turns out.

But that is an irrelevant point given he is merely eight weeks old; ergo, hate of sleep is just a characteristic of puppies and not a life trait.

Sonya doesn't need sleep anyway.

What she needs is a puppy to kick her out of the organizing-to-the-extreme streak she has fallen into, thanks in large part to the influencers she started watching who organize quite literally *every single thing* in their lives.

I actually watched her finish a book about organization the other day, smile with satisfaction, then throw it in the donation bin according to the rule that one must have no more than two books in one's house at any time.

She dragged me to her bathroom once to view her latest project: an entire drawer dedicated to neat straight rows of cotton balls.

Cotton balls.

Last month, I watched her get rid of every item in her house that wasn't cream, white, or tan. All of it. She even tossed out her beloved cans of LaCroix so she could make space for some awful white, fizzy off-brand she *doesn't even drink*.

She needed this puppy.

She needed somebody to shake her out of her latest obsession.

And I have the honor of being her benefactor.

"Doesn't he have the most soulful eyes?" I say, holding him up. "I snatched him up as soon as I saw him. There was this rather manic-looking woman hovering over the crate while talking on her phone, saying something about trading in one of her kids for these dogs, and I told myself, 'Lavender, if you know it's right for Sonya, you've got to do it *right now*.'" I pull the puppy's fluffy little face up to mine. "Now, no pressure, but I'm thinking Bernie. Or Bernard. It's rather regal for a Bernese, don't you think?"

"Where did you *get* these animals?" Sonya is looking down at me like I've gone mad.

I don't like her tone, but then, from the outside looking in, I can see it.

I'm sitting on the concrete floor outside her dressing room in a tangle of leashes. I haven't slept in roughly thirty hours, thanks to a shocking amount of barking and accidents and a general indifference towards all of my belongings. My hair is a mess thanks to falling asleep on the floor and having a dog paw my head. There are mascara streaks beneath my eyes (nothing Chloe can't fix). My skirt from yesterday is on inside out (again, nothing Chloe can't fix). But *look at all these pups*!

"They were at the charity event I went to Saturday!" I exclaim breathlessly. I reach for a drag of yesterday's coffee from my tumbler, which I had set down before knocking, but one of the dogs has tipped it over and started chewing on the lid.

No matter.

"They were doing a fundraiser and these little ones needed a home. When I went back at the end of the night after getting your Bernie"—I pause pointedly—"I was floored to discover that for some *bizarre* reason, there were several left over. The head woman was really disappointed. Said people just went straight for the puppies and overlooked the ones who actually came from the program. Or rather, *had* been in the program before they'd failed out. Can you believe it?"

Her eyes cut to the dog lapping up my spilled coffee. "Hardly."

"And when she said that, I realized *how dare I* point at the splinter in another's eye, when *look* at the log in my own! I, too, am part of this broken system. Picking out this sweet pup when all these other perfectly lovely dogs were left on their own. Judging beings by their looks. Casting others aside just because"—the chihuahua makes a grab for my recently bandaged hand, and I pull it away quickly—"they're a little less *easy*."

"So . . . you took them all," Sonya says slowly. She eyes the one-eyed beagle growling voraciously as it pulls on my leather sandal.

"Lavie." She uses that voice. That you-can't-honestly-think-this-is-a-good-idea voice.

"I have a plan," I reply quickly, just as I've repeated the last ten times to the last ten people who've approached me with the same concern. "I'm not keeping *all* of them. I'm just"—I pause, looking for the right word—"*fostering* them until they find their forever homes. And *this*," I choke out, unwrapping a leash that's been tightening around my neck, "little fella belongs to you!"

I offer Bernie to her. (I mean, honestly, how could he *not* be Bernie? The name fits perfectly.) She pulls away. "Absolutely not," she snaps. "I don't *want* a dog."

"Of course you do."

"They pee everywhere. They *stink*."

"So do babies. But they grow on people too."

"They shed black fur everywhere!"

"Yes, but—" I interrupt myself. I have to take this point seriously. I may have to concede here. No problem. I'll just . . . I look at the dogs. We can start with baby steps. "How do you feel about white fur, then?" I reach for the cocker spaniel staring at a wall two inches from his face and pick him up. "Now he has a little bit of a depression problem—"

"*No!*" Sonya says resoundingly. "No white fur. No black fur. No depressed dogs, no puppies. The only acceptable level here is no fur." And lest I pull a hairless dog out of my bag of tricks, she adds, "Because of having *no dogs*."

"But you would get to make use of that nice new vacuum of yours," I say.

At *this* she pauses.

Considers.

Shakes her head. "*No*. And most importantly, Lavender, *you're about to be late*."

I can see by the way her arms cross that I'm not going to make any headway today.

I press my lips together.

Consider my situation.

"Fine," I say lackadaisically, waving one hand in the air and gathering my skirt to stand. "That's completely fine. I am happy to keep your"—I say the next few words in a rush—"adorable little miracle until you are ready for him to come home. In the meantime"—I gather up my leashes—"if you'll excuse me . . ."

I'm halfway down the hallway when Sonya calls in an exasperated tone, "Lavie, wait."

I spin on my heels.

She nods down the hall.

"Try Kye. He's idiot enough to take on a life-altering responsibility on a whim because you asked him. And then hurry up," she adds, louder, "because I'm not sure even I could fix what you've done with that hair."

Hmm.

Kye.

Well. I had planned to head to the writers room next. Knew several people there who were for a fact lonely, not to mention the fact they could use a room mascot. But Kye *did* just go through a pretty terrible breakup. Yes . . . he probably could use a pup after being dragged through the news. (Is it really dragging when you're to blame?)

I look down at the brood. Doleful eyes look up, and I feel a pang for them all.

Which one? Which one would be perfect for *Kye*?

The scraggly red corgi with the banana eye patch to match his winning personality? The pair of really, *really* large Saint Bernards, who may have barked the past thirty hours (and I must make this *very* clear) without ceasing, but did so with the biggest, sweetest eyes? The fourteen-year-old terrier with a shocking level of bad breath, but who gives the most darling kisses? The Basset Hound puppy who can't stop tripping over his ears—but yes, does have a bit of a psychotic, growling, sinking-teeth-into-people's-skin problem? (Nothing a good first-aid kit can't handle.)

It'll be a mystery. They're all just so perfect.

The dogs tug me down the congested hallway, and I gather up my skirt and tumbler with one hand.

The scent of popcorn trickles down the hall, and I'm nearly hauled right past Kye's door.

At the very last moment, I manage to grab the door casing with the heel of my shoe like I'm rock climbing and hanging on to the ledge for dear life. Barks echo off the concrete walls and down the hall while I call with a feeble, "Kye? You in?"

Now, what I'd *planned* to do was present each dog to his or her future owner in a more ceremonious style. Create a calm environment. Give a little speech. Hold the dog out to the chosen owner, who would take the animal with awe and humble pride (as they should). As if I'd knighted them, maybe. I wanted them to feel the honor bestowed upon them.

Just then, the man with the popcorn rounds the corner and heads straight for us, and the dogs go absolutely wild. The hallway behind Stage 2 is narrow, and the dogs (particularly Basset Hound Flesh Eater) are making it difficult for people to pass. I'm trying my best to get the dog treats out of the tiny leather purse at my hip, and having a rather hard go of it, when Kye's door opens.

The dogs make an almighty lunge for the popcorn and my shoulder makes a loud *pop*. I cry out, biting my bottom lip, then quickly smooth my expression into a smile. "Care if we come in?"

Kye, to his tremendous credit, doesn't hesitate. Brandishing a laugh that echoes down the hallway, he flings the door open.

Kye, for the record, is the love of my life.

At least on-screen the past ten years.

"Lavender. What. On *earth*. Have you done?" he says in amusement.

And in true, born-on-an-eighty-seven-thousand-acre-cattle-ranch-in-Colorado-before-coming-to-LA-to-act Kye form, he takes the leashes in one hand and performs a series of twists, tying them all together to the leg of the leather couch on the wall opposite before I have time to blink. There's a *thud* as two of the four legs of the couch rise and pound against the concrete floor. But the knot doesn't give.

Several of the dogs' heads jerk left and right as they consider this.

Kye's broad-as-a-boogie-board shoulders look even larger as he puts both hands on his hips and stands over them. "*Hush*," he commands, and immediately the two Saint Bernards sit.

The Saint Bernards.

Of course.

My hand, freed up for the first time in . . . well, in about thirty hours, feels like it's been drowning and suddenly has air. The throb is monumental, and I begin to rub it with my other hand.

"So." Kye turns to face me. His eyes dance. "The rumors are true."

I drop my hand and adjust my button-up lilac blouse that had at one point been tucked into the front of my skirt and is now dangling messily on one side. I swipe at my bird's nest of a bun, but it's hopelessly matted.

I spot a stain on the wrist of my blouse.

Ah. And a hole.

Well, the show must go on.

I hold out my not-sprained-in-a-hundred-places hand like Vanna White showing off a new car. "Kye Walker, I'm about to change your life."

"Oooh, fun," he says, crossing his arms excitedly. "I love when you do the speech. Should I sit? Last time you had me sit."

I hesitate.

So yes, *technically* now that I think of it, this may be how I began my speech when I tried to convince him and Sonya to take a last-second drive outside Vegas in that old green VW camper van I'd found on eBay (which ultimately broke down forty miles in). And I might have used similar words last month when I pitched them on buying a series of dying B&Bs. But on the bright side and to his credit, Kye, for one, is always in.

He waggles his fingers as he leans against a chair. "I'll stand. Okay. Go on. Tell me how my life is about to be changed."

I clear my throat. Begin again. "Two days ago I had the

privilege and opportune experience of crossing paths with several hounds in need of rescuing."

He nods. "From a shelter. I've heard."

"Well," I say, "not exactly. They flunked out of dog therapy school. But the cages in their demoted rooms were really quite small. And I hear several of the employees picked favorites."

"The audacity." He presses his lips together and nods for me to continue.

I hesitate, my focus broken momentarily by the way he's leaning with his arms over his chest, his eyes boring into mine.

He can't help it.

He is in very technical terms unnaturally attractive, particularly when he fixes his attention wholly on someone. Something about those shockingly friendly emerald-green eyes mixed with a weight-lifter's masculinity. Kye lifts weights like physicians wash their hands, thoroughly and often.

"And these dogs," I continue, rubbing my hand. "These victims, if you will—"

His eyes tick to the basset growling and ripping the corner of his leather couch. And the corgi who has just lifted its leg and begun peeing on it.

I freeze, and the muscles in Kye's neck twitch slightly, but he doesn't move. "You were saying."

My eyes dart between looking into Kye's eyes and looking around for a paper towel. "They need a place to call home. A forever home. And frankly, I can think of no one better suited for these sweet Saint Bernards, Henrietta and James"—I throw out the names on a whim—"than you."

He's looking at me with the same intensity he employed in season 6, episode 22, when he was trying to decide if he really should throw away his career to tell me he loved me. Well, that, and in season 3, episode 20, when he was trying to decide if he should buy that peacock for a wedding.

I've come to know this look well over the years. The I'm-thinking-carefully-and-meticulously-working-out-a-plan look. And it is best, I've learned, not to interrupt.

Good.

Plan away.

Decide which of the two spare bedrooms in that flat of yours Henrietta and James would prefer to call theirs.

He takes a breath. Moves to the dressing table. Opens a drawer.

I sometimes forget how at odds we are until he does things like this: opens his dressing table drawer.

The one in my dressing room is the color of lavender (yes, admittedly on the nose) and often topped by a fresh bouquet or two. They crowd my efforts to touch up hair or makeup, but I don't really mind, and the scent is always well worth the trouble of searching around blooms for a hidden tube of lipstick. A floral couch from the flat Sonya and I (and four other girls) shared in my earliest days in Los Angeles sits staunchly in the center of the room. Nobody knows quite where it originally came from, and nobody, frankly, is brave enough to ask.

Though it sinks and sags in certain spots, and one side is split right up the middle and patched over with bright purple duct tape, it is probably the most beloved spot in the entire studio. Sonya, Kye, and I cling to this spot. Through ups and downs, highs and lows, whenever one of us goes missing, we typically find him or her there.

It's the place we share our deepest fears and secrets, our moments of glory, and the situations we wish we could wash away with the power of tears. Sonya's parents' divorce. Kye's mum's diagnosis. (The splotch of champagne marks our celebration of her being announced cancer-free a year and a half later.) My own relationship tumbles.

It bears little pink wax stains from blown-out birthday candles and a burned-out hole from Kye's short-lived interest in cigars—a hole formed, ironically, the same night I turned him down during his equally short-lived interest in me.

A giant Persian rug blooms across the floor in front of that couch, a mix of purples and greens and golds. And of course, there is a gigantic coffee station on an old but still functioning record turntable in the corner. Which, given the fact we work for Goodwin, is self-explanatory.

Espresso flows through our veins.

The walls are covered in pictures, some framed of awards won and handshakes given, but most simply taped up—of New Year's Eve parties and wrap parties and late nights squeezed together on the couch stuffing ourselves before jumping back into rehearsal. Of first pets and first loves and some, I know, that probably should be taken down. (Who, after all, keeps photos of their previous boyfriends on the walls?) But every time I begin to, I conveniently remember something else I need to do. When the pictures go up, just like memories, they tend to stay.

(Minus those of me with my latest. The day after we broke it off, I walked into my dressing room to discover all the pictures of the two of us snipped into a thousand pieces of confetti and scattered over the rug. He left a disconcertingly large and dying bouquet of roses on my dressing table. And a lengthy, if not quite lucid, love letter. But that is another matter.)

Kye's room, on the other hand, is the opposite of mine. Tan walls. Black dressing table. Zero photographs of former girlfriends—but then, is there a wall in existence that could manage to hold *all* of them?

Tan leather couch that, up until this moment, had never been tinkled on by person or animal. A single black shelf on the wall with four personal Emmys (i.e., props for wooing), each winged golden lady carrying a huge atom in her golden hands. And drawers that, thanks to his personal assistant and without any credit due him, are meticulously organized and supplied at all times. I don't have an assistant, for the record. I am currently on the train of belief that it's in the best interest of my mental health to have as grounded a life as possible. Ergo, my responsibility to tidy up my own drawers. Ergo, my untidy drawers.

Kye nudges away Henrietta's curious nose while spraying something onto the soiled part of the couch. As he rubs with a crisp black hand towel, he opens his mouth. He says my name as one who has the unfortunate task of relaying bad news. "Lavender. Listen."

Then he makes the mistake of looking at me.

He shakes his head. "Don't do that."

"Do what?" I say innocently.

He points the towel at my eyes. "That. That look."

"What look? I can't possibly have a look. I'm much too sleep-deprived to procure a look."

"Oh, you know. The *Lavender Rhodes* look."

I'm attempting to manipulate him, yes.

It's selfish, yes.

But *I cannot live with ten dogs under my roof for the rest of my life.*

Especially these.

They will eat me in my sleep.

I'm sure of it.

I was quite possibly hallucinating last night, but at one point I woke up and found them all standing over me, hatching *a plan.*

The Lavender Rhodes look must have come through once again, because Kye's resolve softens.

He casts a doubtful glance at the dogs.

Swallows.

"Let me get this straight. You've personally undertaken the task of getting homes for all of them."

My heart skips a beat as I hear his tone. "There was nobody else to do it. Look at them."

He frowns slightly and his eyes tick to the clock on the wall.

I know what he's thinking. We're both supposed to be in our chairs; he in ten minutes, me—I cut a glance to myself in the mirror—two hours ago.

"Leave 'em here."

My hands fly to my chest. "What are you saying, Kye? You'll take the Bernards?"

He draws a line between us with his hand. "I'm committing to nothing, Lavie. But leave them here. *All* of them. I'll do my best to find them their"—he throws air quotes around the words with the merest hitch of his brows—"'forever homes.'"

His voice is rich and deep with assurance, and I know I should push back. I know I should fight tooth and nail to see it all through myself, to claim independence and all that, but frankly, the moment the words come out of his mouth, I feel something inside me crumble. I am a damp towel dropping to the floor. A world-weary traveler who didn't realize just how exhausted she was until offered the opportunity to sit and take off her shoes.

The mental offloading ushers in a wave of relief I didn't anticipate.

I bite my lip.

"If you're really sure . . ."

He nods, and I lunge for a hug around the neck. Squeezing tightly, I grin and say, "What would I ever do without you, Kye Walker?"

He gives a breathy laugh, his arms wrapped tight around my rib cage. "Explode, I suppose."

Chuckles on both our parts mingle in the air, then I break off and make for the door.

It's an inside joke (and by inside joke, it's understood that it's an inside joke between us and three-quarters of America). Those words have circled through our characters across a decade as we've been thrust together and then thrust apart. But it's true, isn't it? Without Sonya and Kye, I most probably, definitely, would have exploded by now. That's what best chums are for, after all.

The dogs begin to bark, and I pause with my hand on the door. I should take at least half of them to my dressing room.

I could pull at least *some* weight.

But as my eyes meet Kye's, he gives a firm shake of the head. "Go on, Lavie. You're telling me that I'm going to space today, and I can't take you seriously with that hair."

I roll my eyes but then remember something. "*Don't* find a home for the Bernese." I point to the fluffball curled up on the floor. "He's for Sonya."

"Does she know that?" he calls after me as I head six doors down the hall.

"Does that matter?" I call back as I throw open my own dressing room door, a free woman.

Ten dogs rescued and one step closer to their forever homes. Another joyous day of making the world just a little bit brighter.

WEEKLY STAFF SCHEDULE

NEIGHBORS

Monday:

9AM Final Script Edits, Writers Room

11AM Shooting Before Live Audience, Stage 2

Tuesday:

9AM Table Read, New Episode, Writers Room

Wednesday: TEAM SPLIT:

9AM Rehearsals, Stage 2

9AM New Episode Script Edits, Writers Room

3PM Run Through Show, Stage 2

Thursday: TEAM SPLIT:

9AM Rehearsals, Stage 2

9AM New Episode Script Edits, Writers Room

3PM First Dress Rehearsal, Stage 2

Friday: 9AM Final Dress Rehearsal, Stage 2

Saturday: Submit Following Week's Script, 5PM, Writer Rotate

Updated List of Contacts:

Creator/Showrunner, Victor Goodwin, *555.152.6724*

Executive Producer, ~~Stuart Smith, 555.633.7723~~ ~~Lacey Hernandez, 555.577.3853~~ ~~John Walker 555.582.4762~~

Coexecutive Producer, Cindy Wright, *555.358.6832*

Coexecutive Producer, Ken Zane, *555.555.1221*

Supervising Producer, ~~Dan Ramos, 555.933.8818~~ ~~Carrie Suja, 555.888.3852~~

Coproducer, Haylie Boxleitner, *555.899.5233*

Coproducer, Paige Rumore, *555.823.1113*

Line Producer, Heath Nelson, *555.385.9928*

Executive Story Editor, ~~Oliver Marshal, 555.582.9359~~ ~~Trey Lane, 555.586.2992~~ Clive Nicols, 555.518.9959

Staff Writers:

Marianne (555.858.2522)

~~Brix (555.686.3424)~~

~~Lori (555.588.2344)~~

Harry (555.823.3423)

Erik (555.313.9592)

Writing Assistants:

Joe (555.581.1232); Alex (555.555.9299); Jenkins (555.525.2349)

Writer PAs:

Stephanie (555.585.2322); ~~Mark (555.119.1295)~~

Chapter 3

Finn

Monday, Script Edits, Writers Room

I've got coffee down my freshly pressed dress shirt.

Not a drop, not a splash on my dark trousers, where it would have just barely been seen if you looked at it from a very specific angle under very specific lighting.

An entire, mind you *entire*, twenty ounces of ink-black liquid poured down the front of my heretofore white oxford. And blue blazer. And blue trousers. And belt.

And a dog peeing on my shoe.

"I'm *so sorry*," the woman repeats for the thirteenth time, crouching down with what appears to be a thousand leashes wrapping tighter and tighter around me. Dogs scratch madly on the concrete floor of the hall, squeezing me beneath a python's grip.

It's my first day, nay, my first *hour* in my new job.

With impostor syndrome clinging to my body like the wealth of cats hanging off my neighbor Mrs. Teaberry anytime she opens the door.

With a notoriously intimidating boss known for his demands

and peculiarities—which I'm almost certain include things like *not* showing up ten minutes late and carrying the stench of urine.

Which I am.

"Again. I'm just so, *so* sorry," she repeats, pulling a leash off her throat as she wipes frantically at my shoes with an old Kleenex. "I tried to hold them back. But you wouldn't believe just how *strong* they are. And these shoes. They're four years old. They have absolutely no traction. I *knew* I should've put on something different, just in case—"

Her cheeks are two blazing red spots, and it's clear from the way she keeps looking at my suit and laptop bag that she thinks I'm someone important.

Which, now that I think of it, I guess I am.

Watching her, I'm sharply reminded of those first days when I, too, was at the bottom of the ladder. I distinctly recall that one story about my supervisor who allegedly threw out a PA on his first day because he commented that he watched a TV show from another network. It turned out to be nothing more than a rumor, but still, tiptoeing around the big names is part of the job description.

I do my best to step back and get her to stop.

Stop with the tissue on my shoe.

Stop with the perception that I am anything besides what I really am: absolutely petrified on my first day.

It's challenging, given I seem to have stepped into a sort of dog tornado, but I manage to break free from at least one leash.

"It's fine. Really." I lie because, of course, it's the only course of action. After all, what can I say? No, it's *not* fine, thank you very much, and yes, I *do* very much wish I had listened to my mother and packed an "emergency" set of clothes for just such an absurd and absolutely-out-of-the-realm-of-possibility circumstance. It turns out ten monstrosities of dog can and do drag young women down narrow corridors and bowl you and your coffee over moments before you open the door and enter into key places where attendance is vital.

But here we are.

And there's no need for her to feel mortified.

I hold steady to the doorframe with my crumpled coffee cup as an angry little dog begins gnawing on the foot of a much larger breed, and the larger breed growls in a way most terrifying. The big dog's twin sniffs at the ground and I jolt as it pushes its head between my legs. A handful of people about to enter the hallway pause midstep, see us, take great pains to pretend not to see us, and turn around.

Wonderful.

You really know who your colleagues are in a moment like this.

The one bright spot in this moment is that the dogs have become temporarily distracted, and in that second I seize the opportunity to quickly maneuver myself over and under several leashes until, at last, I'm free.

"See? Nothing—to—worry—about." I yank my leather laptop bag from a yippy little one-eyed growler.

Check my watch.

Two minutes to nine.

One more hallway to go.

I had originally planned to arrive *much* earlier, but at the very least, I still can make it *just* in time to slide in before nine if I race the clock.

I pull the first of what is sure to be a thousand hairs off my pants today.

"Best of luck," I cast over my shoulder, as I begin striding down the hall at as close to a canter as a human can.

I make it twenty or so steps when my feet slow.

No, Finn.

But there they go, my feet slowing to the cadence of a slow trot. The question lingering.

Why hasn't she replied?

My wheels are grinding, creaking as my feet slow to a full stop.

Barks echo down the hall, the racket terribly loud, but still I hear no reply.

I grit my teeth.

Squeeze my eyes shut.

Look over my shoulder.

Immediately regret looking over my shoulder.

Clamp my eyes shut again.

The young woman is standing, several taut leashes wrapped around both arms. Her red hair looks like she's walked through a wind tunnel. The high, skinny, and incredibly worthless heels she made the most unfortunate decision to wear today are sliding on the concrete, despite clear efforts to stay put.

I have two minutes.

And I'm about to break the one absolute rule Goodwin gave me: don't be late.

But then there's a break in the curtain of her hair. And I see her face.

It's a look of absolute despair. Actually, it's the exact look Bob, my ninety-two-year-old neighbor (I have a surplus of elderly neighbors), had last week when I opened my door to take my dog on a morning walk. Bob was drifting on a large inflatable in the middle of the community pool. Totally stranded after our little party the evening before. Just a man bobbing in a pool of glowing turquoise-green Spanish tiles, clinging for life to the neck of a smiling pink flamingo.

I take a steadying breath. Pull my messenger bag over one shoulder as I head back.

"C'mon," I say, unwrapping a handful of leashes from her arm. Already one of the dogs has claimed my shoe and begun trying to drag me.

"Heel," I say firmly. None of them so much as pause, and I heave a sigh. "Okay. Where to . . . ?"

"Maggie," she supplies, and I hear a small exhale of relief whistle through her lips. "And to the line."

Her eyes are grateful, though she doesn't act entirely out of the woods yet—not surprising considering a dog is trying to lift her skirt while she, with her free hand, is trying desperately to keep him down. But there's a significant lift in her energy. Her breath is steadying.

I frown. "The line," I repeat.

I know the line. The line is notorious around here. The line is also all the way across Wagner Studios to Lot A. And what these dogs have to do with the line is beyond me. Still.

It's not like I can turn back now, and the faster the better. "Okay then," I say, throwing my hand out for her to lead. "To the line."

On her cue I follow, and together we slip and slide our way down four halls, through an outdoor shortcut that includes bypassing (evidently highly alluring) dumpsters, back inside through a back door that after one long hallway gives way to a front door, until here at last we stand.

On the platform.

Before the crowd.

I check my watch. I am ten minutes late now.

My jacket is missing a button.

I'm pretty sure I'll need to see a doctor for my rotator cuff.

I hold my dogs as steady as I can while Maggie holds her dogs as steady as she can. She clears her throat before addressing the crowd.

The line is enormous, like it's Black Friday at the Walmart and the tellies are 75 percent off level. All unsurprising. I pass this line every Monday. People, women mostly, clamoring, wringing their hands, even camping in their little sleeping bags on the sidewalk, all to get into the live shooting of *Neighbors*. To be a part of the real-life experience of the show they attend to with more loyalty than their own jobs.

Several food trucks campaign for their attention on one side while security officers stand guard on the other. Fights break out on occasion. The network briefly considered creating an entire reality show around it. Watch your favorite group of misfit neighbors fall into their funny adventures at 8:00 p.m. central, then catch a slew of middle-aged women in pink *Neighbors* shirts throwing camp chairs at one another at 9:00.

"Would anybody like a dog?" Maggie's shrill voice calls to the crowd.

I cut her a look.

Really? This is her plan?

This is why we came all the way out here?

Nobody, of course, budges.

Nobody even hears.

The short dog with floppy ears at her feet growls at its reflection in a glass door and pounces, bounces, and falls back on itself.

"These are some good dogs here," Maggie calls out again.

The only reason anyone has stopped and paid attention to us is because we exited through the very door where they are awaiting entrance. Now that it's abundantly clear we aren't in charge of opening the doors, they are slowly losing interest.

I get a strong scent of syrup and spy one of the breakfast trucks in the distance. I double up my grip on the leashes. Someone is holding a round platter of pancakes and meandering up the line. Really, we're going to get rid of the whole lot of dogs one way or another here in about two minutes.

"Free to anyone who'll provide a good home," Maggie tries again.

The nose of one of the intimidating Saint Bernards twitches. His eyes zero in on the platter.

Incredible.

I believe he just nudged his twin, who also now zeroes in on the platter.

Quicky I lean down to Maggie's ear. "I don't mean to rush you," I say quietly, "but we're about to have a situation on our hands. D'you have another plan?"

"Um . . . ," she begins unsteadily, then bites her bottom lip. "I don't know."

"A shelter?" I suggest.

She shakes her head. "He said just homes. No shelters."

I pause. "Who is 'he'?"

"Kye Walker. I'm his new PA."

Ah yes. Maggie Goodwin. Goodwin's beloved niece. I knew I'd seen that name on the cast schedule.

I frown. One can almost hear a crack of lightning in the distance as I take a closer look at these animals.

Surely . . . I zoom in on the Bernards as a faint memory of the bins at the party comes to mind. Surely . . .

"And how exactly did *he* come into all of these dogs?"

She shrugs. "All I know is Lavender Rhodes had them this weekend and then handed them off to him this morning."

Lavender Rhodes. *Of course*.

Had a nice little feel-good moment, did she, taking in a bunch of needy dogs at a charity? Enjoyed being the center of attention while people snapped photographs and whispered rubbish like, "God doesn't make 'em like her anymore," and "In my opinion, she is the loveliest person in the world."

Right.

And yet where are the cameras now? Who's watching now that she's dumped the problem on someone else without *any* thought or *any* care for who faces the consequences in her wake?

The people left clinging to buoys, bobbing as she flies by in her gargantuan yacht, adjusting her shiny cat-eye sunglasses. Sun ever shining on her, while her monstrosity of a boat casts a shadow on everyone else.

But I'm doing it again.

I'm digressing from real life to have another one of my Lavender Rhodes mental rants.

I check my watch: 9:22.

Now a whole twenty-two minutes past the top of the hour.

I glance over at Maggie, who has decided to take the one-on-one approach and is making a feeble attempt to persuade a lady at the front of the line. Pointless, of course. The woman is sitting in a camp chair. There's a rolled-up sleeping bag beside her, and from the size of the hiking backpack at her feet and slight scent of body odor, it's clear she's spent several days camped out to claim her place.

No offer of a mad Basset Hound is going to make her give it up.

I clench my fist.

Drop my head.

Five years ago, after Lavender had caused the third—but far from last—major disruption to my life, I promised myself never to speak her name aloud.

I have, in fact, a list I wrote several years ago, written in a moment of utter disbelief at just how *incredibly impossible* it was that she, Lavender Rhodes, of all people, could cause so much irreparable harm to my life. I wrote it during a moment of calculated fury, after the latest in a long line of disasters had struck. I wrote it because deep down I really am a writer, and more often than not the best way I process something is by untangling words. And that day, what I concluded was this: Never, Ever, Ever Be Anywhere Near Lavender Rhodes. Or She Absolutely Will Ruin Your Life. Again.

Some people carry around a rabbit's foot in their pocket. Press a four-leaf clover into a book. Blow on a dandelion or candle and make a wish.

Me? I have the list.

And somewhere, if you go into my closet and dig through my boxes, you will find a list that goes like this:

TRANSGRESSIONS AGAINST FINN MASTERS

Age 17: Transgressor causes broken ankle. Finn Masters forced to step down from leading role. Transgressor seizes leading role. Agent in audience. Agent impressed by transgressor. Transgressor offered representation. Transgressor moves to Hollywood to pursue acting career. Meanwhile Finn Masters endures multiple surgeries, two screws, and four months in physical therapy. No opportunity for agent.

Age 20: Finn Masters makes it to final round of casting calls for *Neighbors*. Dropped from opportunity after transgressor sabotages casting call to get Kye Walker hired instead. Career destroyed.

Age 24: Transgressor stops traffic to do photo shoot in crosswalk, because apparently Photoshop is capable of erasing wrinkles and chin fat but incapable of adding stoplights. Finn Masters is late for important meeting. During important meeting, employer offers job opportunity with salary raise to somebody else.

Age 25: Transgressor swipes meticulously planned dinner reservation at L'Appart with first date Finn Masters is particularly keen on. Finn Masters ends up at Shrimp Barrel. Sharing the coleslaw special. No second date.

Age 28: Finn Masters honored as Welling School graduation speaker for alma mater. Scrapes together vacation days and money for plane ticket. Purchases plane ticket. Mum sends out Christmas card informing every family member down to third cousins of the news. Mum plans surprise party with every person Finn Masters has ever met to celebrate post-event. Finn Masters boards flight to said event. Finn Masters is informed via email somewhere over the Atlantic that transgressor has decided to attend, and consequently, Finn's services are no longer required. Mum still throws party, because "Auntie Agatha drove three hours for cake, and we can't eat it all ourselves." Party becomes the most pathetic four hours of Finn Masters's life.

Age 29: Transgressor destroys three-year relationship two weeks before Finn Masters's planned marriage proposal. Finn Masters loses love of his life.

Call me superstitious. But I do not speak her name, have not spoken her name since the fateful day I wrote the list.

And yet.

I *have* to get to my meeting or she will be the reason I have to dig that list out and add another point.

I clench my fists and growl as I face the crowd head-on.

"Who wants a dog touched by Lavender Rhodes?" I call over the crowd.

It's cheap.

I have no idea if they will be good dog owners.

But I once saw two caterers fired for a scuffle over a lipstick- and guacamole-stained napkin she left behind, so it's a worthy thing to bet on.

And sure enough, ten minutes later every dog down to the one-eyed growler has found its way into the arms of fans anxiously taking selfies with their new "prized possessions."

Several are already fondly calling the dogs by their new name: Lavender.

Or in the case of the exceptionally clever: Rhodes.

Moments later, Maggie and I are back inside, animal-free.

Sheer relief is in her voice. "Thank you so much . . ."

"Finn Masters."

She looks like a different woman now without the emotional, and physical, baggage of ten dogs. She quite literally may have grown six inches.

She laughs with wide, impressionable eyes as she pulls a thick strand of hair from her cheek, tugging it behind her ear.

I grin. "It was nothing."

"No, I believe nothing is what everyone else around here did," she says, smoothing her dress as she inhales a sharp breath. "Really, Mr. Masters—"

"Finn," I correct.

"Finn. Thank you," she says softly.

And for just a moment, there's a hint of interest in her speckled, honey-brown eyes that catches me by surprise.

Something that says there is a real possibility that were I to ask for her number right now, I wouldn't get an automatic no.

But of course even I know Goodwin's beloved young niece is not to be trifled with, no matter how legally available she is.

Still, the compliment in her eyes is a bright spot in an otherwise soggy start to the day.

"Well, Maggie, it's my first day at *Neighbors* and I really have to be clocking in," I say, stepping back. "But should you fall into the urgent task of releasing a hundred rare birds into the wild or purchasing two hundred espressos, you'll know where to find me."

"Right." We share a small smile, then she drops her head with a nod. "Good luck in there. And will do."

I'm panting by the time I halt before the words "NEIGHBORS Writers Room" in neat script on the royal-blue door.

Not merely panting but sucking in deep-until-my-ribs-press-against-my-button-up breaths that I try desperately to control as I put my hand on the knob.

Inhale.

My shirt is damp where the coffee spilled across my chest.

Exhale.

I'm missing a shoelace.

Sweat is itching at the nape of my neck.

But the clock is ticking, and with a sense of urgency, I turn the knob and open the door.

9:32 a.m.

A full thirty-two minutes late.

A dozen new faces simultaneously look up at me from the pages in their hands.

A dozen faces pausing in the commotion of the writers room to gape at the man in the soiled shirt who's heaving like he's just finished a marathon.

The writers room is . . . in a word . . . enormous.

Five times the size of that at *Higher Stakes*.

A whiteboard sprawls across the length of one wall, covered in magnets detailing plot points on specific timelines. Pictures cover the other wall, pictures of absolutely anything related to that rain-laden city of Seattle, where the show takes place. Stereotypes abound: from the magazine cutouts of yellow umbrellas resting in sidewalk puddles to crowded coffee shops filled with rain jackets and half-drunk cuppas. Space Needle. Skyline. Ferry to the great outdoors. Business suits and windbreakers. Office cubicles and kayak paddles. City and forest.

And of course, for the star-studded show that is *Neighbors*, three massive black-and-white headshots of Kye, Lavender, and Sonya, surrounded by a dozen smaller photos of the show's most frequent guest appearances.

Leather chairs surround an expansive mahogany table.

A popcorn machine is in one corner.

Three different types of coffee makers with three different types of caffeine dispensers—espresso, drip, and percolator—are in another corner.

No, four. I spy a Chemex.

Seems we all agree about the importance of caffeine.

Another wall is crowded with shelves of gleaming awards. (*Higher Stakes*, by comparison, has three in total.)

The largest U-shaped sectional I've ever seen occupies a connecting room, facing the largest telly I believe exists. Half a dozen doors stand open around the perimeter, personal offices opening to the shared space. A tiny kitchen lies beyond, with an unearthly number of Yoo-hoos stacked on the counter.

No windows.

I step into the room, and my laptop bag spills my crumpled coffee cup from this morning's misadventures out onto the floor.

I stoop to pick it up.

Stand.

"Ah," Mr. Goodwin says, his eyes still intent on the sheet before him. "Finn Masters, everybody. Here at last."

I wince slightly.

Paula, who looks as overwhelmed and small as a herring that's accidentally landed in the center of an orca pod, opens her mouth as though to say hello.

"I'm so sorry to be late, sir. I had an—"

"C'mon, people, keep moving," Mr. Goodwin says, snapping his finger at the dozen scattered around the table. His attention is on several highlighted lines on a page, and he shakes his head at it.

"Joke's dead," he says and strikes out four lines. "Again. We've got to get it *right*."

Somebody, a writer's assistant no doubt, slides me a copy of the script across the table.

This is as much of a welcome as I'm going to get.

I receive hardly more than a glance from the group as I take an empty chair. Everybody has that familiar pre-deadline look I know only too well from *Higher Stakes*, but with the stress level kicked up a few more notches. It's the cramming-before-exams look. The haven't-slept-in-two-days-and-will-fail-if-I-don't-get-at-least-an-eighty look. The last changes prior to setting the script in stone before the cast takes it to screen.

Only, with *Higher Stakes* being a drama, we didn't have live audiences like they do on *Neighbors*. Still. It seems unnatural and unhealthy for the writers to look *this* intense, *this* on edge over a line needing adjustments on a Monday morning, when this script still has weeks to go before it's polished, given the stamp of approval from an executive producer, and shipped off into the cast's hands.

Nobody's neck is on the line here.

It's 9:32 a.m.

Right?

I glance over at Paula, and she raises one brow as though to say, *Well, what happened to you?* I reply with a slight shake of the head.

So much for good impressions.

I spent all weekend preparing for this very moment. After repeating the entire account to Paula five times and managing to sink into Paula's head what Mr. Goodwin had really offered to me, to us, I zipped home and spent every waking minute planning.

Walked around with my laptop and notebook, playing *Neighbors* day and night, catching myself up. Scribbled notes. Drew the story arc of each and every character. Filled out character descriptions. Researched Seattle and the surrounding areas. Tried to catch up on all I'd missed the past decade.

Tried to learn the idiosyncrasies of the show. To catch the rhythm, the undercurrent. To know where I needed to begin in order to let future ideas flow.

Slept little. Wrote and brainstormed much.

Came up with a dozen trails on which to take the show, and a dozen more that were decent enough for the back burner. My laptop bag is full of them.

Frankly, that brainstorming wall of theirs looks like child's play next to what I put up at home.

But it was necessary.

Because in addition to being a perfectionist in my work, the one tiny thing Mr. Goodwin still doesn't know about me is that until yesterday I was the only person in very likely the whole of America who had not watched a single episode. Not one.

Three years ago, I woke up in hospital from appendicitis surgery to Lavender's face on the telly in my room, and I yelled so loudly the nurse thought I was dying.

No. Just had pulled the tubes out straining for the remote.

Of course, I knew the plot. As with the Super Bowl in this country, no matter how hard one tries, one cannot go without hearing *some* news. But still, up to this weekend, I had truly succeeded in avoiding seeing her act.

The worst part, my greatest disappointment, was that I finally saw Lavender Rhodes was not the overrated actress I had so hoped for.

She was good.

Actually, on acting merit alone, she was excellent. Worthy of every Emmy in her no doubt pompous dressing room overflowing with awards and flowers from her cultlike following. She'd made something of the show despite clichéd scripts and oversimplified character arcs. She'd managed to pull out emotion despite flat side characters and their flat side stories. As far as acting went, she was a writer's dream. Surely these people trusted her to flawlessly deliver the words they poured onto the page. I imagine she delivered the jokes, the heartbreaks, the beats just as they saw them in their minds—or better. I would bet she also delivered the not-so-great words in a way that transformed them from mediocre into something great.

The revelation was awful.

I peer over to the person on my right to see the joke in question.

All around the room people are muttering under their breath. It's a race. War. Fight to be the first to clinch the zinger.

"What if . . ." A man holds his script at arm's length. His forehead is screwed up, as if he's deciphering an ancient map. "What if, just as Kye—"

"Lance," the room replies in unison.

"Right," the man says, lower lip quivering nervously. "*Lance*"—he shoots a glance around—"stands at Resident 3A's door with roses for their first date, Lavende— *Ashley* opens hers across the hall. They catch each other's eye, long dramatic pause for feelings"—he winds his hand—"feelings feelings feelings, and then he looks down at the roses and says, 'Whad'ya think? Too much?' And after a bittersweet pause, *Ashley* gives a tender smile and says, 'They're perfect.' Then she closes the door and walks past the kitchen as the camera pans to the dried roses in her windowsill, a memento from their first date ten years ago. End scene."

Mr. Goodwin throws his glasses on the table and squeezes his eyes even before the man is finished. "*We've done it.* We've done it all before." He throws his script on the table, and the papers scatter like cherry blossoms skidding over water in spring. "I want *bigger*," he says. "Better. Even just . . . *different*."

"It *is* decent, Mr. Goodwin," a woman says carefully. "And clock's running."

Wait. This is for *today's* shoot? As in, they are changing it right *now*?

"If I just wanted *decent*, Cindy"—Goodwin's eyes cut to the woman I recognize from heavy Internet researching as the co-exec—"I'd have created *Everybody's Fine Here* or *10th Street*. Do any of *you* know anybody walking around in an *Everybody's Fine Here* T-shirt?"

He pauses. Waits.

Heads shake around the room.

"Do any of *you* know anybody getting tattoos on their bodies of Suzie saying, 'Better luck next time,' from *Everybody's Fine Here*?"

He waits again.

Heads shake.

"*Good* doesn't cut it. *Decent* doesn't cut it. I want *perfection*."

Paula downs her coffee as if it's a whiskey shot and redoubles her staring game at the script.

Everyone in the room seems to have specific idiosyncrasies for their mind work. The man to my left spins a pencil. Another paces, muttering aloud. Paula drinks coffee like a Labrador drinks water. The woman across from me has fallen into a rhythm of scribbling words furiously and then, just as furiously, scratching them out.

Me? I take out a Rubik's Cube.

Almost as soon as I touch the cold plastic, I feel my wheels begin turning.

My hands twist and turn through the weaving patterns, eyes barely flickering to the blur of red, blue, white, green, and yellow as I reread the scene.

It's all fairly simple.

Unrelatably beautiful girl who always responds with the most unrelatably perfect replies has yet another perfect, unrelatable reaction to the fact that her long-term boyfriend has momentarily broken up with her and is now going—obviously, regretfully—on a date with the new woman across the hall. The breakup is because "he's afraid of commitment" (after *ten* years of an on-off relationship, but who's counting), which, of course, is another way of saying the writers ran out of ideas and needed to make up some shoddy excuse for why the perfect couple would break up, yet again, so they can keep the show going.

So they throw in a convenient backstory about his mother or father doing something wrong in the past, thereby causing his inability to move forward, and she reluctantly lets him go. She goes on some passing date that goes nowhere. But then *he* now, he moves on with someone half as interesting and beautiful as Ashley Krane—objectively speaking here, of course—all the while remaining just as close and having just as many bonded moments with the woman he really loves.

Emotionally married to Ashley Krane while dating everyone else under the sun. Technically not together, ergo, viewers keep watching. Happy writers. Happy viewers.

Throw in episodic mishaps and misadventures (getting stuck in air vents while eavesdropping, nearly accidentally marrying one's first cousin, throwing themed parties at the drop of a hat) and there you are, folks. *Neighbors* in a nutshell.

The reality is, it's all just dramatic and unnecessary action, and it's not remotely plausible that a woman in this modern era would allow a man to break up with her after ten years to then go on a date with a woman across the hall two weeks later. Not at all.

But here we are.

And, of course, Lavender's character is going to take this all on the chin with a smile.

It's nauseating. I am having to swallow to stop from gagging.

This is one aspect where crime drama has the upper edge.

Somebody wrongs you? Kill them off.

Lull in the energy of the show? Someone drops dead.

Murder is almost always the answer.

Here though. *This stuff.*

Get a cup of coffee and talk about your feelings.

Get a cup of coffee and steal so many looks at each other the cameraman gets seasick from swinging back and forth.

Get a cup of coffee and get locked inside your mysterious neighbor's cabinet while snooping.

And then, just as my hands slide the large green Rubik's Cube square into place, I hear the mental *click*.

I look up.

"What if there is no tender moment here? What if, instead of her encouraging him, she slams the door in his face?"

It's not the kind thing to do.

It's not the adorable thing to do.

But *for Pete's sake*, it makes sense.

The room goes silent.

Somebody clutches her chest as if I've just suggested Ashley Krane stab him.

Their mouths aren't just frowning; they're curling down like wire hangers.

"You do realize this is a *sitcom*," a man says, as though I've stumbled into the wrong writers room. "*Lavender Rhodes*, specifically. In a *sitcom*."

He has the audacity to roll his eyes toward Mr. Goodwin, like *Did you really hire him?* Him?

But his expression falls as it lands on Mr. Goodwin.

Who is peering over his glasses.

At me.

He mops his mouth with his hand.

Leans back in his chair.

"An intriguing thought, Masters. Something *nobody* expects. And what exactly would she say?"

This was it.

Barely five minutes in the room and already here I sit before the group, taking the test that will ultimately decide their opinion of me. It was a risk, jumping in so quickly with an idea about expanding the one-dimensional stick-figure character who has put the show at the top of the charts. But that's what Goodwin hired me for. And sure, slamming the door would be a mistake for her, something below her character. Still, that's how a story grows: from mistakes that cause consequences that cause realizations. And from digging out of holes. Or better yet, digging into and out of various tunnels. And—since it's a sitcom—funny, chaotic tunnels, going in all directions, while your character tries every which way to deal with the problem he or she caused. All in the name of growth and character development and story arc. Why?

Because people can admire the sketch of a perfect person on paper, but they relate to, they love, they hate, they weep for, they root for three-dimensional people with both virtues and vices who grow out of the page.

Ashley Krane was too perfect.

She needed to become alive.

And what *would* a woman who had been tossed aside by the man she'd been seeing the past decade say? After watching him hop from obsessing over her to obsessing over every female who had ever wandered into his line of sight?

The postwoman. The florist. The barista. The third cousin twice removed. The new neighbor.

"'I hope you choke on them.' And then," I shrug, "I don't know. Maybe she throws her ring at him."

The room gasps.

Actually gasps.

"Lavender Rhodes would *never* throw the ring he won for her at the season 5 carnival—" a woman sputters, but the lift of Mr. Goodwin's finger stops her.

"What then?" he says.

I ignore everyone's stares.

"Then," I begin, "I suppose she hangs her head for a bit. And next episode, she picks herself up by the bootstraps. Determines to find a date of her own. Maybe even goes apartment hunting. Heaven knows she wouldn't want to be near the two of them ever again."

The man beside Paula snorts. The woman on the other end of

the table looks like she's been holding her breath the past three minutes and is about to pass out.

"Impossible," a man jumps in, as though his point will cut this whole conversation off at the knees. "The apartment is iconic. The show itself is called *Neighbors*. To pull on that thread is to unravel the whole thing."

Several heads begin to nod.

Honestly. Is everybody here new to writing? How often does Goodwin replace these people?

"I'm not saying she *does* move," I toss out. "I'm just saying . . ." I pause, then say airily, "she shops. Takes a step back from this group of hers and assesses the toxic environment she's in."

Which, let's be candid here, it is. Toxic. In the show's ten years, the three best friends have lost twenty-eight jobs and become ultimately credit-card-strapped and penniless. Which is really curious, considering they live in a flat that would let for ten grand a month, easy. They have never managed to land a long-term relationship (which they all so unitedly yearn for) because they cast off perfectly wonderful suitors by the dozens for reasons like "He has this laugh like a hyena" or "Did you see how long he keeps his toenails?" They are so devoted to loyally supporting each other and *only* each other that they are essentially the bullies of the block.

"Toxic?" the woman pipes up. "They're in a sitcom! Of course everything they do is toxic!"

"Ashley slams the door in Lance's face," Mr. Goodwin says under his breath. Then, "'I hope you choke on them.'"

Clouds part in his eyes.

"They'd never see it coming," he says, with an air of *It's just what we need*. "A whole personality shift. It'd be daring, but—"

He puts on his glasses and peers at me, with an even more welcome air of *And you are just what we need too*.

The coffee spill down my shirt feels all dried up.

Several faces turn to me with expressions that say, *Now tell us again, who are you?*

I have taken a risk to outshine the disaster of my entrance, to overshadow the mess and chaos of this morning and make it clear who I am. And as clear as the shine of the mahogany table beneath the fluorescent lights' glow, I know it was the right decision.

Mr. Goodwin is scooping up the idea of not just a line but an entire story arc, and is about to welcome a break in the monotony of the show's narrative.

Everything that has gone wrong so far this morning is forgotten, swallowed in this giant thing that has gone *right*.

For what feels like the first time since Saturday evening, I exhale.

There's a tiny rap on the partially open door and, without looking up from the script, Goodwin grunts, "Busy."

"Sorry, Mr. Goodwin, I'll come back—"

The group unanimously turns at the sound of her voice and gives a collective roar. "No!"

They begin calling out left and right.

Beckoning her.

Telling her that of course *she* is invited in, always.

That of course none of us is so busy as to exclude *her*.

No, that was just a comment for common folk. PAs. Fellow writers. CEOs. Network presidents. Those types of people.

"Are you sure?" Lavender bounces on her toes in the open doorway as if weighing whether to intrude. Her hair is halfway up in rollers, the strands absurdly yellow and roller-skate-floor shiny under the fluorescent lights. Enormous purple rolls cover the left side of her head, where a stylist stands hastily unrolling and spraying at the same time. Her makeup is gaudy. She smells strongly of tropical punch. I'm sure with each blink she loses a dozen of those ridiculous false lashes. Her long, spindly legs look like they belong to an oversized spider, particularly in those black skinny jeans and black flats. In fact, really, she looks like a spider altogether.

"Oh, Lavender. You look especially *beautiful* today," someone breathes across the room.

My eyes cast to Paula. She's nodding like a puppy along with whoever said it. In fact, just about everyone is nodding.

I grab the Rubik's Cube and set the colors flying in my hands.

"Thanks, Chloe," she says, giving her makeup artist a good-natured pat—which pushes the stylist's arm just as she presses the nozzle on her can. And blinds me with hairspray.

All of which nobody notices, or cares.

"I just had a question about this line," Lavender says, holding her script out with a so-sorry-I-hope-I'm-not-ruining-anything-but-am-totally-ruining-everything face.

"First tell me what you think about this idea here," Mr. Goodwin says, beckoning her in with two fingers. He points to me. Or at least, I think he's pointing at me—everything's blurry as I take off my glasses and rub my eyes.

"Say it again, Masters."

Right. Nothing too big going on here. Just trying to halt imminent blindness.

I give my eyes two more rubs and put my glasses back on just in time to discover she has relocated herself and is now settling over my shoulder. Far, *far* too close for comfort.

Honestly, just knowing she lives in the same town this past decade has been too close for comfort.

Which is funny, now that I think of it, because I suppose she and I lived in the same town the two decades before that. In a funny-not-so-funny way, she is very likely the sole person in my existence to have lived exactly where I have lived my entire life. Of all the billions of people in the world, it's us. She and I together. The world's cruel joke.

The glasses are smeared with that tropical punch scent, and I shift in my seat uncomfortably, pulling them off again. Heat creeps up my neck. I'm perspiring at the proximity of her and the way everybody else in the room is eyeing me as I rub madly at the glasses with the hem of my trouser pockets.

I feel Goodwin's impatience as one feels a claw digging into one's shoulder.

Give up on the glasses.

Catch a tiny crease between Lavender's brows as she looks down at me.

Take a breath.

Pull the script close enough that the blurry words straighten up.

Clear my throat.

"Well," I begin uncertainly, "given the arc of your overall character—"

But already Mr. Goodwin is snapping, "Speed up, Finn. Nobody knows Ashley Krane better than Lavender. We've got six minutes."

I drop the script.

The thing is, you don't consult the actors. Nobody consults the actors.

Writing is our job. Acting is theirs.

It's like asking the patient before a root canal which tool the dentist should use.

It's unprofessional. It just isn't done.

"I think Ashley should shut the door in Lance's face," I say bluntly. "And tell him to choke on his floral arrangement."

I don't know what I was expecting. Nothing good, of course. I would never, *could* never, expect anything from our interactions to end up causing anything *good*. But I suppose I didn't expect this.

I didn't expect silence.

Eventually, the lashes over her blue eyes flap a couple of times.

"But . . . ," she begins slowly, "Ashley doesn't do things like that."

I nod.

It's probably going to be best if I avoid talking directly to her as much as possible.

"She never fights with Lance."

I nod again.

It's becoming clearer by the moment that I'm going to have to help her along, so I add, "And as someone playing that character, wouldn't you of all people agree it's time to see her stand up for herself? I mean, 232 episodes of zero character growth must have driven you mad by now, hasn't it? If Ashley Krane has half the intelligence and self-respect the writers have claimed she has, she would've thrown down the ultimatum long ago."

"What ultimatum?" Lavender says.

"That their fate be sealed one way or another. Marry or break up," I say, as if this were obvious. And then add, to make it abundantly clear, "Permanently."

She laughs.

It's a light tinkle of a laugh.

Kind of like one of the twelve windchimes Sally Anne, my other ninety-two-year-old neighbor, put on her patio adjoining my bedroom window that at first seemed innocent but will eventually drive me to insanity.

The BBC once referred to it as "the laugh that stopped a world war." Rumor has it that a door opened during a heated debate among several nations, and on the telly in the hall outside the room was Lavender Rhodes, laughing at some punch line. One by one, the heads of nations turned, and then they started laughing. And half an hour later, a peace treaty was initiated. A rumor at worst, coincidence at best. Whatever it was, here she stands over my shoulder, laughing that terrible laugh while blinking several times, chin up towards the sky.

A Kleenex appears in the stylist's hand, and immediately she is dabbing beneath Lavender's eyes, preventing any moisture from falling on her freshly bronzed cheeks. This must happen a lot. The tears.

"'Choke on your flowers.' Can you imagine *anything* at all more out of character? That's hilarious. But seriously, Mr. Goodwin—"

And while she launches into what she believes is a *real* question with regard to the script, the room around me shifts.

Everything, all the goodwill come my way, goes to pot in an instant.

Faces around the table darken, lips pursed as disgusted eyes squint at me. As if I am some traveling cult leader and they almost, *almost*, got tricked.

With one laugh, with one dab of her eyes, she has effectively shot and killed my idea. She threw out that guffaw with the same disregard she now employs to stand on the strap of my laptop bag, crushing my personal belongings beneath her feet.

I wait several moments.

When she doesn't step off, I speak.

"Excuse me," I say. The stylist's elbow clocks me in the jaw as she pulls down another roller. My body is arched, pressed against the man beside me (who looks only too eager to disassociate himself from me) as the stylist wedges herself in and keeps working. I look down at my strap beneath Lavender's feet. "If you don't mind."

It takes a moment for Lavender to realize she's being addressed. When she does, she follows the direction of my eyes to her own footwear. She steps off the strap quickly. "Oh, sorry."

Her eyes linger on mine, and again that little crease forms between her brows—even as the stylist begins pressing on it with a cream as if wishing it away.

"Do I know you?" Lavender says.

Does she know me.

Does Lavender Rhodes, of Welling School of the London Borough of Bexley, England, know me.

This woman has single-handedly destroyed every single thing in my life she's ever touched, down to my first day on my dream job. I almost don't want to say.

"That's Finn Masters," Goodwin says gruffly, as if I can't answer myself. "He's come in from *Higher Stakes* to take over for Carrie."

"Finn," she repeats, chewing on my name as she turns her attention back to me. An uncomfortable mix of lightning and ice runs through my veins as our eyes lock again. I'm looking the dragon in the eye. I'm finding myself face-to-face with the sea siren herself, knowing full well the plumes of smoke from the distant town are her doing.

I'm momentarily struck by the iridescent green flecks in her marine blue eyes. The sliver of an opening between her full, soft lips. The question mark on her brow as it rises on her porcelain forehead.

Oh, never look her in the eyes!

"Well, Finn," she says, her breath soft and flowery as she raises a hand. She pats me twice on the shoulder. Both times sending electric shocks down my arm. "Nice to meet you. Welcome to the show."

Chapter 4

Lavender

Monday, Film Day, Stage 2

Finn Masters. I know I know this name.

Stage 2 crackles. The electric noise of 250 laughs in the air chases Kye's zippy line, pumping the studio audience with even more serotonin after five hours of nothing but free candy, coffee, and jokes. They're a particularly good group today. Quick to laugh. Quick to sigh. Quick to let you know you are on the right track. Frankly, even if you're not, you wouldn't notice because their laughter just picks you up under the arms and carries you.

Patient. Cheerful to no end. This is when I love my job the most. It's like being six and standing in your living room, very seriously performing something you are making up on the spot for your mum, and believing wholeheartedly that your series of twirls and leaps is so extraordinary that you've actually tricked her into believing this has taken weeks of nonstop practice. And all the while she sits on the edge of the couch, beaming and clapping heartily while video recording you, making you believe you possess a never-before-seen talent.

That's what filming days are like when you have a good audience like this one. But instead of one mum, it's 250 of them.

I have a line coming up, shortly after that a whole paragraph of lines that for the life of me I haven't been able to get just right. A thick blond curl keeps sliding into my eyes, and no matter how trendy Chloe says this curvy, red-headed, smoky-eyed Jessica Rabbit doppelganger look is, and no matter what "magic" it does to my jawline, it's about to *kill* me. I don't know where Sonya's puppy is, and I have this nagging fear that someone's mixed something up and he's gone forever. I'm sitting on the swiveling barstool on set that—mark my words—is going to collapse under me any second. A literal screw is coming loose. And I can't get the new guy's name out of my mind.

Finn Masters.

My awareness of exactly where he's standing in this vast room swarming with people, lights, and panning cameras is equally as distracting. Just off stage right. Arms crossed over his chest. Script in hand. Glasses on. Concentrating with a not-so-unhandsome, bookish face. Broody brows top pale blue-green eyes that are the exact color of the blue-raspberry macarons in this lovely shop I somehow always fall into on morning strolls. Careless, wavy brown hair that curls just below his ears. A long coffee stain down his shirt. A curious missing shoelace I'd like to ask about. And a voice that sounds like home.

Finn Masters.

I *know* I know that name.

His eyes catch mine.

A tiny squint creases his temples—not at all akin to that last bloke in the audience my eyes accidentally gazed upon, who started mouthing *Will you marry me?* and then lifted his T-shirt of a cat riding a shark in space to reveal the question on his stomach in case there was any doubt as to his intentions. Security immediately escorted him out.

No, Finn's macaron eyes are giving off an entirely different look.

One would almost think—this is absurd, really—it's a look of . . . revulsion.

Aimed at me.

But of course, that can't be right. I've only just met the man. Maybe.

I blink and redirect my attention to the scene.

"I'm too nervous. Ashley, you read it." Lance Lewis, aka Kye, sits on the barstool beside me and slides the phone over.

I nearly miss catching it. No pressure, except that we've already had to work through lunch on account of reshoots, many of which, unfortunately, were due to my blunders. (And one due to Kye throwing the scene to wrap his arms around me and declare his undying love, which, of course, the audience died over. He loves getting them riled up.) I'm off my game today, thanks to dog-induced sleep deprivation. Well, and my concentration that keeps slipping out the window. *Finn Masters*. But at the last second my fingers wrap around the phone successfully, and I pick it up.

I wrinkle my brow as I pretend to read the email.

Then pretend to read it again.

This is where I'm supposed to be delighted.

"Cautiously delighted" more specifically, according to the script.

Because, of course, Ashley Krane is rooting for him.

Ashley Krane has always believed in him.

Ashley isn't shocked at all that Lance gets the (totally impossible) opportunity to go to NASA to train for the possibility of leading a deeply important mission (which he, as a midrange engineer, is no more qualified to lead than an eight-year-old with a dozen astronaut posters on the wall). But then, Ashley also accidentally got herself locked in the boot of a neighbor's car last week while trying to eavesdrop on said neighbor and ended up in Vermont.

Miracles abound on *Neighbors*. Audiences gladly suspend their disbelief in exchange for a happy twenty-two-minute escape.

I like that part of the job. It isn't all lilacs and daisies, of course, but making people laugh, helping them see the world through a slightly rosier lens, I do enjoy—even if I'm tiring of the revolving door of shenanigans.

"You got in." I take a heavy breath, letting that sink in. A small smile forms on my lips as I repeat, "You got in."

We stare into each other's eyes for an exaggerated length of time.

We do this, for the record, a lot.

Somebody in the audience sighs.

But honestly now. *Finn Masters*. I *know* I've heard the name.

Kye's/Lance's hands find mine.

I set the phone down on the table.

Feel the broken (props *has* to fix this) barstool wobble with the shift of my hip. Kye gives my hand a squeeze and props one foot on the bottom rung, steadying it. It's subtle enough no one can tell.

I'd thank him silently, but there's a large camera swinging around us, zooming in on my eyes, which are supposed to be full of intensity. So instead I squeeze his hand back.

A *ding* rings out offstage and I pretend, just as he says, "Hang on," and reaches for the phone, to read the text that comes in.

I ignore the camera zooming in even further as my brows furrow. I also ignore the massive curl blocking one eye while I drum up a sense of betrayal to accompany my next line.

I look up from the phone. Back into Kye's ever-startling blue eyes.

"Patricia says she's looking forward to your date tonight," I say weakly.

There's a gasp from the audience. Someone in the audience hisses, "The *floozy*."

Floozy is a bit harsh, given the guest star is playing a blood-donating, plant-loving kindergarten teacher who may or may not end up temporarily engaged to Lance before she joins the Peace Corps.

My voice wobbles. "Guess you'll have to be the one to break the news you're leaving for training in three weeks."

You know, that new guy has a point.

It wouldn't *kill* Ashley Krane to put up a little fuss every now and again. After all, he did *just* declare his never-ending, undying love at the end of last season. Right before "accidentally" snogging with his boss while stuck in an elevator, and believing, due to a series of misunderstandings, the end of the world had come and they were the only two survivors.

By the end of the day today, at the end of this episode, I'm going to be standing at that door, hiding my sadness over the fact that Lance has found himself beguiled by this Patricia across the hall. Once again I'll be using that face that says I'm heartbroken but will move on because within eight episodes we'll be back together—or, at the very least, stealing a few kisses we both declare we regret.

But honestly now. If Ashley were my real-life friend, I'd tell her she really, really, *really* needed to move on.

And if Ashley were Sonya's real-life friend, Sonya would steal her keys, kidnap her, and drag her around to parties surrounded by attractive and available men, demanding she wake up and move on. (Speaking from personal experience here. It's equal parts terrifying and helpful.)

But seriously, how far and how long can an audience suspend their disbelief for the sake of the story before it loses its magic? How much can you stretch the elastic band before it snaps? What was it Finn Masters said again? *"Ashley either needs to stand up for herself or leave him."*

Was that it? Is that why he looks mad at me? Because I turned down his idea?

Well.

Fine.

Let's just take a stab at fixing that and see what happens.

Lance makes a reach for the phone, and I pull it towards me.

"You know what, Lance?" I pitch my voice higher as I clutch the phone a little tighter. "I think . . ." I shoot him a look that says *Kye, bear with me as I go off script* but also pairs nicely with the *Lance, I'm about to throw down some heavy things*. "I think it's time."

Kye's eyes flash, and I could swear that vein on one of his giant biceps grows even bulgier with adrenaline. He *loves* going off script.

He *loves* improv. We don't go there often, because it frays Goodwin's nerves, but when we do, you'd think Kye just flew down a waterslide the way he comes out all grins on the other side.

Improv to Kye, particularly in a live studio, is the equivalent of a hundred-dollar bill to a kid in a candy store.

He checks his watch. "Time? We don't have to leave for the movie for another thirty minutes."

I suck in a breath, figuring the best way to put it. Then I recall Finn's words. "*Time* that our fate be sealed one way or another. I'm . . . tired." I throw out my hands. "Maybe finding out you're leaving the atmosphere gives me a little perspective. Maybe I've just woken up and realized it's time we stop these charades. Aren't you tired of it too?" I say, wrinkling my brow. "Someone told me just today that if I have half the intelligence and self-respect people claim I do, I should've stood up for myself long ago—"

"Who told you that?" he says, moving to stand. "It was Rick, wasn't it?"

"The point is, Lance," I say, touching his arm and settling him back onto his stool. "I'm giving you . . . an ultimatum."

A whoosh of wind blows through the room as 250 windpipes inhale in unison.

Silence.

Silence so complete you could hear a pin drop.

I worry at my bottom lip as the seconds tick by—partly because

I'm actually quite terrible at improv and genuinely in a little distress, and partly because it's at the very least a good action for the cameras.

Kye just sits there. Frozen.

I'm starting to worry he's going to give up with a laugh, or that Mark, the director, will call it, or both.

It's all so tense and heavy, in fact, that I'm about to call it myself with a laugh. Toss my head back. Throw it off as a funny little prank on the audience. Who knows? Perhaps this'll get used for a snappy little blooper during credits.

And just as I begin to put the phone down and throw in the towel, a worrying *creak* sounds from the seat beneath me. I'm about to set my feet on the floor when a flash crosses Kye's eyes that is definitely not scripted, and before I know it his arms lift me off my seat and right into his lap.

His biceps have me entirely engulfed (something the producers have suggested he tone down over the years, given he's supposed to be an engineer, not Thor the Undercover Engineer), barely leaving room for the cameras and audience to see my eyes, let alone anything else.

"What the heck was that?" I hiss in this cocoon built for two.

"What am I doing?" he replies loudly, with a lilt in his voice. "Saving you from disaster, Ashley Krane."

We both look over at the barstool, which is clearly not causing a disaster but sitting rather innocently on its three legs.

He pauses. Kicks the bottom rung with his shoe, and with a crash it falls onstage.

A laugh ripples around the room.

He smiles back at me.

He's so intense, his expression laser focused as he holds me inches away from him. He adds softly, "And giving you an ultimatum right back."

"Me?" I say. "You can't do that. I'm ultimatuming *you*."

"That's not a word, but fine," Kye/Lance says with a soft smile. "But first let me tell you my demands, Ashley Krane. Either you marry me and we live happily ever after in my apartment with the creaky door and the neighbor who rolls bowling balls across the ceiling at 2:00 a.m. . . ."

There it is again. A typhoon-level gust of swoony wind caused by the audience's collective gasp.

I pause. Fight a grin, because I know where this is going and, wouldn't you know, it feels right. We've never actually gotten to this point before. To a real proposal. The writers have always tried to string our relationship out as far as possible, fearing even introducing the concept of a wedding, as if marriage would be the show's doom. I can actually feel a zing of cheer rising in my chest for the imaginary character inside me. Like I've been reading a book about someone who wants that one big thing for ten years and then suddenly, there it is. *At last.*

I swing the briefest look over to Mark. His eyes are narrow. The writers are huddled in my periphery. One has his hands over his head like he's watching the final four seconds of a football game. Two of the younger, fresher staff are flipping pages frantically like they've missed something. Even Mr. Goodwin is standing beside the director's chair, stoic as he holds on to the back of it.

My voice is soft. "Or?"

"Or I marry you and we live happily ever after in yours."

To say the room *erupts* with as much gusto as in season 2, when we kissed for the first time, is an understatement.

And then he kisses me, just as people jump to standing, screaming and cheering, and Mark throws the script in the air.

Papers flutter down around him as I'm enveloped in this embrace, this totally unscripted, out-of-the-woodwork embrace. And out-of-the-woodwork proposal. And out-of-the-woodwork scene.

Kye has gone straight for the Airport Farewell kiss here—a passionate, no-holds-barred style. A logical choice, if a little *too* real.

I take a moment to slam my heel into his foot.

For the record, we have a dozen snogging styles on set. There's the Will That Other Guy Text Me? tentative kiss, where you're in for it at the end of the date but at the back of your mind you're thinking, *But what if this other guy calls?* The Tick Check kiss, where hands are flying, crawling over every (highly appropriate) part of you like hikers after a ten-mile trek. Then of course a least favorite around these parts, the Sloth, where the director *reeeeeally* wants a slow, romantic kiss and you're stuck to each other's faces playing Scrabble in your head while cameras crawl around you. Let me just say, the cameras pull magic out of those shots.

The reality is a little bit nauseating.

At any rate, Kye's choice right here is straight for the Airport Farewell.

It makes sense. It is Lance and Ashley's first time, in all these years, getting engaged.

"End scene!" someone calls in the distance, and the roars and cheers grow.

Kye pulls back, grinning like he's just left the candy store with every gram of sugar in stock. "What was *that?*" he calls over the eardrum-breaking cheers. Then, grinning madly, he pans his eyes across the studio. "Look what *you did.*"

I know.

It's one thing to throw in an occasional line. It's another to change the course of the entire scene.

And the way the staff are looking around at the audience now, I know something big is about to happen.

The room is thundering with applause like we're soldiers just returned from war.

More than one person is actually weeping.

I wince at the writers, who are arguing so loudly over one another they look like they're on the fringe of throwing punches. "I'm not sure if they're going to thank me or kill me."

Kye throws an arm around my shoulder and gives a hearty squeeze. "Chin up, Lavie. If they try, they'll have to go through me first. Well, and Sonya. And you know how terrified they are of her."

I laugh loudly and feel my tension easing up. Because what he's not saying in all this is the truth. Everything's fine. Worst-case scenario—and even that is a very small probability—is a collective frown followed by a reshoot. But my team has my back, and they don't so much as let me get a tongue-lashing around here.

Kye and Sonya. My friends. My family. My people.

In the earliest years after I reached the States, I had nothing. Truly nothing. Except a scribbled address (252 Parker Ave., Apt. B), $200 in cash, and a shiny-but-astronomically-high-interest-rate-to-the-point-it-was-worthless credit card.

I rented a slice of a bedroom in a two-bedroom flat shared by six girls, all Hollywood hopefuls from around the world, all connected by the same agent. I knocked and there was Sonya, holding open the door, all bright and beautiful despite the Pepto-Bismol-pink rollers snaking through her hair and the green mask covering all but her large brown eyes. She had a script in her hand even then.

All of us found jobs in the restaurant business, like every other hopeful in town. But two weeks in, in true Sonya form, she informed us she ran the stats on waitressing, didn't like the numbers she saw, and determined to beat the system.

She started a dog-walking business.

And not just any dog-walking business but a high-end dog-walking business.

Quick money, flexible enough to allow us to make casting calls when we wanted, she declared, and the money, if the business worked, would be 34 percent higher than the wages she'd drawn up figures for in our restaurant gigs. We would walk the dogs and clean their paws with monogrammed towels; she would handle the scheduling, marketing, and accounting.

She didn't know anyone in town, but in the same way she had figured out how to make a five-figure income selling computer paper on Etsy, she was confident she could figure this out too.

She was very compelling. Sonya always is when she walks in with a PowerPoint.

She laid out the proposal to all the girls in the flat; I was the only one who took her up.

And sure enough, the other four girls didn't make it in LA five months.

Sonya, meanwhile, started a franchise.

Sonya has always been the glue in our little group, the leader.

She's the one who took me along to the first LAANG—aka the Los Angeles Actors Networking Group. A group of monetarily challenged actors who couldn't afford classes and didn't have connections (Sonya and I were the lucky ones back then), they met in a basement coffee shop and took turns sharing acting tips learned on wikiHow while secretly trying to gather news about casting calls without giving away any secrets about casting calls.

It was there, at one of these meetings, we met Kye.

And we formed a little pact.

A group of friends devoted to helping one another up the ranks. United on every front. Which is why, when Sonya got news about the audition for *Neighbors*, we all got news about the audition for *Neighbors*. And when the casting director decided that Sonya was perfect for the role of uptight but lovable Maya Ahluwalia, it was only a matter of time before he connected how perfect Kye and I would be for her mates.

Because who better to play a group of hysterically different but loyal-to-the-core best friends than a group of hysterically different but loyal-to-the-core best friends?

I cast one look at the huddle of writers, talking in a rush and snapping their papers, while the audience members crane their necks for an eyeful. They're all so preoccupied by what's happened that the stage manager, Phil, is currently pushing them off to the side like a sheepdog herding a bunch of wayward cows. A woman has overtaken the mic and is doing her best to draw attention elsewhere via half-baked jokes.

Oh, and now there's background music.

And lookee there, apparently juggling.

Attendants start walking down the aisles, handing out sandwiches.

Standard efforts during standard shootings to draw attention elsewhere during breaks.

My stomach churns, reminding me that it's—my eyes scoot over to the large clock on the wall—already three fifteen. We've been at this for four hours and I haven't had a decent bite yet.

I move to the employees' snack table and run my eyes over the spread of breads and cheeses. It's quite impressive today.

Swirls of nuts and cheeses and every fruit color in the rainbow decorate the longest charcuterie board I have ever laid eyes on. Two girls from props stand at the end of the table, engrossed in hushed conversation, though I hear "That set took *months* to make" and "If they *dare* want to change sets on us one more time, that's it, Stella. I quit."

Meanwhile, another girl, Goodwin's niece, Kye's new PA—oh, what's her name? Maddie? Maggie?—is rather obviously keeping her eyes on Finn, to the point that as she reaches toward the spread, she misses the carrots and dips her fingers in ranch dressing.

As she does, I hear a little intake of breath from the shadows.

As Maggie moves along, a woman swiftly steps in from the shadows, replaces a sausage on the board, and swaps out the bowl of dressing for a fresh one.

Fascinating.

So this is how they keep the board looking immaculate. I wonder if she's one of Janie Lane's *If It's Not Perfect, Fix It!* superfans—like Sonya.

"I love the board," I say as I pick up a plate.

The woman gives a startled jump like a mouse caught sneaking into somebody's kitchen. Which is especially on point given her mint-green employee T-shirt that reads "The Miceateers Catering Co." Plus she's currently frozen, holding a toothpick stab of white cheddar.

"Hello, Lavender," a voice behind me says.

I turn.

Finn Masters stands before me looking very much like a man who wishes not to be somewhere but is somewhere, and wishes not to talk but must. "I've been told to tell you that Goodwin would like to see you."

I hear an accusation in his tone. Or possibly frustration that on day one as a producer, he's been demoted to errand boy.

"Really?" I say, raising my brows. I set a carrot on my plate, my stomach knotting. "Good news or bad news?"

"About your little stunt? Jury's still out, but I believe they are deciding to be thrilled. They're just trying to sort out what to do about the last eight minutes of the episode now that the script's been thrown in the river. And apparently," he adds after a pause, "you are just the person they need."

There it is again. A most definite slant on the word *you*.

It's plain as day now. This man has been expelled from the group.

Well. I can fix that.

Awash in relief, I plop another carrot onto my plate with more gusto. "No, you just tell them you can take over from here. This was all your doing after all."

"Me?" His expression is a tangle of pleasure and shock. "I didn't tell you to put up a marriage proposal."

"You most certainly did," I say. "All this talk about Ashley standing up for herself. Growing. Telling Lance to tie the knot or shove off. Of course, shoving off is just much too rude for my character, so I did the only other thing you suggested that made sense: matrimony. The great big bicycle built for two. It'll be much more fun to see them quarrel over wedding registries than see her off weeping into a pillow, don't you think?" I eye the bowl of sun-dried tomatoes surrounded by everything-seasoned pretzels that, quite unbelievably, are all so misshapen I daresay they may well be homemade. I bite into one, and an explosion of garlic, onion, butter, and even—what is that? Paprika? Curry?—floods the senses in the best way.

Amazing.

I'm practically weak in the knees as I begin to load up my plate.

"Did you make these?" I hold up a pretzel to the woman.

"Yes, ma'am," she says in a tight voice. Her hands, which have tucked the cheddar back in place on the board, look taut and ready to spring behind the curtain, where no doubt a bucketful of pretzels waits for the refilling.

I swivel around to face Finn fully, still holding out the pretzel, only to discover he's looking at me strangely, as though both shocked that I've given a smart answer and somehow also repulsed by it.

"Can you . . . would you . . . tell them this?" he says, looking incredibly uncomfortable as he asks for the favor. "That you sprang from my idea?"

I shrug. "They haven't connected the dots? Sure. It's not like I'm vying for your job," I say with a laugh. Which, surprisingly, makes him pale slightly.

"No. They see it more like I'm the guy who came in with the

terrible idea to break up the couple, and you're the one who did the opposite quite brilliantly."

"Thank you," I say. "I am pretty proud of how the improv bit turned out."

"But again, all because I suggested the idea first," he throws in, as though he fully expects I've forgotten what I just said ten seconds ago.

I scoop the pretzel in hummus and take another bite. And honestly (and in a teeny tiny way possibly because with those dogs, it's been days since I've had a proper meal) it tastes better than anything I've eaten in years. I don't even need to go down the rest of the line. I could just pull up a chair right here, shovel the whole supply of pretzels onto my plate, and eat happily. "Have you tried these? They're incredible." I swivel around to the woman. "Would you consider emailing me the recipe?"

I look back to Finn and find he is looking at the pretzel I am holding out for him as though I've just asked him to try clams—which are, for the record, the worst, and anyone who says otherwise no doubt has been swindled into believing so against their will by this culture that insists exotic things are good. They aren't good. What's good is a box of macaroni and cheese. And these pretzels.

"No," he says simply. "So." His eyes tick over to the writers. "You were saying you were going to pop over . . ."

"And tell them my improv moment came by your doing, yes. Really, though," I add, thrusting an entire pretzel into my mouth and speaking through a mouthful, "this may very well be the best thing I've tasted in all my life."

His brow furrows as he watches me until I swallow.

"That is," he responds, unamused, "a dramatic overstatement."

"It's changed my life," I say, reaching for another.

"You should probably reserve those statements for genuinely big moments."

"It's better than a mince pie on Boxing Day."

At this he halts. I hear him clear his throat.

"Nothing," he says quite seriously, "is better than a mince pie on Boxing Day."

He says it as though I just said I thought it was a good idea to kill off the queen.

I pause and then smile. "How would you know? You haven't tried it," I say, holding out a pretzel.

There's one long pause between us.

A silence. A challenge.

And then with an expression that may well have been him crying out, *For the honor of our beloved country, and may God save the queen*, he snatches the pretzel from my hand and pops it in his mouth.

The woman in the corner, for the record, is quietly wringing her hands.

The juggler, in my periphery, has moved off and is making way for two men on skates carrying a curious amount of propane.

"It is not," he says after several chews, "better than mince pie on Boxing Day."

I swivel to the caterer. "Don't believe him."

"I'll have you know I have actually judged a mince pie competition—"

My brow arches. "Which one?"

His head ducks a little as he rushes on, "The Masters Family Christmas. But it's a very large and established group, and believe me, a pretzel can't hold a candle to star-shaped pastries filled with spiced mincemeat." Abruptly, he stops. Looks at the pretzels. "Is there turmeric in these?"

"Why, yes," the caterer says, startled. "You're the first to ever guess." And then, suddenly, this silent mouse of a woman opens up as if he's spoken the secret password. "I mix 500 grams of spelt flour with two teaspoons of turmeric—"

"Unbelievable. Excuse me," he interrupts in a guttural tone. Then, checking his watch, he makes a mad dash for the door.

Chapter 5

Finn

The woman caused me to break out in hives.

More specifically, Lavender Rhodes, with her absolutely *ridiculous* need to make other people try food before she opens up to them about incredibly important things relating to the success or failure of their jobs, *made* me break out in hives.

And quite literally caused me to *run* out of my first day of work to the nearest clinic directly in the middle of a very big and very unplanned shift in the plot of *Neighbors*.

Broken shoelace flapping.

"You know, you really should start asking before you sample treats." Mrs. Teaberry *tsks* as she looks at my face. It's also the sound she makes when she pulls open a can of cat food, however, and at least eight emerald-green eyes pop out from various spots in her living room.

"It was a pretzel. Who puts turmeric in pretzels?"

She *tsks* again, and this time at least three cats jump onto the floral couch. "And I suppose you'd open the door to a burglar and defend yourself by saying, 'He knocked. How was I supposed to not open the door when he knocked?'"

Still shaking her head, she beckons me to the kitchen. "C'mon, Finnyboy. I'm sure I have some Benadryl somewhere."

"Doctor said I'm capped. I've been at the emergency clinic all afternoon."

"*Pssh*, what do they know? A bunch of teenagers who can Google some words. I'll take care of you."

The woman currently trying to become my drug dealer is my neighbor. Eighty-year-old Mr. Teaberry is around, too, though despite everyone's urgings, he still spends weekdays trucking the western states before hitching back home Thursdays for the weekend. On my very first day at the flat, he slipped me a twenty-dollar bill and asked me to keep a lookout for Mrs. Teaberry on the days he was gone. I didn't keep the twenty, of course, but I did keep my word.

Years later, here we are.

Me with a swelling face. She with her spatula pushing cats off the kitchen counter.

I learned early on in my time as a resident of Flat 4, Casa Laguna, that the definition of "looking out" for someone was flexible, and that while I had been initially awkward and bumbling in my efforts to check after her, she was right at home with the notion of caring for me. Letting her do so, mostly in the form of fretting over my state of singleness while simultaneously trying to overmedicate me anytime I so much as sneezed, seemed to be the ticket.

"I suppose you'll be staying for supper," she says.

This is the way she invites me to dinner.

It's never *really* an invitation, always spoken like a mild inconvenience, but if I ever refuse, she'll go on and on about it for days. "No notice, though. And I'm not sure if I have anything good left in the cabinets . . ."

"How about we order in?" I say. I catch a glimpse of myself

in the antique gold mirror on the living room wall opposite and wince. I look like a gang got hold of me in the alleyway. "There's a new Chinese place across the street."

"What are you trying to say, Finn?" She leans in to survey me. "You don't like my cooking?"

I open my mouth to reply that yes, of course I like her cooking, when she waves me away and sticks her head back in the cabinets. "You're just delirious from the attempted poisoning. Chicken and rice it is."

"I like the little peas," I add.

"Fine. Chicken and rice and *little peas*. Just 'cause you look so pathetic."

I nudge two tabbies off my spot on the floral couch and sit down, then drop my computer bag beside it. The bag has several teeth marks from those dogs that *Lavender Rhodes* brought in. It was a present from my brother for my twenty-fifth birthday. A sort of hurrah gift that spoke the unspoken words: he finally supported my life's decision. He never fully grasped why I left home and the family to pursue writing abroad. Well, back then it was acting, but still. Hollywood in general. Sometimes, especially lately with the sting of each photo of my family growing and carrying on life without me, I understand why.

As I take a look around, I get a strong feeling of being watched. I turn my head towards the telly in the corner. A black cat lounges there, beside a potted houseplant.

I squint at it; well, with the one good eye that can currently squint. The other has sealed shut.

Then an identical black cat peeks its head out from behind the other cat.

Oh, good grief.

"Mrs. Teaberry . . . ," I call out slowly.

"Meet Wilma and Fred," she calls back from the kitchen, knowing exactly what I am referring to.

A few moments later she's back in the living room, bearing a suspiciously fully prepared tray of chicken and rice, and yes, peas, steaming from two plates. And salads. And something round and pink that jiggles with bits of orange floating inside.

But sure. Nothing in the cupboards.

"Here," she says, dumping the plates on the coffee table between us. She pours a handful of pills like Skittles into my hand. I dump all of them in the little floral napkin and pretend to knock a couple back.

"So . . . how was it then? How was your first day?"

"Awful. I wouldn't wish such a day on my worst enemy."

She gives a sort of grunt as she presses her lips together. I pick up my fork.

My ears have been ringing since I raced out of the studio. I ignore it. Just as I ignore the headache created by the little dungeon keeper inside my brain swinging his wrecking ball at my cranium.

I've three silent mouthfuls chewed and swallowed when she cracks.

"And what happened?" she says.

"My nemesis released the beasts and then poisoned me."

Frankly, I don't want to repeat the story. I'd much prefer to pretend the entire day was a bad dream. And I'd very much like not to dwell on the fact that it's now six thirty, and my last text from Paula came in at four. Apparently they were going deep into a plotting session and wouldn't be done anytime soon. Probably midnight, she speculated. And while I asked Paula to explain my situation, then followed up when I was freshly out of urgent care, the next text I received (from an unknown number, presumably one of the PAs) read: MR. GOODWIN SAYS NOT TO COME IN.

That's it.

No explanation.

No query or expression of sorrow or "So? You lived?"

No praise for being the one to shove this whole, apparently *earth-shattering*, shift in plot off the dock and into the ocean.

Just: don't come back.

So, to recap: I was late this morning because Lavender released the hounds. I threw out an idea the team loathed. I dramatically ran out for something so trivial as needing to breathe. And *Lavender*, meanwhile, is the heroine. Saving puppies. Suggesting betrothal. Very likely bouncing over to the writers room to hash out the rest of the script and take over my job as well.

But there Mrs. Teaberry is, staring at me, waiting for me to go on.

"As best as I can explain, I was ambushed," I say. "And now, upon Mr. Goodwin's insistence, I quit *Higher Stakes* without formally giving a respectable amount of time—not even seeing it through to the end of the season. Not even giving two weeks' notice. My boss was livid, understandably. But I was stuck between a rock and a hard place."

What I would like in this moment is a pat on the shoulder and some tender grandmotherly advice.

What I get is Mrs. Teaberry spitting over her shoulder. "You can't think that way, Finn. It's a *job*. Did you break a contract?"

"Yes," I say.

"As you had to," she says, not missing a beat. "It's called moving up the ladder. *Higher Stakes* didn't give you the respect you deserved—"

"They've actually always been very good to me—"

"But at the end of the day, who cares about respect? It's about the job security—"

"Goodwin actually made it very clear I may not make it to June—"

"—but really, the workload, the *freedom*. You were worked to the bone at the other place—"

"*Neighbors* is actually going to be twice the load, I think—"

"But what's most *important* in all this," she says, her voice rising shrilly as she slams her hand on the table, "is that you've changed your job. And you know there is *some reason* you changed your job, so we can leave it at that."

This. This is my pep talk.

"I appreciate that," I say reservedly. Now clearly is not the time to dwell on the fact that if all of this falls through, and I lose my job on the first day, or week, or whenever, then I can guarantee I'll be pretty much ejected from the Hollywood community altogether.

I shake my head. Enough talk about me and this day. "How old are those two?" I say, motioning to the two black cats creeping slowly toward our food. "And where'd you find them? And can you take them back to wherever that place is?"

I'm at the point with the spay and neuter clinic at my vet that they want to put my name on a plaque on a bench. I've taken so many cats to the clinic, they started referring to me as "Cat Man."

"Oh, who knows," she replies, batting one away from nosing her plate.

"I think you do," I say. "I fancy you found them . . ."

She waves her hands around airily. "By the trash cans. I couldn't leave them, of course."

She absolutely could leave them, and I have told her so a hundred times.

"You haven't got room for them."

"The world didn't have room for them," she counters, then taps her heart. "Me? I've got plenty of room."

"What does this make?" I say, unmoved. "Twelve?"

"Nonsense," she says. "I'd never have so many as that in my house. Don't try to make me sound like a crazy cat lady."

I look around.

I count at least fourteen.

"You know it's not allowed—"

"And you were allowed to have those two Ukrainians in your apartment last month?"

I frown. "They were refugees who needed a short-term stay until they got on their feet."

"They were two non-tenant visitors sleeping on your couch well past forty-eight hours, and we have a crotchety old landlord." She grins, knowing she got me. "We are the same, Finnyboy. Won't let rules stand in the way of justice."

This is not the same thing.

Nevertheless, arguing will get me nowhere. The best I can do is quell the cat-breeding dilemma.

I sigh. "I'll take—"

"Wilma and Fred," she supplies.

"Wilma and Fred," I repeat, nudging one off my lap, "to the vet tomorrow. I have to drop Miles off anyway before work."

Miles is my eight-year-old Weimaraner. Seventy pounds of lean muscle with a mind as sharp as a tack. Brings the mail to the neighbors. Boosts morale when spirits are low. Stopped an attempted break-in last year. But sure, she has a name for every cat in here and still refers to him as *that dog*.

Mrs. Teaberry agrees to the plan, and after a lengthy supper and gelatin dessert (of which I managed one bite before the cats swooped in), my headache settles to the cadence of a light throb.

Scripts are swimming through my head, though. As are the meds and the need for sleep. I break off for home.

My keys fall into the bowl as I step inside my front door, and the sound of it cracks like a whip. I rub my temples. Miles perks up, his doleful eyes watching as he rests solemnly on the doggie bed. I give his sleek gray head a rub as I pass.

I check my phone again, hoping for news.

Nothing.

Despite the fact that the bed beckons, I drag myself to the closet because I need to gather my thoughts, as well as my things.

I need a failproof plan for tomorrow.

Thirty minutes later, a freshly pressed blue button-up and navy trousers hang on the knob of the closet door. The alarm is set, the second alarm is set, and two bottles of ibuprofen rest at the bedside. The coffeepot is set to brew at 5:15 a.m., and I get (read: crawl) into bed, full of hope.

That tomorrow will be a perfect day.

That my ensemble will be professional and spotless.

That my shoes will shine—with no broken shoelaces.

That my hair will be kempt.

That my creativity will flow.

That I will be quick to produce zingers when asked and fresh thoughts when prompted.

That I will walk into that room *well* before anybody else with laptop ready and script in hand.

That I might even throw a couple dozen doughnuts on the table in a display of goodwill.

I will be Finn Masters, "unstoppable force of creative genius" (Welling's *Daily Gazette*'s "Thirty Under Thirty"). "A forge of wit and wisdom" (again, their words, not mine). "Handsome as they come" (it's possible the interviewer was hitting on me, but again, her words, not mine). Respectable. Innovative. The kind of guy who should be supervising producer at the world's most addictive sitcom.

Tomorrow, simply put, will be perfect.

And Lavender Rhodes, without question, is not going to get in the way.

Chapter 6

Lavender

I open the door and step inside.

"You've got to be kidding me."

I pull down the bill of my baseball cap as I hear a man's words somewhere amid a slew of barking and meowing.

The sound inside the narrow vet clinic rivals the cacophony of buses, taxis, and automobiles blaring horns on the street. The 7:30 a.m. light is bright, beams of sunlight bouncing off car windshields and parking meters, promising that today will be another unseasonably warm February day.

Paper hearts are strewn across the window display of Jones Animal Clinic.

My shirt is on inside out (something I discovered on the way here), but all in all I consider that a success given the night I've had with little Bernie here.

(Shockingly enough, Sonya *still* hasn't come to accept this wonderful gift to her life, and so for a little longer he's bunking with me.)

Which isn't so bad, of course.

He's an absolute sweetheart with those big brown eyes and his cuddle-up-with-you-at-all-times spirit.

And surprising amount of fur.

I mean, it just drops off by the handful. Great big balls the size of mice that end up on your bed. In the bathroom. In your mouth.

It's impressive, really, that he has any fur left at all.

And the house-training situation. Of course I know he's a baby, and nobody can expect a baby to be potty-trained. But really . . . how many times a day can you clean your rugs and couches before they're irreparable? It's a real question. I asked that exact thing of Google when Bernie decided to have a random bout of puppy energy. And scratching.

A really, *really* intense level of scratching. Allergies perhaps?

It got so bad I ended up reaching out to a vet, and luckily enough they *just* had a surprise opening in the schedule for puppy shots and a wellness check the following morning. The veterinarian himself even came on the phone after it became apparent who I was. (For the record, no, I don't like receiving special attention, but in this case, for the sake of Bernie and his scratching, I wasn't going to argue.) He even graciously offered to have me come to his house for a visit right then—which of course I declined, considering it was seven o'clock at night.

So we settled on my bringing Bernie in first thing today. They explained how easy it would be to drop him by on my way to work and pick him up after. And here I am.

The room is crowded, lined with sleepy pet owners clutching tumblers while cats and dogs rest in little cages beside them or at their feet. Someone is handing off her cat in a crate to a nurse in scrubs, who stands guard between what appears to be the waiting area and the back end, where things happen. Everyone seems terribly uninterested in doing anything but chugging caffeine and checking their phones—everyone, that is, except the man in the corner, who has his neck craned towards the blank wall, staring at it as if his life depends on it.

A large gray dog rests obediently at his feet.

The back of his head looks . . . familiar.

Two cats peek out from a small crate in the chair beside him.

I hear my own voice coming from the telly directly above him. Glance up. Recognize the scene immediately.

Funny. The vet did say he was, in his words, "a huge, *huge* fan." Was he playing the show in honor of my visit? Surely not. Surely it was a happy coincidence.

With enormous effort, I half drag, half carry Bernie and get in line, when a second receptionist at the far end sees me and jumps up so quickly her coffee tips over. She slides open the glass partition.

"MS. HUNTER," she cries at least twice as loud as necessary. "DR. ARMENT WILL SEE YOU NOW."

She gives me a little wink, clearly quite proud of the secret name we'd exchanged and how well she'd performed. And sure enough, nobody seems to have recognized me or cared, which is more than fine by me. Most are frowning and checking their phones and watches. One man in a flamingo-print shirt is tapping his shoes like the ticks of a broken clock.

I meet the receptionist at the door. She holds it open with one hand and elaborately smooths her skirt with the other.

"So do I just . . . ," I say, and begin to offer her the leash.

And then just like that, a man appears in the doorway, his fingers stretched out as he holds the door open above her head. His teeth are a blazing white, matching his lab coat and white hair. The blue embroidery above his chest pocket reads DR. ARMENT. He couldn't possibly smile bigger.

"Ser*ena*," he booms. "Let's see if we can get that itching sorted out. You come on through and I'll take good care of you." He winks.

There's something just a little askew in the way he speaks. And I can't help noticing his choice of words. Take care of *you*, he said. Not the dog. I hate to nitpick, but the word sends off a little warning bell in my mind.

(Yes, I am more sensitive than other people. But then again, yes, I have to be.)

"Sorry, if you don't mind, I'm just going to run on." I shake my head, acting as though my memory of last night's phone call was foggy, just to keep things light. I brandish a smile. "I think the plan we had was that I'd leave him with you and . . . come pick him up later?"

"It'll just be a minute," Dr. Arment says reassuringly.

"Yes, but—"

"Five minutes, no more," he interrupts, tipping his head toward the hallway with that overly bright smile.

I'm not sure why, possibly because he invited me to come for a house visit last night, complete with dog bath, but I feel a bit like he's opening up the gates of hades and telling me to skip on down to the party.

And then for a moment, I think he's reaching out for the leash, until his hand settles on my hand.

Which is a hard no.

His thumb slides over the top of my hand, his touch moving in circles and then sliding up past my wrist, sending pinpricks up my arm.

Again, very much unacceptable.

And suddenly there he is, pulling the leash and my wrist toward him and hooking his arm around my shoulder.

It's all so inappropriate, all so bizarre, that I find I'm inhaling an unearthly amount of men's cologne mixed with the scent of kibble, my cheek pressed to his chest, before I've even had time to blink.

"The lady said she has to go," the man from the corner pipes up.

"Finn Masters," I say automatically, because funnily enough

that name has been bouncing around my brain for the past twenty-four hours.

Finn, for his part, looks like he'd rather be doing anything but speaking up right now.

But that's exactly what he's doing, isn't it? And a little tender bloom unfurls in my chest as I realize just how nice it is of him to stick up for me.

I slide out from beneath Dr. Arment's grip.

Dr. Arment frowns. "Who is this? Your bodyguard?"

"Yes," I say with a smile.

"No," Finn says with a frown at the same time.

"That's just the Cat Man," the receptionist chimes in, as though this answers everything.

Dr. Arment's eyes shift from her, to Finn, to me. The varnish is wearing off that easygoing smile of his, and with each passing second I'm getting confirmation that my gut reaction was right. He's starting to give off the vibe of the kind of man who goes to country clubs and laughs really loud as he buys everyone martinis, and then ten years later appears on the front page for money laundering.

"There's no problem here," Dr. Arment says, more to Finn than to me. He squints at the other people waiting along the wall as though trying to spot additional security detail.

How humorous.

He really does think Finn is my bodyguard. This thin, bookish, curly-haired man with glasses and two cats who looks like he's never thrown a punch in his life.

"There wouldn't have been," Finn replies, "if you'd have just let her drop off her beast of a dog instead of getting handsy."

Well. That's a bit harsh, but his heart's in the right place.

I go to rub the top of Bernie's head, but he's dropped off to inspect the cage of cats. Then gnaw on the cage while the cats meow furiously.

Oops. I yank him back.

"I was reaching for the *leash*, young man," Dr. Arment snaps, his voice rising. "And it was merely a *friendly* gesture."

"A clearly unwanted gesture." Finn levels his gaze. "Particularly with *her*."

"I'm friendly with *everyone*," he says, waving his arm around the room. "And your sensitivities have no right to bear down on the freedom of my expression. And who *I* am."

"Funny, I've been a customer for years, and you've never tried to grope me."

And that is how, fifteen minutes of heated debate later, including one rather long argument over exactly who first said, "The right to swing my fist ends where the other man's nose begins," I find myself on the sidewalk outside Jones Animal Clinic with two dogs, two cats, and one very irritated Finn Masters.

Chapter 7

Finn

"Unbelievable."

"You say that a lot, I'm noticing," Lavender says, tilting her head with that horrible smile of hers.

There is—and I can't emphasize this enough—absolutely *nothing* amusing about this moment.

"It's happening," I mutter incredulously, while holding tight to the crate of cats and Miles at my side. My car is the last in a long, long row down the street, where I parked at approximately 6:30 a.m. for early drop-off on the way to work. *Drop-off.* The very standard and normal practice for Jones Animal Clinic, which caters to the busy lives of its LA clientele by offering before- and after-hours services. *Six thirty.* For a drop-off vaccination and grooming session that was supposed to take, and has taken many times in the past, a little over two minutes.

But what happened today?

Lavender Rhodes happened.

Which explains why I got to said veterinary office at six thirty on the dot only to discover locked doors and a handwritten sign that said, "Emergency plumbing issue. Will open shortly. Please be patient."

And so, I was patient.

I stood on the sidewalk with Miles and these cats, alternating between watching the sun and traffic slowly rise on one end, and the staff through the window on the other. They raced around with mops and buckets. Wiped down every surface that existed. Applied tubes of lipstick. At one point, a receptionist used the window I was looking through to check her reflection while adjusting and readjusting her skirt.

And now I know why.

Plumbing issue. Right.

They were all trying to clean up for *her*.

Dr. Arment was off getting his dentures whitened to the point of being able to use them as paint samples for *her*—the girl who skipped to the front of the line while the rest of us, the plebians who'd struggled to calm our caged animals for over an hour, watched.

And now here she is, trotting along beside me like a puppy, while the *actual* puppy she's trying to pull along stops at every crack in the sidewalk.

That's it.

I'm never getting away from her.

This is what I get for not flying home often enough. This is what I get for working through holidays.

This is my life sentence.

A lifetime of *her* ruining my life.

She is my fate.

"Well, that took a surprising turn," she says, as though it is not *7:46 a.m.* and we don't have a pet situation to figure out and we don't have to *get to work*.

"Getting banned for life from a veterinary clinic was not on my to-do list today, no," I reply.

"Thanks for stepping in back there. That was very"—she pauses for the word—"chivalrous of you." Her grin broadens, as though she hasn't used that word in reference to anyone in a while and finds it cute. Finds my actions . . . cute.

"He was much too forward," I say begrudgingly, keeping a brisk pace.

I don't regret what I said. He *did* have some nerve. And *of course* I wouldn't want any woman to be treated that way, regardless of our history.

Still.

That doesn't mean I want to be friends.

"Makes me glad I didn't take him up on the offer to take Bernie to his place last night."

I squeeze my eyes shut and fight the urge to reply.

Do not fall for this woman's charade.

Do not talk.

Do not encourage this conversation.

"But I have to admit, for a moment I considered it," she says, pausing on the sidewalk. She takes over scratching Bernie's side in a spot where the pup had been itching. "Given he was so friendly over the phone and Bernie's been so desperate."

Don't reply.

"But then when he made a little joke about his services including a free bath and grooming, and left a little ambiguity as to whom exactly he was referring to—"

My teeth grind so hard they hit a nerve.

I stop short. "*You* obviously, Lavender. If he was joking, he meant *you*."

"I can see that *now*, of course," she says, with an annoying lack of concern.

I take three more steps and stop again.

Turn. "You of all people shouldn't go walking around assuming people would do anything out of the kindness of their hearts—" I throw up my hands. *No. You're doing it, Finn.* "But of course it's none of my business. Right. Well," I say, quickening my pace as I raise the crate over a sidewalk rubbish bin. "I'm nearly at my car, so—"

"I guess I'll have to take Bernie to work again—"

"I cannot recommend that less," I say and stop impatiently at a light. Miles heels. And then, forced to try to push Lavender elsewhere, I say, "Where's your car?"

"Oh." She waves a hand vaguely as though she can't be bothered to remember. "Somewhere up here."

The Bernese Mountain Dog pup with the ridiculous on-the-nose name tries to lunge into oncoming traffic like the brilliant creature he is, and with a fair amount of struggle, she picks him up. His enormous puppy paws dangle limply at her side.

He looks like he's entirely accustomed to this way of life. Expects nothing less.

"What'll you be doing today?" Lavender asks, nodding to the cats. "Will someone pick them up?"

She really is going to come with me all the way to my car.

"No."

The light turns and we cross.

A few moments later, a horn goes off as a bus rips by. Wisps of Lavender's hair whip around her, then fall gently back into place. But of course they do.

Another car whizzes past, and my pulse speeds up when I see she's practically falling off the curb, tottling along with that animal in her arms.

For the sake of lowering my own pulse rate, fine, I think, grinding my teeth.

And being *extremely careful* to avoid touching her, I move ahead to the curb and edge her over to the building side.

You would've thought I'd launched a cannon.

"Look at you!" she exclaims. "All this talk about people not doing things out of the kindness of their hearts. And yet what do we have here?"

She grins massively.

I don't reply.

I don't want to look at her.

I have just now determined that my goal for the rest of my life (which, fine, may prove quite challenging given my occupation) will be to never directly look at her again. She's like looking at the sun. You think to yourself, *Oh look! A radiant sun!* And then burn your eyeballs to a crisp.

But even from my periphery, I can see she's motioning with those large, innocent (allegedly) eyes, and an exultant smile has crested her lips, and it seems like I just can't help sneaking the teeniest, tiniest glance to see what she's referring to.

"You are *that* person. You do *that thing*," she says a bit breathlessly. (No surprise she's breathless, what with carrying a fully capable dog known for roaming exotic mountaintops and herding sheep in zero-degree weather.)

"I did nothing."

"Yes, you did."

"No, I didn't."

"Yes, *you did*."

I frown. Purse my lips. Look ahead.

"The walk-on-the-side-closest-to-traffic-in-case-you-must-sacrifice-yourself-to-the-stray-vehicle-jumping-the-curb-toward-the-damsel-in-distress thing." She squints at me and announces, "You risked your life for me."

"No," I reply instantly, shaking my head. "Force of habit. That's all."

"You risked your life for me. You've been my hero today now, not just once but *twice*. Look at you!" she says, with a swat on my shoulder as though I should be quite proud. "And it's only nine."

"It's 7:52," I retort. "I did no such thing."

"It's behind us now. You've done it, and you can't take it back," she says happily. "And humble to boot."

"I am *not* being humble," I reply curtly, stepping around a woman with a rolled-up yoga mat in her arms.

Lavender gets blocked momentarily by pedestrians, and against my will, I wait while she catches up. But I need to make this point very clear. There's something about her that makes me want to make this point *very clear.*

"I do this with everyone, I can assure you."

"You do this with your guy chums?" she says. "Swap places when your mates get too close to the road?"

I frown even deeper. "No. That'd be ridiculous."

"Girlfriend then?"

The reference to Delilah on her lips strikes like a viper. For a moment my feet halt, and I feel I must catch my breath.

Meanwhile, there Lavender stands, the wrecking ball to our relationship herself. Cocking her brow as her own feet slow. Looking at me with that playful and completely oblivious tilt of her lips.

"Former girlfriend," I say, resuming my pace. "Yes."

I flip over my wrist to check my watch, and the cats in the crate give a disgruntled meow at the jostling.

"So what is this about you being the Cat Man?"

They say that good befalls those who show kindness to others. Well, I can tell you now, that is a *lie.*

"The cats aren't mine. They belong to my neighbor, who has a stray-cat-picking-up problem," I say, flicking my gaze at her. "Kind of like you."

"She sounds lovely," Lavender says.

"Until someone else has to take over the problem, sure. She's all roses and sunshine. You would like her, I'm sure."

I frown as I slow to a stop at my car. Some idiot driver parallel parked far too close to my bumper, making it impossible to get Miles and the cats into the cargo area. And thanks to my neighbors, the back seat is full.

I'll just have to do my best to inch the car forward.

I set the crate down and drop Miles's leash with the command to *stay*, then step off the curb.

"Finn."

I can hear Lavender calling out to me as I dodge traffic and pointedly ignore her as I hurry around to the driver's side. I slide inside, turn the ignition key, and with laser focus tap the gas pedal to move forward a good three inches.

Lavender's still standing on the sidewalk, massive puppy stretched across her body, when I walk back to survey the clearance. The gargantuan black SUV parked behind me looms ominously despite my three-inch advance.

My chest is starting to pinch at this point, and I can practically feel my pulse ticking along with the seconds on my watch. I'm just going to have to put Miles in the back seat. Which will mean moving two boxes full of paperbacks, two old blankets, and a chair that all need to be dropped off at Goodwill—another task gifted from several neighbors.

I'm just throwing the back door open and heaving my first box onto the sidewalk when I hear a *beep beep* from the parked SUV. I look up.

There is Lavender behind the wheel, slowly rolling the car in reverse. The fluffy black, brown, and white dog's head peeks over the wheel.

Of course.

Of course it's her car.

"I'm going to be late," I retort as I toss the box back in and slam the door. I open the liftgate and usher Miles inside.

She shrugs, elbow dangling out her open window. "You're being a bit dramatic, aren't you? But if you're *that* worried about it, maybe try parking in your slot next time."

"I did. You boxed me in."

"I beg to differ."

My brows furrow and I look down. Sure enough, in my haste I had somehow missed the fact that the road had been restriped and accidentally parked my car on the faded white parking line instead of the clear dark yellow. So my Subaru Forester is now frustratingly covering half of one spot and half of the other.

Well.

"My mistake," I say, grabbing the cat carrier off the sidewalk. I clench my jaw, wanting so much to hang on to my dignity and not say the words, particularly to *her*, that I know I must. "I . . . apologize."

Silence.

She laughs. At me, with me, it makes no difference. "I won't lose any sleep over it. Now, what shall we do with our pets?"

She's using the term "we." As if this is a collaborative issue to be tackled.

"I don't know about *you*," I say. "I imagine *you* have a dozen assistants to handle this sort of thing. In fact, I'm not even quite sure why *you* are personally involved in this scenario at all. As for *me*, I haven't got people to whom I can just hand off tasks. I have to get to work on time or I will be fired. And my flat is forty minutes in the wrong direction. My family is overseas. My workplace demands I maintain a workaholic lifestyle, which has led to all my friends currently being either at my place of employment or being my neighbors—all of whom are senior citizens and drive according to the laws of the 1920s—which, for the record, are terrifying.

"Consequently, I will do the opposite of what is a good plan and attempt to sneak the animals into my closet-sized office. Should I actually succeed in squeezing us all in, Miles will be happy to sit quietly at my feet." I pause and give Bernie a look. "Unlike some dogs I know. And, thanks to my lack of popularity, I do not expect my colleagues to drop in and pepper me with questions such as, 'Did you know you have a dog in here?' and 'Are you aware that

Goodwin's highly allergic to animals?' and 'D'you always sit with two cats on your shoulders?' Of course, my office will smell of cat urine for the next five years, but that'll just be a nice scent people can identify me with. My own personal brand."

"So you've got a plan then. Great."

Her face is a blank slate for a couple of moments, then she cracks a smile. "Your plan's rubbish. They'll all have a party in my dressing room. The pups can hang out together on the couch—"

"I'd rather have Miles whine at my feet—"

"The cats will have an endless supply of tuna sandwiches—"

"Your beast of a dog will eat the cats."

"Will you stop calling him a beast of a dog?" she says, covering his ears. "You're going to give him a complex. And I have a bathroom for the cats." Her bright blue eyes are eager, hopeful. "Come on. It's the least I can do." She waves a hand flippantly. "I don't even care if your pets destroy the room. It'll be fine. We can take turns checking on them throughout the day." Her grin widens. "It'll be like *One Fine Day*. We're just two parents trying to take care of our children, who find that working together is far better than going it alone."

My chest puffs up. "Miles would *never* destroy anyone's room. If anything, your giant dog—"

"Sonya's giant dog," she corrects.

"—will be babysat by Miles, who will keep your . . . Bernie . . . from tearing your stars off the wall."

"Perfect," Lavender says. "It's a date."

It's not a date.

It's not even my plan.

And *everything* within me wants to refuse. Everything in my gut is screaming, *No. No. No!* But I feel a bit like a soldier backed against a wall. There's nowhere to go, and the guy with the loaded crossbow is telling me in soothing tones, "C'mon. Just come with me. It's a plan." And really, what choice do I have? What do I do?

Go with the guy with the big bow, of course.

A chant is on repeat in my brain: *This is a horrible idea. This is a horrible idea. This is a horrible idea.* I start to shut the liftgate. Miles looks at Bernie and gives a mild whine just before it shuts, as if to say, *Really? You're going to put me in a room with that thing?*

I exhale.

Turn to face Lavender.

"Fine. Let's go."

Chapter 8

Lavender

Tuesday, Table Read, Writers Room

Finn Masters is a curious man.

And it's a quarter to nine.

Table readings, where we sit around the writers room and read through the new week's script, are on Tuesdays. Wednesdays we run through the show for the first time. Thursdays and Fridays we run through it with props and makeup just like the real thing. And shoots are on Mondays, when the entire day is spent filming what we worked on all through the previous week.

It's an antiquated way to do things, given most shows dropped live audiences years ago. But Goodwin is an old-fashioned man, and his ways, for better or worse, do gravitate toward success. Personally, I like it. Canned laughter can only go so far. The show's energy thrives on the adrenaline of real people in the audience.

And yes, it is funny to shoot on Mondays instead of Fridays. But that started years ago due to scheduling conflicts when the show was just a baby. It stayed that way due in part to Mr. Goodwin, who assumes we're all just as obsessed with the show as he is. In his mind, *of course* the cast will be honing their lines to perfection over the weekend.

It's been ten years. To my knowledge, nobody has done that.

Sonya spends the weekends dragging me to one event or another, when she's not cycling somewhere mental, like to the desert and back. Kye up till recently spent his weekends with his girlfriend. And before that, his other girlfriend. And before that, the other one.

I've done my fair share of dating on the weekends, but my last boyfriend was a mess, and the one before that, well, we broke off amicably.

Now that I think of it, I haven't checked in since I set him up with that set designer a month ago—but from the way she seems to float everywhere as she arranges fake oranges in bowls and adds new magnets to the set fridge, I wager it's going well.

Matchmaking is actually a bit of a talent of mine. Some people do things like build buildings and remove brain tumors. Me? I have an unusual ability to connect soulmates. In fact, I've been given the credit in no fewer than three wedding rehearsal speeches. It just seems that there is something I can see in people that they can't immediately see themselves. Like a strand of color.

There they go, walking around with a soul that's a very light, light purple, and one day I walk by and recall immediately that other lovely light, light purple soul I met the other day. And of course, given that we all, at our deepest level, just want so much to love and be loved, I can think of no other option but to set them on the right path. Together.

All that to say: Tom, my former flame, was a vibrant orange. And Samantha, one of the set designers, was a vibrant orange too. Now they are vibrant orange together.

It's a wonderful, colorful hobby.

The sun tickles the skin on my legs as I stand at the base of a palm tree beside my parking spot, watching Finn walk down to the first level of the parking lot across the way while Bernie sniffs at my feet. The air is thick with the scent of fresh asphalt. A California scrub jay swoops overhead, calling with a loud *kuk* that lifts Bernie's head. Visitors wearing matching tourist lanyards are seated on passing trolleys, while their drivers spout details over a speaker about the history of Wagner Studios.

It's another beautiful day.

If Finn had a color, it would be a cool gray.

I watch Finn's pursed lips as he grips the cat crate and leads Miles, obviously throwing a silent little conniption over being late to work (to be fair, Mr. Goodwin can be quite scary). A breeze sweeps over Finn's hair and pulls it into an even bigger curlicue on top of those round black glasses of his. He looks so much like his dog. Both so big and thoughtful and calm.

Well, of course, not calm at this moment.

And yet, still, his winsome eyes remind me of home.

It's the accent, of course. Must be. Nobody can know someone for twenty-four hours and already feel they're home.

Put simply, we're two Brits in a very American city.

That, and the way he pushes up his glasses when he's concentrating. And the way he looks so serious as he stares at scripts or throws around a cat crate, or even has my back in a veterinarian's office. Quiet and unassuming, and you can just tell, something about him is wise. He reminds me a lot of my father and two younger brothers back home. He makes me want to call them just for a hello. Just to hear their voices.

Maybe that's why I find myself drawn to him.

He, symbolically at least, makes me feel like I'm right back at the breakfast table at 418 Westbrooke Road, listening to Mum accuse Dad of pinching out the tomato shoots when she's not home, while my brothers elbow each other beneath the table. They're twenty-five now. One married off and beginning a family of his own, the other living in central London, taking the train home to Welling on Sundays for church and potluck lunch. I hear Charlie's three-year-old is going to start playing football in the spring. Wouldn't that be fun to see? Not through a video. Really see.

I take a breath, forcing myself to think of lighter things.

Here comes Finn down the crosswalk from the parking garage, cat kennel in one hand, laptop bag slung over one shoulder. His larger-than-life dog walks obediently by his side, trotting so daintily I squint.

Is he . . . only stepping on the white paint of the crosswalk?

I look down at Bernie, currently chewing through his leash like a rabid chipmunk.

Hmm.

"So who trained your dog?" I say the moment Finn is within earshot.

Finn's brow twitches slightly as he moves past me without slowing down, and if I didn't know better, I would take it to mean, *So . . . we're still talking, are we?* But of course he's new, and stressed, and, like I said, a little bit quirky.

"I did."

"You?" I can't hide my surprise, partly because the dog trotting by Finn's side looks like he's been in dog shows. And *won*.

Meanwhile I give Bernie a tug to come along, and when he refuses, I pick him up. Again.

"You don't dabble in dog training by chance?" I say, only half joking.

He stares ahead so long I feel he must not hear me. Who knows? Maybe he doesn't. I mean, his face is still a little bit puffy from what I understand was an allergy attack yesterday—all the way back to his ears. They're all red and blotchy. Actually, he looks a bit like a fairy from my secondary school's production of *A Midsummer Night's Dream*.

And then I hear myself. An intake of breath so loud and apparently dramatic the trolley across the way stops. I vaguely hear someone ask if I'm okay.

I halt.

Right there in the middle of the road.

As two worlds collide.

"You're Puck!" I exclaim. I suck in another breath, then point at him as my brain tries to compute the slideshow of the past coming to life. "You're the fairy Puck from our school play!" The words sound different in my mouth as I repeat his name. "You're *Finn. Masters.*"

But he doesn't stop in the middle of the road as I have.

In fact, he just keeps staring straight ahead, walking his dog as though he hasn't heard a word.

Blimey.

I jump toward him. A smile overtakes my face as I fall into step beside him.

"Well, look at the two of *us*," I say, pride practically exploding from my chest.

At this, he turns. Looks me over. His expression is one of incredulity. "Look at us, how?"

As though it isn't obvious.

I try to slap him on the chest good-naturedly, but at the same moment Bernie tilts his freakishly large (some would say adorably cartoonlike) face towards me and goes right for my dangling earring. Which, consequently, makes my slap more like a swat at his messenger bag. I feel a concerningly serious tug at my earlobe and drop to the ground, dog still in arms. With my neck crooked toward Bernie and, more importantly, his drooling jaw gripping the gold hoop in his teeth, I carry on talking while I try to pry open Bernie's mouth. "It's incredible, isn't it?! *Both* of us from Welling School. *Both* of us coming here and establishing ourselves in this line of work after all these years. Mrs. Harris would be so proud, don't you think?"

Chapter 9

Finn

Tuesday, Table Read, Writers Room

Don't.

I.

Think.

This woman, this *woman*, who is helplessly on the ground, her Muppet of a dog overtaking her as it tries with all its might to rear back and take her ridiculously large hoop earring with him. Small wonder. It's the size of a glinting Frisbee.

And here she is, on the ground, while pedestrians are slowly coming to a stop around us, having the audacity to look helpless and innocent and infuriatingly unconcerned about being roughly two seconds away from having her earlobe ripped off and needing emergency surgery.

Meanwhile, *again*, I'm about to be late.

And *she* is just looking up at me, careless to her plight, nattering away about all the "happy times" at school that were in fact very, very, *very* much the opposite.

I check my watch. Grit my teeth. Not in a silent way to relieve tension but in a way that declares very loudly, *I am frustrated to the point that I don't care who knows it.*

For me, this is significant.

To other people, I have no doubt this looks bad. A celebrity sweetheart is on the ground getting mauled by a bus-size dog gnawing on her earlobe, and a man is standing above her, tapping his foot impatiently and throwing out his hands in exasperation.

It looks bad.

But looks are deceiving.

"You took my role," I say, rolling my neck in why-me? fashion and drop-throwing the leash to the ground.

The cat crate goes down on the cement.

One knee goes down so I can save the blasted woman from the blasted dog.

"I was not, in fact, Puck," I say, clamping my hand around the dog's mouth to lock him in place, then working to free the earring. "*You* were, if you recall."

Bernie is thrilled I've joined the game. He growls in a puppy-growl sort of way and digs in, his nails clawing the pavement.

"Nonsense. I was your understudy all the way to the end. You were the big hurrah."

The dog tries to jerk his head out of my grip, but when my hands stay firmly in place, he gives a throaty rumble and scrunches up his nose. His razor-blade puppy teeth are clamped around the gigantic hoop.

"And what kind of ridiculous earring is this, for the record? They're as big as Frisbees."

"It's called offsetting my outfit, thank you for noticing," she replies. Honestly, if she were on a sinking ship, she'd be the one standing on the deck with a glass of champagne as she looks over the side and cries happily, "Those waves do look big, don't they? You know, that reminds me of this one time at this great little spot just outside Montecito . . ." Lavender motions towards her denim cutoffs, the strings frayed all along the hemline. Her leather flip-flops, clinging loosely to her toes. "I don't want to be *too* casual."

"So you thought rolls of copper wiring around your earlobes was the answer. Sure," I reply. "And no, I was *not* the big hurrah. My name may have been on the program. Auntie Flora may have wept when we heard the good news. I may have spent three months in front of my bedroom mirror, wearing home-sewn jester ears—and for the record, he's a mischievous sprite, not a mere *fairy*—memorizing my lines. I may have turned down my spot on the cross-country team—because Mrs. Harris said the demands of the role required I choose one or the other. Despite the fact that I was an excellent hurdler with a real chance at earning a scholarship for uni. All facts I chose to ignore."

The puppy begins to wiggle his head ferociously, and I get him into a choke hold. Lavender's ridiculously golden hair is everywhere around me, and I spit some strands out of my mouth and continue. "No, Lavender. I was Puck up until the very last moment. And then it was you."

"Yes. I remember that," she says, her neck grazing my nose and sending the scent of a thousand coconuts directly into my sinuses. "Something about your foot, wasn't it? You broke your ankle?"

"*You* broke my ankle," I retort, holding my breath to keep her offensively tropical aura out. "Technically."

I pry the jaws open at last. Lavender lifts her chin, and the hoop is released.

She collapses onto her backside, takes the hoops from both ears, and pops them into her palm before Bernie can make another go at them.

Then of all things, she laughs.

The world-renowned celebrity is on her backside in the middle of the sidewalk with a pool of hair around her as a swarm of people watching on the outskirts video away.

And she's laughing.

The baseball cap she was wearing is long gone, and the spun-around bun thing she had going at the nape of her neck is now lopsided, with half of her hair fanned around her face. With fresh determination, the dog has locked his jaws around the hoops in her hand.

"Wouldn't this be a funny picture of the two of us?" she says. She laughs again and opens her hand, letting the hoops go. "You and your face. Me and this dog. We should frame a picture of this and send it over to Mrs. Harris. Can you imagine? Esteemed Welling School duo, success across the pond."

I frown, and when it becomes clear she's not going anywhere in a hurry, I hold out my hand to help her up.

"And about me breaking your ankle," she says, grinning as she comes to standing. "C'mon, Finn. That's a stretch if I ever heard one."

"No," I reply, straightening my collar and picking up the cat crate to indicate *we need to go*. The door to the building is twenty feet away, and unless she decides to create another miraculously impossible dilemma out of thin air, we should be at her dressing room in less than five minutes. There I will *promptly* drop the animals at her door, sprint to the writers room, and, with any luck, make it with one minute to spare.

First, I do need to make this point very clear. After all, I've been sitting on this for almost fifteen years. It's my origin story, really. The *why* (well, first why) behind my loathing of all things Lavender Rhodes.

"No, it's not a stretch," I say. "It's an actual fact."

I begin striding.

Lavender tries to follow along but the dog holds fast. A moment later she catches up to me, the dog in her arms, a giant hoop clamped in his mouth like a prize. "You're actually holding that against me? That's what that face of yours has been all about the past few days?"

I stop at the door and swivel on my heel to face her. "I have no face."

"*That* one," she says, pointing with her free hand at my nose. "The one where you look like you've swallowed a lemon. I was wondering if I was just imagining it."

I turn back towards the door and swipe my ID over the handle. It beeps, and I pull the door open.

"You can't actually hold *that* against me, Finn. Yes, I accidentally left the trapdoor open—"

"During dress rehearsal, two days before the performance."

"—but people did that all the time. I mean, I admit, that was my mistake—"

"A mistake in the form of a four-inch-long screw in my ankle."

"—but you have eyes, too, don't you? Surely you don't expect to just walk around, blindly stepping into manholes and blaming the construction worker who forgot to shut the hole? I mean, you can't *sue* for something like that—"

"Legally you can. If a construction worker left a manhole open, that would be his liability."

"—and anyway, it was almost fifteen years ago. Not to mention, nobody's perfect." She grabs hold of me, halting me in the hall. I turn reluctantly, because I have the great sense that if I don't, she's going to nag about this forever.

I meet her sapphire-blue eyes. They're big and wide and innocent-looking and all those other things I've grown accustomed to seeing as I've been forced to watch episode after episode of *her* the past few days. It's the face I have avoided looking at for fifteen years, the face I now live with in my own purgatory, the face I am required to stare at every waking moment. At work. After work. In my dreams. She's always there.

I have dubbed the expression I'm seeing now as the I'm-about-to-tell-a-little-sentimental-story-that-will-have-us-hugging-and-forgiving-and-saying-things-like-"but-the-most-important-thing-here-is-love" face. That face.

I don't want to listen, but at the same time I can't get myself to shake off her hand and walk on. To tell her it's not important. Because it *is* incredibly important, and I would like to see some remorse on that face.

"Finn, I really am sorry," she begins, squeezing my arm. "You deserved that role, and you worked hard for it, and I can see that it meant a lot to you. I was the understudy Lower Sixth, and you were the very big, very tremendously talented Upper Sixth, and for what it's worth, I looked up to you for all that. Tried to match your level of dedication. Studied up just as I saw you were doing. You were quite the role model for me."

My chest swells ever so slightly against my will, and I force it to crumple back down.

No. There will be no winning me over here.

I am a steel wall.

"And that play changed the trajectory of my life," Lavender continues. "So I guess in a very big way, I have you to thank. I don't think either of us would be here today if not for the surprises that came our way back then. And look at us now, you big-time producer."

She's inflating things to soften me up. I know it.

"I don't know about you," she says, a smile tilting her lips, "but I like to think that we landed just where we are supposed to be. Don't you agree?"

Did I agree?

Did I agree . . . that her leaving that trapdoor open without thought or care changed the trajectories of our lives?

I suck in a breath.

Of course.

Of course it did.

For starters, she blew everyone away opening night, which is great and wonderful and just *brilliant*. Then, of course, we have yet to discuss the part about the agent, the aunt of a sixth-form student with a minor role who came and was so impressed by this young understudy, who jumped into the role of Puck with such vigor and a fresh, wide-open face, that she just *had* to talk to her afterwards. Which, four weeks later during summer break, led to Lavender flying to LA to audition for a handful of roles. Which led to her parents' decision to homeschool Lavender for her Upper Sixth year while she flew into the world of acting, arms open wide. All facts I learned about, for the record, while painfully crutching around campus in a cast.

I reach for her hand on my shoulder. Lift it as I look down at her shining, hopeful face. Step back. Let it go. "Third door down, right?"

Chapter 10

Lavender

Wednesday, Rehearsals, Stage 2

So Finn has a chip on his shoulder.

It isn't a healthy way to go through life, carrying that weight around for fifteen years, but who am I to judge? I, too, have faced my own demons, not in the form of grudges but equally self-damaging. Don't we all have our own particular stumbling blocks? I will just make it my job to mend the situation. To help him move on.

I stand offstage during a break, munching on an apple, staring at the wall. I must look visibly off, because Sonya is at my side before I've had two bites, crossing her arms, staring at the wall as if trying to see what I'm seeing. "What are you doing?" she says at last.

"I'm thinking," I reply.

"I can see that. But there's regular Lavender thinking, and there's Lavender-is-off-plotting-something-and-I-should-probably-cut-her-off-before-we-end-up-doing-something-really-stupid-together thinking. What are you scheming up?"

"Nothing," I say. "Well, not yet. It's just"—I hold the partly eaten apple to my lips—"I've just been enlightened to the fact that I've been a thorn in someone's side for the past decade or so, and I'd like to remedy it. I'm just trying to figure out how big of an offering I'm going to need to provide to make up for being someone's object of wrath for so long."

Sonya laughs. "Object of wrath, eh? You know, I think I did see that on a Kay Jewelers flyer recently. A really nice set of pearls beneath the words 'Need to ask for forgiveness for being an object of wrath? Come on by and ask for the Object-of-Wrath Remedy special!'"

I take another bite. Munch thoughtfully. After a long pause, I say, "I think he's more of a watch man, but I like where your head is at. Keep brainstorming."

She shakes her head. Turns to the snack table, where there is no enormous charcuterie board with swirls of lavish meats (and apparently allergy-inducing turmeric) this time, but a much simpler, grabbed-at-the-last-minute deli spread. Sonya begins rearranging the little blueberry muffins by muffin-liner color.

Pink.

Red.

Pink.

Red.

I watch her for a substantial length of time, then switch two muffins when she's not looking.

"So what did you do exactly?" she says, frowning at a man reaching for a turkey sandwich from the lineup of sandwiches she's currently rearranging. She pushes his hand away. Hands him a muffin.

"Well," I say, "he accused me of breaking his ankle and, I gather from his muttering as we walked down the hall, sabotaging his lifelong dreams."

Her perfectly plucked brows jump and her perfectly polished (white, of course) fingers stop stripping the toothpicks of their neon green and red frill. "Did you?"

"Did I sabotage his dreams? Well, yes. Technically. I forgot to shut a trapdoor just before he went onstage . . . and it was pitch-black where he was supposed to be crouching in this little tree prop." I pause, remembering. "And the drop-off was actually through the floor to this whole room below the stage. So he probably fell a good fifteen feet before landing on concrete."

Sonya winces.

"Not to mention the ladder he probably struck on the way down," I add. "Which explains the screws they patched his foot back together with—"

Her face looks a little green now.

"And then of course, there's the whole problem that I happened to be the understudy for his role, and that was how I first met Nancy—"

"Nancy Harra," she says. "Our agent?"

I nod.

"Wait," she says, putting up a finger. "So you're saying he fell fifteen feet and shattered his body because you didn't shut a door, then you took his role, then from said role you landed Nancy as your agent, who brought you to LA and landed you ultimately in *Neighbors*, the number-one most-watched sitcom in television history?"

"It sounds bad when you say it like that," I say.

"And you are trying to make amends."

"Yes." I pick up a muffin. A muffin seems like a good place to start. "I'll take him one of these." I pick up a second one. "Two."

Her brows shoot up. "Wait. He's *here*?" She darts her eyes around the room. "Who is it? Who is this man you've destroyed?"

"Finn Masters." I point across the room to Finn standing in the center of a circle of writers. He looks quite natural there. Maybe it's the midafternoon light, but his face seems less swollen, and though I can't tell what he's saying, I see he's talking. Actually, he looks like he's commanding the room. For the first time since I've laid eyes upon him, he looks very much like he's in his element.

"See. And it clearly worked out."

"The new supervising producer?" she says, mortified. "The one who almost died Monday from an allergic reaction to that pretzel you gave him?"

I pick up a third muffin. "One and the same."

"Good grief. Misfortune follows him around, doesn't it?" She gazes at him for a long moment. Then turns to me. "But he looks like he's recovered from the ankle incident. I'd say he's doing alright now."

"Yes, but I have to do something." I watch him duck his head to look at something somebody is showing him on paper. He starts to nod. I'm not entirely sure how it's possible, but it's an attractive nod. A quiet, I-know-what-I'm-doing nod. Open-faced. Contented. Intelligent.

Ah, and now I'm finding him attractive on top of it.

"I hate to think there's someone out there holding a grudge against me," I say, adding a turkey sandwich to the pile in my hands.

Sonya snorts. It's the kind of laugh she never uses on set. "Only *you*, Lavie. Only *you* would be in this gig for a decade and just be finding out now what it's like to have someone who doesn't adore you. Welcome to the world the rest of us live in."

Finn slips momentarily out of view as Maggie, Kye's new PA, walks by on wobbly heels, hauling a load of coffees. She glances around a little aimlessly as she passes them out, then spots someone. Huh. She makes a beeline for Finn.

A cool-gray shade of a girl if I ever saw one.

And then, just like that, I know how my apology is going to start.

Chapter 11

Finn

Wednesday, Script Edits, Writers Room

I'VE GOT A SURPRISE—

If I look like I've just received a death threat tucked into the liner of a muffin placed anonymously beside my laptop, it's because I have.

I'm just unfurling the slip of paper and reading the flowy, peppy handwriting, feeling the blood drain from my face, when Paula stops talking abruptly. She's sitting with her feet propped up on a chair, waving the Yoo-hoo in her hand as she argues passionately to the rest of the writers about what exactly Sonya's character should do with her failing career, when she eyes me and halts midthought to say, "Finn? What is that? You look like a ghost sent you a muffin."

With trepidation, I unfurl the rest of the roll and read.

—FOR YOU.

I squeeze my eyes shut, hoping with all my might as I turn the paper over that it's signed by a serial killer instead of Lavender.

WARMLY, THE OTHER PUCK AND AUNTIE OF MILES'S NEW BEST FRIEND.

No.

No. No. No. No. No.

What I want to do is drop my head on the long rectangular table where we have been gathered for the last hour arguing through the new script. But I have *just* fought tooth and nail and managed to crawl out of the hole and into the good repute of those around me after a day of hard-earned thoughtful ideas and tactful responses.

After tearing down the hall and throwing open the door to the writers room yesterday at 8:58 a.m., I managed to resist every physical inclination and hold my head high. I sucked in my breath despite the fact I was almost to the point of passing out. Despite every frayed nerve going haywire, I managed to act precisely the opposite of how I felt as I addressed everyone in the room: confident, self-assured, prepared. I was friendly. I was professional. I pretended my first day simply never existed.

I was walking in over my head, but there came a moment around 10:35 when I made a comment and another person started to do something magical. She started nodding.

Then a second person started to nod.

Then a third.

People began agreeing with me. People started listening to and, more importantly, *liking* my ideas.

And then around 11:45 something significant happened.

A PA offered to get me a cup of coffee.

And then I knew I was in.

And

Then

Here

We

Are

One

Day

Later
And
I
Get
This
Note.

I frown as I look at the little heart beside her signature: THE OTHER PUCK AND AUNTIE OF MILES'S NEW BEST FRIEND.

As if *my* Weimaraner would *ever* join forces with her dog.

There's a noise and my head jerks up, fully expecting Lavender's big cheery grin to be swinging my way, a terrible surprise in hand. But what would it be?

Indian curry?

A bouquet of sharpened pencils she trips over and conveniently stabs me with?

It's not her at the door, however.

Someone's just ordered pizza.

But the question lingers. Taunts.

What is it?

What's this horrible surprise?

"Finn," Paula repeats.

I turn. Face her head-on. "Sorry. Just daydreaming." Nightmaring. "Where were we?"

I try to listen while the topic of Ashley Krane carries on.

"I just don't think that's the right move for her," Heath, the line producer, interjects. "She's *engaged* now. We have to pull the elastic on this as far as it'll go. There's available space on outside Lot 12. We could throw some pink ribbon on a few chairs and gazebos. Venue shopping could be an interesting topic for a few episodes—"

"Compared to her getting cold feet after being stuck between two feuding honeymooners on a twelve-hour flight?" Erik interrupts. "Not to mention the hassle of outdoor sets. We'd have to deal with the weather—"

"Oh sure. That one day a year it rains in LA will be a craaaaazy risk," Paula retorts, setting her empty Yoo-hoo can on the growing pyramid in the center of the table. "You know what I think? I think you're all wrong. What Ashley should be doing is having an existential crisis as she narrows down her bridesmaids list. Turn it into some *Hunger Games* bridesmaids' battle involving envelope licking and tackling men who try to stand up during the ceremony—"

"Right after the *Hunger Games* baby-shower battle the girls dealt with six episodes ago?" Erik cuts in. "Do you even *watch* the show?"

An outsider would think they hate each other.

To us? Just another productive brainstorming session.

I set the muffin on the table. I'm going to have to ignore the message. But I turn my chair to face the door.

"Ashley said in"—I lean over, running my finger over the touch pad of my open laptop, scrolling down through my notes—"season 2, episode 13 to boyfriend of failed attempted elopement, Greg Links, that she, quote, 'could never take away this moment from my family. They've been rooting for me since you first slipped that valentine into my desk in second grade that said "I'm Batman. Will you be my Robin?" I can't not let them see how it ends.'"

I look up.

"Let's bring him back. Drop him into a pastoral role at the church where they decide to wed. Have him be Lance and Ashley's counselor during premarital counseling sessions. Find him still madly in love with her to the point of making chaotic decisions. Sabotaging sessions. Causing fights. Kidnapping." I shrug. "The usual."

"Her former fiancé being the pastoral counselor for the wedding?" Paula begins. "I like that."

"Can't," Erik jumps in. "Greg Links was played by Tom Hammon. Rehab."

I frown. "What about the chef from season 4?" I pause, scrolling through the document until I see what I want to see. "Similar breakup story."

"Trent Hathaway. He's booked out on *Cooking with the Stars*."

"I bet we could break him out for a few episodes," Heath says. "Nobody'll miss him. He never gets higher than a two-spatula rating—"

We go round and round into the evening, papers flying, fingers running madly across keyboards and screens. It's crunch time given the massive engagement plot shift. Instead of editing an existing script, we are creating one from scratch. And instead of merely getting words on the page to be edited later, we make great time and, at the end of the day, have it polished to perfection.

We are a team with all cylinders firing. It's my first real day and I already feel as in sync with this team as I did after eight years with *Higher Stakes*.

By nine o'clock, my legs are aching from all the pacing, but I feel alive. I feel good. Plot twists have been conceived. People have fought. Foosball has been played and carpal tunnel has flared. Caffeine has been consumed, fueling thoughts and propelling ideas.

I didn't lead the room at first. Co-execs Cindy and Ken did. But the two stepped out to handle rehearsals with Goodwin halfway through the day, and before I knew it, by title and rights I was in charge.

Before anyone could second-guess it, I grabbed the bull by the horns.

Now all that was left was to hand off the script to Mr. Goodwin on a silver platter (aka printed neatly inside a bright red notebook fresh out of the cellophane wrapping) for his review. And inevitable red-pen slashes.

But Mr. Goodwin would be proud. I felt sure of it.

The tic I'd developed of constantly checking over my shoulder dropped after the second hour, and by the time the full moon was hanging in the ink-black sky, fears of Lavender destroying my life had temporarily subsided.

Never had our paths crossed throughout the day—though that was intentional on my part. I kept close tabs on where she was during rehearsals and snuck away only when they were hard at it. Every time I opened the door to her dressing room, there would be Miles sitting in the corner, watching the great big puppy rip Lavender's pink dress to shreds or throw all the paper coffee cups around as if they were rubber chickens. The place smelled ripe, and the rug in the center of the room sported several new yellow spots. But not from Miles. Every time I'd bring Miles back to the room, he'd look up at me with those big gray eyes as though to say, *Must we? Must we come back here again?*

I didn't even dare go into the bathroom.

The cats had been let loose in there, and I learned via a pink Post-it on the door that they had been supplied with a plate of sushi. Frankly, I'd rather not see the damage.

Suffice it to say, the custodial team will be working extra hours tonight. And Lavender will walk in tomorrow morning, saying something mind-numbingly oblivious like, "Oh! Isn't this a nice surprise. A new pink rug."

But I digress.

"Wow, you really got it done, Finn," Cindy says as she steps inside the writers room and I hand her the latest version of the script. Her eyes flash as she flips through it. She's clearly impressed. "Who said they'd write the next episode?"

"I said I'd do it," I say, pulling my laptop bag over my shoulder.

She looks up from the script.

Purses her lips and tilts her head. "You know you're a producer now. You can leave the first drafts to the staff."

I nod, noting with appreciation that she has chosen to acknowledge my position, even to gently remind me that the uppers don't have to do the grunt work. I know this. On *Higher Stakes*, all of us below producer level divvied up the writing of the episodes, then watched our efforts ripped to shreds by everyone, who then worked the rest of the week putting it all back together, but better. Taking the decent ideas and elevating them to greatness. Taking the mildly humorous one-liner and making it hilarious. It is both grueling and adrenaline-pumping to watch your work be torn apart and analyzed to pieces, then remade into something so much better. Exhausting but exhilarating.

And yes, now as a supervising producer, I would oversee the writing, the shredding, the polishing, and the casting. But.

"I know. But I supported the directional shift for Lavender's and Kye's characters. And I have an idea in mind for the next episode."

Cindy shakes her head, but I can see a little smile playing on her lips. "So you're going to spend your night writing, eh?"

"What else is there to do?"

She chuckles because in LA, unlike back home, there is *anything* to do at any hour. I once passed a heated Lego-building competition on the sidewalk at 4:00 a.m. "You'll fit right in," she says, then stuffs the script in her bag. "I'll call Goodwin and tell him we will have the script ahead of schedule—"

A knock sounds lightly on the door.

Our heads turn.

It's the girl from a few days ago—the PA with all the dogs. Maggie, isn't it?

Well, there are no dogs in Maggie's hands this time. Instead, she's holding a purple sequined clutch quite tightly. The sequins flash from dark purple to light blue as her fingernails roll over them, flipping them over and back.

Like a tic.

Like a nervous tic.

But what is there to be nervous about?

Her eyes land furtively on mine, then drop down.

What?

And then it clicks. I don't know what she said. I don't know what she did.

But I know without a shadow of a doubt this girl is standing here because of Lavender. And it has *something* to do with me.

Inwardly, I hang my head.

I'm on the cusp of stepping forward to address her—how? I don't know, but with something vague that'll draw us out of the room to the privacy of the hall—when Cindy jumps in. "Can I help you with something, Maggie?"

There's a touch of something extra soft in Cindy's voice. Familial. Gentle. Like she's known Maggie a long time, watched her grow up. The way I talk to my nephews when I call home.

"Oh, no thanks, Ms. Cindy." Then she blushes, *blushes*, as she blinks her long lashes my way.

No, there's something else to this. Something seems off.

Didn't I just run into her a couple of hours ago in the hallway? I was in a rush to check on Miles, and without slowing we exchanged niceties. I dropped something trite like, *"No dogs today, eh?"* And she responded with a breathy little chuckle and, *"If I did, would you rescue me again?"* And then she laughed and I laughed and she swept back her hair and—

She's curled her hair.

It was ironing-board straight earlier today.

My eyes freeze.

And is that the exact pink dress I saw Bernie chewing on earlier today in Lavender's room?

It is.

Goodwin's beloved far-too-young-for-me niece has been in Lavender's room, getting a makeover by the unhinged woman herself.

My throat feels dry.

I am not a weak man. If I meet a woman and we hit it off, and it seems like the opportunity is right, I will say the word. Ask the question. But everyone in the entire building is aware that Maggie is the fresh-off-the-turnip-truck favored niece of Goodwin, who has laid down the law: none of his staff are to so much as give her a second look. Not even a first. Our eyes are to pretty much skirt the ground in Maggie's presence.

Her eyes drag to mine.

"Hi, Maggie," I say.

I need to do something.

We're drawing the attention of people now.

Hands are slowing as they pack up their work.

Everybody is curious.

You know what? Running away seems like the best choice here. I just need to leave.

"Well, I'll see you all tomorrow," I say as chipperly as I can and, picking up my laptop bag, nod to everyone in the room.

Please do not follow me.

Please do not follow me.

I'm nearly down the hall, the corner is just in sight, when I hear her heels. "Finn," she calls.

For a long moment I think about pretending I can't hear her.

But then she's calling louder, and I stop.

Hang my head.

Turn.

Several heads behind her pop back inside the doorway, from where they've clearly been watching.

Terrific.

Maggie wrings that purple purse of hers as she walks towards me, chewing on her bottom lip. As she steps up to me she says, "I'm . . . I'm heading out too."

I pause.

Force a grin. "Oh, well, good," I say loudly, formally, like we're two perfect strangers. "We can walk *to our separate cars* together."

With a rather wide step toward the wall to increase the space between us, I continue walking. She follows alongside.

Together we pass several people in silence. We've taken on a corporate look, because as we pass we both nod and smile, nod and smile. Nothing to see here.

I don't say a word, because I cannot for the life of me think of a way to ask such a sensitive question as, "What did Lavender tell you? Whatever it was, whatever she's said, please, just do the absolute opposite."

And then of course there is the wonderful, bright, shiny possibility that this is all in my head. That *of course* Lavender wouldn't do anything as insane as tell this forbidden-fruit-niece-of-Goodwin something on my behalf. That *of course* it is ludicrous to imagine this lovely young lady—who is a full decade younger than me—rolling up her hair into bouncing curls just because she wanted to picture herself with a man who drives a sensible car and spends far too long researching arthritis pills for his dog.

My breaths are just slowing down, each silent step confirming that I am, indeed, imagining things, when we turn a corner and suddenly she's throwing me against the wall.

And kissing me.

And all the while an explosion of thoughts are coming at me, things like, *How is she so strong? Her hands belong to a mechanic!* followed up with, *Well, this isn't the worst thing to have happened to me today . . .*

Kind of like getting a kiss from a nice young lady on the deck of a boat while an iceberg is looming ahead. Sure, hurrah for kissing. But the iceberg . . .

At that moment, the boat crashes.

"Margaret?!"

Goodwin's voice booms down the hall. It's not quite at the I'm-going-to-kill-you level. More like the I-worried-this-would-happen-and-here-you've-gone-and-done-it level. I suspect he's reserving the I'm-going-to-kill-you level for me.

"MASTERS?!?!"

Ah. Yep. There it is.

When I say she jumped back, I mean she flung herself against the opposite wall. I expect she gave herself a concussion.

"WHAT ARE YOU DOING?" he roars.

His formidable eyes slowly swivel from Maggie to me.

This is a top-level-villain look. A serial killer's stare.

"That's a good question," I reply incredibly calmly, because if there's one thing I learned in my eight years on *Higher Stakes*, it was to always remain calm in conversation with serial killers. "To be honest"—I pivot slightly toward Maggie, waiting to see if she wants to jump in—"I was just hoping to find out myself."

I've been sacked.

Or at least, I'm fairly certain I've been sacked, but I'm trying to crawl my way back.

I rub my sandpaper eyes beneath the lamplight of my home desk. Stacks of papers to one side. To the other: a half-completed Rubik's Cube and a glowing computer screen, which informs me that it's now 3:32 a.m. My badge, nowhere in sight. If it remains where I last saw it, that would be skittered across the hallway floor where Goodwin chucked it four days ago.

I press on anyway.

Half the new script is written.

And let me just say, it's challenging to write jokes for a sitcom when you aren't entirely sure you are still employed there. And when you very well may be expelled from Hollywood as a result of what happened four days ago. *Four days.* Has my entire world shattered because of what happened on Wednesday?

It's challenging to imagine that a decade of hard work has led me to such a moment.

Miles's head rests on my foot, and he lifts it to nudge my leg with his nose, as he does whenever I pause in my typing.

"I'm going," I say and begin typing again.

I cling to one certainty: I will work to the bone to earn back my job. I will make this the most polished, perfect draft anyone has ever dropped eyes upon. I will make every attempt to earn my way back into Goodwin's good graces. And then, if by a miracle I should find myself restored, I vow to do one thing and one thing alone, without hesitation.

No more passivity.

No more kindness.

No more avoidance.

No more holding my breath while watching that woman systematically destroy everything I have ever held dear.

No more holding back.

Lavender Rhodes, mark my words.

I will plot a payback.

Chapter 12

Finn

Someone is banging on my door.

It's Wednesday, 2:30 a.m., 153 hours after the Maggie Incident.

Waking up to knocking is a disorienting thing at this hour. My face is plastered to several sheets of paper, and the world is still dark and damp outside the window over my desk.

The moment I come to, I jerk my head up so quickly that Miles perks up. His ears pull back as his wide gray eyes look alertly first at me, then at our surroundings.

I glance at the door, then at Miles.

The flat is still. A silhouette of the lamp stretches across my gray couch. A streetlamp casts a vertical shadow through the blinds over the sliding glass door to the balcony. Papers are littered around me. Leftovers of a midnight snack sit on the counter. You know, this really looks like the scenes we stage when someone gets murdered at home.

But never in all my time at *Higher Stakes* did we introduce a burglar into a scene who knocked first.

Knocking is a move for angry lovers.

Of which I have none.

Knocking is a move for irate employers.

Of which I also have none, as I am so painfully aware.

So the only logical answer is . . . Mrs. Teaberry.

I push myself to standing, reaching for my phone as I do.

The screen is covered with alerts. Missed calls and messages, all from Paula.

Oh. Or Paula.

Paula.

News.

Her voice comes in a raspy hiss pressed to the door. "Finn, get *up*."

I stride to the door. Unlock the double bolts. Open it.

"Well, you actually did it," she says. "Get dressed."

"What?" I say, as she blows past me into the living room and turns. She's already tapping her feet as if annoyed at how slow I'm going. *Slow.* When I wasn't even awake three minutes ago, and now here she is in my living room. At 2:30 a.m.

"You did it," she repeats, throwing her arm out and then waving toward my bedroom as if to say, *Now get going.* "You had me send all those scripts you kept writing, and sure enough, he wants you back."

"Goodwin wants me back?" I take a deep breath. "He liked them?"

"Yes, congratulations, Finn. You've officially become his favorite person. You're the AI we've all feared was going to obliterate our jobs, except you're real."

I begin shaking my head. All the while, my heart is pumping. One hundred forty-three hours writing scripts nonstop, going at the speed of light while also making them as perfect as possible. Throwing together rough drafts, then polishing them so hard the silver began to wear off. The most chaotic six days of my life.

Lance doesn't merely go looking for wedding venues with Ashley—he's blackmailed by an old girlfriend to book their wedding at her failing, terrifying, old-mansion venue, where he and Ashley get locked in the cellar and have to work together to break free as they simultaneously face their fear of being together forever. Maya doesn't merely throw Ashley a bachelorette party—she also receives the wrong ancestry report and falls into an existential crisis while connecting with a long-lost twin who has shown up only for the cheese spread. Lance doesn't merely find the perfect birthday present for Ashley (the promise to show her the world)—he mistakenly takes them to Paris, Wisconsin, after six layovers, four hotels, and a ride in the back of a pickup truck, where he declares on a bouncing hay bale that this life is perfect, so long as they spend it together.

So many empty coffee mugs clutter my desk. So many neglected tasks await my attention. I gave up changing clothes three days ago. I've been in the same maroon sweatpants since the Sunday morning coffee spill. Not even the Monday afternoon spaghetti stain, which I rubbed off with the palm of my hand, was enough to give me pause. Groceries ran out Monday evening, whereupon I turned to canned black beans. Somewhere around midnight I ate a bag of steamed corn. With a butter knife. From the bag.

And it was not for naught.

"Believe me," I begin, reaching for the stack of papers at my desk. I start tidying them, gathering them. "Your jobs are safe. I could never write like that again. I tell you, Paula, I was just about on the ledge. I don't think I could've lasted much longer like this . . ."

And I mean it.

The last six days have been pure insanity.

But there was no chance on earth I was going to be able to get another job in the industry after this fallout. So I took a hard look at the odds and said to myself, "Lavender has already ruined my life. Worst-case scenario has already happened. So why not try?"

So after my ID tag was snapped and I was ordered to stand down, I did the crazy thing nobody expected: I sat at my desk and kept writing. Script after script after script. Paula tried not to take them at first, but I leaned in on the fact that she had gotten her current position from me.

And so, Friday morning—and every morning after that—when I showed up at her house with a printed script in a bright red binder with the cellophane freshly pulled off, she took it, and I could only pray she followed through.

I knew it wasn't easy for her to say, "Here, Mr. Goodwin. Finn has written an episode, if you wanted to see . . . another one," but she is a good friend—and, as evidenced by this moment, loyal.

It was a long shot, hoping I could produce anything in such a short time that could compare. Me against a seasoned team of fifteen putting their heads together every day.

Me against them.

Their collective wit against mine.

No news came for five days.

Nothing to give me hope.

Except for the fact he had not put a restraining order on my efforts.

But I told myself if there was no news by this evening, I would call it. Begin a hunt for a new position under staggering odds. Beg for my old job at *Higher Stakes* with all dignity lost. I had been mentally preparing myself for the past few hours.

And now . . .

"Finn." I realize all of a sudden that Paula has taken hold of my hand. Apparently I've been putting a stack of blank paper in my laptop bag, and she stops me. "Okay." She takes a breath. Frowns at me as if realizing I'm more delirious and sleep-deprived than she'd hoped. "I'm going to get you something decent to wear. You stand by the door—just stand there. Don't do or touch anything. Then we'll go."

I frown. "Okay." But I do have enough pulled together to ask, "Why are we going to work at two thirty?"

At this, she takes a deep breath and shakes her head as she heads down the hall. "You'll see," she calls over her shoulder. "Let's just say you'd better want this job as much as you've acted this week. Because they weren't kidding when they said you gotta be all in."

It's both worse and better than I imagined.

Under normal conditions I would've clued into this truth sooner, as we walked down the hall dotted on both sides by dark and empty rooms. I would've realized it as the noise of shouting grew, choice words echoing down the corridor.

But I was too fixated on fixing everything on my body at that moment, from straightening the button-down shirt, to rubbing the fingerprints off my glasses, to pushing down the curl at the top of my head that had gone into overdrive from lack of showers.

Paula filled me in on the drive, but it's not until I am standing at the open doorway, looking in, that I see the extent of the situation.

The long rectangular table and the floor around it are littered with papers as if a printer has exploded. Coffee mugs and greasy bags of takeout are everywhere. Chairs are tipped over. Nearly everyone is standing, but on opposite sides of the table, as if at war. One of the execs, Ken, is slapping a paper on the table as he's yelling. He sees me step into the doorway. He halts.

"You've *got* to be kidding me." And then he props his foot on a chair. "So you've chosen *him* then, and any crackpot idea he schemes up. Over *all of us*. I'm out."

As he blows past me, coat in hand, he gives a curt nod and says, "Good luck, everyone! I'm getting off this ride!"

I'm still frowning as my eyes follow after him, when I notice a second person, a woman, steal past and trail him down the hall.

A minute goes by in utter silence.

"That it?" I hear Mr. Goodwin's voice and turn my attention back to the room. He's sitting at the head of the table, and his eyes drift from person to person. "Anybody else want out?"

He waits for several seconds.

Nobody dares move.

"Then sit," he commands.

Everyone rushes to their seat. Paula bangs the doorknob as she scurries to sit down.

I make my way toward the empty seat where I sat before.

"Not there," Goodwin says as I touch the back of the chair. "Here, Masters."

He slaps the seat next to him. The unoccupied seat that had belonged to Ken ten seconds ago.

I hesitate.

Then force my legs to move.

Pull the chair out.

Sit.

There's a moment's pause. I open my mouth. "Sir. I just want to say again—"

"No more words. I've read enough of your words the past five days," Goodwin says. "It's my turn, so listen up." He leans forward, his face uncomfortably close to mine now, while the room watches. He raises a finger. "Number one, don't so much as *look* at Maggie again."

I would interject here if I were talking to any rational person, reminding him again that the whole situation was a misunderstanding.

But I am not talking to any rational person.

So I just nod.

"Number two," he continues, giving my back a slap so hearty

it would pop the mint out of a choking man, "congratulations. You're now executive producer. And if anyone so much as looks at you with anything except complete respect, you fire them on the spot. You hear me?"

Me.

Fire others.

I swallow. What I want to do is turn to the rest of the table and whisper, "Of course. Of course I wouldn't do such a thing." But I think it's best at the moment to maintain eye contact.

"Number three," he says, and the chair squeaks as he finally leans back, "is that I want you and everyone else in this room to know you're the best writer here. And from here on out, you own the floor. So take it away."

Chapter 13

Lavender

Monday, Film Day, Stage 2

"I'm sorry."

I put up my hand in a Stop position, halting Kye—currently playing Lance—before he can give me the big white box with the Pete's Doughnuts logo scrawled across the top in red ink.

It's shooting day and the place is crowded. More crowded than it's ever felt before.

Half of the audience's mouths are open, gaping, having just given a thunderous collective *aahhh* as they swooned over our romantic moment. The set has been changed overnight for this scene. Gone is the airport terminal that was set up for the send-off episode we were supposed to have. (Back before the whole plotline of Lance leaving for astronaut training was canned.) Here, in its stead, is the set for a restaurant scene, a quaint little Italian place Lance Lewis is supposedly taking Ashley Krane for Valentine's Day.

And here is Ashley's present.

The Pete's Doughnuts box contains something very unsettling.

The set smells like roses, which isn't surprising given the

designers actually brought in live bouquets to adorn the eight or so tables around Kye and me. Extras are sitting at these tables, having spent the past two hours mouthing words with effusive hands in pretend conversation.

Kye/Lance sits opposite me, looking entirely out of place with his sweeping blond hair tidy and massive shoulders squeezed into a navy-blue suit that looks like it's about to pop.

And here he is. Holding out that horrible box. To me.

I'm certain my temples have started to glisten. I can see Chloe in the corner anxiously stirring her makeup brush in powder, desperate to jump in and do a quick fix.

"Hang on."

The second I speak and pause the shot, she rushes in.

"I'm just . . . ," I say, talking over her and the brush tapping madly around my face, "struggling to see why we need a box of real chickens. This just seems so . . . illogical. I mean, Ashley lives in a shoebox flat in Seattle."

I'm trying to keep it together, but Kye is sitting much too close for comfort, and the box in his hands is chirping. "I just . . . ," I continue, working my words around Chloe and her makeup brush. I'm wringing the white tablecloth now. "I don't see why he should be giving her *poultry* for Valentine's Day."

The room is hot.

The lights are brighter than usual.

I feel almost claustrophobic with the waistband of this dress cutting into my stomach and a powder brush suffocating me.

Hundreds of eyes are on me. Nothing new, but suddenly it's overwhelming.

And all the while, my ears are pounding with incessant, bubbly little chirps that eclipse every other sound.

"Oh, they aren't just *poultry*," comes a singsong voice behind me.

And there Finn is. A warm, friendly smile fills his face as though to comfort me, but really, in this moment, between the pounding of my ears and these lights and the painful press of my heart against my chest, his smile looks almost gleeful. Almost as though he is enjoying my suffering.

His words, however, are clearly an attempt to comfort. "They're chicks, Lavender. Just a couple of sweet baby chicks."

"Twelve, actually," Kye says. "I counted them this morning."

"*Twelve?*" I gasp. And as if we aren't going to believe him, Kye digs into the big box and picks them up one at a time, counting as he goes. I throw up my hands. "I believe you," I say.

"The viewers will love it," Finn says. "We've got a whole slew of scenes already in place with them. Really fun stuff."

I would close the lid, except that would mean I'd have to go near them.

Which could lead to a pointy beak popping out from nowhere. And pecking me.

Which is not a big deal at all.

Except for *pecking me*.

I swallow. "Right. But my script said they were going to be"—I force myself not to sound too intense, and yet even I hear the tremble in my voice—"plastic. We practiced last week . . . with plastic."

Finn is grinning. Pointing at me. "And *this* is why we reserved telling you until the last moment. *This* authentic look of surprise is perfect for the scene. It's so *perfect.*"

My throat feels a bit like it's stuffed with cotton. "Right. But. I was prepared for *plastic.*"

There's a long pause. Finn looks at me for some time, then scratches the back of his head. "Oh. Well, I'm sorry if this ruffles your feathers." He gives a self-congratulatory, breathy chuckle at his pun. But when he sees I'm not moving, he shakes his head a little. Adds, "No, but seriously, Lavender. My apologies if this is throwing you. It *is* challenging when your plans for how something should go are tossed about by someone else."

He's saying all of this like he's very apologetic and wishes to be empathetic, but there's something off with his face. He's smiling. The whole time. Like he's watching a very entertaining circus act.

Finn claps his hands. "Alright, well." He swivels back toward the director's chair, where he's been guest directing all day. (Officially: Mark is sick. Unofficially, I hear Mark received anonymous coordinates to a very secret, highly romanticized, incredibly rare geocaching destination, and so off went the middle-aged, balding man on his *Goonies* adventure.)

Finn addresses the group. "Let's just keep cracking on, shall we? At this rate, I think we'll be done by lunch."

Chloe's makeup case snaps shut like a gunshot, and she gives my elbow a little squeeze. "Doing great, Lavie," she whispers, then scurries back to the shadows.

I, however, am not doing great.

I clench and unclench my fists, though, and try to focus. To get into character.

I am Ashley Krane. On a Valentine's date with Lance Lewis.

And I can do this. I can. I take a huge breath, my rib cage expanding until it presses against the satin bodice of this black dress that feels three sizes too small. *Who picked these outfits? Kye and I are both suffocating here!*

I can pick up a chick.

Sure.

It's *just* a chick.

I am a professional.

"Scene 3, take 2. And"—I hear a long pause offstage—"action."

Kye's demeanor immediately shifts. The difference is almost indistinguishable to the eye, yet it's there. His temples smooth. His eyes hold mine. Without moving a muscle, his expression is all emotion, all romantic tension. He carries on with his line. "You said for so long I'd never commit. Consider this our start."

I pause.

Give an intake of surprised breath.

"Lance, you *didn't*!"

"Cut!" calls Finn. He hops out of the director's chair. And surprisingly, he looks positively ecstatic as he stands, hands on hips. "Lavender, you gotta run your line."

"I did do my line."

"No. You've gotta *take* the box."

I look down and realize my hands are stiffly at my sides. Like a sitting mannequin. Or that extra they dismissed this morning for staring at the cameras with a frozen smile while gripping a steak knife and fork over his plate of fake steak.

Gingerly, as if they might crack, I bend my elbows. Slowly. "Right," I say. *Shake it off.* "Okay."

"Let's do it again. Take three."

Kye jumps into position. "You said for so long I'd never commit." He holds out the box. "Consider this our start."

Against every primal instinct, I force myself to take the box. A series of chirps rings out like little snapping scissors. I hesitate, then with two very cautious fingers touch the top of the box.

Lift.

I'm supposed to be sucking in my breath, but what also comes out is a squeal as one fat brown bird climbs atop the others, chirping madly as it callously sacrifices the lives of the others in its desire to get to me. To bite me. With its tiny disease-ridden mouth attached to its soulless, beady eyes.

"*Ohhh, Lance, you didn't!*" I cry shrilly.

"You always say you miss home in this great big city." He takes the box as the camera hovers over one shoulder, closing in.

"So I wanted to bring a little bit of home to you. Welcome to the first step toward our rooftop garden. I was thinking we could care for them. Together."

"Cut," Finn calls. He pulls off his glasses and rakes a hand through his short brown curls. He hops up the four stairs to the stage as if his legs are made of springs, taking them two at a time.

"You know, it's missing something. Here. Hold this." And all of a sudden Finn sets the box in my hands. He swivels around and motions for the comedian to come onstage. I'm frozen. A box of tiny winged terrors chirps in my hands.

Finn swings back around.

"It's just—I'm having a hard time seeing your enthusiasm, Lavender. Oh. Watch out."

He points down.

To my horror, one of the little birds has pushed its head out of the box and is standing on the precipice, about to jump.

Finn takes the bird in his hands, cradling it, and shows the tiny yellow puffball to the audience. Despite the fact there is a comedian, despite the fact we are not taping, despite the fact nobody should even be looking in our direction, a round of fawning *aahhh*s resounds.

Everybody loves baby chicks. I am, without question, the odd one out.

"It's just . . ." I scramble to put the box back on the little table, then give it a discreet push to edge it to Kye's side. "I'm having a hard time believing poultry is the answer here."

"Oh, of course it is," Finn says carelessly. "It's the perfect addition. Stats show the audiences love to see pets on-screen. Chicks rank number three. Dogs. Cats. Chicks. It's a nice segue into the next phase of your relationship, while at the same time providing a number of comic challenges." Finn waves at Kye. "Big city boy who has enjoyed being the know-it-all prior to meeting"—he waves at me—"small-town transplant who is now going to show off her low-country skills. The road will be riddled with bumps and laughs. Runaway chickens that make it into residents' flats. Lance and Ashley missing a Halloween party, ironically dressed as scarecrows, to do late-night scarecrowing over a threat of hawks. And of course, the inevitable references to the chicks as your children, and the inevitable arguments when Lance forgets his daddy duties. Pool time with the chicks—that'll be a cute one, Lavender. Viewers will love when you take a dip in a plastic tub with all the chicks surrounding you—"

"*What?*"

"Really, this is going to take on a life of its own," Finn continues flippantly. "Goodwin loves it. Props has already been remodeling the existing rooftop set, getting ready for the chicken coop."

I scramble. "But here's a thought." Then pause, hoping something, anything, comes to mind. "Have you . . . have you thought about . . . zucchini? What if his token of commitment was a nice zucchini?"

Finn throws his head back and laughs.

Laughs as though I've just made a hilarious joke. "Zucchini? Do you think Ashley Krane could possibly bond with a zucchini? Oh, Lavender," he says, and there's a twinkle in his eye as he says it, "can you imagine *anything* more out of character?"

For a moment, I'd say he was throwing the words I said upon our first meeting at me.

But then he winks, takes a chick from the box, turns towards the audience, and sets the chick on the ground. Immediately, the big yellow puffball begins tottling and chirping, and the audience laughs and swoons right on cue.

He turns back to me with a shrug that says, *See?*

"Right." I inhale. This is fine. This is all fine. But the bodice on this too-small dress is rubbing at my rib cage and the room is beginning to spin. I push myself to standing. "But first, I have to run to the loo. I'll—I'll be right back."

And before I know it, I'm passing by flashes of silverware and pulling open several doors. I must have forgotten to breathe until I got inside my dressing room, because my chest expands so much that a seam in the back of my top gives a distinct *pop*. I reach back to unzip it, just enough for breathing room, and sink to the floor.

Sometime later I hear the padding of paws across the rug and feel the tickle of Bernie's tricolored hair against my face. His big face presses against mine, and then his tongue is licking my cheek, my neck, my hair. My hand finds his face and begins rubbing his ear.

It is helpful, actually, and I keep rubbing.

"Lavender?"

I look up and realize Finn is standing at the open door, one hand on the handle.

He takes one look at me and shuts it quickly behind him.

"Oh, hey," I say. My voice is soft, light as a feather, as if I just ran into him at a bookshop and am surprised to see him there.

He's screwing up his face, however.

His hands are on his hips.

Actually, he's not looking at me at all. He's looking at the ceiling. Muttering to himself.

"What are you doing?" he says at last. His voice is accusing.

"Just went to the loo and decided to pet Bernie here for a sec," I say. I take a breath. Laugh a little. "Got distracted for a minute."

"It's been thirty."

Finn rakes a hand through his hair and paces to the wall and back.

He looks furious.

I suck in a breath. *Thirty?*

Ten minutes possibly. Twelve at most. How could it possibly have been thirty?

"Oh." I begin to push myself up. "I'm so sorry. I didn't realize—"

"Don't get up." He throws a hand from his temple to me. "Lavender, you're shaking. I just need to figure this out."

Bernie has put his head in my lap, and the weight of his head is somewhat comforting. The rhythmic movement of my palms against his fur seems to force my heart to beat in sync with the slow strokes. I settle back down, my back against the wall, a bundle of satin blooming out around me. The dress is covered in fine white hairs Bernie has shed, and I find that the least I can do is begin to pluck them off with my free hand. One.

Then another.

Then another.

"You said in an *Elle* interview that you don't *like* chickens. Not that you have a legitimate phobia."

Again, he's speaking in an accusing manner, but the way he takes breaths and cuts corners in his pacing, I'm not sure if he's accusing me or himself.

"This shouldn't have been *traumatizing*, Lavender. A mild annoyance at best." He throws out a hand. "Something you could work with," he adds, almost as an afterthought. "For the good of the show."

So he has done his research.

Knows a bit of my past.

At least, one interview.

"Well . . . I am afraid of chickens," I say with a shrug.

"No." He waggles a finger. "No, that's the thing. You're not scared of chickens. What you are is *petrified* of chickens," he replies. Then, as if thinking through all of this and coming to a horrible conclusion, he exhales heavily. "We have to rewrite. Rewrite it all."

Suddenly he is pulling out his phone, tapping madly, pulling it to his ear, muttering to himself, "If I don't get fired for *this too*."

"Now, stop," I say, and with some effort I grab the bottom of my dress and pull myself to standing, using the wall for support. I feel the flap on my back and pull up the zipper. "It's fine. See? I can just get used to them. They're just—just tiny little—things."

"You are supposed to swim with them in a kiddie pool next week."

The image makes me feel nauseous, and I lean back against the wall. "Right. Well."

"Hey, Paula," he says, his attention on the phone. Then taking one look at me, he opens the door and moves out into the hall. His voice is low, but the door is cracked, his hand on the knob. He's speaking low, but I can hear. "Tell everyone to wrap up—we're done for the day. No, not the writers. The audience and cast. We're going to have to do some rewrites. And lay it straight: we're going to go late. Go ahead and plan to bring in some dinner. No, make it worth it. Go for sushi."

He pauses.

One arm is crossed over his chest. His stance is stiff as someone passes by. He gives a curt nod, clearly waiting for them to pass.

"Right, well, let's just not tell Goodwin about this while he's out of town, okay? With any luck we can resolve the whole situation while he's gone. He's the type of man you share these details with after, when it's all fixed up—"

He's overreacting.

Not to mention, taking a whole lot of responsibility for something that is my problem, not his.

Still, the pressure hangs heavy. Never in my career have I been the difficult one. Some people call it people-pleasing. I call it what it is: never letting anyone down if I can help it.

It's logical. A strength, not a weakness.

So yes, I did have a little reaction to the surprise of the . . . the . . . animals, but I will absolutely not let my castmates down, much less the audience who waited so long to get in, much less make the writers throw away words they labored over and stay late on my account. I will just have to snap out of it. That's all there is to it.

I draw myself up and prepare to open the door. But just as I do, I catch a glimpse of myself in the mirror and stop, startled.

Who is that?

I look like the ghost of myself. My face is pale. My dress is covered in dog hairs, the corset top twisted. What was a charming ensemble at first, with the heart-shaped fitted black top melting into a flared skirt, is now a disaster: the dress looks like an exploded chocolate cupcake, the tulle-satin combination puffing out everywhere except where it should. The wall was unkind to me. It has gathered my curls into hairballs.

I lock eyes with myself and step towards the lighted vanity mirror. Have I been crying?

No.

I couldn't have.

I of all people would know it.

But there are two dry streaks running down my cheeks, where tears have cut through all eight carefully applied layers of makeup.

I hear the door open and see Finn step inside as I'm rubbing madly at my cheeks to smooth out the makeup.

Swiftly, I turn. My hands grip the vanity behind me to stay steady. I say with an overbright smile, "Alright. I think we're ready to get back in there."

"You're not going anywhere," he says. He's holding a can of sparkling water in his hand. And with the most resigned voice possible, he motions to the couch. "Here."

I push the water away and move past him to the door. "I'm really *fine*. I just needed a minute."

"Don't." He's shaking his head. "Don't make me have to beg you to sit down. It's already done, Lavender. They've made the announcement. People are leaving."

I can't help it.

A part of me flinches as adrenaline pumps through my veins at the thought of letting down so many people, of being the cause of so much commotion. But another part of me, a more desperate part, can't help but feel massively relieved.

There will be no more of them.

No rooftop scenes.

No pool of chickens.

I take the can of water and sit down on the edge of the couch.

I take a sip.

There's a long moment of silence, aside from Bernie in the corner, who has taken up chewing on the heel of a discarded pink shoe.

"Well. I've got a lot ahead. So." Finn, who looks strung out, stands there as though about to leave, but surprisingly, he doesn't. He keeps standing there, rooted to the ground. Then, looking as though he's conceding something, he throws his hand out toward me. "So what exactly *is* wrong with chickens?"

"Nothing—"

"We both know that's not true. And frankly, if I have to lose my job—again, which I'm just *sure* is going to happen, *again*—I'd at least like to know why. What *exactly* is it that petrifies you? Do you"—he furrows his brow—"eat chicken?"

"Yes. And you won't get let go for this. I'll make sure of it."

"Oh"—he gives a humorless chuckle—"I'm sure you will. Are they too fluffy? Too yellow?"

"No, I just . . . I had a bad experience as a kid," I say, my fingers fidgeting, pushing on the hem of my dress. "My great-aunt and -uncle lived in the country, and when I was a little girl I visited for the summer, and there was this rooster, and it was always chasing me, and one morning it got my great-aunt as she was gathering eggs."

"Right." He's looking at me blankly. "So . . ."

"And it hit a varicose vein on her calf, and I knew I had to run to get help while she was hemorrhaging, but the bloody thing kept attacking her, so I had to pick it up, and it brutally pecked at me the mile to the neighbor's house. Was the scariest moment of my life." I shrug. Glance briefly to the tiny pinprick scars that run up and down my arm. "So. Suffice it to say . . . I don't like birds."

There's a long silence while I'm staring at the carpet.

I don't like to tell people the story.

I don't like to think, let alone speak, of the memory. It feels like I'm contaminating this room, this spot on the couch, and piling rubbish over the good memories. I don't want to sit on this couch and be reminded. I want to think of the good things, the memories taped up on the walls.

I feel him sit beside me on the couch.

His face looks hard, his brow knitted.

His lips are pressed together so tightly they disappear.

He rubs a hand down his face.

His unreadable face.

I can't tell in this moment what his thoughts are. They could be anything from desperately wanting to get out of this situation to judging me for letting one of the hazards of existence cause lifelong fear.

Office supplies could kill you too, maybe, but I don't go around avoiding staplers.

A steaming mug of coffee could kill you, but that won't stop me from owning a bar cart full of it.

Anything and everything in the world has the potential to bring harm.

And, obviously, a few baby chicks can't do anything.

Surely . . . probably. And I know that.

It's all just so *silly*.

My face grows hot as my thoughts spiral.

Already I feel I shouldn't have said anything.

And then I feel the weight of his hand on mine, stilling my fidgeting. His voice is low, serious. "Lavender, I'm really, incredibly sorry."

"Nothing to apologize for."

"No, actually," he says, shaking his head, "pretty much everything here I have to apologize for. I had seen that interview and underestimated your reaction."

"It's fine," I say, shrugging. "I tend to play it down. It's silly, really—"

"It's perfectly legitimate."

I screw my face up into a smile. "Yes, well, easy to say when you are"—I wave my hand around vaguely at him—"who you are."

His brows angle down behind his glasses. "And who do you think I am?"

"You know." I shrug. "The serious producer who has it all together. Even your dog looks like he's better at playing an adult than me. But look at you. I bet you go to bed at some decent hour like ten—"

"Nine." Finn pauses, then adds, "Excluding work events. Particularly of late."

I grin. Shake my head.

Finn studies me for a moment before his lips purse.

He lets go of my hand and pulls off his glasses.

Rubs one hand down the side of his face, then puts the glasses back on with a determined expression.

"Do you know what's silly? I'm a thirty-year-old man, and I can't bear to be the only one in a pool." A smile creeps up my face as he adds, "I play it off, of course, but always in the back of my mind is one of those Goosebumps books I read when I was eight, about an invisible man in the pool, and now, without fail, I'll find a reason to hop out before I'm the last one in."

One corner of his mouth lifts. "Oh look, there's a hot-dog stand. Oh, I'd better go add more sunscreen."

I laugh a little. "You do not."

He puts a hand on his heart. "I once raced my eight-year-old niece for the ladder and elbowed her out of the way. I played it off like it was a game—ha-ha, the good uncle playing with the kiddos—but I was dead serious."

I give a hearty laugh then, and for a moment I can just see Finn Masters duking it out with some innocent girl barely treading water, while the parents' barbecue sizzles.

I feel his hand pat my shoulder as he stands.

"I'll take care of it. And you ought to get out of here before Bernie eats all your shoes."

"I really will make sure to take the fall for this," I say, following Finn as he goes to the door. "I can call Goodwin now, in fact, and—"

He pauses me with a lift of his finger.

"About that. Could you do me a favor?" Finn says, hand on the door.

"Sure. Anything."

"Don't talk to Goodwin. No matter what. Just please. Let's leave this between you and me."

I close my mouth.

"Sure," I say slowly, feeling the hairs on the back of my neck rise as I look into his eyes. "Between you and me it is."

Chapter 14

Finn

And then she says to me, 'I'm sorry. I don't date people who don't care about their *bodies*.'"

My friend (and former colleague on *Higher Stakes*), Chris, is talking. I yawn as Miles races around the edge of the dog park with some golden retriever, then reach for my tea beneath the bench. This is my Saturday. The way my Saturday mornings have gone the past several years, in fact. Only, usually I run Miles from my flat to the dog park. Today it was a slow walk accompanied by the nostalgic, bitter taste of my PG Tips. Because for the fifth day in a row, we've gone to midnight.

It's my own fault, so I'm not complaining.

I had no idea the woman was petrified of poultry. When I first scoured the Internet, I was hunting for something that would parallel to a *degree* the pain she'd caused me. Not full-blown revenge. Just a little payback to help mend my past wounds. Something for a rainy day to think back on fondly. *Has she ruined every possible facet of my life? Yes, but remember her being uncomfortable in a tub of chickens.*

But then she went white as a sheet and conked out for half an hour.

And really, how could I possibly be surprised?

She's so good at ruining my life that of course I should've suspected she could ruin my payback. Take all the fun out of it and leave me to another week of working to the bone, trying to fix the problems this has caused.

Brilliant. Just positively *smashing*.

As I take another gulp, it comes to my awareness that Chris is still here, awaiting my reply. I pop the lid shut. Set the tea back down.

"It was an all-you-can-eat soup and salad bar," Chris retorts. "Someone eating five bowls of tortellini is literally part of their commercials. Not to mention, I'm here after all. At a park on Saturday. Outside. Caring about my health."

I nod, but my eyes flicker to the fried-chicken waffle sandwich in his hand. He picked it off the food truck on our way in. "How very . . . unfair," I say flatly.

He takes a bite and speaks through a mouthful. "I was on a date once with a woman who was *impressed* I could eat that much. We made it a competition."

"Sounds like you should circle back to her then," I say.

"Anyway." He sits back, giving a distracted pat on the back to Tarte, the French Bulldog he inherited from a broken relationship.

"Your dog is named Tarte. She's literally named after food," I reply.

"*Kim* named her," he says, waving his sandwich in the air. "What was I supposed to do? Rename her Butch at three years old?"

I whistle at Miles, and he looks up from sniffing the backside of another dog across the yard. "We both know why you kept the name. If you changed it, where would your perfect pickup line go? How would you ever meet women again?"

And it was true. Chris and I have been coming to this same dog park as far back as I can remember. For quite some time it was the four of us—Chris and Kim, Delilah and me. Then it was just Chris, Delilah, and me. Then just Chris and me.

And although Kim's negligence and spiteful intentions landed Tarte on his doorstep (she never really was an easy one to root for), what she really did was provide Chris with what I believe with all confidence is the most successful pickup line of all time. It's not even a line, actually. Just a word. He can say one single word, and—*bam*—next thing you know he's knee-deep in conversation with whichever female he wants.

Because if there's one thing women in my experience seem to appreciate, it's men who like dogs. Men who take incredibly feminine dogs under their wing in a time of need are especially admired. And men who can show they have taken incredibly feminine dogs under their wing from ex-girlfriends are gold-star caliber.

Responsible, empathetic, confident, caring men.

Chris can get a first date in a heartbeat. (The second, third, or fourth is another matter.)

And all he has to do is say the word. Call her by name. Show the world this dog is his. *Tarte.*

The midmorning sun beats down on the dirt where Miles and a dozen or so dogs race around a large fenced-in area so new that the tags on the fences still whip in the breeze. Light glints off the white Hollywood sign on the hill in the not-so-far distance. A group of tourists pulls in and huddles up outside the fence to take photos with the sign in the background. Parking is brutal, as it always is on Saturdays at the most popular dog park in L.A. But overall, Lake Hollywood Park is manageably underpopulated today, possibly because the late-February wind is bringing us down to a positively Antarctic fifty-two degrees.

Truly.

A woman in front of me is wearing a shining white ski jacket, faux-fur-wrapped hood cinched tightly around her head. A two-year-old is running around in snow bibs.

I roll up my sleeves partway to the elbows.

"So. How's life out of the kiddie ride?" Chris says.

I hesitate.

It's still a bit of a sticky conversation point.

Chris has come to refer to *Neighbors* as a move into the big leagues, while we both know very well he is my former boss—one of several—from *Higher Stakes*. Had I not been hired back on to *Neighbors* two weeks ago, he would've been my only shot at trying to persuade Emmy, the showrunner, to give me back my old job. But then they, too, have a sticky history—she once succumbed to the magnetism of Tarte.

Suffice it to say, I'm just glad I was never put in a position to ask.

"It's good," I say. I hesitate, scratching the back of my neck. "I've been made executive."

He nearly spits out his sandwich. "You're *kidding*," he says.

"Co-exec," I clarify.

It's a toss-up as to how he will take the news. It took him fifteen years to get to executive level at *Higher Stakes*, and we both know staff writers on *Neighbors* get more slaps on the back than anyone at *Higher Stakes*.

But to his credit, he gives a nod of approval.

"That's incredible, man." He throws Tarte a piece of his waffle. "Looks like you made the right move. It's always a gamble, isn't it?"

"A gamble I'm still playing, actually," I reply.

He raises a brow.

"It's fine. I'm just learning pretty quickly why Goodwin keeps a revolving door on the writers room."

He tosses another piece of waffle to Tarte, who takes it and trots off, stubby tail wiggling.

Then in the distance, I hear a woman's voice I recognize.

"*You gotta be kidding me*. Nancy just emailed to ask if I was interested in *Stephouse* for the fall."

"To guest star?"

"No. *Permanently*."

The words float above the grassy field, and without hesitating, I drop to the ground. Miles's ears perk up and he tilts his head, clearly confused as to why I'm suddenly nose to nose.

The answer is simple though.

Trauma.

People do all kinds of bizarre things out of trauma.

Go mute. Avoid escalators.

At this point, I'd jump in the lake on the other side of the park in order to avoid a run-in with Lavender Rhodes outside business hours.

Really, squatting on the ground behind a bench is not even remotely my limit.

And as for how quickly I reacted? Simple.

I have reached the point where I expect Lavender to show up anywhere, at any time. I have taken to locking every door of every room I sit in. I stand against the wall with eyes on the door, all day, at work. I am prepared at every moment, day or night, for Lavender Rhodes to waltz in and flip the platter that is my life upside down.

Only now, of course, I no longer take it sitting down.

Apparently I take it lying down. Behind a bench.

Chris frowns down at me. "Hey, man. You okay?"

Below the bench, I spot Lavender handing a phone to Sonya. "What do you think it means?" Lavender says.

"I don't know, but I'm *ticked*," Sonya replies. "I asked her for an update on next year's contract, and this is what I get back."

"You've just got a new email from Goodwin too." Lavender pauses at the sound of a *ding* and pats her pocket before pulling her phone out. "Me too."

The pair hover over their phones, squinting. Sonya in her trim white jogging suit, with white sneakers and white sunglasses.

Lavender in a blue parka over jeans. Flip-flops. Sonya's frown deepens.

I could outrun her if it came to it.

There's a solid twenty feet between us. Fifty to the gated entry.

But wait. Where is . . . the beast?

The moment the thought bubble forms, I hear the pounding paws.

No, no.

No. No. No.

With his mouth wide open, tripping over his oversized puppy paws, Bernie races toward us. Slams into me as he pulls to a stop. And faces Miles.

Whom he begins licking furiously.

I'm stranded.

Chris says, "What're you doing, Finn?"

What I want to do in this moment is tell him to shut his mouth. What I *need* in this moment is for that puppy to discover a squirrel and run far, far away.

But it appears I have to cut bait.

Abruptly, I stand.

With my back to the women, I gather my things—not so quickly as to attract their attention, just quick enough to get the job done and get out unscathed, but for Bernie pausing every few seconds to excitedly chew on my leg.

Then tumble back on Miles with enthusiasm.

Then turn to jump back on my leg.

I pretend this dog does not exist. "You know what, I'm going to have to run—"

"Really?" he says, flipping over his watch. "It's eight ten. You just got here."

"Yep," I say, holding my back rigid while the puppy takes hold of the hem of my coat and begins a round of tug-of-war. I can see Chris's incredulous face as I snap the leash on Miles and pick up my tea, all while staunchly staring straight at Chris, ignoring the dog. "I was just reminded"—which is true—"how much I have to catch up on for work—"

"Oh look, we're in luck. Hey, Finn!"

I freeze.

Even the sound of Bernie's razor teeth tearing the hem of my coat fades into the background as I see Lavender with her arm raised. A look of delight spreads over her face. Like we're two friends just casually meeting at the top of a ski lift.

Chris does three double takes between Lavender and me before he quietly mutters for my ears alone, "You're kidding me. Less than a month and you're already on friendly terms. With *Lavender Rhodes*."

Lavender's eager expression shifts as she sees her dog yanking on my coat. With a people-pleasing doormat-of-a-pet-owner air, she says, "Oh, Bernie. Get down now. C'mon. *Get down*."

Bernie, of course, ignores her.

Only when she begins to walk towards the dog do I take control. "Down, Bernie," I say firmly. "Sit."

Bernie's big black floppy ears perk up at his name (to his credit, he's not a complete lost cause). He sits on his haunches.

"And you are on friendly terms with Lavender Rhodes's dog," Chris murmurs. There's awe in his voice, and when he turns his attention to me, he sees me through fresh eyes, as if we have been sitting together on a bus and he just now realizes I am Tom Hiddleston.

"Long story," I say, then move to address the two women. Chris moves too. Frankly, for all his time as an exec, working side by side with actors who floss their teeth just like we do, he still looks like he's about to bow.

I suppose I'm not surprised.

Everyone drops what they're doing for Lavender.

Who, by the way, has something green in her teeth.

"You've got something in your teeth," I say, enjoying this small but mighty taste of revenge.

I can see Chris's eyes in my periphery bugging at the audacity.

Sonya's eyes are still screwed to the screen on her phone as she frowns, undoubtedly at the email I ran my eyes over yesterday before Goodwin's PA sent it out just moments ago. A *vision* email.

It's long. Goodwin's words are quite strong about a shift that's needed, a drastic change that's required, for "the good of the longevity of the show." And how we sometimes need to "cut off the moles to save the body." Unpleasant imagery, but effective.

People are throwing fits.

Staff have left—witnessed by myself yesterday when yet another writer walked out. People are tired and overrun and stressed out by both the time demands of the job and the emotional depletion. I can see how it's different from *Higher Stakes*. We had long hours there, but not the emotional and mental grind that working under Goodwin takes. And I can see it now, pulling on Sonya's face as she reads.

"Oh really? Thanks," Lavender says, and to my dismay she says it so cheerfully it's evident I've had the opposite effect, that now she's grateful I am one of those true friends who is willing to be honest. "Where?" she says, pointing at an upper tooth.

"There," I say vaguely.

"Here?" she says and steps closer to me.

"No," I say, stepping backward, already regretting my decision. "Upper right side."

"Where, here?"

And then to my absolute horror, she plants herself directly in front of me, so close that if I but lean in, we could be kissing.

Then she takes my wrist and lifts it, along with the stainless-steel tumbler in my hands, as she tries to look at herself in its reflection.

"I've got it," I say hastily, reaching up and pulling it out of her teeth before she decides to climb inside my coat with me too.

"Thanks," she says. Chris is behind her, a codfish expression on his face. "Oh, and would you look at that," she says brightly, turning her attention toward a tree.

She smiles like a proud parent as she bumps my side, watching Miles and that out-of-control puppy rolling together like they're having the time of their lives. "You were right about this place, Finn. It's *wonderful*."

I haven't told her about this place. All I said during that *awful* day of dog coparenting was that her dog would benefit from some socialization, and then I mentioned dog parks are a place to find such a thing. For the sake of her dog's happiness. Because were it to be left alone with her the rest of its life, it would undoubtedly leap from the top of a third-story building.

There are 181 parks in LA. The odds of running into her here, now, are equal to those of being struck by lightning on a sunny day.

Unless, of course, she is your fate and you're doomed to spend your life with her.

Bernie jumps up from the ground and barks playfully at Miles, and together they race off toward a tunnel.

Lavender sticks out her bottom lip like she's just witnessed the most beautiful thing in her life. Somehow in this moment she has slipped her hand behind my back. And now her hand is actually beginning to do circles on my shoulder blade. "This is so precious. We should do puppy playdates."

I nearly choke on my saliva as I step pointedly out of her grip. "They're dogs, Lavender. This is what dogs *do*. Not to mention Miles is eight," I reply. "My veterinarian—"

"Your old one?" Lavender says.

"—says that's the equivalent of a seventy-year-old man. Far too old for the two of them to be playing."

Miles races past us, Bernie tailing close behind.

"I have a dog," Chris jumps in. He steps between us to put out his hand, shakes hers. "Chris Aggins. Co-exec, *Higher Stakes*."

I know what he's doing.

That obvious-looking bodyguard pretending to be very, very interested in that sign by the gate that says Not Allowed: Dogs in Heat knows what Chris is doing.

Anyone within a ten-mile radius can see what he's doing.

Well, let me *not* stand in the way.

I step back, letting him fully take my place.

I feel like I should warn him, but it's not like he would listen to me anyway.

"Hi." She shakes his hand, then says, "So you worked with Finn then?"

And then I realize her question's aimed at him, but her eyes are working around him, to be on me.

Actually, they're getting closer to me too.

She's walking around him.

Back to my side.

I'm feeling claustrophobic. She's doing it again. She's planes-trains-and-automobiling me. If I don't get out now, I'll end up with her Saran-wrapped to me while we watch Casa Laguna burn down as she apologizes over that little mishap with the matches and laughs about how I don't need the place after all, because isn't it just a little too far from work anyway?

"Yes," I say, then holler, "Miles! Come on."

"Why aren't the contracts in?" Sonya cuts in, her head snapping up from the phone, apparently done reading through the email. There's a significant pause, then she squints and adds, "You're the new guy."

"Finn Masters," I say. I make the mistake of automatically putting out my hand—a poor habit. There's something atrocious about being old-fashioned in a modern town. She looks down at it as if she has never seen nor has any interest in hands. I pull it back and hold the leash.

"He also recently moved up to co-exec," Lavender puts in with smiling eyes and a prompting nod at me.

I will not be fooled by such appearances.

I will not be fooled.

"And I don't know," I continue, keeping a trained eye on Sonya. I have to tread carefully here. She's one of the show's three stars. Her happiness is a key factor, whether I like it or not. I know I am new and, quite frankly as I've experienced firsthand, very much disposable. Everything I do has to be delicate. "That's not really my area—"

Wrong words. Her eyes have become saucers.

"What are you going to do about Ashley and Lance?" she says. "Are they getting married at the season finale?"

"I'm legally bound not to discuss it," I say, then add very, very quietly, shifting my eyes towards Chris, "publicly."

She snaps her head towards him. "Go away."

"Nope," I say, grabbing Chris by the arm. "It's fine," I say calmly. "I can't talk about it *at all*. But I will say, changes on shows are normal. We are at a point where we have to make some tough decisions. The show's been on a long time—"

"Is it because of the ratings?" Sonya persists. Her voice drops with suspicion. "What's Goodwin see in the ratings?"

I tug on the leash. Oookay then. Time to leave. I'm about to be at the center of a crime scene. I can just imagine her storming into Goodwin's office, saying, "Finn Masters says . . ." The less I say, the better.

"Are they thinking of *canceling*?" she says as I begin walking. She keeps pace with me.

The bodyguard across the lawn who was just fascinated with the rubbish bin over yonder also starts keeping pace with me.

Lavender follows, keeping pace with me.

Chris has grabbed his things and is keeping pace with me.

Even Bernie stumbles along, keeping pace with me.

We're one giant, pacing unit.

"I'm sure it's fine," Lavender begins.

"Lavie," Sonya huffs. "We're fifteen episodes into our tenth season. They haven't renewed our contracts yet—and *they're four months overdue*. Let's be honest here." She shifts her focus back to me. Puts a hand out in front of me, which, quite frankly, has the effectiveness of a glowing blue (or red? Possible villain here) lightsaber standing between me and the gate. She levels her gaze. "What do you know, Finn?"

I think I liked it better when she disparagingly called me the new guy.

Now she's using my name like a weapon.

"Nothing," I say. It's not good to lie. It doesn't lend itself to winning trust down the line, so I add, "Well. Not nothing. But enough to know I was hired on to be a fresh eye on the show, which I believe is reasonable for any show after a length of time, and to think of new ways to drive the plot and the characters. I have your best interests in mind, Sonya. We share mutual goals here. My desire is to keep the show thriving, and I hope you can trust us as we strive to do just that."

I end my monologue looking her straight in the eye. She looks back at me without blinking for so long that the bodyguard seems to be calling someone on the phone for backup.

"Aw, look. Our dogs are becoming friends."

Everyone turns to Chris, who is smiling at Lavender, who is looking down to where he's pointing. Bernie has taken the French Bulldog beneath him and is either playing rather forcefully or about to eat it alive.

"Bernie is Sonya's dog," Lavender says.

"It's your dog," Sonya snaps.

"She's in denial," Lavender says, smiling, undeterred.

"*She's* in denial," Sonya replies. She looks at me. "About *everything*, I think."

"Sonya . . . ," Lavender says with a lilt in her tone.

Sonya presses her lips together. Glares from me to Lavender and back again.

It seems like it takes everything in her, but at last she blows out, "*Fine*."

And that's it. Apparently this woman doesn't like to waste breath.

"There," Lavender says, grinning as she gives Sonya a squeeze. "All settled. We're all just *fine*."

"Tarte," Chris calls, and despite the little dog's ears perking up as she begins trotting over, he gives a little Sleeping Beauty-esque musical whistle. It's so loud and long, several people turn. It's like the Samsung dryer song.

He picks her up.

I groan inwardly.

He's clipping that ridiculous pink satin bow on her collar. The pink bow is twice the size of the dog.

But the sound of that clip and the sight of the little pink dog cradled in the crook of his arm does its magic.

The spell is released.

Even scary Sonya's guard drops, and she takes a step forward. "Tarte, you say?" She studies the dog intently, then, after a long moment, reaches out tentatively with her glossy white nails and lightly taps its head.

"You know, if you love dogs so much . . . ," Lavender begins, tilting her head towards Bernie.

"Can it," Sonya retorts. "I'm not taking your dog." Her eyes drift back to the tiny French Bulldog. "Cute bow. Oversized for her tiny frame. How old's your dog?"

Chris shrugs. "Not sure. It was Kim's."

And here we go.

After a tremendous pause, he says softly, "Before she left her on my doorstep. Didn't even knock."

I roll my eyes as Lavender and Sonya both suck in a tiny breath.

"Oh, the poor thing," Sonya says, eyes on Chris, while seeming to unconsciously rub the dog's ears.

Chris gives a tiny and yet oh-so-melodramatic shrug as his eyes drift from Sonya to Lavender. "I'm just glad Tarte's safe."

I push open the dog gate and give Miles a tiny, quiet tug on the leash to let him know. We start our escape.

I'll no doubt be hearing the details from Chris later, how he used the dog to land a date with the one and only Lavender Rhodes. Or Sonya. Or both.

Nobody ever uses *just* Lavender's first name when recounting anything, by the way. She is, in their eyes, too much of an icon. An immortal. A Marilyn Monroe. A Johnny Cash. As though she didn't have the same humiliating prepuberty experiences we all had. Which, of course, she did. (I'm thinking of one photo of her at the age of thirteen, immortalized in our yearbook during a particularly troubling era of braces, bangs, and acne.)

I can hear Chris going into his saga as I step onto the sidewalk and hop the curb. He's deep into the chronicle of his previous relationship (for some reason women love when he rehashes the heartbreak story) when a passing tour bus drowns out his voice. I move to the opposite side of the street.

Despite the tumbler in my hand, it feels like a good moment to run home, and I break into a light jog. Within a minute, my mind swells with blooming ideas as I detangle the struggle of a particular scene I was working on late last night.

In fact, I've almost completely forgotten about the group when I hear a particular voice.

"Finn," Lavender calls out.

I turn before I realize what I'm doing.

And immediately regret it.

Honestly. I have to stop *looking back*.

There Lavender is, dragging that dog beside her, running in flip-flops.

I squint at the dog park, more than two blocks away.

"I believe you are supposed to be back there," I call back without slowing, "falling for a heartrending story about a man with poor judgment in girlfriends who takes in tiny French dogs."

She laughs.

"I'm finding I'm more of a sucker for the big dogs, myself. Can you slow down?"

I grind my teeth.

It's a tricky thing, wanting to be rude to Lavender Rhodes when you are also working with her. One can only be so rude before it's obvious, and when it's obvious, she might get upset and lay blame. And if the star of the show lays blame, then, well, I know which one of us Goodwin would trust.

I stop.

"You might want to tell your detail you have fans," I say, watching a pair of teenage boys tripping along the sidewalk behind her.

She casts a glance back at the duo. "I have no bodyguard," she replies, and as she reaches me, she turns back with a smile, saying, "Hi, guys. I'm just going to take a quiet walk, okay?" And then she gives them a little wink that apparently translates to "So let's just keep this between us."

Sure enough, they give overenthusiastic nods and pocket their phones.

I roll my eyes.

At the light, we stop.

I consider not talking. Wonder how long it will take her to wander off if I go silent.

We're both silent as people and cars pass.

I blink first. "You need a bodyguard."

"Obviously," she says, bright and proud, gesturing at the boys, "I do not."

"Just because two sixteen-year-olds think they're in your best-friends club doesn't mean you don't need a bodyguard. Surely the network has talked to you about this."

Lavender draws herself up. "I don't care what the network has or hasn't said. I don't need a bodyguard. I can have a perfectly normal morning walking through a perfectly normal park on my own, thank you."

"Even Sonya has a bodyguard," I say, nodding with a squint at the man in the Boy Scouts cap who is now very seriously taking pictures of a palm tree five feet from where Chris has handed Sonya his phone. She is tapping something down. "Who looks like she's been suckered into a date, by the way."

"That's her cousin, actually. What you're watching is yet another one of her side hustles," she says.

I frown. "She's started a bodyguard business?"

Lavender shrugs. "She's in the city for it with the contacts for it, and she is the most aggressively type A person you'll ever meet, so . . . I'm not sure why you're surprised. Sonya's big on family. Always gets her family to play a role in the things she takes on. So. Yes." She looks back at the cousin, who has just tripped on a backpack on the ground while trying to get closer to the pair.

I watch him face-plant. "And they agree to it?"

"What?"

I wave a hand vaguely in their direction. "Recklessly participating in questionable business plans?"

"Her friends do too."

"Which explains why she doesn't have many," I say.

She pauses and adds, "You should've seen me when I was a dog walker for her."

At this, I stop pretending to be captivated by passing traffic and give in. Look her way. "You were not."

"Sure I was." She looks up at me as though I couldn't possibly not believe her.

I don't blink. The light has turned, but I remain on the sidewalk. The thought is just so impossible. "I'm sorry, but I believe you're lying. There's just no way that *you* were a dog walker."

A little crease forms between her brows. "And why is that so impossible to believe?"

"You are literally carrying that dog. Right now."

She glances down and, looking quite like my sister, who tends to scour the house looking for her fourth baby while actually carrying said fourth baby on her hip, cracks a smile.

"At best you were a dog carrier," I say. Then repeat, "At best."

The light turns again and another group of pedestrians surrounds us.

"There was one unruly terrier I did tend to carry around quite a bit. But other than that—"

What am I doing?! Pull yourself together, man!

"Sure," I cut in, focusing on the light ahead. No distractions. No chitchat with this woman. "Well, if you'll excuse me, I have a date—"

I am headed to a (practically) blind date, if anyone must know. With a caterer friend of Paula's I met at work and have known for a sum of thirty seconds. Hardly enough time to catch her name, but long enough for Paula to squeeze herself into the conversation and set up a brunch date between her two "favorite eligible single friends."

"With Maggie?" she says, looking intrigued. "That's actually what I chased you down the street to ask about. So you hit it off then?"

"*No*," I reply forcefully. "Specifically *not* with . . ." I pause. It doesn't even feel safe to speak her name. "The young lady, for the record, is Goodwin's niece."

Lavender waits for me to continue.

I don't.

"And?" she says.

"And I'm an old bachelor."

"You said yourself you're about to go on a date."

"An old bachelor compared to women who are as young as your boss's niece."

She laughs. "You're joking. I was on a date with a forty-year-old last week."

"And you're twenty-nine. That's different."

She looks amused. "And how do you know this?"

"We were at school together," I remind her, frowning. "It's hardly rocket science to count down one year."

The light turns again, and traffic begins to flow. I step off the sidewalk and onto the road. "Good-bye, Lavender," I say, training my voice to keep things professional. The goal here is to keep my distance while remaining polite. The *last* thing I need, after all, is for her to officially turn against me. And while I'm not peppy (I will never be "peppy"), I do the job.

But in true leech fashion, she sticks to me.

"Why are you following me?" I say, side-eyeing her.

She shrugs. "I live in the same direction. So who are you going on a date with then?"

"You do *not* live in the same direction," I reply. The area isn't bad per se, but if you recall, both glitter and glue reside in this town, and this area isn't remotely like the famed location where so many of those shiny types reside. Here, we glue people do things like leave our cars on the street. Here we use regular-sized welcome mats for our regular-sized doors.

"It'll take you hours to walk back to your Hollywood Hills mansion from here."

"I don't live in Hollywood Hills," she says.

And I have to admit, she surprises me here.

"I moved to a flat just up the road three months ago. Which . . ." She halts, tilting her head. It's such a commanding halt, I find myself momentarily halting too. It's the kind of motion people make when they've just remembered something very important. Such as the combination to a safe that needs unlocking. Or that vital piece of information the president told you the night before he was mysteriously murdered. "Given the size of this town, I guess that makes me your neighbor. You ought to bring me a welcome-to-the-neighborhood basket. Bring me a hamper of fruit or something."

I frown.

She stares back.

"I'll get right on that," I say flatly.

"I'm honestly surprised you haven't seen me around before. I'm a regular around here now. There's the nice fellow I pass on my walks. Hello," she says, waving at an elderly man bussing a table at an outdoor café.

He frowns and ignores her.

"Clearly," I say.

But as I check over my shoulder, a woman eating her breakfast does a double take. Immediately phones are out. Nobody's going so far as standing to chase her down, but those teens a block back are still there.

They don't look like they're moving. I haven't caught them walking. And yet somehow they are just as close as before.

Which is precisely what makes me feel uneasy.

I have the horrible urge to put my hand behind her back, a sign those boys should back off. Frankly, this urge makes me feel equally concerned.

My pace slows, just a little, to walk beside her.

She's doing it again.

This woman is somehow roping me in against my will.

"So let me get this straight," I say. "You have no dedicated security at all."

"Correct."

"And you live somewhere in this area," I say, looking up and down the street of shops and lofts. "Nothing gated."

"Yes."

I raise a brow.

Take ten or so more paces.

Sink my teeth into my bottom lip.

Hate myself for giving in, but finding it impossible not to care, just a little bit, I halt.

"Are you mad?"

She pauses.

"Not at all," she says. "I have just come to the decision that the world at large is good—"

"It is *not* good. You above all people need to know that it is *not good*—"

"People are kind—"

"I literally watched someone run a pedestrian over for a parking spot the other day—"

"And at the end of the day, humanity wins."

I stare at her.

She makes me want to rip my hair out.

"Are you *serious*?" I hiss at last. "The world is run by maniacs and *the maniacs* win. There are *plenty of stories* where the maniacs win. Have you *never* read a paper *in your life*?"

But Lavender just shakes her head and taps my chest in a way that sends sparks shooting off. "You know what's wrong with you, Finn? You've spent too much time writing for that dark show."

She doesn't sound angry at all. I, however, am getting just a bit wound up.

"No," I reply shortly. "*You* are the one who's clearly spent too much time living in a sitcom. You would do well to start acting in *anything* where the good girl doesn't get it all."

Her lips press together.

I see something shift in her eyes.

For a moment I'm conflicted. Part of me feels I have been too honest, and in my honesty I overstepped, and now I must protect my job. Another part of me, however, feels relief at having spent some pent-up truth. I'm not sure which way this is going to go. But then one corner of her mouth tweaks upward.

She slides her arm around the crook of my elbow like we're school chums.

Or even work chums.

Or just anything besides what we are—which is *not* chums.

"Come on, Finn. Rule one in this *dangerous* world we live in: never gather a crowd."

I look around and realize I have, in fact, been drawing attention. Cameras are out. People are peeking their heads out from doors and windows. We keep walking.

For one long block she holds on to my arm, and for one long block I bristle at the reflection I see in a shop window. She and I together, walking arm in arm with our dogs ahead of us. For once, as though to spite me, her dog trots along obediently beside Miles, and we look quite the pair.

I can't believe my thoughts have uttered those words.

I'm choking on them.

I'm going to suffocate.

I blink away from the window. But it's too late. The view is seared in my memory now, and I'll never experience the gift of unseeing it.

She prattles on about some inane topic—a heart-shaped rock she found? some person she accidentally pushed down a manhole?—but I can't focus, because I'm too focused on how she's successfully Saran-wrapped me to herself. I can't quite figure out how she's done it. My thoughts are muddled by this new situation.

Her hair is crinkly in all the wrong places and swirly and yellow in the breeze, and it smells like an almond pie my grandmother used to bake around the holidays. Her arm rests on mine as she holds to the dog on the leash, and she has this annoying habit of swinging her hand left and right and dragging me along with it as she points every which way while she talks.

I am stranded here, held captive in a haze of almonds as I'm yanked around by this woman, who in one sense has very much ruined large segments of my life, but in another holds the fate of my career in her hands. Pulling away would be rude, but also (oddly) I don't entirely loathe the moment.

That is to say, there are worse torments. Which is really the torment itself, actually, because now she's playing with my mind and even turning it against me.

She's a maniac.

That's what she is. A maniac with nice-smelling hair and a little arm wrapped around mine talking about—what is it now?—*rubbish pickup* days! While having the power to crush me under her thumb.

It's disgusting really, what she's doing.

"I think that's actually a wonderful idea, you know," she says, adjusting the leash on her wrist.

Bernie, I notice, is acting as though Miles is his only friend in the whole wide world. For the moment, Bernie actually looks like a decent animal as he trots along beside him.

I give up. The woman is going to follow me all the way home.

I just know it.

I resign myself to it.

"What is?" I say.

"Getting into something besides the sitcom. I've always wondered what it would be like to try something else."

"Now *don't*," I say, lifting a finger. This is it. This is how she is going to destroy me. She's going to take something I say offhand and use it against me. "I didn't say that."

"That's exactly what you said."

"I didn't mean *that*." I fling a flustered hand in the air. "Stay in *Neighbors*. Keep your head in the clouds and believe the world is full of good and innocent people who will come to your aid the moment you become a damsel in distress. Terrific. But *also* get some security detail." I tug Miles to a stop before the crosswalk, turn, and take the opportunity to pull my arm free. "Do it for the sake of everyone else, if you have to think of it that way. Because if you get kidnapped, then we're all out of our jobs. A lot rides on you, Lavender. Like our livelihoods. And our dreams."

"Oh, believe me, I'm aware." She inclines her head toward Seventh Street. "I'm this way."

I check over my shoulder. See a mass of people walking their dogs, watering streetside plants, carrying grocery bags.

All things regular evil people do when they're not terribly busy being evil.

"I'm acutely aware that it takes all parts to make this show work, and if one piece fails, the whole thing collapses. I was just saying," she continues, "if I had the choice, if I was forced to try something else, I wouldn't be entirely devastated."

What was that?

There is something poignant in the way she said that. A touch of sadness in her tone. Authenticity. Relatability. So much so I find myself inclining my head her way. For once, she sounds human. Truly . . . normal. "What do you mean, if you had a choice? Of course you have a choice, once your contract is up."

I laugh. "Don't tell me you've been doing this all these years because you fear letting others down."

She doesn't respond immediately.

So I add, "Don't."

But to my absolute disbelief, she shrugs. "It's fine. *Neighbors* is a good show. See you tomorrow," she says and turns down Seventh Street.

As if that moment doesn't just *make me want to explode*. "Are you *kidding* me, Lavender?" I call after her. "Are you seriously going to keep working for this show in your prime years while you don't even love it? For *what* exactly? To keep your costars in business? What exactly would you *want* to do?"

I check over my shoulder. Sure enough, those teenage boys are still there.

With a guttural growl, I clench my jaw and give in. *Fine*. Just this *once*.

I rush down Seventh until I'm beside her. A horn sounds beside us and I switch places, pulling the leash, and her, store-side as I move towards the curb. Resume talking. At this point, I have to admit defeat. Tomorrow will be a new day.

Bernie, for the record, appears to be thrilled Miles and I are continuing on the walk.

"It's *fine*, really," Lavender says. "The show is sweet. It's been a dream to work with Kye and Sonya since the beginning. But ten years playing the same character is just . . . well, it's a bit long—"

I check my urge to interject. People would kill for the opportunity to play her role. *I* would've, at one time, killed for the opportunity to play a role. And the job security of a good show is worth a thousand times the instability of a series of failing ones.

Still.

"I wrote for *Higher Stakes* for eight years and was sick of it by the end. I know how it feels to see the same scenarios play out again and again."

"So you get it," Lavender says in a see-we-are-the-same fashion. "But of course, I would never do that to Kye and Sonya. Or the team. I owe everything to Sonya, really. I would never be the one to pull out first."

It's such a striking thought. The world has only ever seen Lavender as Ashley Krane. It's hard to imagine her in any other role. The writer part of me can't help but be intrigued.

"So what would you do? Film?"

Lavender shrugs. Then after a moment, a sly smile lifts her face. "Actually, I'm a pretty big fan of *Higher Stakes*."

I feel a pounding in my chest and make a mental note never to meet Chris at the dog park again.

I can just see it now. Wouldn't it be so perfectly ironic for me to jump ship from *Higher Stakes* in order to work at *Neighbors*, then end up being the one to introduce Lavender to a *Higher Stakes* producer who convinces *her* to jump ship—causing *Neighbors* to crumble while *Higher Stakes* becomes the show of the decade?

Wouldn't that be just. The. Way.

I look back. The teens have pocketed their phones, but they have hoodies up now and keep staring intently our way as they slog along. There's no question about it; they are definitely tracking us.

Which is tricky, because the problem with celebrities is that they are expected to be tracked.

They are incessantly followed and photographed and mooned over. But these boys have a different look, and unfortunately it is impossible to know without question what that look means.

"How much farther?" I ask.

"I'm above that bakery," she says, nodding ahead.

I follow her eyes to the little building in the distance. Aaand *of course* it's this little graffitied building just three stories high. The sign hanging on the shop has a handful of missing letters that says: SHAT LA' BAK R . A window box holds more cigarette butts than flowers. The whole building is a peeling pale pink, reminding me of the color of a rather terrifying Easter bunny my brother sent a video of, along with my three-year-old niece standing beside him in a shopping center screaming bloody murder.

"Lovely," I say flatly.

"Just wait. You'll smell it in a moment. I wake up to the scent of baklava coming through the window every morning."

"Just baklava? You've been lucky."

I take her all the way up to the front door (also peeling, no surprise). It does smell faintly of pastries. The boys have stopped at a distance now, looking so seedy and suspicious as they stand beside one of the parked cars that the owner, who I presume is watching nearby, has taken to clicking the lock button every few seconds. Every time one of them moves, a little *beep* announces a flash of red lights.

I am just about to leave, mentally debating whether to assert myself, when I see a third male meet the duo. This one is at least early forties. Newsboy cap over shaved head. Hands in jacket pockets. Also watching us intently.

Not even pretending to look elsewhere.

"I'm sorry," I say, shifting on my heel towards her.

I want payback.

I want justice served.

But I don't want her dead.

"I cannot sit idly by about this. Lavender, I applaud you for attempting to be"—I wave a hand at the offensive building—"relatable to the rest of mankind, or whatever this is, but you have to see how incredibly unsafe this is. People are *not virtuous*—"

To my incredible irritation, she shrugs with a smile. Makes a little noise that says, *Eh. We can agree to disagree.* Turns. Puts her key in the door.

Meanwhile, the trio has decided to walk this way. And the older gentleman, well, he carries his weight in a way that makes people cross the street to the other side.

I have to admit, my heart is beginning to pound now, and I find I'm trying to gauge if they look crazy enough to attack in broad daylight. "I mean," I say more hurriedly, "not everybody is going to be your knight in shining armor here, should you come to a situation. It's willfully *ignorant* to think so."

Maddeningly, she turns the bolt.

She really is going to ignore me.

"You can't just go in there and expect people to be *good*." I realize I'm raising my voice now, which is in line with the pacing of my heartbeat. The door opens, and she takes a step inside. "Everyone in the world can Google your name and find your address. And *they aren't good*!"

I look up to see an old security camera in the corner of the entry, the wires spliced.

Lavender, at the bottom of a tiny stairwell, turns to face me. Bernie, leash dropped but still attached, takes off up the stairs, banging loudly on each step.

There's a pause as she gazes into my eyes. And then, with a lift of her lips, she exhales.

"Funny that you are so sure there are no knights in shining armor left, when you're right here standing at my doorstep. Your breastplate looks awfully shiny to me, Finn. And by the way, this is Gabriel. My . . . bodyguard."

I halt. Turn and come eye-to-neck with his larger-than-life frame.

"My *discreet* bodyguard," Lavender adds. Then she nods at the two boys. "And Rajiv and Kavish. Sonya's nephews and detail-in-training." She pauses. "Who, I see today, could use a little work."

I freeze for the longest period of time in my life. I'm like an electric robot that's had a hiccup before getting a rebooting.

"Oh." I nod and, for the second time today, mistakenly put out a hand. "Nice to meet you."

Gabriel shakes (incredibly briefly), then grunts in a way that says, *I don't like you, I don't need your approval, and I think you need to leave.*

It feels safer to shift my gaze back to Lavender, so I do. She's smiling. "Sorry. I just, well, I like to limit the number of people who know this. Gabriel has been with me for a long time. He excels at keeping himself in the shadows, and the best thing we can do is keep it that way. I didn't want to lie—"

But already I'm enthusiastically waving her off. I feel ridiculous. *Of course.* "No need to explain. Of course you want to—"

"—but when you decided to be a *knight in shining armor* about it," she says pointedly, "I figured it would be best to let you in. Of course, I would appreciate your discretion."

Already, I'm nodding. "Absolutely." I clap my hands. "Well." I find myself shaking my head, muttering, "Stupid of me. Of course you have protection. I just wanted—"

"—to make sure I got home safe and would be okay. Like a good Samaritan." She says it subtly, all the while smiling.

"Or a good coexecutive producer," I reply. I lift a finger. "Remember that, the next time I get into a scrape."

Probably caused by you.

Her lips part, something dancing in her eyes as she hangs on to the door. "Sure thing, Finn. In the meantime, I'll be waiting for that fruit basket."

I find myself back at my flat, unclipping the leash from Miles's collar and pulling off my shoes as the events of the last hour play through my mind.

Of her taking the twenty-minute walk over sewer grates and past sidewalk cafés instead of hopping in a private car to be taken wherever she wanted to go. Strolling through the residences of

Hollywood Hills is one thing, but stepping over rubbish and passing by the neon-lit vape shops while talking bright-eyed is another.

Of her opting to make the peeling pink loft over top of the failing Lebanese bakery her home and justifying it with the words, "*What's not to love? I get knafeh for dessert and post the mail before breakfast.*"

I never once saw her phone out either. When all the world gives its time and attention to the interrupting *ding*, she just walked along, eyes like a fresh baby's, happy enough to be watching the spindly limbs of a jacaranda tree before bloom.

And there's that one thing I can't stop thinking about over and over as I pull a takeaway bag holding last night's leftovers from the fridge. The hush as she put her hand on mine before she closed the door, and her whispered words: "*But really, Finn. It's important to me that Gabriel is kept a secret. Please don't speak of him to anyone.*" She paused and gave a breathy laugh. "*I guess that's three secrets between us.*"

And despite my best judgment, I'd felt a pang in my chest that was totally out of line with my mind.

There is no denying it now.

I am in her club.

Her secret club.

Now I am not merely the bearer of the ridiculous news that she has alektorophobia, or that she secretly wonders what her life could be like outside the craze of *Neighbors*, but also this little nugget about her bodyguard. Three secrets.

Three secrets about my enemy.

My gut response in the moment was as ridiculous as I imagine the veterinarian's receptionist and the teen boys and all the world would have if they could hear her say those same words. If they could feel her touch their hand.

A *zing*.

A bolt up the spine that imprints the scent of baklava forevermore to this memory. I will never be able to walk by a bakery again and not think of that moment.

I am in her inner circle.

Against my will, yes.

Without asking to be or seeking it out, yes.

Only—and I want to shake myself—I don't *hate* the idea of it like I want to.

I don't *loathe* (as I *should*) the idea that I am among the very few to share a secret with Lavender Rhodes.

The terrible, horrible Lavender Rhodes.

I slap water over my face and tell myself to snap out of it. Because isn't this *just of course* like her? She is turning my heart against myself, against my better judgment.

I need to replay the facts.

No.

I need to find the list.

I ransack every last box in the closet, spitting out mothballs and tearing through old notebooks, but finally I unsnap the clasp on a small leather notebook and flip to the center page.

TRANSGRESSIONS AGAINST FINN MASTERS

I read it top to bottom, nodding and growling and saying such things as "That's right!" and "Oooh, that woman."

When I reach the end of the list, I whip open a drawer.

Find a pen.

Begin scribbling the latest infractions, *precisely*, in every detail. The way she discarded ten dogs and made me late on my first day. The moment she turned the writers against me with her callous comment. My allergic reaction to forced foods. The day she got me sacked.

As the ink runs out, I pop the top off a second pen with my mouth and keep writing.

By the time I've documented my grievances, the contents of the takeaway bag are long gone, and I feel restored in aim and purpose. Looking at the list is the reminder I've needed. No sympathy. No coconut hair. No quietly being impressed by the fact that she wears worn-out flip-flops or comments on the tender blue sky rather than on the pungent lineup of overflowing rubbish bins.

No.

She is a siren.

Beautiful but deadly.

And just to make it absolutely, *abundantly* clear every morning henceforth, I lay the list on my desk beside my laptop, where it will remind me just exactly what happens every single time she's even close to my personal space.

I won't try to ruthlessly sabotage her—although doesn't she deserve it? Just a little bit? I will just see if I can orchestrate a *few* instances of revenge. No, not revenge. That's such a harsh word; it puts all the blame on the one doing the revenging.

Justice.

Just a few instances of justice.

Just a tiny smattering of retribution.

And yes, maybe I'm learning that she isn't all bad. Perhaps, to some degree, she's less specifically evil and more a flighty spirit who doesn't think through how her actions affect others. Actually, she's very much like Puck.

But still. All. Those. Things I've dealt with. On account of her.

Losing Delilah.

Losing career opportunities, multiple times.

Screws in ankles and paw prints on pants and red-faced bosses and ID badges flung down hallways.

She *has* to be held accountable for all that.

And I would be absolutely daft as a doorknob if I didn't take advantage of my position as a writer of her character *just once*.

That's all I'm asking for.

Just once.

Then I can shove the whole thing behind me and move on.

I drop the pen and sit back, then look at the desktop screen. The cursor in the latest script is blinking halfway through a sentence, which is halfway through a paragraph that is halfway through a scene. It beckons me, and for a moment, my eyes skim over the words.

Then I spy the time in the top right corner.

12:45 p.m.

I drop my head.

I just missed my brunch date.

She's done it again.

Chapter 15

Lavender

Tuesday, Table Read, Writers Room

"And I said to her, 'I've appreciated our season of friendship, but the fact is our lives are moving in different directions.'"

I frown at Sonya and pick up my doughnut. We're the first ones in the writers room, seated at the long table. And frankly, I'm only here this early because I was dragged on a jog this morning by Sonya, who apparently decided to call her former running buddy in for a corporate meeting and fire her.

"She said, 'How? What's changed?' and I told her the obvious. She quit running and had a baby. It's not the baby that's so much the problem—you could throw any kid in a stroller—but the *running*."

"Sonya. You can't quit your friendship with someone because they stop running."

"She's all about *ellipticals* now," Sonya hisses. "*Ellipticals*. What am I supposed to do with that?" Sonya drops a packet of sugar into her coffee and begins stirring. "So I said, 'I'm sorry, but my capacity to invest in our friendship has peaked.'"

I rub the palm of my hand on my forehead, then slide a weary hand down my face.

Bite off another bit of doughnut.

Sonya waves her coffee stirrer in the air. "And she gave me the typical, 'I don't understand. This all feels so sudden. What did I do?' Yada yada. So I said, 'I am aware that this may be difficult to hear, but I've been reevaluating the various categories in my life, and unfortunately, given the landscape at this time, I can allot only 12 percent of my time to friendships. And that, unfortunately, means someone has to go.'"

"You're joking, Sonya," I say. I point at her, and through a mouthful of sprinkles and chocolate doughnut I add, "Bad. Very bad."

I shake a finger at her the way I once tried to scold Bernie. He looked so sad I never tried it again.

With Sonya, however, it's easy.

People start trailing in now, and the commotion in the room begins to grow.

One of the new writers, Paula, is walking around the table, dropping scripts. She came to the job with Finn. Word is he insisted she come along when he was hired. A pretty bold move. Goodwin doesn't typically take to stuff like that, actually.

Way back in season 3, Sonya had the idea that she, Kye, and I should form a union of sorts when it came time to sign the next contract. Everybody knew there would be a season renewal; we just needed to get our salaries queued up. That's where the agents would come in, negotiating like their lives depended on it. But when Sonya heard the salary Kye had made the first two seasons, mere shillings to her pounds, she was irate. Stood on multiple soapboxes for the next two weeks about how we were a team, and our work in the show was equal, and we deserved equal pay for equal time on-air. Kye readily agreed, as did I, and it took only one run up the gossip chain for Goodwin to shut it down. Declared he doesn't work with ultimatums. Threatened to drop us all for violating the contract by discussing salaries. Threatened to drop the show altogether if we tried some such stunt as throwing a coup.

Long story short, we did it anyway. Just . . . a little more . . . discreetly. Nancy landed Sonya and me a massive amount. Sonya created a separate checking account that was a direct deposit for all three of our paychecks and had a lawyer divide it up equally biweekly.

And here, apparently, Finn dared to bring on this Paula woman with him from day one. Either Goodwin has lost his fire, or Goodwin *really* sees something in Finn.

I'm not surprised.

In the past few weeks, Finn has raised the bar for the show considerably. Seems every time he speaks, he catches everyone's attention.

Particularly mine.

I look around the room.

Speaking of, where is he?

I reach for the script that Paula just flopped onto the table in front of me.

Sonya fidgets, clearly wanting to finish her story. "Go ahead," I say with a sigh. "Tell me more of your heartlessness."

"And then," Sonya says rapidly, quieter, reaching for her script, "I said, 'I just want to be honest with you so I don't disappoint you. I'm sorry if this feels painful and confusing,' and then she threw a lamp at me and that was that."

I yawn and roll my eyes. "Sonya. It's a miracle you have any friends at all."

"I have seven friends, thank you very much. Pat—"

"Your cousin."

"Montu—"

"Your other cousin."

"Greg—"

"Your trainer."

"Dave and Isabel—"

"Your neighbors. And you only like them because they called the police so much on your other neighbor he moved out."

"And Kye. And you."

I shake my head. "So essentially . . . family. If you tried saying that nonsense to Kye or me, we'd knock you over the head, then steal you for lunch."

Sonya drops the stirrer onto the table. "Precisely. A true friend wouldn't have let me break up with them to begin with. She had to go."

"Well, I'm glad you are decided. By the way, your nonfriend Delilah is meeting us at noon."

She picks up the script, and her eyes begin scanning down the page. She sniffs. "She's not a nonfriend. She's an adjacent friend. A friend of a friend whom I hate less than others. In her case, just a *tiny* bit less."

"Touching. I hope that's how you address her Christmas cards."

"*Please*. Adjacents don't get Christmas cards," Sonya says, flipping the page. "Anyway, heads up, you need to lock in your six thirties for a while until I get a new running buddy."

I slide my doughnut back and forth on the table between my hands. "I have an idea. Why don't you take Bernie?" *And fall in love with him. Your dog.*

"He trips over his own feet walking," she retorts. "Nice try."

And then he comes in.

Our eyes lock.

A little chill runs over me, and I feel like I've swallowed an ice cream cone all at once.

Well. That's new.

He stands next to Paula now, poring over something in the script.

I drop my eyes to my own script, then find my eyes drifting back up to him.

Finn Masters.

What is it about him exactly?

About five nine. Mousy brown hair that curlicues up on his forehead. He's wearing his round-rimmed glasses and, unlike most of the other writers, tends to dress up a bit for his role. Maybe even for life in general. He possesses a quiet sense of professionalism. A personal desire to put on nice shoes in the morning. Not because this is the dress code; no, writers are usually in worn-out T-shirts and comfortable trainers. The cast typically dresses up a little bit more, not at sweeping-gown level but at least a nice pair of athletic shorts. After all, even though we have an agreement to keep phones out of it during work, things have a way of leaking. Writers don't face that kind of pressure, and usually their choice of clothing tends to coordinate with this feeling.

But not Finn's.

He's in a quiet blue oxford today, sleeves not yet rolled up to the elbows (that's something he does several hours in, when he's really getting into it). Navy slacks. Leather laptop bag over one shoulder. Consumed in conversation. And all the while looking very fine. Very fine indeed.

What is it about him exactly?

Kye comes through the door and stops behind him, spots me, and calls over his shoulder, one arm stretched over Finn's body.

Well, it's not his height.

"Lavie," Kye says, pointing at the chair beside me. A young staff writer is just about to set down his coffee in that very spot.

I hate moments like these, but friendship trumps all.

"Hey," I say, putting a hand on the back of the chair. Then, finding that rude, I drop it. "So sorry. Kye was just asking if he could sit here"—I pull a face—"and it really is helpful to sit together during the reading. Would it be okay if he takes this seat?"

Sonya makes a little *pfft* sound, flipping to another page.

The writer moves along, and I shower him with several thanks.

When he's gone, Sonya whispers ten times too loud, "You don't need to *beg* the newbie to let Kye sit next to you."

"First of all, yes, I do. He's a human being, and all human beings deserve respect. Secondly, *that* attitude right there is why they wrote in that random pie-in-your-face scene last season, Sonya. D'you think it made sense for you to suddenly become obsessed with blueberry pies during a wedding and end up facedown in a trash can eating one? Respect the writer, and they'll respect you."

But she clearly doesn't hear me, because her attention is trained on a particular spot in the script.

Sonya cackles.

"Is it good?" Kye says, his eyes alight as he sits down. "What page?"

But Sonya just keeps laughing.

Kye checks over her shoulder, then hunts for the page.

I flip too.

So far, nothing too out of the ordinary.

Lance is building the rooftop garden. Ashley becomes stranded on a ferry for twenty-four hours with eighteen strangers who fall with *Lord of the Flies*–level intensity into two camps, using a currency of gum. The usual ridiculousness.

And then . . .

No.

Kye clearly sees it as well, because his face breaks into a smile, smothered quickly by my glare.

"Oh hon," Sonya says, slapping me on the shoulder with falsely sympathetic eyes, "if all that's true, you'd better put a plug in whatever you're doing to some poor soul in this room. Because given what I'm seeing, you must be trying to blackmail some writer for murder."

Chapter 16

Finn

Friday, Final Dress Rehearsal, Stage 2

"Alright. That's it, Finn. Tell me what's going on here."

I jump at Paula's presence. I've been so focused on watching things unfold from my perch backstage among the shadows, I didn't notice her come up beside me.

"Nothing. I don't know what you're talking about."

"You're grinning like a madman."

"No, I'm not."

But then I feel it. My face, without my permission, grinning so hard it feels like my cheeks have been cranked to this extreme position. They're actually aching, now that I think of it.

"Don't play dumb," Paula says, looking into my face from an inch away. "You've worn that clown-face-behind-the-curtains smile all morning. Clutching your coffee and holding your clipboard, laughing darkly. It's creeping the heck out of the caterers. You remind me of that serial killer we had the hardest time nailing down personality-wise, season 4. What was his name?"

"Gary," I reply without looking away. "And I'm not *laughing darkly*. That's an exaggeration. Darkly chuckling at best. And frankly, if you're going to compare me to any of the serial killers on *Higher Stakes*, Gary is the one to beat. Thanks for the compliment."

"Spill."

I take a breath.

It's Friday afternoon.

I've been emotionally prepping for this moment all week, eager to see how it plays out. Adam hasn't shown up yet, which, given his generosity in agreeing to show up last-minute when he had his own packed week of shooting, is understandable. I personally tasked myself with all but begging his publicist to get Adam to come on the show, arguing from every possible angle how good this would be for him: The money. The very, very little time required of him on set, with just three lines. The boon this would be to his upcoming movie. I even agreed to write in a line or two—they are mediocre at best—promoting *Ships at Apple Bay*. And for the record, it was no small feat to convince the network to accommodate an ad for a historical drama regarding sailors of the seventeenth century in an episode about three modern city dwellers dealing with a gum-on-the-metro crisis and the bumbling construction of a rooftop garden.

But at long last, he agreed.

Adam Glassner is coming. The celebrated ex-boyfriend of Lavender Rhodes. Ties snipped last year. The nation's heart collectively broken when he deserted her for a newer, younger, fresher model.

Payback in motion.

My first successful dabble in payback started this week with coffee. Driving twenty minutes out of the way and spending a small fortune to bring everyone associated with *Neighbors* a special cinnamon latte (something I've heard her order on no fewer than three occasions). And then, when I got to her, *poof*. Oh dear.

Where were all the cinnamon lattes? Did we *just* run out? Of her favorite drink?

It was small. Tiny. But mighty.

Well, until everybody chipped in portions of their lattes and she ended up with forty-eight ounces and appreciative tears welling in her eyes, followed by a spontaneous group-karaoke moment from *You've Got Mail*'s opening scene, "The Puppy Song." I overheard one of the writers saying as we left for the day that it was a highlight of their career.

But for a good four minutes, Lavender was left out.

And that is the moment we are going to focus on here.

Then there was the little mix-up with her dressing room. Silly me, *somehow* that three-tiered cake I sent congratulating her on the news that she'd been inducted into Welling School's Alumni Hall of Fame (I don't want to talk about it) was delivered right on top of her vanity. Wouldn't you know, it was an *ice cream* cake that (with a little help from a hair dryer) left a puddle of strawberry all over the scattered mishmash of beloved cosmetics.

Of course, her response was to hug me around the neck, make a speech about how thoughtful I was, and then force me to lick a dripping mascara tube because the strawberry cake was just "all so, so good."

I ended up in a photo on her wall for that one. Me with a startled look as she scrunched our faces together while holding up a handful of dripping cosmetics with the biggest grin I've ever seen on any face. Like this was the time of our lives.

Needless to explain further, I'm zero for three here.

But. Today is the day.

I check over my shoulder. Nobody is around (possibly because I'm frightening people—I see this now). Just a bunch of unused camera equipment under a thick layer of dust.

Paula, meanwhile, hasn't budged.

"You won't leave it, will you?" I say.

She raises a brow.

My eyes move back to the set, where Lavender is circling Sonya's apartment chair. She's visibly nervous. Her friends aren't being the world's best supporters about all this, and frankly, were I not the one putting up this whole charade, I'd care. I mean, Sonya has actually gotten herself a little bag of popcorn from the snack station and is sitting while Lavender circles her. Kye isn't much better; he's playing on his phone in his chair, merely lifting his leg to let Lavender pass every time she circles him. Regarding that, I'm a little surprised. It's evident he has a bit of a crush on her—given what all the gossip rags have declared for the past decade and how obviously close the two are. I expected more concern on his part.

"You might as well tell me," Paula huffs. "I already have my suspicions. They don't do you any favors."

"Fine," I say, rolling my eyes. "But remember that one time I got you this gig?"

"And remember that one time I dragged you to the party that got *you* this gig? What's your point?"

"Mum's the word."

She purses her lips. Taps her foot impatiently.

I take a breath. "The thing is, I have a"—I lower my voice—"strong dislike for Lavender."

To say she is visibly startled is an understatement.

She blinks several times.

Squints at me.

Her nose wrinkles and she turns to face Lavender.

Looks back at me. "Don't pull my leg, Finn. Be serious."

"I am serious," I say humorlessly. "Deadly serious."

"No no no no," she says, raising a finger. "I've been watching you. That can't be right. You *like* her."

"I dislike her."

"You absolutely *do* like her," she says more adamantly.

"I absolutely do *not*," I reply with equal force.

She gestures toward Lavender. "Then what have I been watching unfold between you two the past few weeks? She follows you around. You follow her around." She pauses. Squints. "Is this a British thing? Is this like one of your British jokes?"

"I am *not* joking," I say, exasperated, then stop myself. "You know what? Forget all about it. You don't need to know anyway, and Adam will be here any moment."

I take a step towards the stage, but she blocks me with her clipboard.

"Halt, Finn Masters. You lay it out for me right now or I'll tell Goodwin about the chickens."

I look down at all five feet of her and the clipboard, which is not the stone wall she seems to think it is. "Are you trying to blackmail me?"

"I'm a happily married forty-year-old mother of four with sixteen years of sleep deprivation who peeled dried macaroni off my hair on the way to work this morning. I need a good story. I *need* to feel the drama."

She looks all red in the face and serious. I gently push the clipboard aside. "Fine. For the sake of your happy marriage."

I tell her everything, starting with that very first incident at the ripe old age of seventeen. By the time I've finished, her eyes have shifted from mirth, to shock, to empathy, to what I see now: an unreadable expression as her gaze frequently shifts from me to my nemesis on set.

"So that's what you're doing then? You're getting payback for the hurt she's caused?"

"I am. I'm not proud of it, but I am."

"But, Finn . . . ," she begins. "Surely you see—"

"That she's not as bad as all the proof in my memory? Well, you weren't there, Paula. It's easy to paint over the transgressions of someone's past when they're not personal. People always want to free the convict who murdered someone fifteen years ago if he has a sappy story. People are quick to forget the actions of the past when they're not personally involved."

"Nobody was murdered here, though."

"And I'm not intending to murder anyone either. Or get them fired. Or kill their dreams entirely—despite the fact certain persons have repeatedly killed mine. I just want a *little* bit of payback. Just a tiny appetizer of—"

"Revenge."

"*—justice*," I correct. "Just a moment of fairness." I raise a hand. "And before you say anything more, please don't guilt me on this. I've lived a good life. I pay my taxes. I take my neighbors' pets to the vet. I just want *this*."

"Who's guilting you?" she clucks. "I think you're being an idiot, but I'm not guilting you. You got Adam Glassner to come here. I'm all for the show."

And just then the door opens, and faces turn.

The room goes silent.

A tall, broad-shouldered man walks down the aisle between rows of seats. He slips his aviators off and lets them dramatically dangle between his fingers. The gray T-shirt is practically painted around his biceps, making Kye's shirt choices look almost baggy by comparison (which is saying a lot). His face is chiseled, as stony and secure as his violently green eyes. By looks and confidence alone it is, without question, understandable that his is the face of the next superhero movie. And, for that matter, why apparently both Lavender and America in general have had their hearts stolen by him.

Perfect.

I feel the tension in the room.

Everyone's minds and eyes are on the same thing: what will happen next.

Paula's nails dig into my arm as she wraps her hand around me. Watching. As if this really is a drama.

I must admit, as his first foot lands on set, and I watch Lavender's clear blue eyes land on his, I feel the first pang of regret.

A little bell is going off in the back of my head.

A twinge that makes me wince.

But then something happens that immediately strips away that feeling, or any feeling besides utter shock.

Because the second he is within arm's reach, he drops to his knees. Wraps his arms around her calves. And cries out through what I can only hope are artificial tears: "Please come back to me, Lavie! *Please!*"

Chapter 17

Lavender

Friday, Final Dress Rehearsal, Stage 2

The thing about strong men is, it's really hard to get them off your ankles when they're strapped around you, begging for your forgiveness.

And for Adam Glassner, it took Kye, Finn, two security officers, and a personal detail, because while his love for weight training was strong, his love for me was even stronger.

Given everything that happened, we wrap up early. Writers are scurrying off in different directions to see what can be done to smooth over the plot hole now that Adam isn't going to be on the show. Nervous PAs run by with phones glued to their ears calling for lists of potential actor replacements and double-checking that I can't sue. Sonya for her part is crossing paths with them, on the phone with her lawyer (despite me telling her to hang up) to see if I can. Kye followed Adam out alongside the officers, as if he were some sort of official who could do anything about anything. Finn went as well.

My heart is still pounding in my chest as I reach the door to my dressing room and turn the knob. I haven't seen Adam in months, not since I made the decision to step back from our relationship. Needless to say, time clearly hasn't healed all wounds.

I open the door to my dressing room, head straight for the minifridge, and grab a sparkling water. The can sizzles as I pop open the lid, and with that the only sound in the room, I sit on the couch and take a breath.

I've taken only a couple of sips when there's a knock on the door.

I open it.

Finn's standing on the other side. And frankly, he looks shattered. Twice as upset as he did last time he was in here. Only last time, he looked worried, angry even. This time, he looks stoic, almost ill.

"Are you okay?" he says.

I give him a long look, then hand him my water. "Here. I look better than you."

He gazes at it for so long I think he's not going to take it. But he does.

He makes no motion to come inside. Instead, he holds the can to his chest without drinking. "I don't know where to begin, but . . . I'm incredibly sorry. Again."

He's rubbing his temples now. He looks so upset, I grab him by the elbow and try to drag him in to sit down, but he's cemented to the spot. "Good grief, Finn. There's *nothing* to apologize for. He's one of those delusional ex-boyfriends who hangs on to your legs and declares he won't let go until you say you love him. Who doesn't have one of those?"

"I was under the impression that he broke up with you."

"He didn't."

"And he broke your heart with that—that young girl—"

"He didn't."

And when he just looks at me with this unreadable mix of emotions, I add, "Haven't you ever been told not to believe anything you hear in Hollywood? Ever?"

And then, when he *still* just flickers his gaze to the floor and keeps it there, falling into what I believe is a deathly sorrowful stare of thoughtfulness, I say the truth. "Adam and I dated for a few months, but when I decided to leave the relationship, he"—I tread carefully here, then say lightly—"struggled. He was also under the impression that it would help his reputation and career if he was the one to leave me, and I was happy to help him out. We kept the breakup a secret for a couple of months, he met that girl you spoke of and began dating her, and voilà. The story went public. The only trouble is that he apparently is not over me, and, well. You can see how he lets his emotions get the best of him."

"Do we need to help you get a restraining order?" Finn says, rubbing his temple. Honestly, he looks so frazzled by the entire situation it's a wonder he gets through life.

I laugh. "Against Adam? No. He'd never hurt a fly." Finn looks dead serious, so I add, "Or even threaten to hurt a fly. He's just dramatic. He . . ." I pause for the right words. "Feels feelings very intensely."

There's silence.

A couple passes by in the hall, and we stand there, mouths shut. He holds the can of sparkling water awkwardly.

At last, I bend down slightly to catch his downcast eyes. "Finn. It's okay."

"I did it," he says suddenly. "I was the one who thought it would be good to have him on the show." There's a long pause. "We'd done it several times with other real-life couples on set. Viewers always loved to see them on-screen. And you two brought so much attention. And I thought, well, I didn't think it was going to be this intense. A little awkward, of course. But nothing . . . well, nothing like that."

"Finn." I touch his hand. It's as cold as the can, nearly as sweaty too. Gosh, he's really worked up about this. A thousand words fly through my head. What can I say to get him to calm down, to see reason, to help him understand this is not the end of the world? It really *wasn't* the nicest idea to throw my feelings under the bus for the sake of ratings, but it also wasn't all that over the top. In the end I settle on this: "I forgive you."

That one lands.

And he looks up.

"No, Lavender. I very much do not deserve your forgiveness."

"Maybe, maybe not," I say, "but that's the beauty of forgiveness. You don't get the say. I do. And I say"—I shrug—"I forgive you. Life's much too short for me to hang on to resentment, especially as none of us is perfect. But for future reference, I don't recommend throwing your actors' personal lives into the script for the sake of ratings. I mean, at least ask us next time."

He runs a hand through his hair. "I don't know . . . what I was thinking . . ."

Oh for goodness' sake.

"C'mon, Finn. We all get caught up in our heads sometimes. I got a little caught up a few years ago. Swept up in"—I gesture around the room, stopping at one of the (admittedly many) shiny golden Emmys I'm currently using as an earring holder—"all this. For quite a few years, I made the mistake of believing this was more than pretty plastic."

He frowns. "That's actually dipped in gold, Lavender. And no, you didn't."

"Hand on heart, I did," I reply. "For a bit, I really believed I was something else."

Suddenly it clicks. *That's* what draws me to him. He has never once looked at me and seen the person I am not. This entire time he has seen me for exactly who I am: just an average person.

An average soul among billions of average souls—and together this way, on this even plane, we are all somehow extraordinary.

"You are *far* too hard on yourself," I say. "Everyone deludes themselves a little when they want what they want. It starts with a little white lie to ourselves, then another one, then a bit bigger one. People rationalize their actions all the way up to genocide, if we want to be grim. You *hardly* can beat yourself up for making a misstep for the sake of the show."

He's shaking his head, so I add, "Or even just for the sake of making yourself look good. You know," I say, "when I first landed the role of Ashley, I promised myself that Hollywood wouldn't change me. I would be the same person, the same Lavender Rhodes—"

"Your name's Mary—"

"Come off it; it's my middle name. I have a point here," I say. "I would be the same person my parents raised me to be. But someone can only serve you as a human side table for your cup of coffee for so long before it starts to get to you. If you let it. And it started to get to me. People laughed at my jokes while they whizzed around doing my hair and makeup, Finn."

He screws his brows together. "I'm . . . not following."

"I'm not that funny. A little funny, sure. But not *that* funny."

At this I see his lips twitch, the tiniest bit of a smile starting to break through the clouds. I grin.

"I mean," I continue, "they'd howl at one-liners you'd chuck your writers out for. D'you know how terrible it was?"

He lifts a brow. "Must have been agony."

"It actually *was*. Because," I say, then pause for emphasis, "suddenly one day I found myself believing it was real. That I *was* hilarious, wasn't I? That I *was* just so extraordinarily witty and pretty and talented and all of these ridiculous things, that I maybe did deserve a human who would hold my cup of coffee for three hours while another did my hair. That maybe I was the best thing since sliced bread."

"I don't disagree that would be annoying. But, Lavender—"

"It's a simple enough leap from there, Finn. I became mean." He starts to interject when I rush on, "Nothing outright, maybe, but subtle enough to get what I wanted. People took on menial tasks for me and I *let them*. People were thrown to the back of the queue on my account. And I *let it happen*. But then someone close to me got sacked over something so stupid that I had let happen. And when I saw how it shattered them, the glass shattered for me as well. I woke up. And since then, I've made it my highest priority to keep things in perspective. It's why I choose not, at this point in my life, to live in Hollywood Hills. Or have a PA. Or do a lot of the things I could get away with. Some people can handle it just fine, but it wasn't good for me."

I take a breath, remembering.

"Speaking of," I say. "I need to find Sonya before she gives the story to CNN. Walk me out?"

I'm not sure he's going to let himself off the hook.

There's an expression on his face as he looks at me. Something I've never seen on him before. His forehead has this long, thin crease across the middle, and his eyes are studying me as if I'm a porcelain doll come to life.

He's silent the whole way out.

Too silent.

Downright broody.

I'm going to have to help him get over this, I can tell.

At the building's exit, I stop him.

"You know what? I've been on the hunt for a way to make it up to you for that trapdoor incident. Now, it probably doesn't carry the same weight, given the whole surgery—"

"Double surgery."

I wince. "—but how about we call it even?"

He's shaking his head. "Forget about it, Lavender. You didn't even *mean* to hurt me. I'm the one—"

"I'll throw in a bonus," I say, smile widening. "Consider it your lucky day, Finn Masters, because I've got a winner of an opportunity for you."

He looks dubious. "What is it?"

"Bernie misses his buddy. Miles, *of course*, feels the same. So how about I'll bring lunch, and we'll have a puppy playdate to make amends?"

Chapter 18

Finn

Never again.

I'm done.

I tried multiple paybacks and failed every time. There is quite possibly no quicker way to sober up than to see the fall-out of your revenge and realize how horribly out of control your head is.

Yes, I suppose I can call it what it was. Revenge.

And to see her reaction to it all, her face as Adam drew near and then clutched her.

She was frightened.

Actually frightened.

And I caused that.

I caused her breath to come in quick pinches and her chest to rise and fall rapidly while her face looked like a sheet of paper.

She put on a brave face and tried to play it off, but there was no getting around it: I was to blame for this. And maybe he wouldn't hurt a fly, but the fact is I meddled in things I knew nothing about and would be absolutely to blame if he *did*.

Maybe she could forgive me, but I couldn't.

Yes, spending an afternoon with Lavender is just like playing

Russian roulette, but I owe her now. And I'll show up for every playdate she wants if it makes up for my actions.

"Oh, you didn't!" she cries when I show up at the park. "This is adorable." Lavender grabs the plaid bandanna from me. "Bernie!" she cries, clapping her hands. Bernie, who is racing around a twig of a tree with no end in sight, makes no sign of coming. She waves the bandanna. "*Bernie!*"

She goes on like this until at last I give a whistle for Miles, so high-pitched the squirrel digging through the bag of popcorn near the trash can a few yards off lifts his head. Miles, who has been leisurely watching Bernie circle the tree, perks up, pulls back slowly on his legs to standing, and begins walking toward me.

Bernie, of course, sees his friend is moving and comes barreling straight for us.

He barrels into my legs and knocks over my tumbler of coffee. Coffee pours out the side, and I quietly right it.

"Here, Bernie, look what we've got for you. Now stay still," Lavender says.

Bernie has gotten quite a bit bigger since I first met him, and from the looks of it, so has his puppy behavior. He jumps up on Lavender half a dozen times, each time stamping paw prints of orange dust along her white denim capris. She doesn't seem to mind, but then, given the massive holes in her dusky-blue jumper, I'm not surprised.

"What a *good dog. Good dog.*"

I raise my brow. Look away.

"What?" she says suspiciously.

"Nothing," I reply, reaching for my tumbler. I take a sip of what's left, which is now only a single drop.

Lavender goes on trying to tie the bandanna around Bernie's neck, but he twists this way and that.

At last I exhale.

"Bernie," I say, reaching into my pocket. I pull out a chew toy.

It looks like a penguin and squeaks with the barest of pressure. Miles hates this kind of stuff (he's far too mature). But I figured—and it seems I am correct given how Bernie lunges for it—the toy was right up the puppy's alley. As he gathers it in his jaws, I quickly wrap the bandanna around his neck, knotting it once before letting go and sitting back.

"Oh, look at *you*!" Lavender cries, and there she is, phone pulled out and snapping pictures as if her fingers are on fire.

One side of my mouth lifts in the tiniest flicker of a smile.

"What?" Lavender asks, jerking her head my way.

I note her finger hasn't stopped tapping for pictures.

"Nothing," I say. "It's just, when you talk to him you sound like a doll who's inhaled a helium balloon."

She draws herself up. "I do not."

"Don't take offense," I say, then point to the woman across from us, who is crouched low, taking photos of her Shih Tzu as it passes through a green tube and squealing as if her dog has just saved someone from drowning. "All of you do it, pretty much."

She raises a brow. "All of us *who*?"

"Enthusiastic puppy owners," I reply.

"Well, there I've got you then, because this isn't *my* dog." Lavender lowers her phone a little, casting what appears to be her first true glance around since we got to the dog park. We're at the same one as before, the one she referred to as "our neighborhood park" on the phone, as though we frequent Lake Hollywood Park together instead of this being what it really is: our second meeting there.

It's more crowded today, what with the March weather creeping into the low seventies and the skies being a cloudless blue. The Hollywood Sign on the hill glints beneath the 3:00 p.m. sunshine. Right on cue, some woman who has just set a dark chocolate Labrador puppy onto the grass beside a pink bowl labeled *Glamorous* in rhinestones begins clapping and cheering it on like she's swallowed a squeak toy when the dog lowers its head and takes a sip.

"It's your dog," I say.

"No." Lavender shakes her head. "I'm just fostering him. He's Sonya's."

"Did Sonya name him?"

"No, but Bernie is the perfect name. Of course she'd approve."

"Does she buy him dog food?"

"It's twenty dollars," Lavender says, giving me an I-know-what-you're-doing look. "Do you know how high my tab is from her? I once *sank her boat*."

I pause. "I'd like to circle back to that story sometime. But to my point: Does Bernie sleep on your bed?"

"Yes, but dang it." She drops her head. Clenches her fists. "Fine. If you must know, I'm starting to believe he's my dog." She raises a finger at me as I start to grin. "But I'm not allowed a dog on the lease, so I'd like to think of it as . . . fostering," she says airily, wiggling her fingers in the air. "I'm helping a friend out. So let's just keep this between you and me."

I laugh incredulously as a little *ding* goes off in my head. How many secrets do I know now about this woman? With me, she's a walking, talking open book. But another, more important question intrudes. "Hang on. Are you telling me you don't own your flat?"

Lavender shakes her head.

"You're *leasing*?" It's less a question than a statement of incredulity, a statement that's so hard to grasp I have to say the words and test them out in the air. "Why on earth are *you* leasing?" I raise my hand. "And for that matter, why are *you* afraid to tell your landlord about the dog? You can't actually be afraid he'd kick *you* out."

"I'm leasing because it made financial sense to try out a new part of the city before buying anything here. I'd rather not pay the Realtor fees and taxes unless I'm certain I love the area. So I'm on a month-to-month lease. And as for being afraid he'll kick me out, I'm *absolutely* afraid he may kick me out. Bernie's a big dog, and . . ." We both glance at Bernie, who is aggressively attempting to shred the penguin.

I know four secrets now. Might as well go for five.

"Alright," I say. "Lay it straight. Are you a gambling addict?"

"What?" Her voice pitches up. "No."

"Do you have a shopping problem? Are you secretly addicted to eccentric million-dollar emeralds in the shape of candy or whatever?" She stares at me, and I throw a hand out. "Or perhaps you accidentally purchased an island or something and now you have to scrimp in order to get by until you can sell?" I pause, then frown, looking at her quite seriously. "Are you being stalked and this is how you stay undercover? Oh!" With another flash of insight, I add, "Or is there something hidden there? Deep inside the walls? And you're tearing the place apart while you hunt for it?"

Lavender laughs, a fresh, bright laugh that makes the gloss on her pink lips shimmer. She shakes her head at me, her eyes smiling. "This keeps you up at night, does it?"

"Oh. Some things do. Not this."

I say it without thinking. She looks puzzled for a moment, but then her face clears. Which is a relief, because I really couldn't say the truth: she has been the one keeping me up. She's the one who invades all my thoughts these days.

She shrugs. "I have the flat because I like the baklava."

She says it with such simplicity. As though *of course* one would trade multimillion-dollar views for a chance to hop downstairs to have your daily cuppa with a nice Lebanese family.

"What about those views? You don't miss them?" I ask.

"No. After I got out of that scrape a few years ago, I did a complete overhaul of my life to make sure it wouldn't happen again. I also felt . . . oddly . . . you remember when Headmaster Tucker hired that hypnotist during exam week to try to lighten the mood and got us all believing that massive basketball player—"

"Trent Howensky."

"—was hypnotized to believe he was allergic to basketballs?"

"Coach Blevins was furious—they had championships the following week."

"Well, it was a bit like that. When I snapped out of it, I really snapped out of it."

"You . . . became allergic to fame and fortune."

"I became allergic to inauthenticity," she corrects, smiling up at me. "I'd rather live in a world where people throw birthday parties with homemade cake and spaghetti smashed together on the same paper plate. I don't need my lonely bedroom wall to slide open to a pool I never use."

"You had that?" I say incredulously.

"I want a dog park I can walk to. I want neighbors who can look into my windows whether I like it or not—"

"Okay, but really? Blinds are a good home staple—"

"I want *community*," she says, overtaking my words. "And a life I haven't got to worry about turning into a pool of soggy sand if and when I stop acting. Or get my first wrinkle. Or the show ends. So as of three Novembers ago, I decided to finally do something about it. And I haven't looked back."

Her smiling eyes look up into mine, and I feel, just for a moment, like time stops.

I take in all of her, from her bright, wonderful eyes to her bright, wonderful words.

Then she blinks. "And before you think I'm getting all philosophical on you, frankly, if I ever wanted to see that view again, I can just pop over to Sonya's. It looks like a castle, you know. She has gargoyles."

"That doesn't surprise me in the least. And you . . ." I hesitate. It seems like I'm pressing this point, but really, I'm having such a hard time getting over it, I just want to ask one more time. "You really don't miss the gargoyle lifestyle? Not one bit?"

"There's a man who sits on my front steps who looks like a gargoyle. His name is Cyle. So look at it how you want, but my gargoyle talks, and hers is concrete. Now, c'mon."

And that's the end of the conversation. Because next thing I know, she's pushing herself to standing, then turning and grabbing my hand with, "Show me that trick you do where you get Miles not to chew up your shoe."

"Ah yes. The don't-chew-my-shoe trick," I repeat. "That one is popular among the trainers."

"That's the one."

And for the next hour, I do.

Because after that grand, terrible mistake on set with Adam Glassner, I ran up the white flag. I gave up.

I recognized I lost.

I'm terrible at paybacks, and more importantly, she is not at all the person I suspected for so long. Even more important, I've learned I'm not the person I thought I was either.

I'm worse.

Up till now, I thought I was doing a pretty decent job at life. I call home every week. Remember my parents' birthdays. Drive the speed limit. Check on my neighbors with meticulous care. But with this? With everything revolving around Lavender Rhodes, I've failed spectacularly.

All this time I suspected she was the villain. But it was *me*.

I was the villain.

And I owe her now.

So. If she wants to take Bernie to the park? Sure.

If I see a little bandanna as I pass a shop window and think she will enjoy it for her pup, so be it.

I will go the distance with her, whatever she wishes.

Well, to a point.

Because when the blindfold was ripped from my eyes during that exchange in her dressing room two weeks ago, something else happened. Not only did I realize just how crippled my own bitterness made me, but I realized how wonderful she is.

Wonderful.

Whereas I've clung to every rotten moment, she lets trespasses slip through her fingers like sand.

Whereas I've spent countless nights staring down at my journal, writing down my woes, she spends her nights looking up, counting the stars.

I grumble; she cheers.

I grimace; she smiles with eyes as bright as the sun.

Somehow I have become darkness, and she is light.

And of course, darkness cannot mix with the light.

Which is why no matter how tempting, I will never hit on her. Despite how I feel looking at her now, with her hair pulled into a ponytail, standing barefoot on the grass as she clings to her leather sandal in a tug-of-war with Bernie, laughing and imploring me yet again to come to her aid.

I will not flirt, despite how aware I am of her every move.

I will look the other way at work, disregarding how I feel whenever Kye rests his arm across her shoulders and whispers something in her ear.

I will never suggest we have anything more than platonic friendship, no matter how caring or thoughtful she is, or whether she might look out for me with that same ferocity she uses to care for others. I have never understood it until now. I know why Sonya and Kye and everyone else in the world treasures and protects her.

I will happily be someone who admires her from a distance.

I will be, if she wishes it, her friend.

"Did you see that? He's sitting!" Lavender cries, swiveling

on her heel. Both her hands are covering her mouth, eyes bright and wide.

The truth is, she has been trying to get Bernie to sit for half an hour. I've managed to do it several times, while she has been successful only in getting him to bounce around with springs for legs while nipping at the elbows of her jumper. She was getting discouraged and needed a win.

So yes, I might have stood behind her, motioning with my hand for him to sit.

Discreetly I toss a treat his way. "Look at that," I say.

"Yes," she says in breathy excitement. "Oh, there's my shoe. I'm going to get it," she says, pointing to her sandal currently stashed beside a tree.

"No," I say. It's one thing to stand there barefoot in the middle of a dog park, and another thing to dodge the miscellaneous gifts left by less conscientious dog owners. "Let me."

As I hand the sandal to her, the two teens who followed us home catch my eye from behind a tree. "I see your entourage is here again. I have to hand it to them, they're getting better. Didn't spot them until now."

"Oh, they're not with me today, they're"—and then she turns around, sees the boys, and drops down onto the bench. A moment later I feel her hand grab mine and tug me to do likewise. "Duck," she urges.

I pause, trying not to laugh at Lavender, who has pulled her legs up onto the bench and is bending over as if trying to melt into it. But she looks so insistent, I, a bit clumsily, fold up like an accordion as well.

"How are you doing this? You're a human pretzel," I say, trying without success to get my nose anywhere near my bent legs like she has done.

"Sonya must be here," she whispers, and peeks one eye over the bench for a millisecond.

"Your best friend, Sonya. That Sonya."

"My very persistent best friend, Sonya, yes. Now if you please, just lower your neck here. That's it." I feel her hand behind my neck as if she is some poor yoga instructor trying to press my head to the ground.

"I'm almost entirely sure my neck was not made to go this way," I manage to say. "Is pinching normal?"

"Perfectly normal."

Several seconds pass.

"The right side of my body is going numb—"

"Shhh." She peeks over the bench.

Her fingers press against my lips. Startled by the intimate touch, I do indeed quiet. They smell of the honeysuckle lotion I saw her rub on her hands from the tube in her pocket. Her nails are a robust pink, with several chips. She's wearing gold bands, but there's one ring on her right ring finger that catches my attention. I recognize the crest.

The seal of a lion, surrounded by a circle of holly and the word *veritas*. An unfurling scroll beneath holding the words *Welling School*.

Her secondary-school ring.

A touch of home. She wears it, all these years later?

"Why are you afraid of her?" I whisper through her fingers, because apparently, this is what we do now: crouch down on public benches like schoolchildren.

"Because she's an incredibly considerate person who cares about my well-being."

I frown. "And that's . . . bad."

"When she kidnaps you by telling you you're going to lunch, and then suddenly you're at an open house touring an estate in her neighborhood every time a house comes on the market, yes."

"But you just said you love your flat. The gargoyle and the spaghetti on paper plates and all that."

"Yes, yes," she whispers hurriedly. "But sometimes there are helicopter pads and hanging grapevines. And Sonya can be very convincing in making you think to yourself, *Why, what about that vague future moment when I'm in a scrape and really could do with a helicopter pad?* and *What else could I possibly do to entertain house-guests if I didn't have that personal vineyard from which to offer a bowl of homegrown grapes?*"

"She's your friend. Just say no."

"Have you ever heard someone successfully say no to her?"

I grin. She has a point there.

Her hand has slipped slightly. Her fingers rest now upon my cheek, her palm cupping the bristles of my five o'clock shadow. She hasn't noticed. I don't move.

For several seconds, I just watch her and the way she holds her breath as she spies over the bench. Her other hand curls over the top of the weather-beaten wood, and for a moment I can imagine what she did after school as a child, running through neighboring backyards, playing games behind bushes. There's a light in her eyes, a childlike glee that outsparks anything she's conjured for the telly. The world may get to enjoy the flat-screen version of Lavender Rhodes, but the real-life version is ten times more vivid.

She has somehow made magic out of the monotonous.

She has turned an ordinary adult day in a dog park into something extraordinary.

And . . . I love it.

I just . . . love it.

"She's coming, she's coming!" she hisses, and drops her hand from my lips. She uncrosses her legs to plant them on the ground and begins rooting aimlessly in her purse. "Look natural!"

"You do realize that technically I am her boss, right?"

And then she elbows me, literally elbows me, right in the gut. "Are you trying to get yourself killed?"

I grin while hunching over for an entirely new reason. "And you do realize you just elbowed your boss too, right? I could get you suspended," I add, then grin wider at her second attempted blow.

"And here she is. Surprise surprise."

I have to admit, Sonya does look a bit like a mob boss as she stands in all white, flanked by two teenagers. Her black hair is in a high slippery ponytail, glossy and long, wrapped in a braid. It looks like a whip. Her long, slim white trench coat is spotless, as are her white pants and white nails. Her sunglasses are enormous. Her foot taps on the dead grass.

"Oh! Hey, Sonya," Lavender says in a startled tone, one hand in her bag. Lavender's acting skills are clearly coming into play here, as every feature on her face rearranges itself into complete and utter innocent, easygoing surprise. She pulls out the penguin squeak toy (we had to hide it from Bernie, as the squeak was turning him into a maniac) as if it is precisely what she has been looking for. "Did you come to visit your pup?"

"He's not my pup," Sonya replies automatically, then taps her phone. "And you're avoiding me."

Lavender gives a breathy laugh as though the notion is absurd. "I'm at a dog park. I'm refreshingly unplugged." She holds her hand out toward the skies. "It's a beautiful day. Isn't it a beautiful day?"

"Yes, it is," Sonya says, frowning. "Just like I said in my text message you left unread, which said," she adds, punctuating each word, "'It. Is. A. Beautiful. Day. I have a great idea. Let's go to Grizzby's and grab dinner on their patio.'"

"Oh yes," Lavender says faintly, putting up her finger. "That *is* a nice idea. But . . ."

"But what? You have a date?"

"No," she says. She stands.

"Is the lasagna too rich for you? Would you rather eat stale potato chips at home?"

"No, we both know the lasagna is magnificent."

"Is the patio too whimsical? Are the rose petals floating in those little cups of water to dip your fingers into between courses too soggy? Is that warm washcloth woven in the Peruvian mountains and placed over your face before the first course too moist?"

"No, you know I always say, 'This is the best moment of my life.'"

"Oh. So you just *want* to wait for another reservation in three months then. You just like waiting."

I get it now.

Lavender drops her head. "You know I think having to be patient is the worst form of torture."

Incredible.

She is going to give in.

I can see it written across her face plain as day. She's even taking tiny steps toward Sonya, drawn in against her will.

Good grief. Sonya really was cast into the wrong genre.

I put my foot out.

Lavender halts when she touches it.

"You're forgetting the thing we have tonight, Lavender," I say meaningfully. I turn to Sonya. "I'm sorry, your dinner sounds lovely, but Lavender's made a commitment."

Lavender blinks in surprise.

Sonya's head jerks my way. "What thing?"

My brain scrambles for something. "Dinner." The last thing I want is to make this sound like a date, so I add, "With my neighbor. It's her eighty-first birthday and she's having me over tonight, and"—I incline my head to Lavender—"when Lavender heard she's such a fan of the show, she agreed to come as well. To surprise her. You know how Lavender is such a good sport."

"So . . . a date. With you and your neighbor. Who's eighty."

"Eighty-one. And no," I reply, almost too quickly.

I hear a terrier's claws across the park scratching into the dirt.

My eyes flick briefly over to Lavender, but she's such a good actress she's not even remotely giving anything away. Unsurprising, but it leaves me with the task of assuming this is what she wants. And hoping that I'm not making a deeper mess for her.

I charge on, remembering her plea moments ago. Frankly, the crick in my neck from hunching down on the bench is reminder enough.

"It's really just a work thing," I say, which I immediately realize is the wrong thing to say.

Sonya's antenna shoots in the air.

"You're discussing *contracts*?" she accuses.

Lavender jumps in with a shake of her head. "No, Sonya. Nothing that serious. It's just a date."

Sonya's eyes dart from her to me. Her mouth—open, ready, and pressurized like a water hose about to be directed onto a burning building—takes several seconds to close again.

"So . . . a date," Sonya says slowly, suspiciously. "A secret date. And you didn't tell me."

She pivots on her heel, facing Lavender head-on. Arms crossed. The two boys flanking her at a distance apparently think it is a good idea to imitate her.

"But that makes sense. Why tell me when you should only be sharing this kind of news with your *best friend*." She taps a toe on the ground. "Oh, wait."

Lavender opens her mouth. And frankly, I have no more clues than Sonya does as to what Lavender will say. "Well." She throws her hands up in the air with a smile. "If you gave me more than five minutes between us making these plans and your arrival, you would've heard the news. But as we have made these plans *just now*, it was a little challenging. Here"—she slips her phone out of her pocket, taps madly for about fifteen seconds, and then slips it back into her pants.

Sonya's phone dings.

Sonya pulls it out. Reads with a monotone: "*I'm going on a secret date tonight with Finn. As best friend with first and only rights, you are the first and only to know.*"

She looks up from her phone.

She's frowning, but sure enough her eyes are a little less sharp.

She really is a bit mollified.

"So you two then," she says, pointing between us appraisingly. Her eyes are narrow. "I can't say I'm surprised. I've seen the way you've acted the past month."

My eyes flicker towards Lavender to catch her expression, and I inhale a self-accusing breath despite myself. She apparently has the same idea, because our eyes meet and bounce off each other like atoms in a great cloud of steam.

Exactly which *you* is she referring to?

Sonya rolls her eyes as if to say, *See? I mean, it's obvious.* But instead of explaining, she says in a disbelieving tone, "So you two. Plus your neighbor. For a date."

"That's right," Lavender says, taking a step toward me and slipping her hand around my elbow. "It's a cultural thing where we're from. The tradition goes back hundreds of years."

She looks to me, and I add, "I've read fifteen hundred, but we can beg to differ."

"So . . . ," Sonya says slowly. "Some kind of courtship thing. An eighty-year-old chaperone for you two adults . . ." She's squinting now.

"He's more keen on it than I was," Lavender says and leans toward me. "He's more traditional than I am."

Sonya turns her attention to me with even narrower eyes. I hesitate but feel Lavender squeeze my arm.

"I'm very old-fashioned like that," I chime in.

"Romantic," Sonya says flatly.

Lavender bites her lip as she attempts to hold back a smile, and

I feel a flash of inspiration as I add, "All my aunts have done it this way and were married off in the first six months. We call it the Brits' Lucky Charm."

I can't help it.

I grin as Sonya's expression grows alarmed.

Her eyes flicker over to Lavender as if to say, *Do you need help escaping this lunatic?*

Lavender, though, presses in deeper to my side and then tucks her chin towards me, looking up fondly as she murmurs, "Now wouldn't that just be something?"

"Does tradition encourage a second guardian here? Because I'd like to volunteer," Sonya says loudly.

My eyes lock onto hers, and simultaneously we say, "No."

My face is tight from smiling and holding in the pressure that has built in my chest, caused by the urge to laugh. Lavender's cheeks are burning red.

"Alright then," Sonya says, curtly pushing her phone into her pocket. "Well, I'll leave you two to it, so you can have your granny date and then call your parents with the big news."

We give a stilted laugh and she gives a stilted laugh, and then she stops abruptly and points a finger in my face. "There'd better not be any *big news*."

As Sonya walks (stalks?) off, I shift on my heel.

"Sorry about that," I begin, just as Lavender starts with an apology.

We both give an airy, awkward chuckle, and she motions for me to go ahead.

"You said you needed help, so I took a leap. I . . . hope you aren't offended."

"Offended? It was *brilliant*," she exclaims. "Oooh, time to wave."

With her arm still wrapped around mine, we look up at Sonya

in the distance. She has turned and is giving us a suspicious look. We wave.

"This'll save you for tonight at least. I assume she'll be calling you this evening?"

"Oh, I have no doubt I'll be getting messages within ten minutes. An irate one because I hadn't clued her in; one asking what happened to Jonathan, that bloke I went out with the other day; one telling me to text back the code phrase if I need saving—it's 'Zinnias always save the day' if you want to know; and one insisting on every detail the moment I get home."

Honestly, I'm like a bucket for her secrets.

"D'you realize that makes at least five secrets you've told me?" I blurt. "You know, Lavender, they really aren't secrets if you share them with everyone."

"I don't share them with everyone." She pauses. Tweaks her brow. Her eyes dance a little as she cocks her head. "So. You're keeping count then?"

I shrug in an it's-hardly-important manner.

"Does it . . . make you feel good?" she says, leaning deeper into my side. "Is it nice to know I find you trustworthy?"

Her eyes are doing a full-on jig now, and I find my chest tightening under the compliment. Although, it's not fair to accept, is it? When I've actually just recently attempted to stab her in the back?

Despite myself, I feel the need to puncture the helium balloon that is my heart. To sabotage myself against hope. "So who is this Jonathan?"

"Oh, he's the forty-year-old I went out with the other day. Hates karaoke, though. There is no future for me with a man who hates karaoke."

"Too bad," I say wryly. "I hate karaoke."

"Extraordinarily good news for you then. Because for chaps

who can keep five secrets, I can make exceptions." She pats my arm with her free hand, then reaches down for her purse—taking me, I note, along with her instead of letting go. I bend with the tiniest resistance and hold on as a fresh wave of her hair tosses over my shoulder as she stands back up. She calls over her shoulder, "C'mon, Bernie."

"Where are you going, really?" I ask, letting her walk us toward the park gate.

"Are you really dining with your neighbor tonight?"

"Yes."

"And is she really a fan?"

"Three of her cats are named Lavender. But to be fair, she owns a lot of cats."

"Well then, it's settled, isn't it? I'm your plus-one."

"*This* is your flat?"

There's shock in her voice and I turn around, pausing with keys in hand, dry cleaning over one shoulder.

She's holding a bottle of wine and a bag of knafeh in her hands, and the bag with the bottle is drooping as she stares up at the old building.

"Yes," I say, unsurprised by her reaction.

The building is pretty well-known. Built in the early 1920s by the renowned architects Arthur and Nina Zwebell, Casa Laguna may be old, and less convenient than the modern high-rises with their fancy amenities, but it's well loved.

Eighteen Andalusian-style flats circle a courtyard, where a tired but functional pool sits among palm trees and terra-cotta pots brimming with succulents.

"You'll have to look out," I say, opening the door to let her and

Miles walk through. "Mrs. Teaberry has gotten the gang started on a carnivorous garden club."

"Oh," she says, cautiously stepping around several pots and beginning down the herringbone brick path leading to the center of the courtyard. "Like that one?" she says, pointing to a vibrant plant trailing up one wall.

"No, like that Venus flytrap by your foot. She keeps telling me they only eat flies, but I'm certain I felt one snapping at my ankle last week. This way."

I unleash Miles and step gently around Lavender. The brick path is narrow, and I find myself touching her shoulder lightly as I pass.

She bristles, her reaction just a flicker beneath my palm.

Not that I *care*—of course I *don't care*—but why does she bristle?

She dodges the oversized Venus flytrap, its vibrant pink needlelike teeth poised to strike.

Was that why her shoulders tensed? Or was it me?

"And who else lives in the building?" she asks casually, turning her head at the various mustard-yellow doors and mint-green stucco walls. "Any other writers?"

"Writers?" I say through a laugh while flipping the key-ring for my key. "Well, Sherry keeps saying she's putting out a novel, but apparently she's been saying that the past fifty years. No. Just me."

I step beneath the little awning that spans my and Mrs. Teaberry's doors, then reach down to move aside the water bowl Miles sometimes drinks from. It's five twenty already, thanks to Lavender insisting I walk her back to her flat to drop off Bernie. She insisted I stay with her, actually, as though afraid I was going to dash off the second we parted and then never relay my address.

Which, to be fair, I might have done—but for her sake as well as mine. It was one thing to rescue her from the clutches of her well-meaning best friend.

It was another to let the little charade go on any longer than that.

And as I absolutely have no intention of telling her directly why I feel it's impossible for us to match up, and as it is *very* possible that she, being the social butterfly, has no intention or real interest anyway, seeing each other more than absolutely necessary will only muddle things further.

Really, because everything is complicated with her.

Because nothing, not a single thing, is simple.

"We'd best get a move on. Show starts in ten minutes, and they get cranky if I'm not there for the start of it."

"They?"

"Well, yes. On Saturday nights, it's more of a they. You'll see."

"So who else lives here then?" she says, pulling up behind me, her back towards me as she scans the courtyard and its surrounding doors. "A lot of people our age?"

I step up to the door.

"I'm the youngest by half a century. The complex is rent-controlled. Once people get into Casa Laguna, they stay. I lucked out years ago when I hit it off with one of the temp actors and he tipped me off about the place before he moved." I wave my key around. "So essentially, it's me and a bunch of senior citizens. And just wait. You'll see how I spend Saturday nights since I got on *Neighbors*. You'd think I was"—I pause—"well, you. Which is why this is going to be fun." I raise one finger. "Just . . . try not to give anyone a heart attack. Bill just got his pacer in. Don't"—I wave my hand around—"touch him. And try not to be so—"

She raises a brow. "So what?"

"You know. So . . . magical. Maybe don't smile directly at him."

"Be less magical and dispense smiles at palm trees. Got it." She reaches down and gives Miles a distracted rub on the head, her attention still facing the courtyard. "So . . . just you then. And you've been here for quite some time."

I'm just putting my key in the lock when she says this.

And then it clicks.

So . . . this is the cause of her bristling.

I take a breath, my eyes on the knob, mind calculating what and how much to say. "Why?"

"I just know someone who used to date someone in this building. She said he essentially lived in a—"

"—in assisted living. Yes. How is Delilah?"

I turn around just in time to see Lavender's mouth pop open. Mrs. Teaberry's door swings open and five women burst out, each carrying casseroles and bowls covered in aluminum.

"Oh, Finn," Mrs. Teaberry says, "Jack just picked up a projector and he's heading this way now. We're moving the party outsi—"

Then Mrs. Teaberry locks eyes on Lavender.

And the entire set of ladies collapses.

Chapter 19

Lavender

I ordered them pizza.

I had to. I insisted.

They fought me on it, but I put my foot down.

And frankly, they were so busy rubbing salsa off their clothes and rushing to their respective flats to find new clothes, they didn't fight me too much on it.

But honestly, to watch five women go down like that, bowls of coleslaw and casserole dishes flying in a mass of hysterics, well. I wouldn't have believed it could be done.

After gathering up the last woman and helping her to her door, Finn puts his hands in his pockets and turns on his heel to face me. "So. We're going to need a new plan to introduce you to Bill."

So, with apparently *much* explanation and forewarning about my presence, Finn and I make our way to the center of the courtyard, where we meet a few more tenants and help set up the projector. Finn proves to be much more technologically inclined than they are, and I prove to be terribly good at gathering patio chairs, and so within thirty minutes, we are all seated beneath the dimming pale blue sky. The courtyard smells thickly of hairspray and perfume (as each woman has apparently decided to give herself a dozen fresh spritzes), pepperonis, and a hint of daffodils, Dutch hyacinths, and early tulips—all flowers that border the walkways. Lights are strung merrily across the projector, and the cerulean pool glints as it laps lightly against the Spanish tile.

In short, it is twice as lovely as Grizzby's on the patio with its three-month waiting list, and frankly, I can think of no other place I'd rather be.

Mrs. Teaberry insists we sit in the two folding chairs provided—and moments later every chair in the place is occupied and huddled around us, as if we are the center of a sunflower and they are the petals surrounding us.

One might even say boxed in. It would be absolutely impossible to get out.

Which is all fine, as everyone passes down offers of pizza slices about every two minutes.

But the best part of the evening is when the show begins.

"You know, I never watch this," I murmur quietly, leaning over to Finn as pictures of Kye clowning around on top of a dining room table flicker on-screen.

His head tilts towards mine, so close I feel the curly hair tickle my cheek. A tingle runs through my body as I smell a woodsy cologne rising from his popped collar. Which means he has dashed inside his flat and put some on somewhere between putting up the projector and laying out the lights.

For me?

"This season?" he whispers, his breath warming my cheek.

Out of the corner of my eye, I spot two elderly women watching us. And the only words I can use to describe their expressions are *maternal glee*.

"Any of it," I whisper back. "I've never seen the show before. I don't like to watch myself."

And to my surprise he laughs, then turns to look me directly in the eye.

It's the closest our faces have ever been. So close I can see little bright blue flecks in his tame green eyes. Light is dancing in them as he says, "You know, before I joined *Neighbors*, I didn't either."

"*Shhhhh.*"

We've been shushed. Actually shushed, by Mrs. Teaberry, who is watching the show—which is currently on a rather close-up view of my face—like she's never seen these people before. Absolutely enraptured.

Finn grins and starts to say something else, but Mrs. Teaberry swats his arm.

His grin deepens and he lets thirty seconds go by before leaning over again, so close his nose pushes back my hair. "Better listen to her; otherwise we'll end up having to listen to a play-by-play of all we've missed."

I chuckle quietly, tilting my head to face him. "Of the show you're writing and I'm in?"

"That's the one," he says, and settles in with his plate of pizza.

And that is when, over the course of the next half hour, I realize I've fallen for him. Really fallen.

Because there Finn sits as the show goes on, and with every single chuckle-moment, the group gives him a hearty roar followed by a dozen hearty slaps on the back. Questions bubble up at nearly every funny jab with, "I'd bet my marbles that's a Finn joke," and "That's my boy!" With every romantic turn of events, the ladies grab their literal pearls or clutch at their hearts. You'd think he was Shakespeare. You'd think this supportive crowd was watching their son take gold in the Olympics.

And with every single pat and elbow jab and quiet or loud cheer, he gives a modest little smile and says a few modest little words.

But his ears are pink.

And his cheeks and eyes are glowing.

And he has a quiet enthusiasm about this entire scene.

And that is when I realize I am all in.

Because this isn't just a sweet little get-together, do-gooder thing he does for his neighbors. He *loves* this. Truly loves this. *He loves them.* They haven't just adopted him; he has adopted them as well. I can see it in the way he so casually picked up dry cleaning on the walk here and dropped it off at Mr. Hankins's door. In the way he subtly glanced past me while I spoke, then wordlessly moved a tipped terra-cotta pot out of the way just before Mr. Phillips came by with his walker.

He can say all he wants about the unbeatable rent and high ceilings and Spanish architecture, but the fact is, *these* are his people, and he has achieved something in reality that my entire job has revolved around all these years: neighbors who are family.

Delilah had explained it to me as her boyfriend's strange obsession with living in an old folks' home, but now I see it for what it really is.

Perfection.

And frankly, if a flat came open, I'd drop my own place in a minute.

Because *this.* This is what I've been searching for since the moment I snapped awake. This . . . is real community.

And I have a feeling Finn has a lot to do with creating it.

I look at him and the cat who has found its way to his lap. He is distractedly rubbing it as he watches the show.

Apparently, I've fallen for a man who's an old soul.

Finn catches me smiling and raises a brow. "Okay?" he whispers. "They can be a bit much."

"What, the twenty people packing us in so we can't get out? No. No, it feels cozy. Like a blanket."

A woman pats my knee and points. "There's you!" she whispers energetically, just as she has every other minute of the past twenty.

"A really tight blanket," I add, grinning, "but still cozy."

"Really, Lavender. Whenever you want to go—"

"Don't try to get me to go," I say, settling back, eyes on the screen. "You couldn't get me to go if you tried."

"Oh, believe me, I've learned never to get in your way."

We watch the show a few more minutes, then after a bit I find myself tapping him in the side with my elbow. "I did like that part. That was funny."

To which he smiles and says after a pause, "You know, I did come up with that one."

"Pipe down, you two, or we're going to have to start it all over," Mrs. Teaberry calls over her shoulder. "You are taping it, aren't you, Finn?"

"Yes, ma'am," he replies, then gives me a little grin as if we are two children caught cutting up on the playground.

A few minutes pass by, but I find myself watching his arm resting on the edge of his folding chair. The cat sits on his lap, the tabby rubbing its head on his forearm, begging for attention.

I set my paper plate on the ground.

My hair falls over one shoulder as I reach in, my face just an inch from his, and then I see it. I even hear it.

How he holds the air in his chest as I pick up the black tabby cat from its perch and bring it to my seat.

"Hello, you," I whisper, settling the tabby on my lap. I shift position and swallow that last inch of space between Finn and me.

His arm matches mine, shoulder to wrist.

A minute passes.

Another.

Another.

"You stole my cat," he whispers, leaning down. His breath tickles my ear, even as the live-audience laughter booms through the speakers.

I move to reply, and my lips graze his cheek before reaching his ear. "You weren't giving him enough attention."

There's a moment's pause, and I add, "Also, I have to hand it to you, Finn. You put on a lovely date."

He laughs quietly, but the tips of his ears are stinging red. The heat?

My eyes dart to Mrs. Teaberry, who's sitting frontmost in the audience, a truly die-hard fan. "I will say, I'm not sure about your chaperone, though," I whisper. "She's not terribly good at her job, is she?"

"Well, it's a tricky thing when you've been waiting for Ashley and Lance to get engaged for a decade," he replies. "Can't be too hard on her." He puts a hand to his chest. "And to my credit, I do provide excellent backup," he says, his eyes flicking to the group around us. "According to tradition."

Someone coughs to get us to lower our voices.

I grin. "Is it always like this?"

"Always like what?"

"You know"—my eyes dance around the group—"this intense? This tight-knit a community?"

"If you're asking if we have bingo nights on Mondays, no. They're on Tuesdays. Mondays are for arguing over which terrifying plant to introduce next into the community garden."

I laugh, which causes Mrs. Teaberry's hands to fly up with demands to rewind. Finn has to remind her it isn't taped yet, so that's impossible.

"This must be nice," I whisper, after Mrs. Teaberry has turned back around. "Must feel like home away from home."

"When was the last time you went back?"

"A year ago." And my voice softens as my thoughts drift to the family left behind. "Too long."

"Agreed." His tone says he knows the feeling.

I shrug. "You know how Goodwin is now. You see. Even when the world is on holiday, he's having us work. I love it, but . . ." I take a breath. I don't like to complain. I don't like to think negatively, but this is a pain point. "I missed my childhood best friend's wedding last year. Then right when I got back to LA, Dad went in for emergency pancreatic surgery. I had a time begging off to go back. Even then, I only managed to skid in at the very last second of his hospital stay. I've got a niece who has a baptism next week. They aren't the biggest things, and he makes allowances for the truly big emergencies, but you know how it is. Everyone's a team. And when you stop, the whole machine stops. Still, though—"

"You'd like to be there, I know." Finn nods knowingly. "I have two nephews in weekly football games. I'm always hearing about them but never getting to see with my own eyes. No one in their right mind would let me take time off to travel 'cross the globe just to see one, but I would. I'd fly there in a blink.

"I'm in the same boat as you here. I'm aware of what I'm missing." He takes off his glasses. Rubs his nose. "They're little blips on the screen, these dinners and games and weddings, but all these blips put together are what makes up the video of our life."

I nod, my chest swelling as I look at him.

This man *gets it*.

This man knows better than anyone in my life, even Sonya, what it feels like to love what you do, feel grateful for what you have, but also feel such a massive hole in your heart for the world you've left behind.

He gets me.

Finn smiles lightly. "Guess we missed that day in drama class, didn't we? The consequence of traveling 'cross the globe to follow your dreams."

He puts his hand on mine.

I take in his grin, and the warmth of his eyes, and the stabilizing weight of his hand on mine, and I shake my head.

Delilah truly misrepresented this man.

Of course, Delilah also described the spa she went to on her birthday as a dump, and she had a caviar lunch there, along with a custom-made 24-karat gold facial mask. Appreciation isn't her strong suit.

"For what it's worth," I say, "you deserve better than Delilah."

He raises a brow. "Big words coming from the woman who broke us up."

I wince. "You knew about that, did you?"

He's too gallant to answer, just gives a little shrug.

I almost don't want to ask, but the question will linger forever if I don't. "How long have you known?"

"Oh," he replies, taking in a breath, "I believe your name was dropped in her breakup speech."

I squeeze my eyes shut. "Sorry about that. Not that it's any excuse, but her description of you was . . . well . . ." I struggle to find a word that doesn't knock a blow to him.

"Made me sound like a maddeningly dull, unadventurous old man who was wasting the prime years of her life on crossword puzzles and farmers markets, depriving her of the full life she deserved in the most adventurous city in the world?"

"No. Of course not."

But yes. That was exactly how she described him.

He shrugs. "Words straight from her mouth. It's okay."

I wince again. "I'm sorry. She's run in my circle a long time, but she can be . . . well. I've learned not to be surprised."

He shifts in his seat to face me fully. "Let me ask you something. What does Sonya think of her?"

I laugh at the change of course. "Why?"

"Idle curiosity."

"Well." I pause, thinking of how to say it. "She declares she's not sending Delilah any Christmas cards, if that's any indication."

The corners of his eyes crease as he smiles. "I like Sonya."

"She is the friend who would shovel the hole for me in a pinch, no questions asked."

He raises a brow.

"Which she hasn't. *Of course*," I say with a laugh. "Well. Once. But that was for an ill-timed hamster versus dog situation early on in my dog-walking days. But other than that, *absolutely not*."

"Has she said anything of me?" he says, eyeing the phone in my pocket. "This woman with such keen judgment?"

"Let's see." I slip my phone out.

My eyes run down the lines of messages.

Then fall on one, at which I pinch my lips.

He straightens. "What? What'd she say?"

"Nothing," I squeak, keeping myself from laughing as I put my phone away.

"What?"

I shake my head.

"Fine." He turns to face the show.

Seconds tick by.

I exhale.

I lean over and whisper, "She says she's done a quick background check and that I should be pleased to know you're apparently not on any list."

"Ah." He bolts his attention back to me. There's a flash in his eyes. An energy. "That is good news."

"But," I say, raising a finger, "she's also been scouring your social media the past hour and she's becoming fretful because you haven't got any online presence to speak of. Is this true?"

He shrugs. "I don't need a social presence. Look around, Lavender. I'm up to my ears in social presences."

I grin.

"Well, I think she's currently narrowing you down to psychopath or sage recluse. Either way, it's not looking good."

"What's not looking good? Tell her I'm more of a sage recluse."

"Won't help."

"Why?"

"Nothing." I pinch my lips together again.

He adjusts his glasses. Refreshes his look as he lowers his voice. "Why?"

I open my mouth, grinning despite myself. "She says you have worrying eyes."

Finn frowns. "What's the matter with my eyes?"

And then he's looking at me full in the eyes, through his big round glasses with flashes of light from the screen glinting in the blue of them. And I take in Sonya's words as I gaze into them, looking, maybe even hoping, to see what she sees.

Should I tell him what she said?

Do I dare?

"She says you have forever eyes."

And there it is.

A flash crosses his expression as his eyes turn from curious and inquisitive to surprised, and then settle into a look that makes my stomach fly all the way up to my chest. I squeeze the cat so tightly it meows against the pressure.

Admission.

A look of being found out.

A balloon swells inside me. The pressure so tight I feel it'll pop any moment.

There's silence between us, a space filled with the sound of my own televised talk, and then he leans over. "I hate to bring it up, but you are a terrible first date."

I put my hand on my chest. "Me? I just told you you were wonderful at it!"

He *tsks*. "Here I am, following all our very important traditions, having gathered chaperones by the boatload, and you go off mentioning *forever*."

"Me? You're the one giving the marry-me eyes, evidently," I retort. I laugh, which does release a bit of that pressure in my chest.

"Next up, I suppose you'll say you want children along with another slice of pizza."

"Two, actually. I would like each to have a friend. And pepperoni, please."

"Two. Very thoughtful," he replies, picking up my plate from the ground and passing it to the man beside him, who passes it down until one of the ladies drops a piece of pizza and it begins its return. "It's settled then."

He grins, then drops his arm on the armrest, skin to skin at my side.

And for the rest of the show, up to the final laugh, Finn and I stay in this position. Him keeping his hand resting on mine as if it's been stapled there. Me keeping mine there because, of course, the cat needs me not to move. At all. And as we sit side by side, eyes on the screen, I take it all in.

The glint of the pool water.

The sitcom laughter.

The pats on the backs—his and mine—and the scent of shared lemonade cookies and the purr of the long-haired tabby on my legs. And him. And me.

Daring me, it seems, to breathe.

This is really happening, isn't it?

And it feels *right*. Really *right*.

"That was *tremendous*," says a woman with friendly blue eyes and a cloud of short white curls around her head. She grabs my hand in hers and gives it a warm squeeze, a dozen gold rings pressing into my hand. "Look at you." She leans in conspiratorially, and I'm swallowed up in her perfume. "Just between us two, what happens next?"

I laugh.

It's the question I get more than anything else in life, and yet with this group, part of me really does want to answer.

"Don't be trying that, Ms. Gregory," Finn says, interjecting himself into the conversation. "You know she's under an NDA."

And then a thought forms.

An idea. I feel a swell as I nod. "True, but there is something to be said for just . . . *practicing*. Getting some work done, making sure those lines feel right"—I wave my hand around the courtyard—"in the privacy of your own home." I give a significant pause. "We can't help it if people *happen* to see."

It's amazing. For all the men and women who claimed to be hard of hearing and made Finn turn up the volume to a blaring 65, the absolute *halt* of movement and turn of heads is intense. They are children who've just been told an ice cream truck is waiting outside.

"A *show*! What a *splendid* idea!" one cries, and the next calls out after, "Quick, William, move the front chairs out of the way."

"No. Now, everyone—"

Finn goes on for a minute, trying to stop the mad shuffle that's begun, but it's no use. Eventually he gives up and lifts a brow at me. "Now look what you've done. You've got them all worked up."

"And we mustn't let them down," I say, grinning. "Think of Bill's new pacer."

"We haven't finished up the script—"

"Doesn't matter. Consider this a true work date. We're working." I nod my head to Mrs. Teaberry, who is shoving chairs out of the way faster than a Boy Scout. "All we need now is a script."

"And some actors," he says. "You expect to go up there and play all the roles yourself?"

"Of course not. Why, Finn," I reply, and know my eyes must be dancing as I reach for his hand, "let's not forget—you're an actor too."

Chapter 20

Finn

She's done it again.

Foiled every one of my plans. Shattered them into a million pieces.

Like the imaginary plate she's just thrown down between us.

Her eyes dance as she stomps her feet, mimicking, it seems, the sound of the plate that would be crashing.

"Opa?!" she cries, and there's an arch in both her brow and her tone as her eyes meet mine, one arm flung into the air and the other gripping the baby script that has existed fewer than twelve hours. It's rough to say the least.

Riddled with plot holes.

Phrases needing tightening all over the place.

Erik finished it just this morning and sent it over. I was going to take a look before we took an axe to it Tuesday morning in the writers room. It's three episodes past the show we filmed earlier this week, so baby-fresh it will be unrecognizable from the final product, which is the only reason I'm really letting us stand up here now, running roughshod over our confidentiality clause, acting it out. I may as well have pulled out a fan-fiction chapter from the Internet. It would be closer to the real thing.

"*Opa? Really?*" Lavender says under her breath as she takes my arm and begins to swing.

"Your downstairs neighbor is at a Greek wedding. We had to get Ashley and Lance together again after the zucchini incident."

"There's been a zucchini incident?" Lavender says. The world is spinning, flashes of golden light from string bulbs and faces swirling around us. The sound of the concrete fountain bubbles behind us just beyond the winding pathway, the heady scent of perfume and flowers all around. The sky is a square of black above us, dim stars blinking as though they are watching too. Just like every occupant of Casa Laguna.

And to me, it feels like the whole world.

Lavender is the only thing centered in my sights, cheeks flushed, eyes mirthful, golden curls bobbing and dancing as we spin. She's sucked me into her spell. And I can't even care anymore. At this point the intrusive thoughts whisper I should throw a dishrag over tonight and let it be how it will be.

You can try again tomorrow.

For tonight, you can pretend.

"I told you it was rough," I grunt as she elbows me in the ribs and faces the group. Her eyes drop momentarily to the script, and she tucks in her lower lip, biting it with her teeth to keep from laughing as her eyes scan the line before speaking out loud. Attempting to keep character. "Oh, Lance!" she cries shrilly, clutching her chest. "If you keep dancing with me like this, what will Patricia think?"

"Patricia comes back?" she hisses.

"An alternate reality episode," I whisper, to which she nods her head understandingly with an "ah."

"I wondered that!" Mrs. Teaberry called, pointing. "She won't like it *one bit*!"

"It's just dancing."

Lavender puts a hand on my bicep, the firmness and familiarity of her grip sending a thrill down my spine. She raises a brow. "Is it, though?" She takes a step closer, her voice husky, her eyes mirthful to the point of beginning to brim with tears. "Is it?"

I purse my lips, arching a brow of my own.

Okay.

Yes, this script is bad, but the melodrama isn't helping. "A little over the top, aren't we?" I murmur.

"But don't you wish"—she bites her lip again, tears wetting the corners of her lashes now as she fights back laughter, reading the script—"just sometimes, Lance, that this night would never end? That we could just go back in time, and do this all over again . . . the right way?"

She looks up at me, her smile as bright as the moon, her face nothing but open. All I want is to scoop her up. And yes, have this night never end.

My eyes don't flicker to the script but stay on hers. "Sometimes, yes," I say. "Sometimes in moments like this."

Our makeshift audience is completely hushed, and suddenly something shifts in Lavender's expression. A little smile tugs at the corner of her lips, and unprompted, she takes a step in. The circle has closed with my arms around her. My fingers, somehow, have found the small of her back, the softness of her eyelet top rubbing against my palm. Stray strands of her hair dance around my face, tickling my chin and cheek. Her tidewater eyes draw me in like a riptide, and suddenly I feel as though there's nothing I can do but follow the script. To the letter.

Which instructs: PASSIONATE KISS.

It feels as though she's waiting for me to.

The audience is waiting for me to.

Mrs. Teaberry with her hands clutched together, hunched over as she stands, murmuring what seems to be a chant, is waiting for me to.

Or for Lance to. To be honest, I'm not sure which.

I hesitate.

"And then . . . we kiss."

I mean to say this loudly.

I mean to let go of her and tell the group.

I mean to.

And yet here I am, realizing that I haven't released Lavender as we stand nearly nose to nose. I'm not addressing the group. Instead, I've murmured.

Lavender raises a brow. "I'm aware of the prompt, Finn."

Do not kiss her.

I hold steady.

I'm letting her go.

I'm telling her, without saying it, *We can be done now. We've played the game for everyone. We don't need to go so far as to kiss.*

With great self-control my fingers loosen their grip.

I'm moments away from releasing her entirely.

From stepping back, out of this haze, to say the show has ended.

Then a tiny crease forms between her brows. Her next words are hushed. "Oh come now, Finn. Are you a real actor or not?"

Her words break what little self-restraint I had with the force of a hammer on a sheet of glass. I close the gap between us.

Distant cheers ring around us.

My hand finds the back of her neck.

And we are kissing just like it says on the page. Passionately.

Just like Ashley and Lance should be, as they realize they have found each other once more and don't want to give each other up ever, ever again.

My lips find hers and catch fire, startled by how perfectly they mold to mine. Papers flutter to the ground as I take her by the waist and draw her closer, breathing her in. The world around us slips away until it's us. Just us. Lavender and me. As, in a way, for me, it has always been.

If I don't break this off, I'll go up in a blaze and be reduced to ash. I sweep over the softness of her cheek, the tenderness of her temple. The ear that listens to the song of the goldfinch in the morning and offers up an appreciative smile. The chin that lifts in gleeful defiance in conversation as her eyes cut my way.

I realize as we break apart that I'm breathing raggedly. "Is that enough acting for you?"

Her smile twists, face as flushed as I know mine must be. Her own chest rising and falling rapidly. "Nearly."

Nearly enough acting, or nearly enough kiss? I want to ask, but instead I scoop up the fallen script to hide my question. "And that's the end of a pretty rough scene," I say to the group. My lips are still tingling. My jaw aching. Heart pounding. "As I said before"—I point my script at each member of the group—"*no snitching*. Alright. Let's clean up."

The group gives us resounding applause, and with energy to spare (and enough embarrassment to last a lifetime) I pick up the closest thing to me to put it away.

A jug of orange juice and stack of cups.

I don't want to admit what just happened.

My mind right now is a disco band. Glittering lights and noise everywhere, so that no single distinct thought has the opportunity to rise above the others. All I know is I'm a mess. Lavender Rhodes takes my well-laid plans and throws them out the window, and no matter what, I can't ever seem to take control of the situation around her.

I plan to destroy her but backtrack to the point of apology.

I plan to stay as far away from her as possible but end up beside her.

I plan to hate her but somehow fall in love with her.

I plan to help her and respectfully keep my distance but end up kissing her surrounded by twenty surrogate grandparents.

If I even *think* about leaving LA, we'll probably elope.

I chuckle as the thought raises its head, while feeling an uncanny zing at the thought.

No.

Just stop thinking.

Thinking is simply not allowed tonight.

The beauty of what's just happened is that I kissed her under duress. I was challenged to play a role, and I played the role. My abilities were questioned, and she could just consider me the most competitive person around, unable to let that lie.

If I were worth my salt as an actor, I could string together a dozen sentences to tie up that lie nicely. I could make her believe the whole evening really was just a silly little game beneath the stars. It had nothing to do with how I really feel about her and everything to do with proving I am the actor she doubted me to be.

Which is exactly the plan I am weighing before Lavender picks up a stack of paper plates and meets my eyes.

Just as Mrs. Teaberry stops to pat Lavender on the back. "Thank you for the loveliest evening, young lady."

Lavender smiles. It's a warm smile. Something in her eyes flashes even brighter at the words *young lady*, making her seem even softer. As though she accepts and appreciates being called something so casual, so familiar, instead of *Lavender Rhodes* as all the world knows her.

"You know," Mrs. Teaberry continues, clutching an empty pizza box between her arms, "I've seen you do a lot of kissing on that television screen the past ten years. And correct me if I'm wrong, but I believe this was your best one yet."

Chapter 21

Lavender

I saw the list.

Saturday, at Finn's place, I saw it.

After the showing of *Neighbors*, everyone was packing up. We had our hands full returning tables and chairs and projectors to their proper spots, and as we gathered up everything, Finn and I took on separate duties. I saw to the boxes of leftover pizza in Mrs. Teaberry's feathery arms and insisted I walk with her to her kitchen. She assented, saying something about still recovering from a hip surgery of some months ago. I walked slowly beside her as she struck up a detailed analysis of the men I'd kissed on-screen over the course of the past decade, along with rigorous snogging tips. After all, she was a self-declared guru with "sixty-two years of experience with one very lucky man."

By the time I was cleaning dish soap off my hands and the casserole dish that had earlier gone flying out of her arms was drying on the kitchen counter, I was simultaneously turning down "sketch support"; smiling as she informed me, "If I had a rating system, I'd say you were a solid 8, but needing a little practice"; and nodding heartily as she advised, "Now if I were you, I'd practice more with Finn. Because he clearly knows what he's doing, and when he placed his hands on the back of your neck, I gotta say, I felt chills . . ."

Believe me, we both did.

Just as she was suggesting coming on set herself as support crew, my eyes fell on the manuscript rolled up and sticking out of my linen pants pocket, and I whipped it out faster than a canary could sing. "I'd better get this back to Finn while it's on my mind. NDAs and the threat of losing our jobs if leaked and all that. Good night, Mrs. Teaberry."

"Pop this in his fridge when you go," she said, handing me what remained of a chocolate pie. I reached for the aluminum to cover it as she added, "It'll make a good midnight working snack. Heaven knows he could use some fattening up."

And that's how I left Mrs. Teaberry, who watched me with an expression that said, *There's his open door and the pie is melting*, and entered Finn's flat. For the first time. Without Finn.

I had paused in the open doorway but took Miles's greeting to mean, *Look, I live here as well. Come on in.*

Keeping the door respectfully open wide, I walked tentatively through the open living room, casting my eyes about quickly but with interest. There is something nice about getting to see inside someone else's home without them watching you.

You don't have to hold your face in a smile while looking at some terrifyingly dark piece of art. You don't have to nod encouragingly at the massive sketch of a skull over a fireplace and say things like, "Yes, I do see why you purchased that for your life inspiration. And what a perfect spot for it too."

And of course, the more interested one is in a person, the more interested one is in his home.

Because flats tell secrets.

Intentionally or not, I had stumbled into Finn's flat before he could ensure I see only what he would want me to see.

We'd come straight from my flat after the dog park. My visit was unplanned. Everything about today was a surprise, right down to that very real and very unplanned kiss. Consequently, the world around me was his natural habitat.

I feasted my eyes upon it.

My mouth dropped open a little as I took in the Spanish architecture of the room. Surprisingly high ceilings. Narrow arched windows and two French doors that opened onto a concrete patio. Books with brown and black spines spilling out from the built-in bookcases framing an old fireplace, a pile of ashes surrounding three charred logs. I squinted for clues. It didn't take long to see what I was looking for. I stepped toward them.

Framed pictures—older ones, mostly—of younger Finn in his English world. Finn standing among a group of people who looked strikingly similar. They huddled together on a cold, windy beach, arms tucked into sweatshirts, hair whipping, smiles wide.

Finn beneath a pile of children in Minnie Mouse nightgowns and plaid jammies beside a Christmas tree, the rug around them littered with wrapping paper. He looked the most carefree I've ever seen him.

Finn sitting around a writers table surrounded by coffee cups and laptops and take-out bags, looking sleepy and exhausted but happy.

A family man, loved children, enjoyed his work.

Essentially, perfect.

Miles nosed the aluminum pan holding the chocolate pie, so I moved along towards the kitchen.

It was small and outdated, but like the rest of the flat, a comfortable level of clean. A couple of dishes and an empty coffee mug in the sink, but tidy counters and a broom in the corner, recently used. I opened the fridge.

Orange juice. Half a pint of milk. Three apples. A few (ignorantly placed) potatoes. An abundance of condiments. Some takeaway containers.

He had never struck me as a cooking kind of guy, and his fridge confirmed this impression. Made sense. And frankly, I live similarly. After all, why slave away over a cooktop when you could just drop downstairs for a world-renowned pastry? There are too many things to do in this great, wide world besides cook. And too many people who have perfected the art of it for me to be loyal to boxed spaghetti. Isn't it nice to live in a world where so many can specialize in their gifts, and we can enjoy the fruits of each other's labors?

Laughter tinkled through the outside window. I closed the fridge and turned towards a little cubby, holding the rolled-up script.

His desk was littered with papers, and whereas the rest of his space was tidy, this certainly was the spot where he surrendered to the whims of his creative mind. His laptop rested on top of a stack of papers, which teetered precariously on a stack of writing and screenwriting books—from which so many bookmarks poked out that he may as well have highlighted every word.

Script pages strewn about bore his handwritten notes.

Blunt slash marks and unforgiving Xs aggressively cut out whole paragraphs of old pages.

The recycling bin beside the laptop was stuffed to the brim with crumpled papers.

A writer told me once that words on a screen read differently than the words on a page, and it was clear Finn felt the same way.

I laid the rolled-up script on his laptop, then paused, struck by the desire to snatch it back, to make a sort of scrapbook of the evening. A memento.

I was just picking up the script when my eyes fell upon a page beside the tower of books and papers. Something in my chest thudded as I read the heading, "Transgressions Against Finn Masters," and banged all the way down to my toes as I read the words that came after.

Chapter 22

Finn

Wednesday, Rehearsals, Stage 2

"Has my office always been blue?"

Paula halts the rant she's been on the past half hour about why exactly it is "necessary to the plot" that we bring on Julia Roberts as a guest star.

She looks up from the PowerPoint on her laptop, which she's been holding out as she perches on my desk, her oversized T-shirt of Roberts's face with the bold letters: BIG MISTAKE. BIG. HUGE.

But I'm not looking at her. No. I'm studying the walls with absolute wonder.

"This is a beautiful shade. What would you call it? Robin's-egg blue?" I crane my neck and cry out, "Well, *look at that*. They even got the ceiling!"

"Finn."

I look down to discover she's frowning at me, her finger poised over the bullet point on the paragraph titled "Reason #33 Julia Roberts Is Perfect." She says warily, "It's always been blue."

"No," I say, pursing my lips and looking around again. "Can't be."

She drops her hand. "Are you alright?"

"Of course." I wave my hand at her. "Carry on. I'm listening."

She plops the laptop onto the desk and stands. "Yeah, that's the thing, Finn. You *are* listening. I'm on slide 46."

I raise a brow.

"Slide 46," she repeats. "I'm getting bored of myself. Honestly, I didn't expect to get you past slide 10. I was hoping you'd do that thing where you halt me and say, 'Fine, whatever, Paula, just let me go to the bathroom,' and then I'd go off and spend half our yearly budget on Roberts before you have time to blink and change your mind." She starts flipping through the remaining slides. "See? I didn't even *finish* 50 to 150. I just wanted you to see the number at the bottom of the screen and panic. So *what is going on*?"

"Nothing," I say, reaching for my coffee. "It's just a good day."

She frowns at me. Her eyes flicker to my coffee.

"You've got a dead fly in your coffee."

"Oh," I say, chuckling as I fish it out. "So there is."

I take another sip.

Paula's eyes look like they are about to bug out of her head.

But at the deepest level, I suppose, her suspicions are not off.

I walked Lavender home Saturday night.

She was quiet for most of the walk, which made me feel uneasy, the kind of uneasy that makes you flip through your actions of the last twelve hours and spiral downward. Was I too honest? Did she regret that kiss? Did she see through my facade of platonic friendship, deep down to my true feelings? Was I too eager? Was I too boring? I had said that thing two minutes back about not caring for cheese.

Stupid, stupid comment. Everybody loves cheese.

What was I thinking?!

Pair that with my karaoke comment and I'm the dullest man alive! Who wants to spend time with a man who hates lasagna? Nobody, Finn. NOBODY.

But as she stood on her doorstep and opened her door, she turned abruptly. Took a breath. Said, "D'you think you can invite me to next week's community showing?"

I casually quirked a brow but on the inside felt awash in relief. "I'm pretty sure you invited yourself the first time. What's stopping you now?"

And she shrugged. Then fell quiet again. Then said with a touch of softness, "I just wonder what it would feel like to be properly invited. Without Sonya around."

I smiled. Tried very hard to ignore Gabriel and his angry muscles strapped over his chest, standing in view from the open doorway. And said with a little bow, "Lavender Rhodes, it would please me very much if you would come to our exclusive gathering next Saturday night at seven. And if you could bring some of that baklava, that would be even better."

For one stomach-plummeting moment, she just stared at me.

I'm not sure what was going through her mind, but this exchange suddenly felt much bigger than our friendly little game. Facing the sudden possibility that she may not actually accept, I was met with the pounding fear that she didn't want to. That getting me to ask was just a cruel joke.

But then the moment was over, and a little smile lifted her lips.

She nodded. "I'm feeling keen for enchiladas. I feel it must be enchiladas."

For one fleeting moment, I considered joking back, "I guess you won't be coming then." But I smashed it to bits, saying instead, "Anything or nothing, Lavender, we will always want you there."

"We?"

"Yes."

"Everyone?"

"Always."

"Always?"

The question lingered, light as a feather in the air. I grabbed and anchored it with firm resolution before it could fly away.

"Always."

A smile blossomed on her lips that was the most beautiful thing I'd ever seen.

And before I knew it she kissed me on the cheek. Patted me once on the chest. Turned.

"Good night, Finn."

"Good night."

So *yes*.

Maybe I was having a good day.

Maybe I was letting myself linger in the haze of the past weekend.

Maybe I was happy deluding myself for just a few hours before I slapped myself across the face and reminded myself it was technically never going to happen.

I push up from my desk.

"I'm going to check on Lavender about that line. It still seems a bit off." I suck in one more sip of coffee, then set it down. Swipe some curls away from my face. Take off my glasses and drop them on the desk.

Decide the world is too blurry and put my glasses back on. "Right. See you in a jiff."

"Finn?" Paula's gaze follows me out my office door. I pass through the common room, where the table is covered in a Petro's taco spread and people are scattered about standing, sitting, huddled over computers while munching nachos or clutching coffee. I check my watch. One fifteen. Lunch break.

I have walked through Lavender's door—let's see—three times for the same purpose in the past four hours.

But so what if I'm heading to Lavender's to ask her opinion on the word "haberdashery" for the third time?

I am a producer.

I care intently about my job.

I am merely going above and beyond for that which I love.

Which is, for the record, my job.

I'm not going to say I am whistling as I stroll down the hall. But there are tiny distinct, off-key noises zipping through my lips as I round the corner nearest her door.

Kye's door is open, and my head naturally inclines towards it before registering what I am seeing:

Kye, hands gripping young Maggie's shoulders, leaving absolutely no room for a sheet of paper between them.

My feet slow to a stop.

After standing in the hallway for what feels like an eternity, my feet start to move again. And with great care, I file what I've seen in the back of my mind, fully intending never to think of it again.

But then the post-lunch rehearsal happens.

Kye steps on set and slips his arm around Lavender's waist, and he whispers something in her ear with all the cockiness of the last living male among a sea of available ladies at a Bridgerton reenactment ball, and that . . . that is when I snap.

"You know, it's just, now that I'm thinking about it, it strikes me that *wouldn't it just be so grand and unexpected* if Lance went to space after all?"

It's late Wednesday afternoon and there's a script in my hands. The writers room is stiflingly hot. I'm convinced the HVAC is broken despite the fact I've checked on the thermostat three times.

My eyes ache from kneading them.

My foot has somehow found its way to the seat of my chair,

where it's perched as though I'm captain of a ship setting sail for America.

I tore my glasses off an hour ago, and now they rest flopped down beside my laptop and a stack of papers I've been throwing around for the past hour. The sleeves of my button-up are rolled up to my forearms in the most *ridiculously* stereotypical working-man-trying-to-emphasize-he's-a-working-man-by-slapping-the-sheets-in-his-hand-while-rolling-up-his-sleeves way, but here we are.

"But Ashley and Lance have just gotten together, *again*—" says Erik.

"Oh, and what's new?" I say, waving him off. "What's bloody new? No, what we *need*, I think"—I snap the script against the table—"is something *actually new*. And I'm thinking . . . space."

Now that's an idea.

Separate scenes.

Separate sets for separate scenes.

Separate times for rehearsing separate scenes for separate sets.

Separate dates for separate times for rehearsing separate scenes for separate sets.

Him in a makeshift aircraft. Her somewhere off in the apartment, sitting by her phone. Zero faces or arms or hairs within reach.

"We already thought about space. You said it was absurd."

"Ah"—I put up a finger—"yes. But that was before we considered including . . . a *sloth*."

Erik frowns. "A sloth?"

"A friendly space sloth," I say gleefully. "Everyone loves sloths. It's a trending animal. People adore them."

Kye, for the record, hates sloths.

He made it absolutely clear that he "had a bad experience" once during a Los Angeles Zoo publicity event for season 4. And yes, perhaps I'm "backpedaling" in my growth. Perhaps I haven't entirely learned my lesson after all that's happened with plotting against Lavender. But this is a two-steps-forward-and-one-step-back kind of thing. And plotting against Kye to decidedly ruin his life will just be my one step back.

Paula's eyes are shooting at me as if to say, *Hey, sweetie, we're nodding but you sound a bit manic.*

This isn't because of jealousy, for the record.

It's *not* because I want Lavender to myself, no.

To prove it, I should let you know I even had a plan in case she asked, "So remember this weekend when we kissed in front of all your neighbors?"

I would smile serenely and tell her never to challenge an actor.

That I was competitive. I wouldn't be proved wrong.

And yes, perhaps the whole thing was a stretch, but at the end of the day she would believe me, because time and resolve would be on my side. With time, she would grasp that we were simply acquaintances. Work friends. Dog park friends.

Perhaps, one day, even close friends.

As with Delilah, I would end up dating someone, and Lavender would end up accidentally meddling in our relationship and ultimately destroying it. I had accepted this fate. I planned to live my life happily-ever-after in it.

She would carry on dating quite literally anyone in the world she pleased.

Even Kye, with his frequent, not-so-subtle hints.

But then Kye went off kissing Maggie, and then Kye came back on set to take every *single* opportunity to touch Lavender, to invade her space, and to coo under his breath in between every page rehearsed.

I could no longer surgically remove any emotion from my expression as I followed the lines and diverted my attention elsewhere as needed.

I cracked.

"You know what?" My eyes widen as a new thought pops into my mind. "What if things get really interesting. What if he just *dies*?"

Cindy frowns, as she has done the entire past hour as I've been steering this ship through this storm. "We can't kill off Lance Lewis."

"Sure we can. It'll be the spin nobody expects."

"He has a contract."

"The season's nearly up and we're set for contract renewal." I throw my hands out with a grandiose shrug. "Nothing is set in stone. And I think we can all agree here that his biceps would be better suited to other channels."

"Lance has been Lavender's love interest for *ten* seasons."

I snap my fingers. "Correct. All the more reason to introduce Joey, that new neighbor downstairs."

"The forty-five-year-old telemarketer with the parking problem?" someone says.

"Oookay." Paula jumps up, and before I know it her hands are on my shoulders, pushing me up and out of the writers room. "I think we've stretched our minds to their creative limits for one day. We've had some great brainstorming here"—she says this to the room as if to emphasize I am not crazy but just doing what is very, very standard for our jobs, so nobody needs to mention my momentary lapse in sanity—"and I think we ought to go home, have a nice night, and bang at it tomorrow."

I don't resist as she pushes me through the door, gives everyone a friendly see-you-all-tomorrow-because-this-is-absolutely-normal wave, and slams my office door.

She wheels around. "*What* is going on?"

"Nothing," I reply. "I am just trying like everyone else here to get this season off to a spectacular end—"

"By turning a sitcom into *Higher Stakes* and killing off your main characters."

"Is he, though?" I retort. "Can we really say with all honesty he's a *main* character?"

"Yes," she replies bluntly, crossing her arms over her chest. "On the page. And in his contract. And on-screen."

"See"—I raise a finger—"that's where I think we may differ in our viewpoints," I reply. "Because the way I see it, it's Lavender who's actually carrying the show. Frankly, if she turned to a cash register as her next love interest, people would write songs about it."

"Is that what this is?" she says, her voice hushed. "Are you honest-to-goodness trying to sabotage the show to get back at this poor woman?"

"No." I rake my hand through my hair. The conversation is settling over me like a wet blanket over the fire that has been burning in my chest. A tiny bit of reason is starting to show its face. "No." I turn to the desk. "I just *really* prefer he not shoot cupid's arrow at every woman he meets."

Her eyes widen. "Wait. Now you're *jealous* for Lavender?"

Her words ring through the room far too loud for my liking, which makes me grit my teeth and growl, "I am not *jealous*. I just don't like his overstepping professional boundaries to flirt with Lavender every second he can."

"I *knew* it." There's a gasp and a sudden punch in my arm that, were I Kye, would probably bounce off like a ping-pong ball, but as I am not Kye, and I don't spend five hours a day lifting weights to impress *multiple* ladies, it hurts. I reach up to protect my arm from another swing.

"You *like* her," she accuses.

"I *appreciate* her," I correct. "And I was wrong before, and—"

"Are you going to ask her out?" she says, apparently dropping the point of this conversation and going for the newer, shinier point of interest.

"—and no," I continue. "I have no intention of asking her out."

Her smile wilts into a suspicious frown. "Why?"

"Because I respect her too much. More specifically, because I don't think I can forgive myself."

"So you think she deserves someone better. Like Kye."

"I think she absolutely deserves someone better. Most specifically anyone else *besides* Kye. I just caught him feeling up that intern in his dressing room—"

"The one you felt up?"

"I was the victim of hallway stalking."

"Interesting," she says, her eyes narrowing. "Maybe that's what Maggie did to Kye too. Maybe she's just lurking, pouncing on men every chance she can."

"Yes, well, whoever started it, it was clear Kye wasn't planning on ending it anytime soon. And then, five minutes later, he hops on set and tries to do the same thing with Lavender."

Silence settles around us. Paula takes this in and, from the way she's watching me, I know she's deciding how to address me. I am trying to force the tightness in my chest to ease up to a rational (at least breathable) level.

"Lavender's a kind person," I say quietly. "Sometimes, I think, too kind for her own good."

"Lavender's her own woman." Paula considers me. "But if you really feel this way, why don't you try doing the one thing you haven't in all of this?"

"What?" I say.

"Talk to her." Paula shakes her head. "If you haven't noticed, for whatever reason, she trusts you. Maybe before throwing Kye into space, you try having a candid conversation."

I don't move.

To be frank, I have no intention of moving, until she adds, "And for the record, considering everyone is heading to their cars to spend the rest of the night as they please, now may be a good time."

I'm very nearly jogging as I see the glint of Lavender's golden ponytail slip into the driver's side just before her car door closes. Automatically my eyes swivel to the passenger seat, hoping nobody is in it.

I squint, but the glint of light against her windshield makes it impossible to see.

This whole ride-into-the-desert-at-sunset plan feels more and more impossible with each step. But reason, it seems, flew out the window the moment I saw Kye with Maggie. And now it's too late to call it back.

The car door pops back open, and Lavender looks at me as she climbs down from the SUV, a question in her eyes.

I began this day with the intent to stay cool and detached.

And now here I am, running after a woman after declaring we kill off a man.

"Finn? What's wrong?" she says, just as I'm putting a hand behind my neck and pulling to a stop at the car door.

I hesitate.

"Nothing," I say. I take in a breath, hands on my hips as I suck in lungfuls of air. "Nothing . . . just . . ."

How am I going to say this?

How am I possibly going to open up about this?

"Look. I think there's something you should know."

And then she blinks, and her expression shifts as if to say, *I know. I know what you are about to say.*

"Right now?" Her gaze darts to a group of tourists in the distance, several of whom have phones out as their guide directs them onto Stage 4. "How about we talk at home?"

She means her home. *Obviously* she means her home. But the familiarity sends a zing up my spine that I have to neutralize to maintain my composure. I find I'm shaking my head.

"No." I realize I sound brusque and add, "I have to get back to work. I just . . . I saw something today and think you should know."

"Oh." And at this her expression turns to puzzlement, as if the conversation is taking an unforeseen direction. She shifts subtly away from the phone cameras, shielding her face by my chest. "What's up?"

"I saw . . . Kye."

She blinks. Blankly.

"More specifically, I saw Kye with Goodwin's niece, Maggie, in his dressing room."

"Oh." She seems to take this in, chewing on my words. "And . . . this makes you feel . . ."

"Incredibly frustrated," I admit. Is that a curtain of disappointment that falls over her face? "On your behalf," I finish.

She blinks a few times, her forehead creasing. "Mine? Why are you frustrated for me?"

"Look, I'm not blind," I say. "I'm aware of how, how close you two are. And it's evident how much he wishes to"—I fumble for the polite words—"to know you more . . . intimately—"

I've never seen a hand move so quickly. She posts it like a stop sign in front of me. "Hold on right there, Finn. Let's get a few things straight. Starting with: I don't care about him and Maggie snogging in the dressing room."

"You don't?"

"No. Now would I prefer Kye keep his attention on one woman at a time? Sure." Her voice hitches up. "But that conversation's been had with him, and he doesn't listen to me, or Sonya, or really anyone with a head on their shoulders, and hopefully one day he'll wise up. But the point is"—she shakes her head slightly—"Fine. Whatever. The intern's a sweet girl and frankly he could do much worse." She pauses. "So. Now that that's cleared up . . ."

She's waiting for me to say something.

To add to this.

I scratch the back of my head. "So. Well. Terrific. It's just . . . I didn't want your heart to get trod on—"

A flicker of a smile passes over her face. "Nope. My heart isn't with him, so never fear."

"It's just . . . you do realize how heavily he hits on you?"

"Yes, well, 90 percent of that is to keep the papers guessing, and the other 10 percent I suppose happens when he's really in a dry spell and has to aim his cupid eyes somewhere."

"And that"—I hesitate—"doesn't bother you? You're fine with his attentions? I just want to make sure. As your producer. I want to take care to look out for you and make sure he's respecting your boundaries."

"As my producer," she repeats back. "Ah. Well, yes. I mean, I could do with a little less touching of late—"

"I'm on it," I say, nodding curtly, my hand inching toward my phone. "I'll have a word with him right now."

My hand is actually reaching into my pocket, my feet ready to pivot, when her hand grips mine, stopping me. "I can handle that myself. Particularly as I've set my sights elsewhere. But thank you all the same. As my producer. Who is looking out for me."

She hasn't let go of my hand, nor does she seem inclined to.

This is the part where I'm supposed to ask her where exactly she *has* set her sights.

This is the moment when I should throw away my resolve and quit denying her hints.

But this is also the moment when I will most assuredly *not*.

For her sake. Because a woman like her deserves the best.

Today I will stay strong.

Gently, I free my hand from hers. Take a small step back. "I'm glad to hear it, Lavender," I say, then add with the most sincerity in the world: "Because, quite frankly, I believe you deserve a man far better than Kye Walker. Frankly, the more I know you, the more I'm convinced you deserve the best in the world."

With a curt nod, I take another step back.

Turn.

Go back inside.

Chapter 23

Lavender

"Alright. I need answers."

To be clear, I did not *intend* to cause Paula to throw up her arms and release an explosion of papers, covering everything from the hood of her car to the parking garage floor. A few flutter over the wall of the third level like paper money thrown off a balcony.

Looking at it from her angle, I suppose it is my fault. It's dark. She's alone in the parking garage. And her back was to me as she pulled out her car keys.

But that's the thing: I wasn't thinking about it from her angle.

I was entirely in my head at the moment, fueled with pure adrenaline after sitting in my car the past half hour without having the motivation to put it in Reverse. The whole Finn situation is baffling. First, the list that gave every indication he hated me. At one time, perhaps. In the past, I could only hope. But if that was the case, *why* was the paper on his desk? *Why* was he hanging on to a list of grievances against me?

Then this conversation about Kye today.

Was he overcome with jealousy? Protectiveness? I saw him

today when Kye leaned in between takes to say something for my ears only. I saw Finn's jaw clench. His hands too.

Then he came out here, claiming to be looking out for me "as my producer."

Just a few days ago we kissed.

Not a stage kiss.

Not something meaningless.

Something real. *Quite* real.

But now here he was, after I'd opened up about my feelings, backing away.

He told me I deserved the world.

And then he ran inside as if the place was on fire and he had to rescue a box of kittens.

Of course, the list is most troubling.

I wanted to discuss it with him, put it all out in the open, clear the air, but the way he reacted to my suggestion we talk at home is enough to tell me I need backstory, and I need it now. I am done playing games.

So I charged up the parking garage stairs on foot, looking for one particular woman. Eventually I found her.

Alone on level three beside a sliver of sunset streaming over her Honda Odyssey.

In retrospect, I can see how sneaking up behind a woman and making demands as she's trying to get into her car is probably not the best way to approach the situation.

"Oh, *Paula*," I spurt, dropping to my knees and reaching for her arm. "I'm so sorry. It's *me*. Lavender."

She flips over onto her back like a fish that has flopped onto a pier, breathing heavily. "*Lavender.* Good *grief.* Are you trying to *kill* me?"

"Sorry about your papers. We probably ought to go grab them before they fly off."

She waves them off. "Just some half-baked scene our new writer was playing with. Worthless stuff. Leave it."

She brushes herself off, then regards me. "So. What are you looking for exactly?"

"I'm looking for you." I take a breath. "I'm looking for answers about a list."

Her face is a statue for 6.2 seconds, and then all at once she's popping open the driver's side door of the minivan and motioning me to the other side. "If this is about the list I'm thinking it is, get in."

I never knew the inside of a car could smell so strongly of jalapeños.

I hear the crunch of more than a few fast-food bags beneath my feet. Something jabs me in the back. At least ten empty to-go cups are stacked inside one another in a cup holder. And at least six gold medals hanging from the rearview mirror on red, white, and blue ribbons clank against one another when she puts the car in Reverse.

"Where are we going?"

"My son's wrestling match." She peels out of the space so rapidly my hand snaps for the handle, which is suspiciously sticky. "He has a meet at six. If you want to talk, you're going to have to talk on the drive. That alright with you?"

I have my choice of at least a dozen napkins littering my surroundings.

"Sure," I say, wiping my hands and trying to decide exactly how desperate I am to get answers tonight. "Fine."

As she squeezes us into the flow of traffic, a move I had hitherto thought would be impossible, she gives me a sidelong glance. "So. What do you know?"

"That's what I'm hoping to find out from you. What do *you* know?"

"My car. My rules," she says. "And while we're at it, don't waste our time holding on to your cards. You flagged me down in the parking garage. You're in my car on the way to a wrestling match, where you're about to be swarmed by a bunch of thirteen-year-old males. Let's not play games."

"Fine," I say. I'd respect her more for all this big talk, except for the fact I am sitting on potato chips. "To put it bluntly, I may . . . do . . . have feelings for Finn."

"I knew it!" The childlike thrill in her voice throws all her respectable big talk out the window. Now she's wagging her finger. "I *knew* you did. You *had* to."

"Had to?" I retort. "Well, I wouldn't go that far." I do have my dignity.

"Of course you did. Look at the way he looks at you. I haven't seen him like this since . . . well . . . since ever." She's shaking her head as she swerves unnervingly into the next lane and, I'm 99 percent certain, clips the car in front of her.

Her words boost my spirit, however, and a warmth creeps to my cheeks. "Oh, I don't know about that. There was that Delilah he was pretty chummy with once upon a time."

"Oh, *her*," Paula says, her lips puckering as if I'd suggested spoiled taco meat as a refreshing appetizer. "No. She was more like a shadow."

"Of what?"

"Of you. Of the real thing."

I'm starting to recognize a pattern among the people in Finn's life. I saw it several days ago when visiting his flat. Everyone speaks of him like proud owners of a pristine lawn, smug gardeners of perfectly pruned azalea bushes, openly gushing about the number of birds that like to visit this beautiful landscape each day.

People in his life care about him, take pride in him, are anxious to see and rejoice in his success. It makes him look wonderful.

If he ran for president, they'd vote for him.

Out of loyalty.

"Well, here's the thing, Paula. The way I see it, there are two problems." I squeeze my eyes shut and pray for dear life as she cuts off a tractor trailer to swing towards an exit. "One, he is giving me mixed signals. And two, I stumbled upon this list."

"Those aren't two problems. It's one and the same. He's giving you mixed signals *because* of that list." After a pause she adds, "Which, for the record, I *can't* believe he's kept all these years and which, for the record, I'd like to say was the effect of a momentary lapse in sanity. Really, honey, he's the stablest man I know. It's just . . . when it comes to you . . ."

"I apparently drive him mad. And it's somehow causing him to want to stay away."

"Oh, honey, you don't know . . ." Her eyes widen. Like she's just now putting together that all this time I have been clueless as to the missing key. "You don't know the big thing," she finishes. She clicks her tongue and looks at the traffic ahead. Considering that good driving skills are the only thing she seems to have *skipped* so far, I take this as a clear indicator she's deep in thought. Probably about whether she should tell me.

"From your response just now," I say, jumping in before she decides to back out, "you seem to be in support of Finn and me having a go at it. And on my end, at least, I'm getting nowhere—unless you count that kiss a few nights ago—"

"You two *kissed*?" she sputters.

I get it now. I get why she is a writer. She *lives* for the drama.

"Well, I sort of coerced him into it, to tell the truth."

She shakes her head, all the while grinning madly. "Let me break it down for you. They are the list of your offenses that have shaken up his life."

I nod, following.

"And all his life he's gotten along just fine dealing with his own troubles by trying to ignore the pain you—his words, not mine—caused. Then one day he's approached by Mr. Goodwin and given the offer of a lifetime. A job on *Neighbors*. Too good to pass up."

I nod again. Easy enough.

"But then he could avoid you no longer. And then another series of unfortunate incidents involving you occurred, down to getting him fired at one point—"

"I got him fired?" Well. This is news to me.

"Right after he started. Some misunderstanding involving Goodwin's niece. But then he dug himself out of that. And I think after all of that he just . . . momentarily . . . snapped. And"—she hesitates—"attempted, against all my advice, to plot a payback."

"*What?*"

We are driving roughly fifty-five miles per hour two inches from the back of a truck overloaded with what appears to be someone's entire dorm room, including an unsecured mattress, a dresser, and a thousand coat hangers loaded with T-shirts hanging over the side, flapping in the breeze. The shock of what she just said stunts my ability to focus on the chaos before me.

I snap my attention to her. "Explain."

"But his every attempt at being the villain failed horribly, because at Finn's core he is a stuffed teddy bear. Ultimately, after a few spectacular flops, he was consumed by guilt and remorse. He has since decided he does not, and will not, ever, deserve you."

"What payback?" I say. My wheels are spinning. I can't think of any— "Hang on. Is this about the chickens?"

"Yes," she says in a sympathetic tone. "Well . . . and Adam."

"He wanted Adam to come for payback?" I spit out. "That was *his* plan?"

But no, this doesn't make sense at all. He was so upset about it in my dressing room afterward. Just like he was about the chickens. But.

Ah.

The memory strikes me.

I see it all in a new light.

The way he looked so tortured. The way he raked a hand through his hair, absolutely in a state. At the time he seemed protective of me, even overzealous. I thought he cared about me so much that he was distressed to see me struggle.

Now I see it through another lens. It was guilt. A guilty hand raked over his face. Taut muscles as he refused to pass through my door, because he knew he was the cause of whatever had happened to me, and—

Well.

I suppose he felt bad.

"He didn't want those things to affect you as much as they did. They were poorly executed. His attempts to merely irritate you escalated quickly, as pranks often do."

I don't think I've ever been plied with so much popcorn and Coke in my life.

As it turns out, Paula carries the weight of other people's guilt as a habit and tries to release said guilt via gifts of food. Considering I was not only hit with the unfortunate news that the man I like has a history of loathing me but also swallowed up in a near trampling of teenage boys in leotards asking me to their prom (you do it for *one kid* six years ago . . .), Paula ensured the concession stand was a fountain of Raisinets and popcorn and Sour Patch Kids endlessly flowing my way. Every time a kid said a shaky "Miss Lavender Rhodes . . . ?" behind me, she'd slip me a Reese's. And frankly, between my pent-up energy and Paula's worried eyes, I ate it.

I've never had a better-deserved five-thousand-calorie day.

Which accounts for half the reason I'm slowly drooping in here on Thursday morning, my stomach a fistful of knots and streaks of fire rising up my windpipe. As I step on set, I give a bleak nod to Paula. She was awfully kind to answer the questions I lobbed at her every few minutes throughout her son's match, evidently deciding it was better not to prolong my agony.

"So break down for me exactly the story of the things on the list. How exactly did I do all these things?"

"So how does he feel about me now? Really?"

Between the gurgling mix of Coke, candy, and popcorn in my stomach and the rehashing of every minute with Finn up till now, needless to say, I spent the night staring at the ceiling, thinking.

Considering.

Fingers drumming the blanket in cadence with my restless thoughts.

What to do now . . .

By two in the morning, I leaned toward one direction over another.

By three thirty, I had a plan.

By five, I had confidence in that plan.

Now here I am, Pepto-Bismol bravely floating on the crashing waves of a Coke-and-candy sea, pale but determined.

Where is he?

The set is littered with people. Everyone is moving quicker than usual. I assume this is an effect of my slow-as-molasses pace. They zigzag around each other with folders, papers, makeup brushes, and phones in hand.

Actually a lot of phones.

In fact, most everyone has a phone.

A guy whips around me, head bent, lips moving as his eyes

scan the words he's reading on-screen. I can feel something new, something heavy. It's quiet. Much too quiet for a typical Thursday morning.

And then, all of a sudden, it's loud.

A cacophony of noises and words rises as one person, then another, cries out. People are whipping their heads around, looking for comrades, gripping wrists, speaking fervently.

"Lavender!" Sonya cries. And then I, too, have someone gripping my wrist. Her eyes are bright. She studies my expression and knows I'm in the dark.

"What is going on?" I say.

She pushes her phone into my hands. Just before my eyes drop to her screen, I catch a glimpse of him.

Finn stands in a cluster of writers and producers, a gathering of eight or so, huddling and talking excitedly. But his eyes are on me, and as our gazes lock, a small smile lifts his lips.

I'm about to take a step toward him when Sonya pushes the phone closer to my face.

Now I feel my own phone dinging in my pocket. Emails are flooding in. Texts.

Something big has happened.

And then my head falls . . . oh, of course. How could I have forgotten?

Our agent's name is at the top of Sonya's email. The subject shouts "CONTRACT UPDATE."

Sonya's foot is tapping madly, her impatience clear.

I pick up the pace.

> Terrific news. Network agreed to terms at the ninth hour, which as a reminder include a 12.9% salary increase from last year. And better, they want you to sign on for a THREE-YEAR CONTRACT at this rate. This is *unbelievable*, Sonya. Honestly, I didn't

> think they had it in them. See attached updated contract and let me know if you have any questions. I know we've gone point by point a dozen times, but in case you need a reminder, I'll lay it out below.

Quickly I scan the remainder of the email, the details of everything from taxes to vacation time to publicity commitments.

Then I pull out my phone. Read through the details of my own email.

The answer to my most burning question comes halfway through a paragraph:

> Now I know you were hoping for more time off, but they just wouldn't budge. I did, however, manage to get you a couple more days, Lavender, and I hope you'll find the little conciliation prize I was able to snag as something to ease things: Dressing Room 4A opened up, and it's yours. Bigger space. Full remodel.

By the time I've finished reading, Sonya's foot is tapping so madly she's close to making a hole in the floor. When I look up, her face looks like it's about to absolutely *explode*.

"Three more seasons!" Sonya cries, and in very un-Sonya-like behavior, she throws her arms around me.

"Yes." I exhale. She squeezes like a python. I'm pretty sure one of my ribs is cracking.

"And the raise!" she cries in a frisson of excitement. "Can you believe it? Goodwin really took his time there." She laughs, then pulls back to look at me, saying in a confessional tone, "I was actually beginning to panic." Then lowers her voice further. "I was considering taking the interview at . . . *Stephouse*."

As words flow from her in an adrenaline-driven barrage,

I notice a bizarre feeling has overcome me (in addition to the other bizarre feelings I've had all morning).

I don't feel thrilled.

No, if I had to nail it down, I'd say I actually feel numb. Which isn't the right way to feel at all in the face of such news.

Three more years. That'll take me into my thirties before I'm up for another contract renewal, or the chance to get out.

Get out.

Those aren't the right words to say in this situation.

I should be elated. The room is crackling with electricity. Every single person around me is bursting with smiles. Jobs saved. Stress spared. Stability, nay, even raises given.

And one can't forget: a new dressing room.

"Lavie, you okay?" Sonya says. Her flow of words abruptly stops, her eyes zigzagging as she scans my face. "Hang on. Are you seriously *not* thrilled?"

I take a breath. The swell of bustling bodies crowds me. The hopes and dreams of others sit on my chest. I push the claustrophobic feelings aside.

I will not think about the contract.

I will not think about the number of years I am going to remain in this exact spot, playing Ashley Krane, dancing around the same problems, playing with the same lines.

I will not think about the missed weddings, birthdays, retirement parties, and funerals. I will not think about Thursday nights when Mum slides herself in front of the telly to watch *Doc Martin* or wonder when I'll next see Dad poring over his petunias.

What I *will do* in this exact moment is exactly what I do for a living. Act. Lie. And if there's one thing I'm certain of, it's that I can lie flawlessly.

I let my eyes crinkle at the corners, feel the muscles from my cheeks to my chest tighten in a manipulated burst of projected energy. Excitement. My smile brightens. Wide. I take a little anticipatory breath, and when I speak it's in a breathless, I-can't-believe-this-incredible-news-and-will-be-celebrating-for-days rush. "This is *amazing*."

"I know—12.9 percent!" Her nails press into my palms. She's so overjoyed, she doesn't even notice. "The ratings must be through the roof."

I shake my head, eyes twinkling from the inside out. "It's all . . . just absolutely . . . perfect."

Chapter 24

Finn

Thursday, Rehearsals, Stage 2

She's lying.

Lying through her teeth.

While Sonya parades around the room, uncharacteristically hugging everyone in sight, Lavender trails along.

The set has transformed into a party. All thoughts of work have been thrust aside. The writers have begun brainstorming ways to mark the occasion, clamoring for the biggest and best idea until words like *flights* and *air balloons* and even *group tattoos* (with the curlicue *Neighbors* logo) all become mainstream.

Everyone is over the moon about the new reality: this contract is going to propel *Neighbors* onto the list of longest-running live-action sitcoms in US history.

I have all the more reason to be thrilled: I received an additional email from Goodwin himself with a subject line saying "Meeting" (which, to be clear, caused a temporary panic attack), followed by a short message: "Meet me at my office tomorrow at noon. It's time to talk salary."

So, in many ways, I am more excited than anyone here, ready

to get the *Neighbors* logo plastered permanently somewhere as well—specifically, onto my laptop. Or perhaps a water bottle.

But there's Lavender.

I can't keep my eyes off her.

Nor off the specific thing I read in her face, the thing nobody in the room seems to see: she's disappointed. No, *disappointed* is the wrong word. *Claustrophobic.*

There's tension at the corners of her eyes. She swallows her breath every few minutes. An unconscious tic worries her bottom lip.

Exuberant words flow from her lips only after a split second of hesitation.

These are all variations of the same thing.

And every minute I watch her, I see the feeling of claustrophobia in her grow.

She is going to go through with it.

Even though she is the woman with all the talent and the world before her—the woman who could quite literally say, "I want a new job," and field offers for hundreds. Thousands.

Everybody wants her in their court. She could go anywhere. Do anything.

But no, it's clear as day she's spinning herself into a cocoon, wrapping her beautiful wings up tight around her body, drawing herself into a dark shelter, so as to please everyone else.

And it makes my chest ache.

Worse, it gives me resolve.

Paula sidles up to me, scratching the back of her head. "Cindy's saying we ought to cut loose today. She thinks at this rate we're just going to have to give up the day. Come back tomorrow."

"Yeah. Whatever everyone wants," I say distractedly, the wheels in my head whirring as I make a mental grab for courses of action that could fix Lavender's problem. I try ideas on for size, thinking through the consequences of said actions.

Unconsciously I find the mini Rubik's Cube in my pocket and pull it out. Begin twisting and turning it, the colors barely more than a flash in my periphery as my eyes stay on her.

"Everyone's starting to talk about going somewhere to celebrate. Cindy wants to go to Pica Rita's, but I told her we wouldn't get through the door with a party this size—and Ken would kill us if he heard everyone went out to celebrate and he missed it on a sick day."

The yellows click into place. I have a sheet of perfectly uniform yellow squares.

Kill us.

Murder.

A new idea comes to mind, entering as quietly as a mouse, and sits straight in front of my mind's eye. I ignore it, considering other less dangerous paths.

"Do you think we ought to see about planning an official celebration?" Paula continues.

I flick through a couple of options to their logical dead ends. The mouse idea sniffs.

"PR could coordinate something. Sonya told us we could use her place under the stipulation that"—she pauses—"everyone takes off their shoes and drinks only neutral-colored liquids. Apparently she thinks we're all toddlers who can't hold our juice steady on her white couches. I'm game if . . ."

After a few more pale ideas whiz by to their inconclusive, undesirable ends, I finally lock eyes on the mouse and give it my attention.

And in a few moments, I know.

It's the hard road.

There's a 90 percent chance (and that's generous) it'll flop, and if it doesn't flop outright, it'll flop by the end, dragging me along with it.

And of course, it'll take time. Much, *much* more time than I have.

Unless I go absolutely right . . . this . . . second.

I cast my eyes sidelong onto Lavender.

Urgency explodes in my mind, just as Lavender locks eyes with me. She hesitates. Then takes two steps.

"Paula. I need your help," I say.

Paula halts. Barely has time to blink before saying, "I'm in. But for what?"

"I know how we can end the season."

And then I'm turning, pacing towards the exit. Paula's falling in line with me, her short legs racing to keep up with mine. "And the show."

Chapter 25

Lavender

He left me.

Not only left but drove off the side of a cliff, apparently, to stay away. At least, that's the latest wild rumor. No one has seen Finn or Paula for the past ten days.

Speculation includes them having a simultaneous meltdown from the pressure (logical, given we've all seen it happen before) or finding love together and running off to some balmy paradise.

Of course, neither is a remote possibility. Finn loves the work and the frenzy. I've seen the way he ducks his head to his computer, madly typing new thoughts and ideas in his office. And of course I've personally witnessed Paula in the center of her family huddle: mountain-man husband and beefy sons surrounding her on the gymnasium benches. She is the queen of her own island.

I did have a short run of text exchanges with Finn:

LAVENDER: Word on the street is you and Paula have made a run for it.

FINN: Have we now? Short and terrifying has always been my type.

LAVENDER: Where are you? Text "SOS" if she's got you cornered and you need help.

FINN: ZINNIAS ALWAYS SAVE THE DAY.

LAVENDER: Okay, well, this didn't go at all as planned. I was sort of bluffing. You really don't want me in a real-life emergency.

FINN: She scare you too?

LAVENDER: I watched her thirteen-year-old throw a kid onto the ground and put him in a choke hold. And she chanted the whole time. Cheered when the kid couldn't get up.

FINN: I believe that's called wrestling.

LAVENDER: The chanting was disconcerting.

FINN: Supportive?

LAVENDER: Is she making you say this?

Ten minutes pass.

FINN: No.

FINN: She is confiscating my phone now. I'm sorry but

And that was the last I heard from him.

For days. I ventured by his flat, but Mrs. Teaberry said he was gone. She didn't know where.

I take a breath perfumed with vanilla and coffee beans. The dog park has a fresh crop of grass, and lawnmowers hum in the distance. It's an April Saturday in LA, and I sit on the bench, my fingers anxiously wrapped around my cup of coffee.

I was told to be here at ten. I arrived at nine thirty.

Bernie has done his best to play alone. He zoomed by the trees a few times, but his energy quickly petered out. Eventually he settled in the shade of a tree. For the first twenty minutes his eyes ticked around, looking for his pal. Eventually he gave up, and now his eyes are closed, head on his paws, nothing to indicate he's even awake except for the occasional flick of his ears when a loud bus or running dog passes.

A Schnauzer comes by and gives him a chummy little sniff.

He flicks his ears and turns his head away, not even bothering to open his eyes.

"Poor bud," I say. "I miss them too."

And I have missed them pretty sorely. I couldn't have anticipated how much.

Work, home, dog parks, cafés. Bernie and I still frequented them all, just without Finn and Miles. The colors of the day muted slightly, everything feeling a little less vibrant.

And then late last night I got a text from Finn.

"Dog park tomorrow? 10AM?"

So here I am.

I check my phone for the fiftieth time and exhale. It's 9:59.

Bernie's eyes pop open, and his head lifts off his paws as if zapped by an electrical shock. My brows crease as he stares at something behind me, and I feel a tingle up my spine.

A second later he stands, and I take in a breath, steady myself, and turn my head.

Bernie's racing feet pound as he goes to meet Miles.

And a man at the end of the park is just shutting the gate. Finn looks subdued today. A breeze sweeps through, showering the ground with white confetti blooms from the evergreen pear trees around him. He takes off his glasses and gives his eyes a quick rub before putting his glasses back in place. Turns. Takes a breath.

He looks weary. His clothes are nicer than his usual Saturday morning attire, as though he just left a meeting. His laptop bag is slung over one shoulder. There's a five-o'clock shadow on his chin, something so utterly atypical and yet so attractive I find my breath momentarily stifled. No, this is more than a five-o'clock shadow. He's gone days without shaving.

The tension grows as he closes the gap between us. When our eyes lock, I catch a shy twinkle in his eye, and all the nerves in my body tingle from my heart to my fingertips like an electric shock.

I can't sit any longer, so I stand.

He seems to feel likewise because his stride lengthens.

And then, suddenly, he halts a foot from me, so abruptly one would think he bumped into an invisible force field.

But I know better.

I rise on tiptoe and wrap my arms around his shoulders until the air really does leave him. His body tensely receives me, but after a few seconds I feel his shoulders release, his muscles melting into the hug.

"Good grief, Lavender. I haven't gone to war."

"It's been nearly a month—"

"Not even two weeks."

"Spring is practically over—"

"Literally ten days."

"Do you know how hard this has been on Bernie?"

His hands touch my hips as if to push me away, but I anchor myself to him. He gives a weak attempt at pushing himself back, then gives in.

He looks down at me, his scratchy beard tickling my forehead. His eyes are bright, humorous, as though I'm a ferret who has settled on his shoulder. Honey flecks within his blue-green eyes dance. "Well, I'm sorry this has been so challenging for him. But I assume he's fielded plenty of offers from other dogs."

I shake my head. "A few. No one sticks."

His brow rises. "That so?"

I grin. "He knows what he wants."

The world around us goes silent for a long moment, nothing but the two of us taking in each other.

And then he places his hands around my wrists, and with

resolve this time, he unlocks my arms from around his waist and step out of our bubble.

"I have something for Bernie, actually." He turns and unzips something from the bag over his shoulder.

Bernie is in full jump-on-jump-off mode with Miles forty yards away, the very picture of how I feel.

"Oh, well, he looks awfully occupied—" I begin.

"Bernie!" Finn calls, then gives a short but effective whistle. Bernie drops Miles's ear and begins pounding the ground as he races over.

"Unbelievable," I murmur. "You've been gone a year and he likes a stranger more than his owner."

"So you're now in the acceptance stage I see."

I shrug.

Bernie collides with Finn's legs. "I see we still have trouble stopping," Finn says, then begins wrapping a bandanna around Bernie's neck. It's blue gingham—a surprising choice, to be honest.

Then he stands back, assessing, as if this is exactly what he expected. Not pleased. Not displeased. And there he goes, taking a photo. Then he quickly steps a few feet away and calls to Bernie with a low and subtle, "Bernie. Come." He actually *videos* the dog making a beeline for him. Finn shakes his head. He tries again, saying this time, "Slow, slooow," to no avail. The dog runs like a racehorse and knocks into his legs each time.

He taps something on his phone, then slips it back in his pocket before turning to me.

I'm standing with my head cocked, having watched this moment unfold.

"What was that?"

He shrugs. "Nothing. Can't a man give a nice gift to a friend's dog and capture the moment?"

The *ding* in his pocket betrays him.

His eyes lift, but he says nothing.

"Blue gingham?" I say.

"Maybe I'm a blue-gingham kind of guy," he says. "Maybe I saw it in a shop window and thought to myself, *Now, this is exactly what Bernie needs. He'll match the blue-gingham suit I plan on wearing tomorrow perfectly.*"

"Matching you?" I say, reaching down to adjust the bandanna on the dog's neck. "Can you imagine wearing something like this?"

My fingers pause on Bernie's neck.

A very curious feeling is rippling through my stomach, and I straighten. "Who were you texting?"

Finn is sitting on the bench now, leaning down, rapidly pulling items out of his bag. There are folders in various bold colors. All are labeled.

"Come sit, Lavender. This is going to take a while."

He pats the space beside the growing stack, and I sit, bewildered.

"Now, if you don't mind," he says, readjusting his glasses as he picks up the folders, slipping a few in front and behind, "I'd like to just start in order."

"In order of what?" I say, eyes roving from the stack to Bernie now craning his neck, unsuccessfully, trying to get the gingham bandanna off.

"First things first, here."

He hands me a blue folder with a single word over the center. *Script*. Normal enough. I get scripts every week. Just got another one to go over for the next week yesterday. But this—

I stare at the first line.

"Murders are just *so* tedious."

My eyes drift down the page, catching on words and phrases I have, quite frankly, never laid eyes upon in my career. *Weapon* and *host* and *rain spitting on the black asphalt of the streets of Seattle*. Dark alleyways. Littered corners of dark alleyways. Sirens.

Honking taxis. Whereas *Neighbors* was all about cozy nooks and hidden restaurant gems and pizza nights and Seattle-cityscape gazing among found family, this is all *knives* and *reports* and *chalk outlines*.

I look up. "What is this?"

His eyes hold mine before he answers, and I realize he's been watching me closely as I pore over the pages. Looking for my reaction. Now I see the tension at the corners of his eyes. The way he's leaning toward me, stiff and subtle, hands clenched together, wrists on knees.

He's waiting to see *my* reaction?

But I don't even know what *this* is.

"Are you writing for a new series?" I say. And then with a sickening feeling in the pit of my stomach, it dawns on me. He's leaving the show. He's turned down the *Neighbors* contract, and he wants to know if I'm happy for him. This must be what he was doing the past ten days. Perhaps he flew out for interviews. Why? Was he really *so* intent on getting away from me, all on account of that list?

I know he wants me to be pleased for him. Perhaps it's some grand promotion, perhaps he gets his own show, but my face is betraying me, because I can't rally the energy to think about him leaving. I've had ten days of not being around him on set. And now it will be forever. "This is . . . great." My eyes dust over the pages again, because I can't keep eye contact as I try to draw up enthusiasm. "I'm guessing you've moved on to a different show—"

"Your show, if you want it."

My attention flips back to Finn.

"I don't understand."

"If you accept, the pilot will run in a month," Finn says. "Now, your character would stay the same. You'd still be Ashley Krane, but that's where the surprise comes in. Ashley would keep stumbling into murders, and while the same sweet person at heart, she ends up helping to solve them. There is a serial killer on the loose in your apartment complex. Who is it?"

"A drama," I breathe, looking back to the pages with fresh eyes.

"What would it be called?"

There's a beat of silence before he says in a low, serious tone, "*Neighbors*."

"*Neighbors?*" I say, my voice hitched.

"No," he says, shaking his head. And says again with a distinctly low and mysterious tone, "*Neighbors*."

I can't help it. I'm laughing at the absurdity of it all.

He rolls his eyes, then adds, "You sound just like them. Fine. There's actually a *The* in front of it, so it'd be *The Neighbors*, but wouldn't you know I fought hard for the same title. Goodwin kept telling me it was one step too far, that people would be spending the next twenty years sitting down at night on the couch to ask their spouses, 'So what shall it be tonight? *Neighbors*? Or'"—his voice drops an octave to a sonorous level—"'*Neighbors?*' I thought it was genius. But"—he shrugs—"I could only ask for so much."

A thousand pinpricks ripple all over me, jabbing my skin the moment he says Goodwin's name. Everything gets more serious. Even the air feels thicker. "Wait a minute. Goodwin has seen this? Goodwin—Goodwin is *in* on this?"

It's less of a question than a confirmation that I am hearing what I am hearing.

There's a bit of shy pride in his eyes. "He hired me on to think out of the box. I just fulfilled my promise."

I feel the weight around me lifting, along with my body. I feel like I'm floating as realizations flutter down.

"So you're not trying to leave me and dash off to a new show?" I say.

"What?" he says with a laugh, then pauses, taking me in. He

shakes his head, and more seriously he says, "No, Lavender. I'm not leaving you. I'm simply asking you, do you really want to try something? Because if *you want to*, we'll make this happen."

For me.

He is throwing down this whole idea, this opportunity, for me.

"Yes." The word is rushed, and I feel my hand gripping the script tightly, protectively. "Yes. I'd love it. But . . . but what about Sonya? Kye?"

"Want to know a secret? Something so secret, in fact, you'll have to promise to take it to the grave—or to the show's finale, whichever comes first?"

His eyes dance.

"What?" I say.

Finn leans forward. His breath is hot on my ear. "Sonya is the murderer."

"What!"

He sits back and laughs, looking exceedingly proud of himself. "I know. Frankly, I think I've been wanting to recast her since the day I came on the show."

Sonya. A secret serial killer.

"It's perfect," I breathe.

"Should we go for it then?" Finn asks. "It's a risk, but . . . it could be just the thing—"

"Should we? The idea of all of this is a dream."

"Good, because it comes with some stipulations," he says, then pulls out a red folder. "First, we'd shoot in Seattle."

"What?"

I flip open the folder to see set location and hotel location and a bunch of other brochures spilling out of the pockets.

"We skip the trial pilot. Frankly, your names and the concept alone guarantee a viewer rating, securing us at the very least one season. We'd leave in three weeks. Sonya would be there, of course." After a pause, he adds in a monotone, "Kye too. The staff would be the same. Same writers. Same stylists. We'd retain just about everyone—even Paula, although she's planning to go virtual for about half the season and bring the family out the other half. Her son Liam, the seventeen-year-old you saw the other night, would be cast as a young detective. He's over the moon at the very idea, as you can imagine. Now, I have a few apartment options to lease here, but between you and me, I'm letting you choose." He gives a subtle smile. "Pick whichever suits you. I'll lease it for the cast and staff."

"So . . . we're all literally going to be in a complex?" I say. "Neighbors in Seattle on a show about serial-killer neighbors in Seattle?"

"Correct." He taps one of the sheets in my hand. "And if you pick this one, you reduce the likelihood that Sonya will murder us all in our sleep by 30 percent."

"She'll like this one?" I say, holding it up.

"It's entirely floor to rooftop in white and there are not one but two gargoyles. So. Yes."

Every moment my heart is beating quicker.

Every word that spills from Finn's mouth is only getting more exciting.

I flip through a few pages, scanning the listings, then hold up a sheet with what appears to be a rooftop helicopter pad. "Yes, but you know I have a weakness for helicopter pads."

Finn shrugs.

"Pick any of these you like. We'd only be there six weeks."

"*What?*"

Finn's voice is barely contained. "Two shoots a year. Three months each. Three weeks in Seattle. The other two and a half months on set in LA. Two months in preproduction. Three months filming. One month in postproduction. What you do with the other six is up to you."

Instantly images of home come to mind.

Mum leafing through her latest novel by the garden gate.

Dad on a stepladder with a drill in one hand, YouTube pouring directions from the speaker on his phone in the other.

Six months.

I could go home. *For three months at a time.*

I could plant a garden.

I could spend half my life there.

"How did you *possibly* get Goodwin to agree to this?" I say.

"Ah. Well, that was the easy part," Finn says. "Detective dramas are easier to shoot without the live-audience aspect. And after I initially came to him with my idea and he fired me for even thinking such an insubordinate idea—"

"He *sacked* you?"

"Again," he says, as if this is as routine as saying, "I get meatball sandwiches on Mondays." He continues, "But the way I saw it—"

"How did you see it?"

"I saw that you were secretly miserable."

I freeze. So I didn't escape his notice that day.

"And frankly, you are too good a person, Lavender, to go around life secretly miserable if there is something I can do about it. So I did."

I can feel it, my cheeks turning a rosy hue. "And how did he respond?"

"He cut my employee badge in half. Again."

I wince, but he goes on with a wave of his hand. "But then . . . he read the script. And after that, he heard me out. And finally came to see that, at best, we have three more years in a sitcom staying where we are. But if we jump now, with this cast, with this crazy idea and the current hype we have behind us, we just might get another seven- to ten-year run."

He takes the red folder from my hands, then slips a dark pink one into place. "Which brings me to the last little thing."

His phone dings and he slips it out of his pocket, then briskly nods. "Bernie's just been accepted to the short list as your dog on the show—"

"*Neighbors?*" I say lightly.

He corrects me with a guttural, "No. *Neighbors*," and when I look at him like he's gone mad, he adds, "I told you viewers love the comedic relief of a good animal."

I look at the jumble of folders on my lap. All neatly organized and labeled.

"So this," I say, motioning to them, "is where you've been? Dashing around writing scripts and talking up this madcap plan to Goodwin?"

"Pretty much. Except I was running around the country, actually. I left for New York on the red-eye to meet with Goodwin in person about this. It was too important to leave to a call, and too important to wait until he got back from his meetings."

"Why?"

A don't-you-know? look crosses his face. "Because you deserve someone looking out for you the way you look out for others, Lavender. You deserve someone who just wants to see you happy."

I tug on my lip as my heart swells, and his blue-raspberry eyes linger on mine before a smile breaks forth, and he rubs his nose, saying quietly, "And I do hope this makes you happy. Again, and I can't reiterate this enough, *the choice is yours*."

"Y-yes," I say, my voice cracking beneath the weight of the word. "Yes, I would like this. Very much."

"Good." He pats my hand, which rests on the folder atop my knee, then holds it, his large hand encompassing mine, before giving it a little squeeze. "Goodwin will be glad to hear it. We'll get cracking on this right away."

"Finn."

"Hmm?"

"Thank you."

"No problem. What are . . . good friends for?"

His words are weak, but he gives no sign of letting my hand go anytime soon.

I clear my throat. "Friends. Right. About that." I release his hand and turn to my purse. "As we are reviewing paperwork today, I do have something to bring up as well."

"Oh." He looks startled and takes the folded sheet of paper from my hand. He unfolds it.

His brows furrow.

His Adam's apple bobs as he swallows.

"What's . . ."

When his voice trails off, I go ahead and jump in. "Right, so. Let's just kick off by laying it all out there. I saw the list."

To say his eyes become as dark as a crow is an understatement.

"And you . . . you copied it," he manages at last. "Here."

"Right. You see, the problem is, you didn't finish it. So I took the liberty." I lean over and point to the words on the page. It's a replica of his list, the one I took a picture of on my phone. In deep-red ink, I've scribbled my own additions.

"About being the cause of your broken ankle years ago and not even apologizing," I begin. "That is deeply regrettable, and frankly, I have no excuse. I was young, and everything happened too quickly what with scrambling to stand in for you the next day, and then rushing off to LA and flipping my life over the next month. Despite all that, it was inexcusable and should have been at the forefront of my mind." I take both his hands firmly and look him straight in the eye. "I'm deeply sorry, Finn Masters, and I hope you can forgive me."

"Lavender, please," he says, looking obviously uncomfortable. "It's fine—"

"No, it's not," I say, holding—almost vise gripping, really—our hands steady. "It was childish and selfish."

He's shaking his head.

"*Finn*," I say brusquely, "I'm apologizing. Shut up and listen. Now, as for making up for that, I believe the traumatizing-chickens experience nailed that one, so we can cross it off."

He winces, momentarily squeezing his eyes shut. "Paula told you."

"Of course she did; she's a good friend. Also, I cornered her in a parking lot and scared her so much she possibly peed her pants. She was bound to tell me anything. She's surprisingly skittish for having five men in the house—"

"Chalk it up to eight years writing murder mysteries."

I cross out number one and scribble *traumatizing chickens* in blue ink beside it. I finish off with a chipper little check mark. "Now, on to number two. You made it to the final casting audition for *Neighbors*."

Finn drops his head as if I've caught him stealing candy from the local drugstore. "Lavender, *please*."

"Now this one is tricky," I say, "because I had no idea you were in auditions. I was just trying to be a supportive friend to Kye. *But*, I can absolutely see how that would be quite the punch to the gut."

"Again, I've learned from this," Finn says, almost pleading. "You aren't at fault here. Honestly, without that experience I wouldn't have been driven to writing—"

"It's your true passion, yes, yes, I know," I say, waving him off with my pen. "Still, there needs to be recompense. So I'm thinking the maniac ex-boyfriend visit would cover that—"

Finn groans and throws both hands over his face. My grin is a mile wide as I strike out number two and scribble the words, *Coordinate a stalker-ex visit.*

"Now, as for number three. Breaks up three-year relationship two weeks before you were set to propose. That's a big one. Gosh."

"Lavender," Finn growls through his teeth. "You have nothing to make up for. I'm the one who should make up to *you*."

"See, now one could argue that I saved you there," I say, "given she had *no* appreciation for your lifestyle choices. You were just blinded by loneliness, or good looks, or *something* at the time, and I really think I helped you dodge a bullet. Do you know she makes her husband wear coordinating costumes for every holiday?" I pause significantly, then add, "And they do *karaoke*?"

He peeks through two fingers, his voice strangled. "What can I do to get you to stop?"

"I think we both know," I say, and continue on. "So how about we just go ahead and strike that one out and call it a win," I say, giving it a firm strike-through and adding: *Rescued from unhealthy relationship*. "Now I do have one idea here, though," I say, "regarding the time I swiped a dinner reservation out from under you—"

Coming to a breaking point, Finn takes his hands from his face, lays them on my cheeks, and pulls me in. His lips press against mine, muting my words. And what at first is a very obvious, forthright attempt to stop me from speaking melts moments later, as we both truly, fully come into the moment. His hands slip down my face, one onto my neck, the other cupping one shoulder. Gentle. Tender.

We stay in this moment, beneath the spring sunshine and the thick air of cut grass, his scratchy could-be beard tickling my cheeks. Only when Bernie tugs on Finn's corduroy pant leg does he release me, our eyes locked.

Baby birds chirp in a tree in the distance.

A puppy barks playfully as it chases a ball.

The sky is a brilliant blue, with streaks of white clouds zigzagging overhead.

All forever a part of this memory.

"It only seems logical," I continue, crumpling the sheet in my hand, "I take you out to dinner. Where is the restaurant where I swiped your reservation?"

Finn groans and leans down and kisses me again. He makes a grab for the list, but I tuck it out of reach behind me. "Nice try, but it's memorized," I say. "And I've got a lot of apologizing to do. In the form of dates." I peck him lightly on the lips. "In the form of puppy playdates." One more kiss. "You won't be able to get me out of your hair there will be so much making up for. *Years* of it really. Apparently we have a trip to my cousin's wedding when this show—"

"*Neighbors*," he says lightly.

"*Neighbors*," I repeat, "wraps up—"

"We?" Finn raises a brow.

"Of course. This *is* your opportunity to be my plus-one at a family wedding, which seems like an awfully nice gesture to make up for"—I scan the list—"number twelve."

Finn scratches the back of his neck. "You really can forgive me for plotting against you?"

"Easily," I say. "Everybody needs a good how-we-started-dating story. We'll be the life of the wedding party."

Not twenty minutes later, as we're making our getaway plan, I realize one more thing in this avalanche of a day.

"Hang on," I say, brows furrowed as the new realization dawns. "Finn," I say accusingly. "This means you have to go back to writing a detective series."

"Right?" he says, as if he doesn't follow.

"But you said you hated doing the detective series. You told me you were tired of the same old plot. You said you liked the snappy humor of *Neighbors*—the sitcom. *You wanted out.*"

"Oh, that. Well." He shrugs. "I'm good at it. It's my expertise."

"Yes, but you wanted out."

"Yes, but you wanted Nancy Drew."

"Yes, but *you* shouldn't have to give up your dream to carry on mine."

"That's where you're wrong." He lets a few beats pass between us, stilling the charged energy, settling my racked nerves that have tightened with my fear of stepping on someone else's path. It's the same choke hold that seized me when the new contracts arrived, this fear that I would be stuck in something I no longer wanted. Only this time I feel it for his sake.

"Here's the thing, Lavender. If there's one thing I've learned of late, it's that dreams can shift, can change. They grow and evolve into new and different dreams—sometimes fashioned by outside forces, sometimes by change of heart. I've learned, from you actually, how my dreams could change due to external forces. And it's not a bad thing. But this time, it's a mix. I saw an opportunity, and I reached for it. Sure, I'm going back to a detective series. But I'd do it again in a minute. Because you are my bigger dream now. I don't care what I'm writing, so long as I get to share my days with you."

I scrutinize him for so long Bernie nudges my feet. "So you're saying murders won't be so tedious after all."

He grins. "Of course not. As long as I'm solving them . . . with you."

Epilogue

Finn

Saturday, Casa Laguna Courtyard

"You're all *out of your minds* if you didn't see that. It's a clue, I'm telling you!"

Mrs. Teaberry cries out so loudly, Paula's middle son startles and his bowl of popcorn tumbles onto the ground. It's a typical Saturday night. Everything is exactly the same as it's been for three years, only roughly a hundred times louder and twice as cheery since the day Lavender and I married and she moved in.

Season 3 of the hit series *The Neighbors* has gripped the nation. (Incidentally, people have dropped the article over time, so people really do differentiate the shows in conversation by their tone. This gives me profound joy.) The success has been an unintentional blessing to my career, actually. What started as a way to help Lavender escape a typecast turned into my being recognized as one of the "Top 10 Self-Made Starters in Hollywood." I appreciate the support, even more so the joy of having become showrunner of my very first show. But it all pales in comparison to the true thrill of it all: working by her side.

Lavender sits in the center of the folding-chair huddle, grinning madly as she accepts pats on the back every time she says a line or the camera pans to her face.

"What an expressive frown, Lavender!"

"Oh! Don't pick up the phone! Don't pick up the phone! LAVENDER, WHY DID YOU PICK UP THE PHONE?!"

She is more proud of their praise than of her growing number of Emmys.

Sonya stands at the food table, allowing herself a dark and somber smile as she watches herself on-screen. Geez. Even the way she's stabbing the little hot dogs with toothpicks and reorganizing them on the platter makes her look like a serial killer. She really is going to go down in history when this is all over as one of the greatest villains of all time.

Kye cannonballs into the pool beside us, and his date—Candy, I believe her name is?—cries out and wipes her face as if he really did something there (which, given she is literally treading water *in the water*, is a stretch). Then she starts giggling. Half a dozen long *shhhhh*s come from everyone watching the show.

"Luke, you're coming up now," Paula murmurs, eyes on the projector screen like she's watching a wrestling match unfold. She rises from the folding chair, hands clenched at her sides. "C'mon, Luke," she mutters as the camera swings toward the sound of a knock on the door. "Let's go," she says, rising a few inches higher but still squatting as Ashley goes to open it. "This is your big moment," she says as Ashley turns the knob. The door opens. Paula is standing now, hands fisted at her sides, transfixed by the two men in police uniform. "We're looking for Ashley Krane," Luke's character says in a low rumble, and Paula's fists punch the air. "That's my *boy*!" she cries, then turns to the real-life Luke and drops down for a half dozen kisses on the cheek.

"That's your boy with twelve more lines this episode, hon. Sit down," her husband says, peeling her off their son so the rest of the group behind them can see.

"Oh, here comes the surprise!" Lavender says, clapping and pointing. A moment later, none other than Bernie, in a striking blue-gingham bandanna, lifts his one-hundred-ten-pound body off the ground and saunters to the door.

"*BERNIE!*" everyone cries in unison (yes, it's taken nearly three years to train him to a point of being on the show and even still he has a habit of knocking down caterers). Cheers lift to the sky, the noise so loud I wouldn't be surprised if it travels all the way to the moon.

"That's my boy!" Lavender says proudly, and rewards Bernie, who is sitting beside Miles at her feet, with the crust of her pizza.

We linger for a couple of hours after the show and then pack up for our flight. It's near midnight by the time Lavender and I have our luggage set beside the front door. There are far too many bags, despite how often we travel. But there always are.

"Oh. My carry-on," Lavender says, lifting a finger just after I've locked the door. "You'd think I'd be better at this by now," Lavender says as I unlock it again, and she dashes through.

"Soon as we close on the house, we won't need to," I reply. "Things here. Things there. We'll just jump on a plane and go."

Lavender shoots off a little smile at this latest development in our lives.

I'd suggested we get a second place, a little place to call home during those weeks and months we spend in England. But it took time to find the right spot. *"We'll know when the right home pops up,"* she'd said. And finally, it did. A little one-story stone cottage built on the back side of a little hill overlooking fourteen acres. The moment we stepped out of the car and I saw the roses trailing up the tired picket fence (and GPS declaring it was a mere eleven kilometers from her parents), I knew.

"Are you tired of it yet?" she says, reaching down for her massive suitcase. She also totes a gift bag stuffed to the top with white paper as we start down the sidewalk.

"Of traveling?"

"Of weddings. I told you I had a lot of cousins."

I shrug. "Everyone has their hobbies. The Rhodeses are wedding folk. There are worse ways to spend a weekend." I whistle. "C'mon, Miles. Bernie."

The dogs shift from sniffing at the bushes to trotting along beside us. Gabriel opens the door of our SUV, squinting at me slightly (I don't believe he will ever decide to like me). The dogs jump in and pace back and forth in the back seats, peering excitedly out of one window and then the other. They absolutely know where they are going, and Nana and Pop Pop, Lavender's parents, absolutely spoil them with treats. As I duck in after Lavender, I feel her hands gripping my shirt and pulling me inside.

The door shuts. She kisses me and doesn't release me until I see the green signs that say the LAX airport is two miles off.

I raise a brow at her. "What was that for?"

"Sometimes I just feel overwhelmed with happiness," she says. "I have to release the energy somewhere."

I wrap my arm over her shoulder and pull her close, and together, we watch the signs fly by, the looming lights of the airport nearing. I take a breath, feeling the whisper of her almond-scented hair tickle my nose, thinking of how far we've come. From broken hearts and bones and bitterness, to paybacks and regrets, to a chest that aches these days not because of hostility but because of joy so full it hurts. "Me too, Lavender," I say, kissing the top of her head. "Me too."

Acknowledgments

This is the book where I've fully come to realize what exactly authors mean when they say their writing is a group effort. Or, as Finn says in this book, "It was a joint effort. Everyone in the writers room is essential." Maybe before I've just had my nose stuck to the screen as I typed (or been too busy being pregnant, ha), but recently I took a moment to sit back and look around, and can you believe it: as of 2023, there are nearly four million books that go into print *each year.* Unbelievable. Insane. I mean, how is it remotely *possible* that more than my mother and mother-in-law read my books when there are *millions and millions* of wonderful books to choose from? How?

The answer is simple. It really is a group effort.

And so, allow me to show my profound gratitude for getting to enjoy my days laughing (read: cackling) alone with my feet propped up on pillows, grinning as my fingers spin on my laptop about the scene unfolding in my head. I love "my job." I love that my little contribution to this world is getting to help people laugh and smile and feel a little bit happier in their days. A little more hopeful. A little more at peace. So without further ado, my gratitude goes to:

The Thomas Nelson team. Margaret Kercher, Amanda Bostic, Becky Monds, Laura Wheeler, Kim Carlton, Caitlin Halstead, Nekasha Pratt, Savannah Breedlove, and the incredible sales team. *Wow.* It feels like both an hour and a lifetime ago since I joined forces with you all, and all I can say is I am still so overwhelmingly grateful and happy you chose to work with me.

To the cover designer, Amanda Hudson of Faceout Studio. I *love* your vision for this story and how bold and beautiful it came to life through your art!

To Erin Healy, thank you for preserving my voice in my books while working so hard with me through edits.

Special shoutout to my lovely and insightful editor, Laura Wheeler, the first and for a long time the only one to see and *care* about my secret stories. I appreciate you!

To my amazing agent, Kim Whalen, stalwart advocate for both my books and me, thank you for always believing in me more than I even believe in myself. I am so very grateful to have you in my corner.

Special shoutout to my marketing manager, Kerri Potts. You, Laura, Ashley, and Kim keep me going! I love our calls and strategy sessions and always will be grateful for your kindness, patience, and friendship.

And to Ashley Hayes, I don't even know what to say here that could possibly sum up how much I love our friendship. Few friends can cover multiple territories. But you are an all-in-one package. Work friend, sympathy friend, mom friend, faithful encourager, the one who laughs with me one moment and schemes up some brilliant business plan the next. Perhaps God knew you had to live across the continent—otherwise we'd never get anything done.

To Valarie Cox and Shelby Edwards, the moments you love on my kids so that I can write are so important. Thank you for helping me keep my sanity!

To my author friends and general encouragers (you know who you are), thank you. To my awesome VAs, Amanda, Megan, and Katie, who keep my plates spinning so I don't have to (*quite* as much), thank you. To my awesome influencer manager, Mariah

Zingarelli, who has made my life so much easier, thank you. To Christine Berg, for your unwavering support all these years, thank you. To Gabriela (@gabbysletsread) for giving such great insight into my first chapter, massive thank you! And to Madison (@madisonfavoritebooks) for reading my draft and giving such wonderful encouragement, huge thank you!

To my extended family and mama who keep reading my books, thank you. To my husband for your endless support all these years, thank you. To my children, for giving my life such sheer happiness and blissful chaos, thank you.

And to God, for creating me with hands that type and eyes that see and an imagination that never wants to power down, thank you. For giving me opportunities and resources that have allowed me to pursue this lifestyle, thank you. For both opening and nudging me through doors I didn't even realize I would want one day, thank you. I love the life you've given me and hope to spend the rest of my days on this earth loving you and others with a fraction of the love you've showed me.

And lastly, to the readers, bookstagrammers, librarians, bookstore employees, BookTokers, and everyone else who has supported me online and in reviews: You are incredibly influential in my career. Thank you, thank you, thank you for responding to my IG stories and commenting on my posts. Thank you for adding my book to Goodreads TBR lists and writing reviews. Thank you for asking for my books at your libraries and reading my books in your book clubs. I spend a lot of time in my little room writing, and the daily interaction with you all on my socials has been more of an encouragement than you know. I recognize many of your social handles and smile when I read your comments. I see you sharing my posts and love and appreciate you for it. Thank you for making such a difference in my life. I hope you enjoy reading Finn and Lavender's little story just as much as I did writing it.

Discussion Questions

1. Finn Masters faced several hiccups in his life that were difficult to get over. Have you ever had a moment in your life when someone swept something out from under your feet? How did you react both in the short and long term?
2. What is the range of emotions and thoughts you have had when you've had to forgive someone? Have you ever identified with Finn and his struggles, and if so, how?
3. Where would you rather live: in a town like the one Finn and Lavender grew up in or in Los Angeles? Why?
4. Which scene or moment in this book made you chuckle? Why?
5. Do you think you would enjoy Finn's career? Why or why not? Do you think you would enjoy Lavender's?
6. Finn learned that sometimes dreams change. Have you ever experienced a moment where your dreams have shifted?
7. What would you do if you suddenly had the chance to write the actions out for your real-life enemy? Would you act on it or not?
8. Which character's weakness do you identify with most? Why?

9. Which character's strength do you identify with most? Why?
10. When and where exactly does Finn learn a life lesson that changes him? How?
11. Who is your favorite character and why?
12. Lavender was the unknowing victim of a lot of judgment. How quick are you to judge others? How often do you yourself feel duly or unduly judged? How do you handle the criticism in a healthy manner?
13. What is your favorite scene and/or quote and why? *(Side note: I would love to hear your answer to this! Please don't hesitate to message me on Instagram or tag me with your answer at @our_friendly_farmhouse. —Melissa)*

About the Author

Taylor Meo Photography

Melissa Ferguson is the bestselling author of titles including *Famous for a Living*, *Meet Me in the Margins*, *The Dating Charade*, and *The Cul-de-Sac War*. She lives in Tennessee with her husband and children in their growing farmhouse lifestyle and writes heartwarming romantic comedies and children's books that have been featured in such places as *The Hollywood Reporter*, *Travel + Leisure*, *Woman's World*, and BuzzFeed.

She'd love for you to join her at www.melissaferguson.com
Instagram: @our_friendly_farmhouse
TikTok: @ourfriendlyfarmhouse